MURDER IN THE
STORYBOOK COTTAGE

D0035598

Praise for Ellery Adams's Previous Novels

Murder in the Locked Library

"Creating a group of suspects that will keep readers intrigued until the last page, Ellery Adams has proven one thing with this book: this is one series that should and will go on for a long time to come. In fact, the author has done such a brilliant job, readers will find themselves wanting to live in Storyton, no matter how many people end up dead there."

—*Suspense Magazine*

"Ellery does a wonderful job in capturing the essence of this whodunit with a visually descriptive narrative that not only lends itself to engaging dialogue, but also seeing the action through the eyes of Jane and her fellow characters."

—*Dru's Book Musings*

"In *Murder in the Locked Library* . . . there is a very old pile of bones, an old book buried with the bones, and plenty more bodies are discovered. There are laugh-out-loud moments along with the serious, which makes for a most enjoyable read. Avid readers will keep this novel on their keeper shelves! Ellery Adams is a marvelous writer; she intertwines famous quotes, famous authors, and famous books to create mystery magic."

—*RT Book Reviews* TOP PICK

The Whispered Word

"A love letter to reading, with sharp characterizations and a smart central mystery."

—*Entertainment Weekly*

The Secret, Book & Scone Society

"Adams launches an intriguing new mystery series, headed by four spirited amateur sleuths and touched with a hint of magical realism, which celebrates the power of books and women's friendships. Adams's many fans, readers of Sarah Addison Allen, and anyone who loves novels that revolve around books will savor this tasty treat."

—*Library Journal* (starred review), Pick of the Month

"Adams kicks off a new series featuring strong women, a touch of romance and mysticism, and both the cunning present-day mystery and the slowly revealed secrets of the intriguing heroines' pasts."

—*Kirkus Reviews*

"This affecting series launch from Adams provides all the best elements of a traditional mystery . . . Well-drawn characters complement a plot with an intriguing twist or two."

—*Publishers Weekly*

"Adams's new series blends magical realism, smart women, and small-town quirks to create a cozy mystery that doubles as a love letter to books. Readers will fall in love with Nora's bookstore therapy and Hester's comfort scones. Not to mention Estella, June, hunky Jed the paramedic, and Nora's tiny house-slash-converted-train-caboose . . . a book that mystery fans—and avid readers—won't want to put down until they have savored every last crumb."

—*RT Book Reviews*

MURDER IN THE STORYBOOK COTTAGE

ELLERY ADAMS

KENSINGTON BOOKS
KENSINGTON PUBLISHING CORP.
www.kensingtonbooks.com

KENSINGTON BOOKS are published by

Kensington Publishing Corp.
119 West 40th Street
New York, NY 10018

All Kensington titles, imprints, and distributed lines are available at
special quantity discounts for bulk purchases for sales promotion,
premiums, fund-raising, educational, or institutional use.

Special book excerpts or customized printings can also be created to fit
specific needs. For details, write or phone the office of the Kensington
Sales Manager: Attn.: Sales Department. Kensington Publishing Corp.,
119 West 40th Street, New York, NY 10018. Phone: 1-800-221-2647.

Kensington and the K logo Reg. U.S. Pat. & TM Off.

First Printing: May 2020
ISBN-13: 978-1-4967-1567-8
ISBN-10: 1-4967-1567-5

eISBN-13: 978-1-4967-1568-5 (eBook)
eISBN-10: 1-4967-1568-3 (eBook)

10 9 8 7 6 5 4 3 2 1
Printed in the United States of America

This book is for all the parents, grandparents,
teachers, librarians, babysitters—
to anyone who ever read to a child.

To gift a child with a love of reading
is to open a magic door.

"Obsessed by a fairy tale,
we spend our lives searching for a magic door
and a lost kingdom of peace."
—Eugene O'Neill

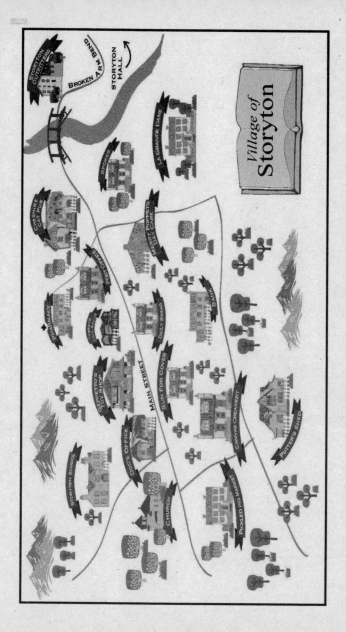

Welcome to Storyton Hall

OUR STAFF IS HERE TO SERVE YOU
Resort Manager—Jane Steward
Butler—Mr. Butterworth
Head Librarian—Mr. Sinclair
Head Chauffeur—Mr. Sterling
Head of Recreation—Mr. Lachlan
Head of Housekeeping—Mrs. Templeton
Head Cook—Mrs. Hubbard
Spa Manager—Tammie Kota

SELECT MERCHANTS OF STORYTON VILLAGE
Run for Cover Bookshop—Eloise Alcott
Daily Bread Café—Edwin Alcott
Cheshire Cat Pub—Bob and Betty Carmichael
Canvas Creamery—Phoebe Doyle
La Grande Dame Clothing Boutique—Mabel Wimberly
Tresses Hair Salon—Violet Osborne
Pickled Pig Market—the Hogg brothers
Geppetto's Toy Shop—Barnaby Nicholas
Hilltop Stables—Sam Nolan
Potter's Shed—Tom Green
Storyton Outfitters—Phil and Sandi Hughes

CHILDREN'S BOOK CONFERENCE ATTENDEES OF NOTE
Birdie Bloom
Nia Curry
Gunnar Humphries
Sasha Long
Reggie Novak
Todd and Tris Petty
Gloria Ramirez

THE GOLDEN BOOKMARK WINNERS
Max Gilbert
Alika Gilbert
Fern Gilbert
Peter Gilbert

MISCELLANEOUS VISITORS
Zoey (Mrs. Templeton's niece)
Malcolm Marcus (book dealer)
Dr. Brandon Parks (Gloria Ramirez's fiancé)

Chapter One

Jane Steward, manager of Storyton Hall, a five-star resort for bibliophiles, distributed Wonka Bars to the members of her book club.

The Cover Girls examined the chocolate bars in wonder.

"Are these real?" asked Betty Carmichael. She ran the Cheshire Cat Pub with her husband, Bob, and wasn't surprised by much.

Jane smiled. "You can try a bite, but we're having a full tea spread in a few minutes."

Betty put the candy bar in her handbag. "I'll save mine for later."

"A fictional candy bar? As long as it wasn't made by an Oompa Loompa, I'll eat it," Violet Osborne whispered to Anna. Violet owned Tresses, the village beauty salon, while Anna was working on a doctoral degree in pharmacy. Between work and school, she hadn't attended many book club meetings for the past six months, so her friends were delighted to have her back.

"If T. S. Eliot dared to eat a peach, then I dare to eat chocolate," said Eloise Alcott, Jane's best friend and proprietor of Run for Cover bookstore.

Mabel Wimberly, who owned a women's clothing boutique called La Grande Dame, slipped her chocolate bar into the pocket of her fuchsia cardigan. "No need to twist my arm. This will be dessert tonight." She turned to Mrs. Pratt, the most senior member of the book club and a retired educator. "If you're not going to eat yours . . ."

Mrs. Pratt jerked her candy bar out of Mabel's reach. "If you want mine, you'll have to pry it from my cold, dead fingers. I make it a rule never to share men or chocolate."

The women laughed.

Jane peeled off the purple paper label of her chocolate bar and showed her friends the gold foil inside. "The labels were made by a graphic designer specializing in literary designs. Each label has the Storyton Hall logo on the front and a quote from *Charlie and the Chocolate Factory* on the back. I hope the kids coming to Storyton for this weekend's Family Valentine's Celebration like them. As far as the chocolate? It tastes like a Hershey bar."

Eloise turned over her candy bar. "My quote says, 'What you imagine sometimes comes true.' I'm pretty sure Grandpa Joe said that. I remember reading the scene where Charlie finds the golden ticket like it was yesterday. I was ten or eleven, and I got so excited that I jumped up and down on my bed. My grandmother came rushing in to see what was going on. She'd never heard of the book, and I begged her to read it when I was done. After that, she read everything I read. Sharing those books brought us closer."

Mrs. Pratt put on her reading glasses and studied her label. "The quote on mine is 'We are all a great deal luckier than we realize.'" She peered at Jane over her glasses. "Isn't that a bit philosophical for children?"

Jane shrugged. "Their parents will get chocolate bars too. I want guests of all ages to feel lucky this weekend. Speaking of which, I'm going to put all the goodies for our first Golden Bookmark winners in the Fairy Tale Suite. That way, when the Gilbert family goes into their room, they'll see all of them at once."

"I remember when you first mentioned the Golden Bookmark program," said Eloise. "The idea of giving a free Storyton Hall vacation to a couple or family who couldn't afford it is so like you, Jane. It makes me proud to be your friend."

Compliments embarrassed Jane, so she smiled and kept talking. "Do you gals want to share your contributions before we have tea?"

Mabel clapped her hands. "I thought you'd never ask. As soon as you told me about the Storybook Supper, I contacted the Gilberts to find out who their favorite children's book characters were. After that, I started sewing."

As usual, the women were gathered in the living room of Jane's house. She lived in what had once been the hunting lodge on the original estate. Like the manor house, the hunting lodge had been dismantled from its original seat in the English countryside and rebuilt in a remote, bucolic valley in Western Virginia. The front half of the lodge no longer housed guns and dog kennels, but Storyton Hall's fleet of vintage Rolls-Royce sedans. The back half was home to Jane and her twin boys. The twins, Fitzgerald and Hemingway, were currently upstairs in their room. Eloise had gifted them with several new comic books, and the boys had raced off to read them.

Mabel shot a glance toward the stairs before opening the lid of a rubber storage box. "I have the twins' costumes in here too. I want them to be a surprise, so I'm only showing you what I made for the Gilberts. I think you'll guess which book they love best." She pulled a pair of denim overalls and a flannel shirt out of the box. "These are for

Max, the dad. Mom's next. Her name is Alika. Betty, would you grab the other end?"

Betty helped Mabel hold up a black poncho with a glittering white spiderweb design. Mabel put the poncho aside and pulled out a hat shaped like a spider. The spider had a sweet face. She had two eyes instead of eight, pink cheeks, and a kind smile.

"If you haven't figured it out yet, Peter's outfit will give it away," said Mabel. She showed the Cover Girls a pink pig costume designed for a young boy.

"*Charlotte's Web*?" Anna guessed.

Mabel gave her a thumbs-up. "Yep. The daughter, Fern, was named after the little girl in E. B. White's book. That's why she has overalls like Uncle Zuckerman, aka Max Gilbert. And I put a rubber rat in the bib pocket of Fern's overalls. I had to make sure Templeton made it to the party. He's my favorite character."

"Mine too," said Violet. "Whoever thought a rat could be so likeable?"

"Mrs. Templeton would disagree," said Jane, referring to Storyton Hall's head housekeeper. "Not even a shared surname could save a rat from her broom."

The women chortled. They talked about the Gilberts' costumes, the *Charlotte's Web* animated film, and their favorite fair foods until Mabel reclaimed their attention.

"Both of the Gilbert kids are named after book characters. Alika named Peter after the little boy in *The Snowy Day*. Alika read it aloud every day of her pregnancy, and when Peter was born, he loved seeing a book character that looked like him. Alika was excited to hear that some of the picture-book conference events are open to the public. The panel on diversity in children's books is right up her alley."

Phoebe pointed at the pig costume. "Wait. You said that Alika named Peter. Not Max *and* Alika."

"The Gilberts are a blended family," Jane explained. "Fern and Peter are step-siblings. Though they look nothing alike, their parents say that they're thick as thieves."

"And they're only a year apart, which made it easier to pick out books for them." Eloise held up a box set of paperbacks. "My contribution is this Roald Dahl set. Fifteen books in total."

The book club members complimented Eloise on her choice.

Phoebe held out an envelope. "Mine's not very colorful. I have a gift certificate for free drinks and frozen custard."

"Don't worry, Mrs. Pratt and I have the colorful part covered." Anna gestured at a gift-wrapped package on the coffee table. "We bought a pair of sketch pads and two art sets from Geppetto's Toy Shop."

Betty picked up the basket by her feet. "I have a lovely bottle of merlot and a tin of cheese straws for Max and Alika. The parents can have wine time while the kids have Picasso time."

"Where were you when the twins were finger-painting my bedroom walls?" Jane gave Betty a playful nudge. "I could have used a bottle back then. This single mom never had enough wine time."

Violet was the last Cover Girl to share her contribution. "I'm offering to do the family's hair and makeup before the Storybook Supper. If any of you ladies need a special hairstyle to go with your costume, let me know. I'll add you to my list."

All the women spoke at once, eager to talk about their plans for Valentine's Day.

"What about Edwin?" Mrs. Pratt asked Jane. "Wouldn't the two of you rather have an intimate dinner with candlelight and roses? It's the most romantic day of the year, and you're going to spend it with a roomful of kids, parents, and people who make children's books?"

Jane got to her feet. "The whole point of the event is to provide an alternative to the candlelight and roses cliché. I'm looking forward to celebrating with my guests, my friends, and my family. As is Edwin. What could be more perfect than a night of good food, whimsical costumes, and a charming play?"

Mrs. Pratt frowned. She was about to press her point when Jane held up a finger. "I'm going to put out the tea spread. When I'm done, you can tell us about *your* plans."

Someone whistled, and Mrs. Pratt blushed.

Eloise followed Jane into the kitchen. "I'll brew the tea while you arrange the food." She scanned the selection of finger sandwiches and sugary treats. "It's a good thing I won't be wearing a swimsuit for another few months. I want one of everything."

Jane placed a tray of finger sandwiches at one end of the table. Next came the treats. These included almond scones, white chocolate raspberry macaroons, date cookies, and miniature angel food cupcakes. Eloise added two teapots to the table before returning to the kitchen to fetch teacups and napkins.

"Teatime, ladies!" Jane called.

The women filled their cups with winter chai or spiced ginger tea and carried their loaded plates into the living room. As soon as they were settled in chairs or on the sofa, Mrs. Pratt peered at Jane over the rim of her teacup. She wanted to talk about her beau.

Eugenia Pratt and Roger Bachman had met when a group of historians had come to Storyton Hall for a conference on the Great War. Mrs. Pratt and Roger had been partnered in a wartime cooking class. Their mutual attraction had taken them both by surprise, and though Roger lived and worked in New York City, their relationship was still going strong.

"Is Roger coming to Storyton this weekend?" Jane asked.

Mrs. Pratt loved the spotlight. She took a dainty sip of her tea, drawing out the moment, before answering Jane's question. "Yes. He has big news that he wants to tell me in person. He hopes that it will make me happy."

The room echoed with *oooooooohs*.

All eyes were on Mrs. Pratt. She wore a dreamy expression, and her mouth curved into a secretive smile.

"Do you think he'll propose?" Violet asked. "You've been together, what, five months?"

Anna didn't give Mrs. Pratt the chance to answer. "What about the fact that it's been a long-distance relationship? How well can you know someone when you only get together every few weeks?"

Eloise looked at Mrs. Pratt. "I thought you didn't want to marry again."

Mrs. Pratt moved her shoulders in the ghost of a shrug. "I don't. I'm *very* set in my ways. I had a long and happy marriage to a good man. After he passed, I didn't plan on sharing my life with anyone else. I've given my heart to Roger, but I don't want to open my home to him."

Mabel nodded. "I tell you what. Even if Idris Elba asked to move in, I wouldn't want him underfoot. You all know that I can be messy, but there's an order to my mess. A purpose to every pile. I can't imagine changing things to accommodate a man."

Jane thought of the bundles of yarn, mountains of fabric, and spools of thread in Mabel's shop. They seemed to migrate to every room in her house, turning it into a wonderland of color and texture. Like most of the merchants in the village of Storyton, Mabel's brick and stone cottage was both her business and her home. The two-story cottages marched in a neat line down Main Street, boasting lush front gardens enclosed by a low fence and a small lawn in the rear.

As she topped off Mabel's tea, Jane said, "You're like the miller's daughter in Rumpelstiltskin. Instead of spinning straw into gold, you spin cloth and thread into beautiful clothes. Magical shawls, enchanting dresses, charming hats. I can't wait to see the twins in their costumes on Saturday."

Eloise gazed down at her empty plate. "Speaking of costumes, I won't be able to zip mine if I have a second scone. And I'm not giving any hints either."

Betty offered to carry the teacups and plates to the kitchen. When Mrs. Pratt held out her teacup, Betty took it and said, "Jane and Edwin don't cohabitate, and their relationship hasn't suffered, so you and Roger should be fine." She looked at Jane. "If you ask me, you and Edwin seem more in love than ever. Why don't you get married?"

Jane could feel the weight of her friends' stares. As much as she hated to lie to them, she had no choice. Only Eloise knew about Edwin's secret life. Last fall, he'd finally told his little sister that he was a Templar. He went on to explain that he was a Robin Hood of book thieves. He stole incredibly rare books and documents with the sole purpose of returning the items to their original owners or their descendants. And when he wasn't stealing things, he was cooking exquisite food at the Daily Bread Café.

Edwin went away for weeks at a time to carry out missions for his order while posing as a travel writer. Jane loved him with her whole heart, but he wasn't good father material. His life was filled with duplicity. Despite the fact that the twins adored Edwin, Jane had asked him to distance himself from her sons. They were the most important people in her life, and she wouldn't see them hurt. They came before everything. Even her own happiness.

However, the Cover Girls knew nothing of the challenges Jane and Edwin faced. Only Eloise knew the truth. And just as the silence was on the verge of being uncomfortable, she came to Jane's rescue.

"Jane said that she'd never marry again after losing William, remember? No matter how much time goes by, it must still hurt."

Jane shot her a grateful look. "It does. It kind of catches me off-guard. One of the boys will make a certain face, and I'll see William in the expression. It makes me feel a bunch of emotions at once. I'm happy because I know that he lives on through his sons. But I'm also sad because they'll never know their father."

Anna took Betty's hand. "Not everyone gets to marry their high school sweetheart. You're one of the lucky ones." She turned to Jane. "Love is complicated. Just ask me. Being in love with your boss takes complicated to a whole new level."

Violet looked at Jane. "I know you're excited about this weekend, but I don't like Valentine's Day. It's not a fun holiday when you're single." She forced a smile. "Maybe whoever bought the Spokes cottage will turn out to be my dream guy. If not mine, then Phoebe's. She and I are competing to see who has a longer dry spell when it comes to men. Neither of us wants to win."

"You're both amazing, and any man incapable of seeing that is missing out. Not to change the subject, but I didn't realize that Spokes had moved to its new location," Jane said, referring to the town's bicycle rental and sales company.

"Their old place is already under contract. No one

knows who the buyer is. Believe me, I've asked. All I got from the Spokes guys is that he isn't from around here."

"He?" Jane arched her brows. "Maybe it *is* your dream guy. We'll just have to be pleasantly surprised. And speaking of surprises, I have one for all of you. You'll have to bundle up, though. We're going outside."

Mabel pointed at Jane's front door. "You have a surprise for us out *there*?"

"Yes. I wanted my friends to be the first to see it. Other than the twins and the staff members who created it, no one has experienced Storyton Hall's newest attraction."

Betty gasped. "Is it the spa? Have you opened the relaxation area?"

"That's scheduled for later this week." Jane clapped her hands. "Come on, ladies. If you don't button up and get outside, we'll miss our ride."

"Is it a she-shed?" Phoebe guessed. "I've always wanted a she-shed."

Mrs. Pratt pulled on her gloves and joined Jane by the door. "Since you started our meeting with Roald Dahl chocolate bars, I'm guessing your surprise is related to him. I just hope you didn't recreate *his* shed. He kept a piece of his own hip bone in there. Why he kept that bone, or a giant ball of chocolate wrappers, is beyond me."

"Novelists are strange creatures. And thank God for that," said Mabel. She tugged a wool cap over her ears and raised a warning finger. "Jane, I know how much you love literary quotes. Doesn't *The Book Thief* have a line about a snowball to the face being the beginning of a lasting friendship? Because I do *not* want a snowball to the face."

Jane laughed. "We already have a lasting friendship. But I'm glad you mentioned a book about kids because this attraction is all about books and kids."

When her friends were finally out the door, Jane called

upstairs to tell the twins she'd be back soon. She then steered the Cover Girls to the middle of the Great Lawn, which was blanketed in several inches of pristine snow.

Suddenly, a pair of horse-drawn sleighs appeared from a path in the woods.

"Oh!" exclaimed Mrs. Pratt. "Is this for us?"

Jane grinned. "Yes. Sam started offering sleigh rides in December. Hilltop Stables doesn't generate much money in the winter, so we thought of a way for him to earn a little cash while treating Storyton Hall's guests to some cold-weather magic."

Phoebe watched the approach of the two sleighs, her eyes glittering with anticipation. "I've heard about these rides through the woods. They've been a big hit with your guests."

Sam Nolan eased his horses to a stop. His assistant, Deacon, followed suit. Sam, who was handsome in an all-American way, flashed a brilliant smile. His gaze lingered on Eloise. He'd been in love with her since they were kids, but he was slowly coming to accept that her heart belonged to Landon Lachlan, Storyton Hall's head of recreation.

As he helped Eloise into the sleigh, she greeted him warmly. She then arranged a blanket over herself, Phoebe, and Mrs. Pratt.

Jane made sure her friends were comfortable before taking a seat next to Sam. He made a clicking noise with his tongue, and his clever horses began to walk.

"They've adjusted so well to the snow," Jane marveled.

"They have." Sam grinned like a proud parent. "I had to outfit them all with special snowshoes, but they love it. Sometimes, they play in the snow like little kids. They run and toss their manes and roll around on the ground."

Behind them, Deacon began to sing. He had a deep, rich

baritone that floated over the snow-covered lawn and drifted into the barren trees.

Jane didn't recognize the song, but Sam did.

"It's Queen. 'A Winter's Tale,'" he said.

With Deacon's song filling the air and the landscape gliding by, the sleigh ride took on a feeling of quiet enchantment.

By the time the song was done, Sam was leading the horses into the woods. The wide walking path was covered with packed snow, and the sleighs headed for the clearing where hikers and nature lovers enjoyed picnics during the temperate months.

As the sleighs rounded a bend, lights came into view. There were thousands, twinkling in the tree canopy like a sea of fallen stars.

"How lovely," Eloise cried.

As the sleighs drew closer, structures appeared in the clearing. Jane pivoted in her seat to catch her friends' reactions as they recognized the diminutive buildings.

"Is that a giant shoe?" Mrs. Pratt asked.

"A shoe-shaped house?" added Betty. "Like in the nursery rhyme?"

Eloise giggled. "Yes! And there's Rapunzel's tower and the gingerbread cottage from Hansel and Gretel. Look at the gumdrop shingles and the candy-cane shutters."

Sam pulled on the reins, and the horses came to a stop next to a carpet of false grass.

"Welcome to Storybook Village," said Jane, jumping down from the sleigh. "It might be wintertime in the woods, but inside the village, it's always spring."

Jane waited for her friends to join her on the green carpet.

"How are you keeping the snow out?" Anna asked, glancing overhead.

"The entire area is covered by a canopy. The underside is painted to look like an evening sky and is woven through with fairy lights. The canvas drops down around the sides of the village as well. We tried to camouflage it with silk trees and blooming vines."

Beckoning to the Cover Girls to follow her, Jane led them inside the gingerbread cottage. The interior was crowded with child-sized tables and chairs. Gas logs burned in a small fireplace, and a battery-powered lantern sat on each table. In the kitchen area, a menu board listed the hot chocolate drinks and iced cookies available for purchase.

"A staff member will man the kitchen this weekend," Jane explained. "You should see the cookies Mrs. Hubbard baked. She made gingerbread boys and girls, scary witches, magic wands, unicorns, crowns, fairy-tale castles, princess gowns, and frog princes."

Mabel pointed at the menu board. "Snickerdoodle hot cocoa? Yum. Is there an age limit for customers?"

"As long as you're young at heart, you can enter the Storybook Village. Come on. I have more to show you." Jane led her friends to Rapunzel's tower. Inside, there were chairs facing gold-framed mirrors. Another menu board listed the services offered for princesses-in-training.

Violet's eyes widened. "Fairy hair? How cool! What colors can they choose from?"

Jane opened a cupboard at the back of the tower. "All colors of the rainbow."

"What's fairy hair?" Betty asked.

"It's hair tinsel," Violet explained. "You tie a strand onto your own strand of hair, near your part, and then cut it to the desired length. It's shiny and colorful. Like tinsel."

Phoebe examined the display of strands in the cupboard. "I love the rose gold."

"There's no age limit here, either," Jane told her friend.

"What about the boys?" asked Eloise. "Won't they feel excluded?"

Jane put a hand on the ladder leading to the second floor of the tower. "If they climb the tower, they can get an airbrush tattoo. The activities are open to both genders. The parents will decide who does what."

The next building was a ramshackle structure with a straw-covered floor. A replica spinning wheel sat in one corner. A large worktable occupied the rest of the space.

"This is Rumpelstiltskin's workshop," Jane told her friends. "Kids are invited to make no-sew crafts including a pillow, potholders, placemats, or a dog toy."

Mabel stared at Jane. "You do realize that we all want tattoos and fairy hair. We want to drink hot chocolate and weave placemats. We might never want to leave."

Jane gave Mabel's shoulder a pat. "The village will be open for business on Friday."

"Is there an activity in every house?" Eloise asked.

Jane shook her head. "Two of the buildings are playhouses. We have a dress-up station and a funhouse mirror wall in Cinderella's mini castle and a climbing wall and spiral slide in the cottage of the Seven Dwarfs. We plan to keep this village up all year, but it will only be staffed during kid-centered events. I think you'll like Belle's house, Eloise. That's where our youngest authors can write and assemble their own storybooks."

Eloise's eyes danced with delight. "Show me."

Jane waited for her friends to gather on the grass carpet once more. She'd just opened the door to the next cottage when she spotted a splash of bright red on the faux wood floor inside.

A pair of rocking chairs partially obscured her view, but there was something familiar about the red shape.

"Wait here," Jane murmured to her friends and walked to the far side of the cottage.

As soon as she cleared the rocking chairs, she realized that the red thing on the ground was a coat. A long, wool coat.

Jane noticed a dozen details at once. Black leggings. Black boots. Curls of long, dark brown hair. The curve of an elegant neck. The roundness of a cheek. The lack of motion.

Jane rushed over to the woman and abruptly halted.

The woman in the red coat lay on her side, facing a waterfall display of picture books.

Jane stared and stared. She was so focused on the woman that she didn't hear the Cover Girls tiptoe up behind her.

"Is she asleep?" someone whispered.

"She's not Aurora. She's more like Red Riding Hood," Mrs. Pratt murmured. "See the basket for her grandmother by that velvet cushion?"

No one replied, and suddenly, Storybook Village felt eerily still.

Eloise tiptoed up to Jane and whispered, "Is she okay?"

Jane looked back at her friend. Her eyes were dark with fear. "No. She's dead."

Chapter Two

Jane took out her cell phone and looked at the screen to confirm what she already knew.

No bars.

They were in the middle of the woods, which was why her staff members would carry walkie-talkies when Storybook Village opened to the public. Jane didn't have a walkie. Why would she? She hadn't expected to find a dead woman on today's tour.

"Eloise, can you run back to Sam and have him drive you to Storyton Hall? Find Butterworth and tell him we have a Rip Van Winkle in Belle's cottage."

A question appeared on Eloise's face, but she didn't voice it. Instead, she turned on her heel and ran off.

Jane assumed the question had to do with the Rip Van Winkle reference. Later, if she had the chance, she'd explain that it was code for a guest who'd passed away inside Storyton Hall or on the estate's grounds. Most hotels had a code name for such incidents, which occurred more often than people realized.

Mabel and Betty had their arms looped, comforting each other with proximity.

"Do you know her?" Mabel asked.

Jane's gaze swept over the woman's fair skin and long,

dark locks. Her sky-blue eyes, which reflected the ceiling light, were framed with lush lashes. Her lips were full and plump. Too plump. To Jane, they appeared swollen.

"What a shame. Such a pretty girl," said Mrs. Pratt.

Jane was annoyed by the comment. She wanted to swing around and say, "And if she wasn't pretty? Would it still be a shame that she's dead?"

But she knew that Mrs. Pratt was grieved by the young woman's death. She was saying that the stranger had reached the end of her life too soon. Even in death, she was colorful. There was her bright, red coat. The floral scarf bundled around her neck. The delicate pink blush on her cheeks. Her red nails. Her tawny eye shadow.

As she studied the woman, Jane noticed the blue tint to her lips. The woman was losing the hues of the living. These subtle shades were slowly ebbing. Soon, her skin would go from creamy white to ashen gray. It was already a bit waxen. Within the hour, she'd no longer look like a grown-up Red Riding Hood. She'd look like a marble statue, stiff and colorless.

Once again, Jane turned to face her friends. "You need to go back to my place in two waves. Deacon can't take all of you at once. I'll wait for the sheriff." She hesitated before adding, "I'm sorry that you had to see this. It wasn't how I wanted your magical tour to end."

"We're sorry too," said Betty. She stepped forward and touched Jane on the shoulder. "For you and for this poor lady. The only consolation I can come up with is that she left this world after seeing this wonderful springtime oasis. Better here than the winter woods."

Jane acknowledged Betty's words with a nod. It was all she could manage because a lump of sorrow had formed in her throat. Part of her grief was for the dead woman, but the rest came from a sudden loss of hope. Jane had begun to believe that Storyton Hall would no longer be the setting for violent crimes. She thought she'd established a good plan—measures to ensure the safety of her children, friends, employees, and guests.

You failed, whispered a niggling voice inside her head.

For years, Jane had been the Guardian of Storyton Hall. She'd been its manager and its steward. But it wasn't until her great-aunt and great-uncle gave her the key to a secret library housing untold treasures that Jane became the Guardian. Uncle Aloysius had explained that every Steward swore an oath to protect the contents of the secret library, which was housed in the highest turret of the manor house and accessed only by inserting a key and turning a lever in the back recesses of Aunt Octavia's closet. This action would cause the bookcase in their living room to swing away from the wall. This created a narrow opening, allowing a person to slip into the dark space behind it. From there, the Guardian could ascend the spiral staircase leading to an impenetrable steel door.

Jane remembered her first sight of what she now thought of as the Eighth Wonder of the World. She'd been rendered speechless by the wondrous, one-of-a-kind materials stored in the temperature-controlled, fireproof attic vault above her aunt and uncle's apartments.

She'd pulled out drawers to discover unpublished Shakespeare plays, gilt-covered Gutenberg Bibles, and sequels to some of the world's most famous novels. There were dozens upon dozens of drawers filled with documents, books, maps, and scrolls. These priceless treasures had been entrusted to the Stewards for a host of reasons, such as preventing theft or damage during times of war or other conflicts.

A small percentage of the material had been given to the Guardian to be hidden from public view. These works were filled with disturbing and dangerous ideas. Jane had stumbled on books recommending the mass sterilization of all females without a genius IQ, a treatise on the supremacy of the Aryan race, and detailed suggestions for keeping minorities "from rising up."

Though Jane understood why the previous Guardians had misgivings about releasing these materials into the world, she'd never agreed with their decision to let the rest of the collection languish in the dark.

Over the years, she'd had passionate but fruitless arguments with Uncle Aloysius on this subject. And over the years, a host of villains, thieves, and miscreants had journeyed to Storyton Hall in search of the secret library. They'd blackmailed, kidnapped, and killed—all for the chance to get their hands on the literary jewels in the attic turret. Jane and her Fins, a group of men sworn to protect the Guardian and the library, had stood their ground against these criminals. Despite their efforts, innocent people had been caught in the cross fire. Innocent people had died.

Finally, Jane had decided to act. As Guardian, the fate of the secret library was in her hands, and she'd decided to sell or donate its entire contents. If it no longer existed, her family, friends, and guests would finally be safe. It would take a year or two to accomplish this goal, but Jane had made enormous headway over the past few months.

And yet, here was another body.

Another death.

"Jane?" Phoebe's voice sounded very far away. "Are you going to look in her basket?"

Jane snapped back to the present, her gaze traveling from the dead woman to the picnic basket. The basket was on its side next to an oversized pink velvet cushion. One of the compartments had fallen open, depositing an object onto the edge of the braided rug.

"It's a book," Jane said. "I can't see the title from where I'm standing, but I'm not going to move any closer. We need to leave everything as we found it."

Anna shot Jane a puzzled look. "Do you think this is a crime scene?"

Jane wasn't in the mood to be peppered with questions. "I don't know. I don't know who this woman is or why she died in a storybook cottage in the middle of the woods. Would you all go back to my place now? Sam will drop you off, and it's probably best that you go on home from there."

After murmuring brief words of comfort and support, the Cover Girls left Jane alone with the dead woman and her mysterious book.

Jane didn't have to wait long for Butterworth, Storyton Hall's butler and a Fin. He approached with his customary brisk stride and inscrutable expression. He carried a thermos in his right hand.

"It's quite cold, Miss Jane. May I pour you a cup of tea?"

The dulcet tones of his British accent complemented the fairy-tale setting. In his Storyton Hall livery, it was possible to forget that the fifty-something butler had once been an analyst in Her Majesty's Secret Service. However, Butterworth's stature was formidable. He also possessed the musculature of a man half his age. He was one of several men who'd helped raised Jane. As a child, she'd been comforted by his unwavering strength. She was still comforted by it now.

"That's very thoughtful, Butterworth, but I can't. Not in her presence."

Butterworth dipped his chin. "I understand. Sheriff Evans will be here any moment now. The good doctor is accompanying him."

Jane relaxed a little. "I'm glad I came clean with the sheriff last fall and that I don't have to concoct an elaborate lie to feed him. He knew there was something off about the number of bodies that kept turning up inside or within sight of Storyton Hall."

Butterworth grunted in disapproval. He'd been opposed to the dissolution of the secret library and to Jane's decision to take both Sheriff Evans and Eloise into her confidence.

"The wider our circle of trust, the easier it will be to break," he'd warned.

Now, as she stood guard over another dead stranger, Jane wondered if Butterworth had been right.

"She had a book in her picnic basket," Jane said as a means of distracting herself. She pointed to where the basket and book had fallen, regretting that the antique-style candelabra affixed to the walls weren't more powerful. But then she reminded herself that the cottage was meant to be Belle's house, not an operating room.

"I'm sure you're on tenterhooks to learn the book's name."

Jane gestured at the woman. "And hers."

Butterworth cocked his head. "I believe the cavalry has arrived."

Sheriff Evans, an honest, intelligent, no-nonsense lawman in his late fifties, appeared in the grassy alleyway between the two cottages. He removed his hat, ran a hand through his salt-and-pepper hair, and paused to let Doc Lydgate catch up.

Doc Lydgate had fifteen years on the sheriff and moved a little slower. He was a fixture in Storyton and had been the Stewards' family doctor for as long as Jane could remember. Though his hair and beard were cloud-white, he showed no interest in retiring. He loved his patients, and they loved him. Luckily for Jane, he'd encountered Rip Van Winkles at Storyton Hall before.

"What have we here?" Doc Lydgate set his battered black bag on the ground and gave Jane's arm a paternal pat.

"I saw her while I was showing my friends around the Storybook Village."

Sheriff Evans gave his utility belt a tug and edged closer to the body. Jane noticed that his slight paunch had grown a little larger over the holiday season.

I told Mrs. Hubbard not to send him all those Christmas cookies and cakes, she thought.

"Did you touch her?" Evans asked.

"No. It was clear that she was beyond our help." Jane pointed at the floor. "I knelt right here. My friends stayed behind me."

The sheriff glanced around. "Is anything out of place?"

"I hadn't finished the tour, so I don't know if the rest of the cottages are as they should be," Jane said. "Would you like me to check?"

"We'll do it together. It'll give the doc a chance to examine his patient."

Leaving Butterworth with Doc Lydgate, Jane and Evans entered one playhouse and, seeing nothing amiss, breezed through the other. Next, they examined the inside of Geppetto's Workshop, which housed a trio of small puppet theaters and a trunk stuffed with hand puppets.

"Everything's as it should be," Jane told the sheriff.

He replaced the dragon puppet he'd taken out of the trunk and followed Jane to the final cottage.

"This is the Little Pigs' House," Jane explained. "Here, kids can build houses using different materials. We have cardboard bricks, tongue depressors, paper straws, etcetera. They can test the strength of their houses by blowing on them. We'll give them headbands with wolf ears so they can go from being a little pig to the Big, Bad Wolf."

"It's neat as a pin right now. I don't expect that will last once the village opens."

Jane looked at the sheriff. "About that. Can we still open on Friday?"

"Let's see what Doc Lydgate has to tell us," Evans said. "On the phone, Mr. Butterworth said that the dead woman is a stranger."

"I've never seen her before. No one in my book club has either."

The sheriff managed a small smile. "Well, since your book club friends own half of the businesses in Storyton, it's probably safe to say that the woman is from over the mountain."

"Over the mountain" was a catchall phrase for outsiders. Storyton was a tiny town located in a small valley in the Blue Ridge Mountains. It was not easily reached. Visitors either drove or took a train to the nearest station, which was forty-five minutes away. Every business in Storyton was independently owned. There were no box stores or shopping malls. No hospitals or universities. It was a place that time seemed to have forgotten. Which was exactly how the residents liked it.

Of course, plenty of children grew up and left Storyton, eager to experience life over the mountain. A small percentage would eventually return, claiming that nowhere else on earth could rival Storyton's tranquil beauty.

"I don't understand why she's in this village," Jane said

as they headed back the way they'd come. "With her red coat and basket, she looks like a storybook character."

"Red Riding Hood?" the sheriff asked. "Wasn't she carrying food in her basket? For her grandmother?"

"Yes, which is why I really want to know the title of the book our grown-up Riding Hood was carrying."

When they returned to the grassy alley, Doc Lydgate was shining a penlight into the dead woman's mouth.

The sheriff squatted next to the doctor. "What do you think?"

"Ten to one we're looking at an allergic reaction. There's overt swelling to her throat, tongue, and lips. Like she'd been stung by a thousand bees."

Jane shuddered at this unpleasant image.

"Not a bee," said Evans. "It's the dead of winter."

Doc Lydgate glanced at him. "An appropriate phrase. Did you know that it was coined in the sixteenth century to describe the lack of life and activity due to the darkness and cold? The shortest days of winter felt like death. A silent stillness."

The sheriff stared at the dead woman. "If not a bee sting, then what?"

"My guess would be food. She appears to have suffered from a fatal case of anaphylaxis. I took the liberty of searching her clothes for an EpiPen, but her pockets were empty. Perhaps her basket contains a clue."

Jane's gaze roved around the cottage. The children's books, rocking chairs, and colorful floor pillows were in perfect order. "Where's her purse?"

Sheriff Evans wriggled his hands into a pair of examination gloves and stepped toward the basket, scanning the floor as he moved. After photographing the basket from several angles, he directed the beam of his flashlight into its interior.

"Only thing inside was the book." He read out the title, "*Grimms' Fairy Tales*."

A chill ran through Jane's body. She crossed her arms over her chest and hugged herself, but it didn't help. There was no warmth to be had. The idea that this woman's death hadn't occurred naturally sat between her, the sheriff, Doc Lydgate, and Butterworth like an undetonated grenade.

"I need backup to process this scene," Evans said. "Ms. Steward, can you get the doc back to his office? Mr. Butterworth, can you make a list of guests who checked out this morning as well as those checking in this afternoon?"

"Certainly." Butterworth stood a fraction taller. "Doctor? May I carry your bag?"

Doc Lydgate shook his head. "I'm old, but I can still tote the tools of my trade."

Jane felt like she should say something before they left. If Sinclair, Storyton Hall's head librarian, were here, he'd recite a short poem or literary quote. Though Jane didn't have his photographic memory when it came to literature, she still wanted to convey her regret to this stranger—to say how sorry she was that her life had ended too soon.

Out of the blue, Jane recalled a passage from *Fahrenheit 451*.

Everyone must leave something behind when he dies . . . a child or a book or a painting or a house or a wall built or a pair of shoes made.

This woman had left a book.

Jane looked at the woman and whispered, "I don't know your name, but I'll find out who you are. As long as your name is spoken, you'll live on."

Sheriff Evans, who'd removed his hat while Jane had been speaking, solemnly nodded.

As Sam drove them back to Storyton Hall, the sharp air stung Jane's face and hands. She huddled deeper into her coat and stared into the winter woods. It was a bleak landscape made of gray tree trunks, a stone-gray sky, and white snow.

This is it, Jane thought. *The dead of winter.*

She entered her house to find that all the Cover Girls had left.

The twins were still upstairs. When Jane went into their bedroom, she gasped.

It looked like a tornado had blown through a comic book store. Comics were strewn across every inch of the floor. More were scattered on the beds and nightstands.

"What happened?" Jane demanded. "I thought you boys wanted to keep these in good condition?"

Fitz, who'd been flipping through a comic at the desk, cast a nonchalant glance around. "They're okay."

Hem sat on the floor with a comic on his lap. "We're trying to prove who the strongest character is," he said. "Fitz says it's Hulk, but that's dumb. No one can beat Thor. He's a *god.*"

Fitz immediately listed the attributes that made Hulk more powerful than "that stupid Viking." Hem immediately retorted, his face growing flushed with anger, and explained all the ways Thor could flatten Hulk into a green pancake.

"Stop!" Jane shouted over the bickering. "You have exactly five minutes to clean up this mess. If you aren't downstairs, with this room clean, in that time, you'll lose dessert for *three* nights. Grab homework, a book, or something to keep you busy while you're with Uncle Aloysius and Aunt Octavia."

Hem opened his mouth to complain, but Jane held up a

warning finger. Her son wisely closed his mouth and began to tidy up.

Jane went into her bedroom and called her great-aunt and great-uncle's private number.

"Hello, dear girl," Uncle Aloysius answered.

His voice was filled with such warmth and affection that it nearly brought tears to Jane's eyes.

"I'm sorry to be the bearer of bad news, but we have a Rip Van Winkle in the Storybook Village."

"Oh, my." The two words were heavy with solemnity. "I thought the village didn't open to the public until Friday. It's only Monday."

Jane was impressed. Her great-uncle might have stepped down as Guardian, but the octogenarian knew what was going on at Storyton Hall at all times. And what he didn't know, Aunt Octavia could find out through her network of informants. Jane was always amazed by how quickly her great-aunt was able to ferret out information, whether it be the day's tea menu or the name of the guests with the ill-mannered child who'd pushed a plate onto the floor in the Madame Bovary Dining Room.

"It isn't open. I was giving my friends a tour when we found the female Rip Van Winkle. Sheriff Evans is with her now. I was wondering if the boys could stay with you while I assist the sheriff."

"We'd be delighted. I'll have my beautiful bride call down to the kitchens and arrange for a special supper. I've been craving a cheeseburger and Mrs. Hubbard's home-made potato chips."

Jane heard the smile in her uncle's voice and felt a momentary flash of envy.

If only simple pleasures like a cheeseburger and chips were foremost on my mind, she thought. Aloud, she said, "See you in a few minutes."

Fitz and Hem were waiting for her downstairs. They'd donned their coats and were standing by the front door.

"If I went back upstairs and opened your bedroom door, what would I find?"

"We cleaned up," said Fitz. "Promise."

"Really fast," Hem added. He was in a phase where he wanted to have the last word in any exchange. "We were like the Cat in the Hat at the end of the book."

Jane put on her hat and coat. "Don't forget the moral of that story. Don't make a mess when Mom's away. *Or else.*"

Together, the threesome crossed the Great Lawn and entered the massive brick mansion through the terrace door. Next, they ducked into the staff corridor. This dim, chilly passageway was one of many. Once, the corridors had been the thoroughfares of Walter Steward's servants. They'd carried food, fresh flowers, and laundry from one floor to another, moving around the manor house like ghosts behind the walls.

Storyton Hall employees still traveled the same paths, their feet landing on stones worn smooth by the hundreds of workers who'd come before them. The installation of electric lights had made the space a little less gloomy, but it always felt cold to Jane. The boys, unfazed by the drop in temperature, chatted away about laying a new track for the train set in Uncle Aloysius's office.

They took the staff elevator to the top floor. When they stepped out of the cab, they saw that the door to the apartment stood ajar and a pair of hostile yellow eyes were glaring out at them.

"Hello, Muffet Cat." Jane leaned over to pet the portly tuxedo cat blocking their way.

Muffet Cat, who'd been named before Jane and her family learned his gender, flattened his ears and redoubled his glare.

"Okay, so you don't want to be touched. Fair enough. But can we come in?"

"*Kitty treat!*" trilled Aunt Octavia from inside the apartment.

There was a flash of black and white fur as Muffet Cat abandoned his post.

The boys trotted into the living room, tossed their coats on the sofa, and kissed Aunt Octavia on the cheek. After shouting for Uncle Aloysius, they raced into his office.

"I'd like to bottle their energy!" cried Aunt Octavia. "At my age, it's a trial to get out of bed and shuffle into the bathroom. These old bones just want to sit in a soft chair. Add a cozy blanket, a hot cup of tea, a book, and Muffet Cat on my lap, and I might not move for hours."

"Nor should you," said Jane. "You and Uncle Aloysius have done enough work and dealt with enough worries for two lifetimes."

Aunt Octavia started digging in one of the pockets in her housedress. Mabel designed and sewed all of Aunt Octavia's dresses. She knew that Aunt Octavia preferred bold patterns, bright colors, and lots of pockets. Today's dress looked like an oversized Hawaiian shirt. It had a teal background and a neon-pink hibiscus print. Lime-green lizards raced around the hem.

Muffet Cat watched his favorite human pull out a pair of reading glasses, replace them, and try another pocket. When he saw the brown rectangle appear between her thumb and forefinger, he issued a soft meow and jumped onto the sofa.

"Our Jane needs cheering up," Aunt Octavia said to the cat. "Show her your new trick. Give me a fist bump."

Jane was floored when Muffet Cat raised his right paw and pushed it against Aunt Octavia's closed fist. He was rewarded with a treat, which he scarfed down in record time. He then shot Jane a look that seemed to say, *Yes, it's undignified, but those tuna-flavored things are irresistible.*

He turned in a circle and began bathing his hindquarters, making it clear that he was no longer interested in socializing.

"What about you?" Aunt Octavia reached over the cat to pat Jane's hand. "I know the pressures you face. As manager, mother, and Guardian. Aloysius had me. We shared the burden of that position together. You shoulder it alone."

Jane gave her aunt a reassuring smile. "No, I don't. I have my family, the Fins, my friends, and Edwin. I'll survive this next challenge, don't worry."

"I know you will. But I want more for you than survival. When you were a little girl, you were always humming or singing. You never walked. You ran, skipped, or danced. And when your energy was spent, you'd flop on a patch of grass or a comfy chair and read until the sun went down. Every day of your youth, you were a firecracker waiting to go off in a burst of sound and color. You thrummed with joie de vivre." Aunt Octavia's eyes grew misty. "What your uncle and I want for you is less stress and more humming."

"I had a fairy-tale childhood, it's true," Jane said. "I was the luckiest girl in the world. Storyton Hall was an ideal setting. I lived in *The Secret Garden* and in Daddy Warbucks's mansion. Now, it's more like *Brideshead Revisited* meets an Agatha Christie novel. There are always things to worry about." Jane pointed at the bookcase. "Maybe, just maybe, when that's empty, I can hum a bit more. But it'll take years. We can't dispose of the contents too quickly, or our enemies will become suspicious and hordes of villainous book thieves will descend on us."

Aunt Octavia knew Jane wasn't gesturing at her collection of Meissen porcelain teapots affixed to the cabinet shelves with museum wax, but to the contents of the secret library. Like Butterworth, Aunt Octavia had balked over the idea of donating or selling these priceless materials. After Jane had put her in charge of donations, however, Aunt Octavia had been so delighted by the expressions of awe and gratitude from museum curators across the globe that she'd come around to Jane's way of thinking. Now, she looked forward to sharing their treasures with the rest of the world.

"The rooms of Storyton Hall are filled with books," she said. "We have thousands of them. You learned most of life's most important lessons from books, my sweet girl. I know you need to rush off. I know something terrible happened and you must work to make it right. But as you work, as you grapple with these difficult things, consider C. S. Lewis."

"What about him?"

"When he was ten, he read fairy tales in secret because he was ashamed. They were too childish, you see. It wasn't until he was fifty that he openly read fairy tales. We all need to believe in the magic of those stories. In happily ever after. What the stories don't tell you is that happily ever after isn't a single moment. It's a million little ones. Like bubbles in a bottle of champagne."

"It's hard to find a happiness bubble with a dead woman on our property," Jane said glumly.

Aunt Octavia smiled. Every inch of her radiated love. The curve of her lips. The crinkles on her cheeks. The fan of lines around her eyes. The softness of her gaze. Still smiling, she whispered one of C. S. Lewis's most memorable lines, "'Courage, dear heart.'"

The words wrapped around Jane like a shawl. As she stepped into the hall, she held on to them as if they were a jar filled with fireflies, illuminating her way. She felt lighter in her heart as she headed downstairs to search for the name of the woman in the red coat.

Chapter Three

Back in her office, Jane found copies of the lists Butterworth had made for the sheriff. He'd printed a spreadsheet showing the guests who'd left that morning and those who'd checked in that afternoon.

Jane focused on the column showing the number of occupants in each room.

"No female single occupancies departed today," she murmured.

There were a few single-occupancy arrivals, including the owner of Peppermint Press, Gunnar Humphries. Anyone who read children's books had heard of Peppermint Press. The company had published hundreds of bestselling titles, all sporting the famous red-and-white pinwheel candy logo on the spine. Jane was excited to meet the man who'd launched so many careers and produced hundreds of wonderful books. She was equally excited to meet his right-hand woman, Nia Curry.

Nia and Jane had spoken on the phone and exchanged dozens of emails regarding this week's conference. Ms. Curry was smart, funny, and incredibly organized. She'd be traveling with Gunnar Humphries. Like her boss, she'd also booked a single-occupancy room.

Please don't be the woman in the red coat, Jane thought as she searched for an image of Nia Curry online.

It took one glance at a photograph of Nia taken at last year's BookExpo America for Jane to confirm that she wasn't the dead woman. Nia was in her late forties. Her skin was the color of polished chestnuts and her eyes were nutmeg brown. Her short hair was dyed an icy blond, and she had a tattoo behind her left ear of a bird with two sets of wings.

Though Jane was relieved that Nia was alive and well, she knew that the dead woman might still be connected to the children's book conference. Even if she had no connection, she mattered. People somewhere cared about her. People would mourn her loss. For their sake, Jane needed to find out who the woman was and how she'd ended up in Storyton.

She dialed the sheriff's cell phone number.

"I don't think Red Riding Hood is on the list Butterworth gave you," she said. Before the sheriff could reply, she added, "Sorry, but I'd rather call her that than Jane Doe. Were there any clues inside the book?"

"Nothing. No notes. No letters. Not even a bookmark."

"Would you send me an image of the copyright information? I'd like to see if there's anything special about the edition."

The sheriff agreed. In turn, he requested that she let him know if anyone came to the front desk in search of a missing loved one.

"She might not be a registered guest, but she could be the guest of a guest," he said.

Jane had considered this possibility as well. It would be dark soon, and if the woman was expected for dinner, either at one of the eateries in Storyton Hall or a restaurant in the village, then her dining companion or companions might begin to worry when she didn't show up.

"We're getting ready to move her," the sheriff went on. "We'll use the service road. Let me know me if anything comes up."

Sheriff Evans ended the call and, seconds later, Jane received a text with two images of the book. She printed both images in color and headed to the Henry James Library.

A fire crackled in the large hearth and guests occupied every reading chair. No one looked up when Jane entered the room, and the sight of so many people lost in their books made her smile.

Glancing around, she spotted Sinclair. He wasn't helping a patron find the perfect read or shelving strays. He was putting the final touches on a special display. As he stepped back to assess his work, Jane moved to stand beside him.

She pointed at the diminutive book at the end of the row. "*Gashlycrumb Tinies*? Isn't that a bit ghoulish for February?"

Sinclair responded with the faintest of shrugs. "Parents are strangely attracted to that book. Who knew that Mr. Gorey's imaginative destruction of children would be so popular?"

"What's the theme of this display?"

Sinclair showed Jane a small sign that read EMBRACING YOUR INNER CHILD.

"I thought it would be nice for parents and their children to buddy read this weekend. Some of these selections are too advanced for children, so I'll encourage their parents to read the stories aloud. If the family gets hooked on one of these books before they leave, they're likely to purchase the title or a similar title from Run for Cover. Eloise and I colluded on this display."

Jane wasn't surprised to hear this. Sinclair was a thoughtful person, and if he could help Eloise's business, he would. "I came to talk to you about another children's book. An old edition by the Brothers Grimm."

Sinclair's eyes sparkled with interest. "Oh? Which edition?"

Jane handed him the printouts.

After adjusting his silver spectacles, Sinclair scanned the images. "You know I have a soft spot for Arthur Rackham illustrations."

The head librarian looked like a man who'd have a soft spot for Victorian illustrations. His dapper ensemble included polished Italian loafers, wool trousers, a silk bowtie, and a tweed suit coat, with a handkerchief peeking out of the breast pocket. Sinclair was the only Fin who'd eschewed the Storyton Hall livery in favor of custom suits, and though he looked like Sir Arthur Conan Doyle, he was as dangerous as Moriarty. Sinclair could kill a man with a well-aimed strike from his hands or feet. Jane and the twins had been studying martial arts under his tutelage for years, and they were constantly amazed by his speed and power.

After making sure that all the guests were still engrossed in their books, Jane leaned closer to Sinclair and whispered, "This book is part of a larger mystery. Can we go into your office for a minute?"

Sinclair led her to a door on the far side of the library. The door was so skillfully concealed in the floor-to-ceiling wood paneling that most people never noticed it. Sinclair fit a brass skeleton key into a small keyhole, unlocked the door, and waited for Jane to precede him inside.

The office was a long, narrow space comprised of a long, narrow counter, two chairs, and a series of wall-mounted corkboards. The corkboards were covered by printouts listing facts on every guest, as well as photos of their current driver's licenses. Jane studied the photos, one by one, in search of a woman resembling Red Riding Hood.

"Mr. Butterworth told me about the sad discovery in the Storybook Village, Miss Jane. I was hoping this year would be a fresh start for you. A year without violence or drama."

"Me too. Every time I feel like I'm in control, something like this happens."

Sinclair gazed at her with paternal affection. "Life is unpredictable. All we can do is focus on the present—the page where our bookmark rests. Right now, I can tell you that Ms. Riding Hood's basket held a rare and valuable book. Give me a moment, and I'll have its estimated value."

Setting the printouts aside, Sinclair sat down in front of his computer.

Technology was not permitted in any of the estate's public areas. These spaces were meant to serve as pockets of peace and calm for readers or for those conducting a quiet conversation, working a jigsaw puzzle, playing a board game, or indulging in an afternoon nap.

Guests were welcome to use their smartphones, laptops, or handheld devices in the privacy of their own rooms, but when in the company of other guests, they were asked to respect the no-technology rule. Storyton Hall was a sanctuary for readers. It was meant to be a place where people could unplug and take a deep breath—a place where they could enjoy the beautiful surroundings or bury their noses in a book.

Like any other large resort, Storyton Hall relied on

technology. It was equipped with a state-of-the-art security system and the most advanced computers on the market. However, these machines were kept behind closed doors to help preserve the illusion that Storyton Hall had been transported to another period in time.

The dead woman didn't seem to exist in their computer system or on Sinclair's wall.

"She's not here," Jane said when she reached the end of the row.

Sinclair glanced away from his screen. "No. Mr. Butterworth reviewed these profiles before returning to his post. We also examined the profiles of our incoming guests. There was no match for Ms. Hood. The book in her basket was printed in 1909 by Constable and Company of London. Bound in crimson Moroccan leather with a gilt-decorated spine, raised bands, and marble endpapers, the book features forty illustrations by Arthur Rackham and is worth over five thousand dollars."

Jane whistled.

"Judging by these printouts, I'd say that it's in fine condition. Very fine, perhaps. Which raises the question, why would anyone carry such a valuable book in a basket in the middle of winter?"

"My only guess is that it's a prop—something used to reinforce the fairy-tale theme. A woman in a red coat. With a basket. In a storybook village."

Sinclair knit his brows. "Mr. Butterworth told me of the anaphylaxis and the good doctor's theory that the woman had a fatal reaction to something she ate. There was no food at the scene though, correct?"

"Correct."

"Which makes the fairy-tale elements somewhat inaccurate. Red Riding Hood was carrying cake and wine to her grandmother. In the original Brothers Grimm story, these items were tied up in her apron. There was no basket."

Jane sighed. "There's no cake or wine in our village either. Nothing about this makes sense. Where did the mystery woman come from? Why was she found with a basket and nothing else? Where's her purse? Her phone?" She looked at the photos on the wall. At the rows and rows of faces. Another batch of guests. Another group of strangers. "It'll be dark soon. We'll have to wait until someone reports a friend or loved one missing. What else can we do?"

"In *Atonement*, Ian McEwan wrote that waiting was 'one person doing nothing, over time, while another approached.' Another person will approach, Miss Jane."

Jane frowned. "That's what I'm afraid of."

By six o'clock, it was already one of those frigid, lightless winter nights that make a person yearn for a blazing fire and hot food. The guests dined on soup and roast meats and sipped whiskey cocktails in the Ian Fleming Lounge. The hours passed, but no one came forward with a missing person report.

With the twins feasting on burgers and fries with Aunt Octavia and Uncle Aloysius, Jane would have loved to share an intimate meal with Edwin. However, he was in Gibraltar on Templar business, so she wandered into the kitchens.

It was the height of dinner service, and the place was a riot of sounds and scents. Jane carried her plate to an out-of-the-way corner and watched the kitchen staff. While savoring a meal of pot roast, mushroom grits, and garlic broccolini, she listened to shouts, the hiss of steam, and the clank of pots and pans. She smelled sautéed butter and fry oil. And when a pastry chef opened the oven to remove a tray of dinner rolls, the fragrance of baked bread filled the air.

Mrs. Hubbard, Storyton Hall's head cook, seemed to be everywhere at once. She tasted sauces, barked at servers, and added seasonings or garnishes to dishes before sending them to the dining room. Her round cheeks were pink with exertion, and her eyes twinkled with pleasure. Food was her passion, and she never grew tired of preparing it.

Cheered by the energy of the kitchens, Jane took the stairs to her great-aunt and great-uncle's apartments to collect Fitz and Hem. The three of them walked home where the boys requested ice cream for dessert.

Later, after they'd gone to bed, Jane found her copy of *Grimms' Complete Fairy Tales* on the top shelf of her bookcase. Though her edition was a far cry from the one found in the dead woman's basket, it was still beautiful. The illustrations were copies of those done by Arthur Rackham in the 1909 version, which meant that Jane's book would look very similar to the older, far more valuable edition.

Jane put on her pajamas, got into bed, and turned to the table of contents. She ran her finger down the page until she found the listing for *Little Red Riding Hood*. She turned to the page and saw that the story was accompanied by an illustration of a small girl in a red coat speaking with a scruffy, black wolf in a remarkably inhospitable forest. The brown trees were misshapen and bore few leaves, creating a feeling of decay. The only splash of color in the scene was the little girl's hooded cape.

From the story's first line, "Once upon a time, there was a dear little girl who was loved by everyone who looked at her," Jane was struck by how time had altered the Grimms' most famous tales. She'd become so accustomed to the newer versions that she'd forgotten the unique tone and poignant details of the originals.

For example, Jane didn't remember the wolf telling the little girl to pause long enough to look at the pretty flowers. The girl agrees and admires the flowers. Being a considerate child, she decides to take her grandmother a nosegay. While the girl goes deeper and deeper into the woods in pursuit of the prettiest flowers, the wolf runs ahead to the grandmother's house and devours her.

Having read the entire tale, Jane decided to examine the illustrations more closely. Turning back to the drawing of the little girl and the wolf in the woods, she noticed that Rackham didn't show the cake and wine in the girl's apron. Instead, he drew her holding a woven basket. No wonder all Red Riding Hood stories featured a little girl carrying a basket. The power of the written word had been overshadowed by the power of an illustration.

The next illustration depicted the wolf in the grandmother's nightgown, cap, and glasses. Even though the little girl's red cape was meant to draw the eye, Jane fixated on the wolf's long snout and curved fangs.

She then reread one of the lines describing the wolf. "'Red Riding Hood did not know what a wicked creature he was, and was not at all afraid of him.'"

The Red Riding Hood created by the Grimm brothers was a child. An innocent, fictitious child. The woman in the red coat whose body had been discovered inside a storybook cottage was no child. She was a young woman in her mid to late twenties.

Did you meet a wolf in our woods? Jane wondered as she turned off the light. In the darkness, a second thought came to her. *If you did, were you afraid of him?*

* * *

The next day, the authors and illustrators attending the five-day conference began trickling in. A few had arrived yesterday afternoon, like Gunnar Humphries and Nia Curry, but Jane had been too busy with the Red Riding Hood situation to welcome them in person.

She tried to be in the lobby whenever a large group arrived. She enjoyed seeing people admire the colossal floral arrangement on the center table or the sweeping curve of the main staircase. She liked how they were drawn to the grandfather clock that had been in her family for generations. But what she loved best was the look on their faces when they first stepped into the lobby. Butterworth, who stood in his usual position by the massive front doors, would give them a few seconds to get their bearings before offering them champagne in a crystal flute.

It didn't matter how worldly or well-traveled the guest, they were all impressed by their first sight of Storyton Hall. After traveling on a quiet highway that wound through dense woods and rolling blue hills, they'd pass through a pair of tall, wrought-iron gates emblazoned with Storyton Hall's motto. The Latin translation was, *Their story is our story*. The motto referred to the priceless works guarded by the Steward family and to the books lining the mansion's numerous reading rooms.

After passing through the gates, the now eager guests would progress down the long driveway. For several minutes, they'd see nothing but the encircling mountains and a vast sky, until finally, Storyton Hall came into view. Its two wings spread outward like open arms. In the center, above the massive front doors, a clock tower stretched toward the heavens. The mansion's tall windows glittered in welcome. At night, the windows were illuminated by yellow light, turning Storyton Hall into a beacon in the darkness. Spacious lawns, lush gardens, and dozens of walking trails surrounded the mansion. The grounds of the estate went on as far as the eye could see, creating an oasis of tranquility and beauty.

Jane was used to seeing dazed guests entering her ancestral home. This group, however, was boisterous from the get-go. They laughed loudly and often. Theirs were the most colorful clothes and hair Jane had ever seen. They were like birds with showy plumage. Parrots, peacocks, and toucans.

Butterworth, who rarely encountered guests with multiple facial piercings or sleeve tattoos, men with dyed facial hair, or women with mohawks, struggled to maintain a straight face.

After a woman in a canary-yellow dress and a blue wig accepted a glass of champagne and walked away, Jane told Butterworth to picture their guests as exotic birds.

"I'm British, Miss Jane. The word *exotic* evokes visions of poisonous snakes, stinging insects, unbearable humidity, and malaria."

Jane laughed. "Most of these guests are artists—authors and illustrators who use their imaginations to create stories for children. Without them, many children might not learn to love books. They might never become readers. Isn't that thought more unsettling than a neck tattoo?"

Butterworth muttered something that sounded like "point taken" before turning to offer champagne to a bespectacled bald man with a hot pink mustachio.

The man took his glass, raised it in the air, and declared, "To you, sir."

Hearing the man's British accent, Butterworth performed a small bow and almost smiled. Almost.

After introducing herself to most of the guests, Jane either directed them to the front desk or, if they'd already checked in, told them how to find the Agatha Christie

Tearoom. Mrs. Hubbard had planned very special tea service to welcome the conference attendees, and Jane wanted to be sure that Gunnar Humphries, head of Peppermint Press, was one of the first people in line for the tea service.

She found Gunnar seated in one of the lobby's conversation areas. He was a tall, lean man in his seventies with silver hair and cobalt-blue glasses. He wore a cardigan over a dress shirt, which made him look less like the founder of a successful publishing house and more like an aged professor.

Jane was immediately drawn to Gunnar's cane. The cane's shaft lanced the middle of a metal basket, which was stuffed with peppermint sticks. Gunnar's palm rested comfortably on the cane's knob handle.

The older gentleman made to rise when he saw Jane, but she motioned for him to remain sitting.

"Your cane is so whimsical. Do children follow you around the streets of Manhattan?"

Gunnar chuckled. "Other than the occasional grade-school field trip, we don't get many chances to interact with children at work. That's why this weekend will be such fun. This hotel will be filled with our target audience. It'll be a nice change from memos and meetings."

"Oh, our meetings aren't that bad," said the black woman standing behind Gunnar's chair.

"Nia!" Gunner waved at her. "Come say hello to our hostess, Jane Steward."

Nia deftly maneuvered around Gunnar's chair and gave Jane a hug. "After all our emails and phone calls, I feel like we're friends. A friend who lives in the most amazing place ever."

"It'll feel like home to you in no time." Jane pointed at

the grandfather clock. "Speaking of time, I thought I'd accompany you both to the tearoom."

Nia issued a little squeak of delight. "I spent the last two weeks eating celery sticks and kale so I could gorge myself over the next few days. I've seen pictures, and I want it all!"

"Then let's get you two to the front of the line."

Jane led Gunnar and Nia to the tearoom. The door was closed, and a member of the waitstaff stood in front of it. Jane explained that she was letting her special guests inside a few minutes early.

Nia had her phone out and was ready to snap photos, but when she stepped inside the tearoom, her hand fell to her side and she gasped in astonishment.

As for Gunnar, his eyes widened with childish delight.

"Nia, you said that you wanted the events for this conference to be fun and colorful—to have a magical quality," Jane said. "Because Peppermint Press is sponsoring this conference, we wanted to make your wishes come true. This Rainbow Tea Service is only the beginning."

Mrs. Hubbard and the kitchen staff had created a breathtaking spread. There were finger sandwiches made of colorful cheeses, rainbow veggie pinwheel wraps, and a platter of rainbow fruit skewers.

The dessert selections were even more impressive. There was a rainbow trifle, squares of rainbow fudge, rainbow sandwich cookies, rainbow Jell-O parfait, and of course, a magnificent rainbow cake. The cake was covered in a rainbow of icing rosettes. When the server cut the first piece, the guests would be treated to the sight of six interior layers. Each layer had a different flavor. Jane knew this because the twins had been Mrs. Hubbard's official batter testers. Fitz had liked the lemon layer best. Hem's favorite was cherry.

"Wow," Nia said. "Do you eat like this all the time?"

"Though every tea service is delicious, they're not this colorful." Jane gestured at the wall clock. "Now we can invite everyone in."

The authors, illustrators, and book publishers were clearly impressed by the tea service.

"It's like a scene from a Seuss book," said one.

"Or something Fancy Nancy would dream up," said another.

Jane circulated around the room. Though she made it a point to chat with incoming guests during the tea service, she always left by the time the twins got home from school. Tea with her sons was one of the highlights of her day. They would talk about school and their friends, while Jane asked about homework and tried to limit their consumption of sugary treats.

As she headed to the kitchens, her phone vibrated. She'd missed a call from the sheriff during the tea service. Quickening her pace, she appeared in the kitchens just as the boys raced in through the back door.

"Hey, Mom," Fitz greeted her with a smile.

Hem dropped his bookbag on the floor and asked, "What's for snack?"

"Rainbow fruit." Jane pointed at the plates of fruit skewers Mrs. Hubbard had made for the twins. "I have to make a quick phone call. After that, you can tell me all about your day."

"We both got As on our spelling tests," said Fitz.

Jane smiled at her sons. "Really? In that case, I think you've *both* earned a rainbow sandwich cookie. Wash your hands, please."

"Yes!" Hem cried. He and Fitz exchanged high fives.

Jane was still grinning as she closed the break room door and dialed the sheriff's number.

"I called to give you an update on the case," Sheriff Evans said. "But first, I wanted to see if anyone came forward today to report a missing person."

Jane's grin vanished. "I'm afraid not."

"We're hoping to get a hit on the woman's fingerprints, but it could take another day or two. In the meantime, the ME found something. I wouldn't normally share this information with a civilian, but this situation is unique."

Lowering herself into a chair, Jane said, "Go on."

"The ME found a piece of apple lodged in the victim's throat. It appears to have caused the allergic reaction. The ME is running tests on the fragment, but I wanted to ask if you kept track of your produce. Would you know if a single apple disappeared from the kitchen?"

"No. We also put out fruit bowls in the lobby near the front desks."

Evans thanked her and promised to check in again soon. Before he could end the call, Jane said, "The apple. What's it being tested for? Poison?"

"The ME explained that some people are allergic to the protein found in apples. She's never heard of the allergy being fatal, but there's always a first time. People with mild apple allergies get an itchy mouth after one bite. In more severe cases, the throat swells. The ME needs to determine if the victim was allergic to the apple itself or to something inside the apple."

Jane sat very still. "Either way, she was essentially poisoned by an apple. Which takes us out of Red Riding Hood's story and puts us in another fairy tale."

"Which one?"

"Snow White. A witch gave her a poisoned apple. After taking a single bite, Snow White fell down dead."

The sheriff grunted. "And Storyton Hall is currently filled with people who create these kinds of stories."

"Not really. Today's children's books are careful to limit violent content. That's why kids don't read the original *Grimms' Fairy Tales*. They're too dark. Too disturbing."

"But that book was in the victim's basket for a reason," said the sheriff. "Did it belong to her? Or to someone else?"

When the call was done, Jane closed her eyes and tried to focus on the comforting noises coming from the kitchens. However, the clock mounted on the wall behind her overshadowed the other sounds. Its rhythmic ticking seemed to grow louder as the seconds passed.

A word began to echo in Jane's head, repeating over and over in sync with the ticking of the clock. It was an ugly word. A poisonous word.

Killer killer killer.

Jane opened her eyes and rushed from the room, but the word followed her.

Chapter Four

Once again, the Cover Girls gathered at Jane's house to prepare for the All of the Colors cocktail party. While the twins ate dinner in the kitchen, Jane and her friends flitted between her bedroom and bathroom, filling the spaces with chatter, laughter, and perfume.

"I feel like I'm about to step onto a Paris catwalk," Eloise said as Violet clipped a silk rose into her honey-blond hair.

Betty leaned close to Eloise and began to hum "The Lady in Red."

"That'll be in my head all night now," Eloise grumbled good-naturedly. "Anna, you'll have to sing something else while we're working."

Anna would be standing next to Eloise at the cocktail party. Her dress was the color of a fresh clementine. The A-line, knee-length taffeta gown flattered her curves, and the dainty monarch butterfly pins in her dark hair added a playful touch. Mrs. Pratt was wearing a wide-leg jumpsuit and a green fascinator with leaves and peacock feathers.

Violet beckoned Phoebe to the vanity stool. When her friend was seated, she deftly wound a blue bandeau around her hair. She then pulled out a few wisps of hair to frame her friend's face before calling Betty over. Violet's plum-colored hair was in ringlets and her 1950's-style satin dress swished when she moved.

Betty shot a brief glance at Jane. "How are we doing on time? We need to make sure that the hostess gets her hair done too."

"We're right on schedule," said Jane.

Violet used bobby pins to secure an enormous yellow bow in Betty's hair.

"Okay, Miss Pretty in Pink." Violet waved Jane over to the vanity stool. "I'm going to weave a pink extension into your hair and braid it. It'll end where this string of pink flowers begins on the other side. You're going to look like a fairy princess. Or a cupcake. We'll see."

Betty and Violet laughed. Jane wanted to join in, but she couldn't manage it. She wanted to be jovial, but her thoughts kept returning to the woman in the red coat.

Violet bent close to Jane's ear and whispered, "Are you okay? Did Sheriff Evans find out what happened to that woman?"

Jane shook her head. "He's waiting on a fingerprint match. It could take two or three days. I just wish the conference wasn't starting today. It's hard to focus on entertaining when I don't know that woman's name or what she was doing in Storybook Village."

"Well, we've got your back if you need anything," said Violet. "I know it won't be easy but try to have fun tonight. Edwin is away. You have a lot on your mind and something tragic happened. But there's a time to worry and a time to let it go. If only for a little while."

"Are you misquoting Corinthians?" asked Mrs. Pratt.

Violet flashed her a grin. "You have the hearing of a superhuman. Or a schoolteacher."

"Thank you," said Mrs. Pratt. Catching sight of Jane, she

clasped her hands to her chest. "If only Audrey Hepburn could see you now. She's the one who said, 'I believe in pink.'"

Jane didn't usually wear hot pink because she thought it clashed with her strawberry-blond hair, but she loved how the toga-style dress made her look taller and leaner than she really was. The chiffon fabric was airy but not transparent. It was a fun, flirty dress, and as Jane studied herself in the mirror, she decided that Violet was right. She should enjoy tonight's party. She couldn't do anything for the dead woman right now, but she could celebrate with her friends and treat her guests to an unforgettable evening.

After thanking Violet for her handiwork, Jane looked around for Mabel. "It's almost time to go. Where's our rainbow?"

Just then, Mabel threw open the doors of Jane's closet and bellowed, "Ta-da!"

She was resplendent in a dress with a blouse-like white bodice and a floor-length skirt of rainbow batik. There was no ornament or embellishment in her black hair, but her face looked like a painter's palette. Her blush was orange and yellow, which looked amazing on her coffee-colored skin, and her eyes were rimmed with green, blue, and purple. Her lower lip was red, and her upper lip was pink.

"You're a rainbow goddess!" exclaimed Jane.

The Cover Girls clapped in admiration and Mabel responded with a courtly curtsy.

"Before we go, is there anything we should know about these book people?" Eloise asked.

"Keep an eye out for Gunnar Humphries, the founder of Peppermint Press," said Jane. "He's an older gentleman who looks, well, totally bookish. You'll be able to identify him by his cane. It's rigged with a basket filled with peppermint sticks. His company, which is sponsoring this conference, awarded scholarships to a dozen aspiring authors and illustrators. These folks didn't have to pay for their travel or hotel room, or the registration fee for this conference. Because he's been so generous, I want to make sure Mr. Humphries has a memorable stay at Storyton Hall."

"What's more memorable than a rainbow of gorgeous women serving colorful drinks?" asked Anna.

Even the twins were impressed by the Cover Girls' looks.

"You're pretty," Hem said shyly and was rewarded with at least four hugs and two hair ruffles.

Jane reminded the boys to load the dishwasher after dessert. She then reminded Ned, the staff member who often watched the boys when Jane had to work late, that it was a school night.

"They'll use flashlights to read, so you'll have to check on them," she warned.

After saying good night to her sons, Jane and her friends put on their coats and, hunching their shoulders against the cold, hurried across the Great Lawn toward Storyton Hall.

The conference attendees were already in the lobby, waiting for Jane and her troop of volunteer bartenders. When she and the Cover Girls appeared, the guests burst into exuberant applause.

Jane accepted a handheld microphone from Butterworth and said, "Welcome, ladies and gentlemen. I hope you were able to explore Storyton Hall this afternoon and that you'll be inspired during your stay. Tonight, I invite you to sample our colorful cocktails or mocktails. We also have a little game for everyone to play. Think of a children's book that includes a rainbow." She smiled and pointed at Mabel. "Write down the title and give your entry to our own rainbow, Ms. Mabel Wimberly. We'll draw a name before we break for dinner. The winner will be treated to a Winter Wonderland spa service."

This announcement elicited another round of applause.

Jane handed the mic back to Butterworth and took her place behind a long line of tables. Her table, which was covered by a pink cloth, featured several silver ice buckets and a row of empty champagne flutes. Jane's colorful cocktail was easy to serve. "The Olivia," named after the adorable storybook pig, was simply pink champagne poured over fresh strawberry slices.

Jane had barely reached for the first bottle when her first customer appeared. It was Barbara Jewel, the best-selling romance writer. Barbara had moved to Storyton several years ago after falling in love with Tobias, the youngest of the three Hogg brothers. She and Tobias had been inseparable ever since.

"Good evening, Barbara." Jane poured champagne into a glass flute.

"This brings back lovely memories," said Barbara. A stocky woman with nut-brown hair, Barbara often dressed like the heroines in her novels. Tonight, she wore a turquoise gown with a corset-style bodice. The dress was a frothy, lacy, puffy affair, and was too formal for the occasion, but Barbara wore it with confidence.

"How's *The Devil and the Duchess* coming along?" Jane asked.

"I'm almost done. I think it's my best book yet and I've had such fun writing it. Oh, here comes *my* handsome devil." She pointed at Tobias, who looked uncomfortable in a dark gray suit. "Did you hear that he's written a children's book?"

Tobias and his brothers ran the Pickled Pig Market. Tobias was the friendliest Hogg brother by far. He created delightful window displays, slipped free pieces of candy to the children when his miserly brothers weren't looking, and spoiled his miniature potbellied pig.

The pig was clearly on the forefront of Tobias's mind. "Is my lovely lady telling you how she convinced me to write a book about Pig Newton?"

Jane pointed at the sign describing her cocktail. "You're at the right table for pig talk."

Tobias laughed. "I'm going to the pitch session tomorrow. Barbara's already given me great advice, but is there anything you can add? I'm really nervous."

"I might be a voracious reader, but I'm not in the book business. Why don't you practice your pitch on Eloise? She could give you a book buyer's point of view."

Tobias shot a glance at Eloise. She was manning the table to Jane's left. Her cocktail, "The Clifford," was far more complicated than Jane's. It was a mixture of raspberry vodka, cranberry juice, grenadine, and a splash of lime juice, and Eloise was trying to measure ingredients with one hand while pouring liquid from a drink shaker with the other. To her left, Anna was being far more cavalier with her "Fantastic Mr. Fox" cocktails. After pouring vodka, Cointreau, and orange juice into a tumbler, she added club soda and an orange peel. When her current customer sampled his drink, his eyes rounded in surprise.

"Whoa! You have a generous hand," he said. "I'll be coming back to your table."

Anna batted her eyelashes and told the attractive young man that she'd be waiting. As soon as he walked off, she leaned to her left to whisper something to Betty, who was serving the "Chicken Little" cocktails at the yellow table. Mrs. Pratt wanted to know what they were talking about, so she thrust a "Grinch"—a sour apple martini—into the hands of a female guest and scooted over to the end of her table to listen in.

Watching them, Jane smiled. She'd hit the jackpot with the Cover Girls. Her friends were smart, funny, loyal, and generous. They were book lovers. They worked hard and knew when to cut loose. For example, Phoebe was stealing sips of her own "Pete the Cat" cocktail. She'd asked to run the blue table because she was fond of margaritas on the rocks. Blue Curaçao turned these margaritas a sea-blue shade, and each glass had a blue sugar rim that was now staining Phoebe's lips. Jane stifled a giggle and leaned over to see how Violet was doing.

Violet had the most labor-intensive drink because she was good at multitasking. Her "Harold's Purple Crayon" was made of muddled mint and blackberries, vodka, and sparkling water. It was also quite popular, and a long line had formed in front of her table.

When Jane turned back to her own table, she saw that she had a customer. It was the man with the pink mustachios.

"How nice of you to make a drink that complements my facial hair," he said with a smile. "I'm glad I changed it. It was mustard yellow last week—not a good color for cocktails."

Jane poured him a glass of pink champagne. "Do you dye it often?"

"I'm influenced by whatever book I'm illustrating. The mustard yellow came from a scene I did of a Cuban boy who wants to become a professional baseball player. I couldn't stop seeing a ballpark hot dog with mustard. Now, I'm painting mice wearing—you guessed it—bright pink tutus."

"Your current project inspires your mustache color," said Jane. "Why not?"

"Exactly! Why not?" The man beamed. "I'm Reggie Novak. Thanks for the drink."

Jane knew the name of her next customer. Anyone with kids would recognize the famous author, and Jane tried to act casual as she served the petite blonde with a pixie cut and enormous hoop earrings. But she couldn't let Birdie Bloom walk away without gushing over her work.

"Your books are so popular in our Beatrix Potter Playroom that we buy a new set every year," she said. "*Cooking With Cheetahs* is my personal favorite."

"I like that one, but *Ironing With Iguanas,* which is coming out next month, is my fave."

Jane whistled. "All the kids will want an iron for their birthday."

Birdie winked. "I hope so. That's the point of my books—to teach kids that chores or other kinds of work can be fun. All they need is a little imagination."

"Can you skip ahead in the alphabet?" Jane asked. "I could use *Vacuuming with Vampire Bats* to convince my sons that vacuuming their room once a year isn't quite enough."

"I haven't thought that far ahead in the alphabet, but I love the title." Birdie raised her glass and said, "If I make it to V, I'm dedicating that book to you!"

Jane had no doubt that Birdie would complete the entire alphabet. Her books had sold millions of copies and delighted readers of all ages across the globe.

Most of the other guests smiled or said hello to Birdie as she maneuvered through the crowd, but Jane saw a middle-aged couple glaring daggers at the author's back when she stopped to speak with Gunnar Humphries.

Jane couldn't focus on the couple for long because she needed to serve another guest. As she and her friends poured drinks and exchanged small talk with authors, illustrators, and aspiring writers, the noise in the lobby escalated. The sound of dozens of competing conversations was interspersed with low guffaws and shrieks of laughter. The guests were clearly feeling the effects of multiple cocktails.

Eloise waved for Jane to come over. "Clifford the Big Red Cocktail was a big hit, but I'm almost out of cranberry juice. And you're down to two bottles of champagne. Isn't this party supposed to be over by now?"

Jane looked at her watch. Eloise was right. The cocktail party had been scheduled as a two-hour event, but it was well into its third hour.

"Peppermint Press paid for the supplies, so we'll keep serving until we run out," Jane said. "By this point, guests are usually bored or hungry and end up wandering off to find something to eat. This group doesn't seem interested in food."

The guests seemed perfectly happy to talk and drink. When their glasses were empty, they went back to one of the colorful tables for a refill.

The din grew louder and louder, until eventually the Cover Girls ran out of booze. As soon as they abandoned their posts, the party began to break up. When most of the guests had left the lobby, Jane told her friends that one of the corner tables in the dining room was being held for them.

"Dinner's on me," she added. "I couldn't have done this without you. Go ahead and order. I'll join you in a minute. I want to touch base with Gunnar and Nia about tomorrow first."

Gunnar sat in a wing chair facing the grandfather clock. The couple who'd glared at Birdie Bloom sat in the loveseat across from Gunnar. Jane noticed that the coffee table separating the chair and loveseat had been pushed against the wall and the loveseat had been moved forward so that the woman's knees were now nearly touching Gunnar's.

A staunch proponent of personal space, Jane was irritated on Gunnar's behalf. One couldn't tell by his posture that the woman's forwardness bothered him. He sat very still with his hands crossed over the knob of his cane. And though his body seemed relaxed, his face revealed his displeasure. His mouth was stretched into a thin line, and his eyes were wary.

Neither he nor the middle-aged couple heard Jane approach. The man and woman were speaking in rapid, whining tones. Though they were closer to fifty than five, they sounded like petulant children who weren't getting their way.

"You keep shining the spotlight on Birdie, but we've been with Peppermint Press for twice as long as she has," said the man.

"Twice as long, but with *half* the advertising budget," complained the woman. "You can't expect us to—"

Gunnar raised a hand to silence to her. He got as far as, "Tris," before she plowed on. "We've made you boatloads of money, but you still treat us like second-class citizens."

"Does it take rainbow hair or a nose piercing to be an important author in your eyes?" the man demanded. "What happened to quality over quantity?"

Birdie didn't have dyed hair or facial piercings, but Gunnar was obviously in no mood to argue the point. Slowly, he rose to his feet and said, "This isn't about our other authors. You're disappointed that we passed on your latest proposal. I understand your disappointment. But as I wrote in my email, the market has enough Goldilocks variations. Nia and I agree that yours is too similar to Jan Brett's. We're looking for something fresh. Exciting. A hook that grabs the reader from the first page. You two are talented. Go back to the drawing board and see what you come up with. Better yet, talk to some kids this weekend. Ask them about their hobbies, their favorite foods, their best friends. You never know what inspiration you'll find."

After politely excusing himself, Gunnar walked away. He was obviously eager to escape his present company and limped as quickly as his weaker leg would allow toward the elevator banks.

Jane was about to follow him when she saw Nia exit the ladies' restroom. Her gaze landed on Gunnar, and she hurried to his side. They spoke for a few seconds, and then Nia looped her arm through Gunnar's and steered him into an elevator cab.

I'll catch up with him tomorrow, Jane thought.

She signaled to Butterworth to join her by the grandfather clock. As soon as the author couple left, she wanted to return the furniture to its original position. However, the man and woman were still in the same positions. They were both casting glares at the elevators.

"I told you," said the woman named Tris. She had bear-like eyes and stringy, wine-colored hair. Her bangs were short and severe, and her lips were the same hue as her hair. In the midst of so many bright colors, she looked dour and drab. "You can't have a civil conversation with that man. Mark my words, he's going to reject every proposal we come up with. Or Nia will. She must be sleeping with Gunnar. How else would a black woman be in her position?"

Jane's mouth dropped open. Had Tris actually said that?

"She acts more like a wife than his bit on the side," the man answered. "Always fussing over him. Anyway, Gunnar's still signing the checks, so we need him to come around. Our proposal *is* original, and it's nothing like Jan Brett's. What the hell does Gunnar Humphries know about kids anyway? He doesn't even have any."

"Oh, Todd. You're wicked." Tris swatted his arm.

"He's old, Tris." Todd's face was flushed and puffy. He was a man who enjoyed his liquor. "He's too focused on market trends. Parents want morality tales. We handed Gunnar one on a silver platter, and he turned us down."

"What should we do? Try to come up with a new idea?"

Todd reached down and picked up the glass he'd put on the floor. He stared at the red liquid inside and said, "No. That peppermint-stick-carrying bastard is going to offer us a contract on our current proposal before this weekend is over. If things need to get ugly for that to happen, then I'm fine with ugly. We deserve better than this, Tris. The old man will agree to our demands before we leave, or he'll be sorry."

Todd downed the contents of his glass and suggested they relocate to the Ian Fleming Lounge for another round.

Jane cringed as she heard Tris say, "You're so sexy when you're angry. Let's order drinks and take them back to our room."

The couple walked away without seeing Jane.

Butterworth had crossed the lobby in time to overhear this remark. He directed his disapproval at the coffee table. "It's rather impolite to rearrange the furniture in someone else's home," he muttered as he and Jane returned the table and loveseat to their proper places.

"They're beyond rude," said Jane. "They're awful. And quite possibly dangerous."

She repeated the conversation between Gunnar and the two authors, ending with Todd's implied threat.

"Will you tell Mr. Humphries?" Butterworth asked.

Jane wasn't sure. "Maybe tomorrow. I think he's had enough excitement for the evening. As for me, I'll be in the dining room."

With Ned taking care of the twins, Jane didn't feel the need to rush through her meal. She savored every bite of her blackened salmon while listening to the Cover Girls swap stories about the authors and illustrators.

"The highlight of my night was meeting Birdie Bloom," said Eloise. "I acted like a total fangirl. I even asked if she'd stop by the shop to sign books. Guess what she said?'"

"Yes?" guessed Betty.

"Even better. She's going to sign both my personal copies and the books I have in stock. She's a lovely person. She even promised to do an impromptu story time if any kids were in the store when she showed up."

Eloise was glowing with pleasure.

"That's great, Eloise. I had fun hearing about Tobias's book," said Phoebe.

"Me too," agreed Violet. "I love the idea of a potbellied pig needing glasses."

Jane, who hadn't heard any details about the book, asked for a summary.

"Tobias is a veritable encyclopedia of pig facts. I still can't get over that he's a Hogg and owns a pet pig." Mrs. Pratt giggled.

Anna gave Mrs. Pratt a playful poke in the arm. "Leave Tobias alone. He's one of the nice guys. And I enjoyed learning about pigs." She turned to Jane. "Did you know that they have terrible eyesight but a superior sense of smell?"

"I did not," Jane admitted.

"His story focuses on that detail," Anna continued. "A litter of kittens is born in the barnyard. During a terrible storm, the smallest one gets frightened and crawls away from his mom. He falls into a stream and is swept downriver. No one can find him. Not the farmer's dog, who is supposed to have the best hearing. Not the sheep, who brags about having the best eyesight. Not even the owl, who is supposed to be the smartest animal in the barn.

Nope, it all comes down to the potbellied pig who wears glasses. The animal who was always teased by the other animals turns out to be the hero. In the end, he and the kitten become best friends."

Jane got a little teary-eyed. "That's so sweet."

"Don't worry, we all got emotional after hearing it," said Mabel. "Oh, before I forget, the raffle entries are under the table. Do you want to draw the winning name?"

"Someone else should do it," Jane said.

Mrs. Pratt raised her hand. "I volunteer. No one can accuse me of favoritism because I hardly know anyone at this conference. There weren't many locals at the party either. Tobias isn't the only aspiring children's book author in Storyton, is he?"

"No," Jane replied. "Our mail carrier wrote a book about a female postal worker's friendship with a grumpy dog. One of our front desk clerks wants to pitch a series about a little girl and her imaginary friend. We also have a prep chef who came up with a book on baking for kids. I hope their publishing dreams come true."

"Should I pick a winner before our dessert comes so that someone's *spa* dreams can come true?" asked Mrs. Pratt.

Jane told her to go ahead, laughing as Mrs. Pratt closed her eyes and stirred the pieces of paper in the box. Finally, she dug down to the bottom and pulled out a name. "The winner, with a book title of *The Rainbow Goblins*, is Tris and Todd Petty."

Without warning, Jane reached across the table and snatched the piece of paper out of Mrs. Pratt's hand. She tore the paper into tiny pieces and dropped them on her plate.

"Draw again," she said. "This isn't a couple's prize."

The Cover Girls stared at Jane in astonishment.

"Those two don't deserve a complimentary pampering session. They need a whole new attitude, which will probably never happen because they're totally closed-minded." Jane stared at the pieces of paper on her plate and realized that she didn't want to spoil this moment with her friends. Very gently, she said, "Please pick again."

After exchanging stunned glances with the other Cover Girls, Mrs. Pratt reached into the box and selected another name.

Chapter Five

The next morning, the authors, editors, illustrators, and literary agents attended a presentation given by a group of children's librarians. After that, the agents and editors headed to various conference rooms to hear pitches from aspiring authors.

Standing in front of the fruit bowl in the lobby, Jane couldn't escape the thought that a piece of poisoned apple had killed the woman in the red coat. She wished she could do something to help, but all she could do was wait for word from the sheriff.

Searching for a distraction, she entered the Shakespeare Theater and was met by a shriek of microphone feedback.

"Turn it off!" a woman shouted over the painful noise.

Thankfully, the sound came to an abrupt halt.

Jane saw Mrs. Templeton, the head housekeeper, standing stage left with her hands on her hips. In addition to her many duties, Mrs. Templeton also directed the Storyton Players, the amateur theater company comprised of Storyton Hall employees and village residents.

"Oh, Miss Jane! I wish you weren't here to witness this disaster in the making," cried Mrs. Templeton. "We'll never be ready in time! Everything, and I mean everything, has gone wrong. When we tried to inflate Violet Beauregarde's purple costume, the air pump malfunctioned, and we nearly blew her into bits. The actors are forgetting their lines. Costumes aren't fitting right. What a mess!"

Jane suppressed a smile. Mrs. Templeton was one of the calmest, most level-headed people around. Until the days leading to the performance. From the second the cast took the stage for the first dress rehearsal until the final curtain, she'd be a total basket case. And with all the scene changes and ensemble numbers, *Charlie and the Chocolate Factory* had been a challenging play to produce.

"Did you solve the Oompa Loompa problem?" Jane asked.

Mrs. Templeton brightened. "As you know, we couldn't use children in our production because they're in school, so we're borrowing from Chinese thespians by adopting the practice of shadow puppets. The overall effect is fabulous."

"Will we still hear their theme song?"

Mrs. Templeton rolled her eyes. "I hear that wretched song in my sleep."

Jane laughed. "And how's your niece doing?"

Mrs. Templeton glanced away, but not in time to hide a look of misery. "I'm having a hard time telling the difference between Zoey and Veruca Salt. They're both spoiled, impolite, and pushy. Basically, my niece is a brat." Mrs. Templeton shook her head. "I know I shouldn't talk about my sister's daughter that way, but Zoey has been living with us for a month, and she never lifts a finger to help. She asks for money all the time. She even asked to be paid for being in the play."

Jane was stunned. "She wants to be compensated? It's amateur theater."

Mrs. Templeton snorted. "Zoey expects payment for everything, whether it's loading her plates in the dishwasher or making her bed. She's seventeen going on seven."

"What does your sister say about all this?"

"I haven't told her. My sister isn't well, and I don't want to cause her more stress. My brother-in-law has enough on his mind, what with taking care of my sister and their two other children. They sent Zoey here because she was acting out at home. That's what they call it these days when a teenager breaks all the rules. *Acting out.*"

Jane felt sorry for Mrs. Templeton. Her niece sounded like a piece of work. "Does Zoey like the other cast members? Maybe one of them can talk to her—find out what's going on in her head. Maybe she's behaving this way because she's worried about her mom."

"Zoey hasn't been very nice to the rest of the cast. She openly criticizes their performances." Mrs. Templeton sighed. "She must be terribly lonely, but I don't know how to get through to her. She seems to dislike everyone in Storyton, including me."

Jane wanted to help Mrs. Templeton. The woman had enough to worry about without adding a belligerent teen to her list.

"It sounds like Zoey isn't interested in connecting with people right now," she said. "Maybe she'd prefer the company of animals. I'll talk to Lachlan about introducing her to one of the birds. If that doesn't work, I could ask Tobias if she could give Pig Newton a bath."

"She could bathe Muffet Cat. I'd pay money to see that."

Both women threw their heads back and laughed. Muffet Cat was as prickly as a cactus. He'd scratch a person into ribbons before they got him within ten feet of a bathtub.

A stagehand called Mrs. Templeton's name. She thanked Jane for cheering her up and hurried off to put out another fire.

Since Jane had a few hours left before the Golden Bookmark winners were scheduled to arrive, she drove a Gator down to Storyton Mews.

Landon Lachlan was good at his job. He knew how to steer guests into choosing the perfect activity, whether it be a fishing excursion, mountain hike, kayak or canoeing trip, bicycle ride, cross-country skiing, or a falconry lesson. But other than Eloise, he preferred the company of animals.

The falconry program, which was entirely Lachlan's idea, had been an instant hit. Guests loved learning about the raptors. Even those opposed to seeing wild birds in captivity came around when they discovered that every raptor had some kind of debilitating injury. If Lachlan hadn't rescued the birds perched in their clean and spacious aviaries, they'd be dead by now.

Some of the raptors had been trained by Lachlan. A few could even be handled by members of the public. The rest remained as wild as the day they'd been struck by a bullet, hit by a car, or electrocuted. The only human the hawks, falcons, and owls trusted was Lachlan. They'd eat from his hand, jump on his arm, and allow him to stroke their feathers.

They'd missed Lachlan during his two-month tenure as an inpatient at a treatment center in the Northeast—one that specialized in PTSD. At times, the condition had made Lachlan as skittish as his raptors. But no matter what he'd done, the horrors he'd witnessed as an army ranger had haunted his dreams and kept him from opening his heart to the woman he loved.

All that was in the past. Thanks to the professionals at the treatment center, Lachlan had learned coping mechanisms. He'd returned with renewed energy and a positive outlook on the future. Eloise was thrilled to have her man back. She told Jane that there was an easiness to their relationship now—a level of comfort and trust that made Eloise fall in love with Lachlan all over again.

"I'm glad you're here," he shouted when Jane stopped the Gator next to the mews.

Lachlan was wearing a down vest over a flannel shirt. There was a long leather glove pulled up to the elbow of his left arm. Perched on the glove was Cillian, the resident merlin. Cillian was smaller than their saker falcon and had a few bald patches where his feathers hadn't grown back after he'd plummeted from the sky, straight into an electric fence.

According to the staff at the wildlife rehabilitation center, the merlin's survival was miraculous. Another miracle was the attachment he'd formed with Lachlan. If a bird could fall into a depression over missing a human, then Cillian had been depressed the whole time Lachlan had been away. Now that his human had returned, the merlin's eyes were bright and alert, his plumage looked fuller, and when he leapt into the air on a short training flight, he cried out in unfettered joy.

"It's nice to see him in better spirits," said Jane. "Uncle Aloysius tried to cheer him up, but Cillian gave him the cold shoulder."

"At least Horus loves your great-uncle. He wouldn't kill a mouse for just anyone."

Jane smiled. "Is that the raptor definition of love?"

Lachlan raised his arm in the air and Cillian leapt from

a tree branch on the other side of the clearing and flew back to the mews. He landed on Lachlan's gloved forearm, shook out his wings, and opened his beak to reveal his pink tongue. He issued another cry before turning his head right and left as if searching for threats.

"Um, speaking of demonstrations of love, I could use some advice," Lachlan said as the merlin adjusted his grip on the leather glove.

Jane's eyes traveled from Cillian's talons to Lachlan's face. Noting the blush creeping over his cheeks, she asked, "Does this have anything to do with Valentine's Day?"

"All of my days," said Lachlan. "Let me put Cillian away and I'll explain."

Minutes later, Lachlan stepped into a small room that doubled as an office and maintenance closet. After dropping his gloves on the desk, he opened the top drawer and took out a small jewelry box.

Jane inhaled sharply. "Is that a ring box? Is it for Eloise?"

Lachlan's cheeks reddened even more. "You can open it."

Jane's heart was racing. Eloise, her best friend in the world, was about to receive a marriage proposal. And she, Jane, was about to see the engagement ring. She opened the lid and stared.

The center stone was a brilliant blue oval-faceted sapphire surrounded by ten round-cut diamonds. The platinum band was made of rope links, infusing the ring with a sense of strength and stability. It was feminine, elegant, and extremely beautiful, just like Eloise.

"You couldn't have chosen better. And I'm not referring to the ring alone. Eloise is one of the finest people I've ever known. I love her like a sister, and I'm thrilled that she's found someone who appreciates her like I do."

"She's my whole world," said Lachlan.

Jane smiled, and when Lachlan reached out to reclaim the ring, she closed her hands around his. "You know that I'll kill you if you ever hurt her, so don't. Other than issuing that very serious threat, I'm really happy for you. For both of you."

Fear stole into Lachlan's eyes. "When I ask her to be my wife, I want that moment to be unforgettable. I was planning to ask her on Sunday. Will you help me?"

Jane nodded vigorously. "Were you thinking of a book-themed proposal?"

"Yes. *Jane Eyre*."

Picturing the Anne of Green Gables Gazebo illuminated by a thousand fairy lights, Jane said, "You can count on me."

She'd been so distracted by the happy news that she almost left the mews without talking to Lachlan about Mrs. Templeton's niece. When she asked if he'd be willing to introduce Zoey to the raptors, he readily agreed.

"Anger and hostility are a natural reaction to hurt," Lachlan said. "Whether it's a wild animal, a military vet, or a teenage girl, anger is a defense mechanism. If the birds and I can show Zoey that she's safe here, she might let her guard down. That'll be a start."

He's one of the good ones, Eloise, Jane thought as she headed back to the manor house.

She was giddy with delight for her best friend and wanted nothing more than to spend the afternoon parked in front of the computer clicking on images of romantic gazebo scenes. However, Jane didn't want to miss the arrival of the Gilbert family. She was excited to take the Golden Bookmark winners on a tour of Storyton Hall and to show them the surprises waiting in their suite.

The family of four entered the lobby with identical

expressions of wonder. Butterworth offered champagne to the parents, Max and Alika, and hot cocoa to the kids, Fern and Peter. Jane gave them a minute to look around before welcoming them to her ancestral home. After making sure that a bellman was seeing to their luggage, Jane started the tour.

At first, the whole family was quiet. They stared at the Great Gatsby Ballroom and the Madame Bovary Dining Room without uttering a word, but when Jane took them to the Henry James Library, they exchanged enthusiastic whispers.

At the entrance to the Walt Whitman Spa, Jane heard another flurry of animated whispering behind her. Being excluded from the conversation was a little disconcerting.

"Is everything all right?" she finally asked.

Alika looked abashed. "We're sorry. We're just . . ."

"We can't believe this is really happening," Max finished for her. "We saw pictures of this place online. We read reviews. But nothing prepared us for what's it's really like. We're having a serious fish-out-of-water moment."

"It's like being in a castle!" Fern exclaimed.

Peter peered up at Jane through a curtain of dark lashes. "Do you have dragons?"

"We have gargoyles on the roof. I guess they're like small dragons," she told Peter. "We have lots of treasure though."

"You do?" Peter's brown eyes widened. "Like gold? Diamonds?"

Jane pursed her lips in thought before saying, "I tell you what. On Sunday, before you leave, I'm going to ask if you found any treasure during your stay at Storyton Hall. You can tell me if you found gold or something else. Something different. Deal?"

"Deal."

Jane put a finger to her lips. "We have to be quiet in the

spa, but I wanted your parents to see where they'll be spending their afternoon. After tea, of course."

Fern looked worried. "Where will we go?"

"The kids' club is going on a magical scavenger hunt this afternoon, and I thought you'd like to join them." Jane lowered her voice. "I can't say for sure, but I heard they're searching for a secret door. I also heard a rumor about butterbeer and chocolate wands."

Fern and Peter exchanged excited glances.

"Can you see why we feel like this is all a dream?" Alika asked, smiling.

"We're just getting started," said Jane, inviting the Gilberts into the spa's atrium. While the kids gawked at the wall of water that gently trickled from ceiling to floor, Max and Alika selected their spa treatments. After the couple decided on chocolate facials and rose oil aromatherapy massages, Jane led the family to the elevator bank. Fern and Peter argued over who should push the floor button, and Max shook his head in embarrassment.

"This is nothing," Jane told him. "I have twin boys. They fight over everything. Lately, they've been going through a 'which is best' phase. Pancakes or waffles. The Hulk or Thor. Dumbledore or Gandalf. Cookies and cream or cookie dough ice cream. It goes on all day."

Fern and Peter immediately began to debate the merits of their favorite ice cream flavor. Jane mouthed *sorry* to Max and Alika, but they were laughing too hard to reply.

Luckily, the sight of the Fairy Tale Suite rendered the argument obsolete. The twin beds in the kids' room were shaped like boats and had ocean-themed bedding. The mural behind the beds featured fairies napping in oversized flowers, a knight on horseback, a castle on a hill, and a flying dragon. The wall opposite the beds was painted with an underwater scene featuring colorful fish, mermaids, and the wreck of a pirate ship. The ceiling was covered with lights that glowed like tiny stars in the darkness.

Jane gestured for Max and Alika to step through the connecting doorway into their room. The canopy bed, with its gauzy white curtains and fluffy white comforter, looked fit for a king and queen. The crown-shaped headboard was covered in gold toile, and vases stuffed with white hydrangeas sat on each nightstand. The spacious room included a sitting area with a television and a writing desk. The desk was heaped with gifts from village merchants.

"I'll leave you to get settled," said Jane.

Max was too overwhelmed to speak, but Alika threw her arms around Jane and whispered, "Thank you. This is beyond amazing. We really needed to get away—to find a reason to smile. And right now, we can't *stop* smiling."

Jane returned the hug and then slipped away before she cried in front of her special guests. She'd picked the Gilberts from a large group of applicants because they'd been through a terrible ordeal. Like many of the families hoping to receive Golden Bookmarks, the Gilberts were facing financial troubles. However, they were also recovering from the loss of their unborn baby. At a routine checkup in Alika's eighth month, the doctor couldn't find a heartbeat. Max's letter describing their crushing sadness had moved Jane to tears, and she wanted to ease some of their sorrow.

As she descended the staff stairway, her heart was full, and her tread was light. She loved the feeling of giving to others, which was another reason why she wanted to donate the contents of the secret library.

She returned to her office with plans to check emails and catch up on paperwork. She placed a few orders with their regular food vendors and replied to several event booking inquiries. She was in the middle of composing an email to a woman who wanted to secure a block of rooms for a family reunion when Sheriff Evans called.

"We've identified Red Riding Hood," he said.

Jane braced herself.

The sheriff continued, "Her name is Kristen Burke. Does the name ring any bells?"

"No," Jane said, her fingers moving over the keyboard. "According to our records, she's never been a guest at Storyton Hall." After a pause, she said, as much to herself as to the sheriff, "Could she still be connected to the children's book conference?"

"I don't see how. Ms. Burke worked in a coffee shop in New Jersey. I spoke with the manager, and though he didn't know much about her personal life, he said that Ms. Burke didn't have children and never showed any interest in writing a book or working in publishing. He didn't think she had any food allergies, but she always brought lunch from home. The shop serves mostly prepackaged baked goods. No apples. He knew nothing about her coming to Storyton. She told everyone at the coffee shop that she was spending a long weekend in the Poconos."

"She missed the mark by a few miles."

"Three hundred and sixty. Which is why I'm trying to figure out why she lied to her coworkers."

Sheriff Evans asked Jane to keep her eyes and ears open and ended the call.

Jane sat in her chair and thought about the dead woman in a red coat. She thought about fairy tales. Of forest paths and poisoned apples. Of wolves and of witches.

The dead woman was no longer a stranger. She had a name. And now that Jane knew it, she vowed to find out why Death had followed Kristen Burke to Storyton.

Chapter Six

That night, the conference attendees were free to have dinner wherever they chose, which meant Jane could spend the evening at home. She liked to cook, and though she couldn't hold a candle to Mrs. Hubbard, there were a dozen dishes in her recipe box that never failed to please. Her cottage pie was one of them. As was her apple streusel tart. And though two pies seemed a bit indulgent, Jane decided that nothing would warm their bellies better on a cold February night than a hot meat pie with a browned mashed potato crown followed by a warm apple tart topped with vanilla ice cream.

Having told the twins to set the table, Jane tidied up while the cottage pie cooled a bit. She started by sweeping potato and apple peels off the cutting board and into the garbage can. One of the apple peels curled around her thumb like red ribbon, and Jane thought of the apple piece that had been lodged in Kristen's throat. Had tonight's apple tart been inspired by a stranger's death?

Discomfited, Jane pushed the peel into the bin and rinsed her hands.

"We're ready, Mom," said Hem.

Jane dished out servings of cottage pie and joined her

sons at the table. As was their custom, they shared the highs and lows of their day.

At one point, Jane asked if they were having a class party that week.

Fitz shrugged. "I don't think Ms. Miller likes Valentine's Day."

"I only like the candy," said Hem. "I don't like all the cheesy romance stuff."

"It can also be about helping someone when they're down," Jane said. "Lots of people feel sad or lonely on Valentine's Day. We can help by surprising them with a little treat. For example, Mrs. Hubbard bakes special Valentine's cookies for some of our staff."

The boys, who'd continued eating while Jane had been talking, paused to exchange confused glances.

"You want us to make cookies for Ms. Miller?" Fitz asked.

"You're both smart and creative," said Jane. "I'm sure you'll come up with something."

Later, when the twins were watching *Doctor Who*, Jane headed to the kitchen to cut the apple tart. After taking the vanilla ice cream out of the freezer, she paused to look at the postcard affixed to the door.

Like most of Edwin's missives, this one contained a quote from Rumi, the thirteenth-century poet. Edwin had once given Jane a real literary treasure in the form of an original Rumi poem. Jane couldn't read Persian, but Edwin knew every line by heart and had read the poem aloud to her. That was the night he'd whispered, "I love you," and told Jane that he was hers until the end of time.

Since then, he'd communicated his feelings using Rumi's poetry. Mostly, these were short but powerful lines written on the back of a postcard. Jane cherished each and every one, including the lines on the back of the card in her hands.

If you find me not within you, you will never find me.
For I have been with you, from the beginning of me.

That was all Edwin had written. He hadn't even signed his name. But for Jane, it was enough to know that the man she loved was thinking of her. He was sending her an embrace and a long, lingering kiss using Rumi's words. She felt his love in each loop and curve made by his pen, as if the ink had flowed right from his heart onto the white cardstock.

As she sliced the apple tart, she wondered if Kristen Burke had her own Edwin. Was someone missing her at this moment? Was someone looking at her photograph and hoping to see her soon?

Jane served dessert to her sons, but she didn't want any. She'd suddenly lost her taste for apples. Instead, she waited until her twins had gone to bed before pouring herself a big glass of wine.

Jane was excited about the event taking place the following morning. The illustrators were all participating in a paint-off. They'd be given blank canvases, paint, brushes, and an hour to complete a new piece of art. The finished paintings would be sold online, with all proceeds going to the Kids' Book Bank. This nonprofit organization focused on delivering books to low-income neighborhoods where, in some cases, there was only one book per three hundred children.

Jane had grown up seeing thousands of books every

day, so she couldn't think of a better cause than gifting young readers new books to call their own.

The theme of the paintings was still a mystery. It would be up to Fern and Peter Gilbert to share their ideas with the artists. The Gilbert kids didn't know it yet, but they would also be allowed to pick their favorite painting from the finished pieces. There were prizes for the illustrators too.

Jane paused by the urns in the lobby to fill her coffee cup before entering the ballroom. The large space was buzzing. The artists, already at their stations in the center of the room, were chatting as they organized their supplies. Conference-goers and curious locals were selecting seats in the rectangle of chairs around the artists.

Catching sight of Betty and Mrs. Pratt, Jane wandered over to say hello.

"There's an advantage to working evenings," Betty said to her. "I can't name all the fascinating events I've attended at Storyton Hall while Bob is home watching sports or getting ready to open the pub. Murder mystery scavenger hunts, literary costume contests, Great War reenactments, Christmas tree lighting. The list goes on and on. Your guests are lucky, Jane, but your friends are even luckier."

Mrs. Pratt vigorously nodded her head. "It's true. And I'd never have met Roger if it hadn't been for one of your events. Why do you think I refused to marry Gavin and move to Florida? Does anything in Florida hold a candle to Storyton Hall?"

Jane took the question seriously. "Disney World?"

Mrs. Pratt snorted. "I refuse to be within a hundred miles of that many children. Hordes of screaming babies and tantrum-prone toddlers. Harried, impatient parents. No, thank you."

With a wry grin, Jane said, "You do realize that this resort is going to be full of kids."

"I fully expect the children coming to Storyton to be like my former students," said Mrs. Pratt with a sniff. "After all, their parents are undoubtedly readers, which means the children could be readers too. A child with a book in his or her hands is immediately more likeable, don't you think?"

"I need to run. The Gilberts are here," Jane said.

After greeting the family, she smiled at Fern and Peter.

"It looks like the artists are ready to make their magic. Are you two ready to give them their assignments?"

Peter jumped up and down. "I am! I am!"

Fern bobbed her head. "Me too."

Jane asked the Gilberts to accompany them to the lectern. She then plucked the microphone out of its stand and smiled at the crowd.

"Welcome, everyone," she began. "This is our very first paint-off, and I can't wait to get started. Neither can our celebratory judges. Please welcome the Gilbert family." She gestured at the Gilberts. "Max, Alika, Fern, and Peter. Fern and Peter have spent a lot of time coming up with the themes for today's contest. Artists, please look at the top of your easels. If you have a green star, you'll be painting Fern's theme. If you have a blue star, you'll paint Peter's theme."

Jane gave the artists a few seconds to locate their stars. The spectators began to exchange whispers as Jane held the mic out to Fern.

Shyly, Fern unfolded a piece of paper and read, "My theme is Magical Cooking School."

Her announcement was followed by a burst of applause and more animated murmurs.

Next, it was Peter's turn. He was clearly thrilled to speak into the mic, and his voice boomed across the room. "My theme is Dinosaurs in Space!"

After another round of applause, Jane thanked the Gilbert children and made a big show of looking at her watch. "Now, I'll count down to the start of your sixty-minute painting window. Good luck! Brushes ready? Ten . . . nine . . . eight . . ."

Jane reached zero, and the artists got to work. Some sketched their scenes in pencil first while others dove right into their paint palettes and began covering the canvas with color.

As intrigued as the rest of the onlookers, Jane wandered the perimeter of the room. When she stopped behind Mrs. Pratt and Betty, Betty turned around in her chair and whispered, "It's like having a peek inside the worlds of *Girl with a Pearl Earring* or *Claude & Camille*."

Jane gestured at the painting directly in front of them. "A hippo in a polka-dot apron has come to life while we've been talking. Even if I had hours to work and an image to copy from, my hippo would end up looking like a polka-dot rock."

Suddenly, Reggie, the man with the hot pink mustachios, yelled, "Make a little noise, folks. We're not used to working in a museum atmosphere."

As the minutes passed, the scenes on the canvases began to take shape. Jane saw a kitchen filled with animals wearing witch hats. She saw a T-rex in an astronaut suit trying to grab hold of a brontosaurus's tail. Both dinosaurs were in the middle of space and were dangerously close to a black hole. In another kitchen scene, a wizard had animated all the food. Carrot sticks were jumping in and out of the ranch dressing bottle, the roast chicken was waltzing with a celery stalk, and the donuts were stacking themselves on pretzel rods. The food was making a mess, but the wizard didn't seem to mind.

Jane was amazed by the detail in the paintings she'd

already seen, but the solar system and the dinosaur-piloted spaceship in the next piece were incredible. As were the floating cupcakes in the magical kitchen scene. A little girl stood outside the kitchen window, using magic to transfer the cupcakes from the counter into her red wagon. Her freckled face was filled with mischief, but her drooling dog stole the show.

"Ms. Steward?"

Jane turned from a painting of dinosaurs and aliens eating lunch on the surface on the moon to find Nia Curry of Peppermint Press looking at her in concern.

"Sorry to bother you. It's just that I'm supposed to be a guest judge along with Mr. Sinclair and Gloria Ramirez of Baxter Books. But I don't see Gloria anywhere. I know what she looks like, and she's not here."

Jane glanced at her watch. The paint-off would be over in twenty minutes.

"I'll call up to her room," Jane told Nia. "If I can't locate her, I'll find a replacement."

Pulling Butterworth aside, Jane explained the predicament.

"I'll see to it," he assured her and left the room.

With ten minutes remaining in the contest, Butterworth returned.

"Ms. Ramirez didn't respond when I knocked on her door. She doesn't appear to be in the library or any of the reading rooms. By this point, it would be prudent to select someone else."

"Mrs. Pratt works well under pressure. I'll ask her."

Butterworth dipped his chin in approval and Jane walked back to where her friends were sitting. Betty had her hands clasped over her heart, and Mrs. Pratt was smiling from ear to ear.

Jane leaned over and shared her problem with her friends.

"Do you want me to step in for your missing judge?" asked Mrs. Pratt. "I can do it as long as there's a rubric."

Jane had no clue if someone had come up with criteria for judging the contestants. The entire event had been Gloria's idea. Without her, Jane didn't know how to pick a winner.

With Mrs. Pratt following close behind, she walked back to where Nia stood.

"I have a substitute judge. Did Gloria provide any parameters about the judging process?"

Nia's concern deepened. "She sent me a message a few days ago. I'm pretty sure it had an attachment, but I got busy and forgot to open it. I'd have to use my phone to do that."

"Do you mind stepping out into the lobby? If there's something we can print, the front desk clerk will take care of it. We have four minutes until the contest ends."

Nia hurried out to the lobby, trailed by Butterworth. There was nothing else for Jane to do but watch the seconds tick by.

When the hour had officially passed, she struck the dinner gong with a mallet. The high, tinny sound echoed in the vast space.

"Time's up. Put your brushes down, please!" she said into the microphone.

She waited for the artists to comply, her gaze straying to the door. Neither Butterworth nor Nia had returned to the ballroom. Pasting on her managerial smile, Jane gestured to where the Gilberts were sitting.

"I'd like to thank our guests, Fern and Peter, for the gift of their imaginations. Without them, our artists wouldn't have had such lively scenes to paint."

Jane waited for the applause to die down before continuing. "Fern and Peter don't know this yet, but because they're our special guests, they'll each get to keep one of these paintings." She turned in time to catch the looks of surprise on the kids' faces. "You don't have to make up your minds right away. You can walk around the room. In fact, why don't we all take a few minutes to view the paintings?"

Mrs. Pratt made a beeline to Jane. "Are you stalling?"

"Totally."

Sweat beaded Jane's forehead as she stared at the closest painting and tried to think of categories. Luckily, she was saved by the return of Butterworth and Nia. Butterworth had three clipboards in his hand. After whispering in Sinclair's ear, the butler led the two judges over to Jane.

"It's a good thing I rarely clean out my emails," Nia said with a laugh.

Jane introduced her to Sinclair and Mrs. Pratt.

"These categories are fun," Nia said. "Should we get started?"

The three judges examined each painting, marking down scores as they moved. It took them less than ten minutes to finish with their assessments. After huddling in a corner, they came up with their final decisions and delivered the score sheet to Jane. Butterworth stationed himself at the prize table, preparing to bestow goodies on the winners.

Jane scanned the sheet and grinned. Some of the categories included Most Huggable Animals, Best Use of the Color Blue, Most Zany, and Most Action-Packed. When Jane finally met Gloria Ramirez, she'd congratulate her on such a wonderful event. Not only had the artists and spectators had a ball, but children in low-income neighborhoods would soon receive brand-new books thanks to her ingenious idea.

Picking up the microphone, Jane read the winners in each category. The artists, no matter how famous or successful, were thrilled to have been chosen. After that, it was time for Fern and Peter to choose their paintings.

Peter didn't hesitate. He ran over to the artist who'd painted the dinosaurs and aliens dining on the moon. The artist, a young woman, turned the canvas over and wrote a dedication to Peter.

Fern seemed to be torn between two paintings, but finally selected the painting featuring the cooking school for magical animals. Reggie was the artist, and he was obviously moved that Fern liked his best. He signed the back, gave Fern a hug, and then presented her with the painting.

Jane wrapped up the event by thanking the artists for their participation. After a final round of applause, Butterworth opened the ballroom doors. The spectators and artists streamed out, talking animatedly as they left.

Storyton Hall staff members were standing by to clean up each artist station and return the folding chairs to the storage area behind the stage. Jane and Sinclair carefully moved the paintings from the middle of the room to the stage. They would soon be photographed and sold online.

Jane was just about to grab the painting with the astronaut T-rex when a familiar voice said, "Let me get that for you, milady."

She swung around to find Edwin smiling at her.

She wanted to throw her arms around him and kiss him. She wanted to whisper, "I missed you," into his neck and inhale his scent. She wanted to feel his fingers in her hair and his breath on her face.

But she didn't do any of these things. Not only was the room full of staff members, but Jane had never been prone to public displays of affection.

"You came back early," she said, trying to convey everything she felt with her eyes.

"I came back for you," said Edwin.

And before Jane could protest, Edwin pulled her to him and kissed her.

She forgot about the other people in the room. No one existed but Edwin. He was home, and he was holding her as if he'd never let her go again.

She melted into him like sun-warmed snow.

Chapter Seven

After a moment, Jane stepped out of Edwin's embrace. "Want to have lunch in the kitchens? Mrs. Hubbard will be thrilled to see you."

"She's already seen me," said Edwin. "I figured I could only surprise you if I came in through the kitchen door. Besides, I wanted to give Mrs. H the spices I got her in Morocco."

Jane rolled her eyes. "She doesn't need more reasons to sing your praises. I get tired of hearing about how wonderful you are."

Edwin grinned. "I could listen to her all day. Unfortunately, I can't stay because I promised Magnus that I'd help with the lunch service. He's taking next week off, which means tonight is the only night I'll have time to make a special meal for you and the boys. Will you bring them for dinner? Please? I have gifts for them. Just souvenirs. Nothing big."

Months ago, Jane had told Edwin that he needed to distance himself from her sons because she was afraid that they were beginning to see him as a father figure and Jane couldn't have that. Edwin's secret life was replete with danger, criminal activity, and prolonged absences. It was one thing for Jane to risk loving him, but it was quite another to expose Fitz and Hem to disappointment or heartbreak.

To protect her sons, Jane had asked Edwin to change the parameters of their relationship. Edwin would no longer come to her house. Instead, they'd go out on dates or hang out at Edwin's apartment. Jane accepted Edwin as he was. In return, she asked him to understand that her sons always came first.

Though Edwin had understood, awkward moments like this kept cropping up.

He was the first to break the silence. "I'm going to reserve a table for my best girl and her two wildlings. Since it's a school night, how does six o'clock sound?"

Jane smiled. She'd missed Edwin. So had the twins. What was the harm in taking them for a meal at Edwin's restaurant? "We'll be there."

After giving her a feather-light kiss, Edwin jumped off the stage. He landed as nimbly as a cat and strode out of the room.

Knowing that dinner was bound to be lavish, Jane decided to have a light lunch. But Mrs. Hubbard had other ideas.

"I made a plate for you, my dear. There's nothing like a sandwich and a nice bowl of soup on a blustery day. Apple and fontina grilled cheese and tomato bisque. I was dying to try one of my new spices, so I added a dash of cumin to your soup."

After her delicious lunch, Jane headed for the conference room in hopes of catching the opening remarks of the session entitled "3D Storybooks: Pop-Ups, Lift-the-Flaps, and More."

Today, the conference attendees had a choice between afternoon sessions: "3D Storybooks" or "Poetry in Picture Books." Judging by the lack of empty seats, Jane guessed that she'd picked the more popular session. She was glad she'd made arrangements for the speaker to give a hands-on lesson on making pop-up books to the twins' class when the session was over. It was bound to be a hit.

Jane was instantly captivated by the slideshow presentation, which featured one dazzling book after another. There were pop-up books with ocean and jungle scenes. Others had buildings that looked as if they might rise out of the pages and touch the ceiling. There were entire dollhouses, exploding volcanoes, and ornately decorated Christmas trees.

Fitz and Hem would have destroyed them trying to see how they worked, she thought.

Apparently, she wasn't the only one who questioned the "readability" of such a book.

"Is there a market for books that can be easily damaged?" one of the female authors in attendance asked. "Don't get me wrong. They're beautiful and super fun, but my toddler would rip King Kong off the top of the Empire State Building in five seconds flat."

Her remark elicited a ripple of laughter from the audience.

"Based on the amount of text per page, I assume these books are for grade-school kids," the woman went on. "But parents could buy several chapter books for the same price."

The speaker nodded. "You're right. These books cost more to produce, which is why they tend to be marketed as gift items. The majority of sales occur during the holiday season, which is why you'll see titles like *The Nutcracker* show up in bookstores in October."

A man seated at the very back of the room, close to where Jane was standing, slowly rose to his feet. The overhead lights were still off because the slideshow wasn't over, so Jane couldn't see the man's face.

"These aren't books for children," he said. His voice had a sharp edge. "Books for children don't require pop-ups or flaps. Sounds or lights. They require a good story paired with good illustrations. A child's first reading experiences shouldn't be about bells and whistles. The story and the pictures get them hooked on books. Not *gadgets*."

"You have a valid point, sir," the speaker said without rancor. "But I believe that children should be able to choose from a wide variety of books. That's how we'll get a book in the hands of reluctant readers. If we make books irresistible, we'll create a new generation of book lovers."

"Pfffah," the man growled. "These aren't books. They're toys in disguise!"

After delivering this ruling, the man headed for the exit. As he hobbled Jane's way, leaning heavily on his cane, she recognized Gunnar Humphries. His mouth was twisted in disgust and his eyes blazed with anger.

Jane hurried to open the door for him, but he didn't thank her. He didn't seem to see her at all. He just limped down the hallway. The runner muffled his footfalls, but his cane struck the hardwood floor with every step. The steady *click, click, click* echoed, filling the air with a hostile rhythm.

Because the spell of the presentation had been broken by Gunnar's mild outburst and subsequent exit, Jane decided to work in her office until the twins' class arrived.

At half past two, she walked to the middle of the lobby. She was going to wait for the school bus by the front door when she happened to glance to her right in time to see Fern and Peter exit the elevator, their faces bright with anticipation. Jane had invited them to attend the pop-up book workshop and was pleased that they'd decided to come.

The elevator doors hadn't even closed before Fern cried, "Oh, no! I forgot my camera!"

"We can go back up." Peter rushed to press the button.

At that moment, Tris and Todd, the author couple who'd complained to Gunnar about their supposed mistreatment, approached the elevator.

When the doors opened, Fern and Peter darted into the car and politely held the doors for the couple. Instead of thanking the children and stepping inside, Tris pursed her lips as if she'd just bitten into a lemon, and Todd leaned forward and muttered something to the kids. Jane couldn't see Peter, but she caught a flash of hurt on Fern's face.

Jane suddenly remembered Todd's bigoted comments about Nia. She also remembered Tris taking delight in them.

If those cretins insulted Fern and Peter, I'll send them packing, Jane thought, her hands curling into fists.

"Mom!" Fitz shouted from the behind her. "Ms. Miller said that we were having a surprise field trip, but we didn't know we were coming *here*!"

"Yeah, what are you showing us?" asked Hem.

Mrs. Miller and the rest of the class were streaming into the lobby. Jane looked at her sons and smiled. "You're having a workshop with one of our special guests."

The kids in her sons' class crowded around the center table, eager to hear what Jane was saying. By the time she glanced back at the elevator banks, Tris and Todd were gone.

Jane vowed to deal with them later. For now, she needed to introduce Mrs. Miller to the artist conducting the pop-up book workshop.

The workshop was meant to guide the kids through the process of making a four-page pop-up book based on the theme "Things I Love" using construction paper, printer paper, glue sticks, and scissors.

Jane didn't have time to sit through the entire workshop, but when she dropped by the conference room to see how things were going, she noticed that Fern and Peter weren't among the children happily constructing books.

I knew it! That horrible couple said something to upset those children.

Fuming, Jane used the phone in the lobby to call up the Fairy Tale Suite.

Alika answered the call.

"Hi, Mrs. Gilbert. It's Jane Steward. I was calling to see if everything was okay with Fern and Peter."

"They changed their minds about joining the rest of the kids," Alika said in a guarded tone.

Jane wanted to ask if Todd had said something to offend Fern and Peter. She couldn't get Fern's stricken expression out of her head. And though she wasn't sure how she should broach the subject she decided to forge ahead. "I didn't want them to miss the workshop, but the real reason I'm calling is that I saw your kids near the elevator. A couple spoke to them right before the doors closed. I was too far away to hear what was said, but I caught a glimpse of Fern's face. She looked upset. I want your family to feel safe and welcome at Storyton Hall. If there's ever a single moment when you don't feel welcomed by everyone you meet, I'd like to know about it. That way, I can set things straight."

"I appreciate that," said Alika. "But we're good. Thanks for calling to check on the kids."

"If Fern and Peter are interested, my sons could show them how to make the books. The four of them could have tea together. My boys, Fitz and Hem, can meet your kids by the grandfather clock in the lobby at 3:30. If they'd rather not come, that's absolutely fine."

After promising to deliver the message to her kids, Alika ended the call.

Though Jane was still troubled, she couldn't do much about her undesirable guests right now. Later, she'd seek out Sinclair and ask for his advice on how to handle Tris and Todd Petty.

Not long after Jane's phone call to Alika, the pop-up book workshop ended. Mrs. Miller's class lined up in the lobby, happily chatting and showing off their handiwork. Butterworth opened the door, and a blast of cold air rushed inside. The children shrieked and hurried out to their bus. After waving good-bye to Fitz and Hem, Ms. Miller followed the rest of her students into the winter afternoon.

"Hey, we're home early from school," Hem said to Fitz. "What do you want to do?"

"Let's go see Mrs. Hubbard."

Jane held out a hand to forestall them. "Before you go dashing off, I have a favor to ask."

To their credit, the boys didn't complain when Jane led them to a nearby sofa. Very quietly, she told them that another guest might have been mean to two children named Fern and Peter.

"I can't say what happened for sure," she admitted. "All I know is that Fern and Peter were supposed to join us for the workshop but decided to stay in their room instead. I have extra supplies. Would you show them how to make a book?"

"Sure," said Fitz.

Hem gave an absent nod before asking, "Can we work in the kitchens?"

Jane knew exactly what he was thinking. "Yes. But remember the rule. Sweets for teatime or sweets for dessert.

Not both." She pointed at the grandfather clock. "Fern and Peter will meet you there in five minutes if they're coming."

An hour later, after Jane had crossed off several items on her to-do list, she went to the kitchens for a cup of tea. Mrs. Hubbard was in the middle of a pre-dinner service meeting with her staff, so Jane filled the electric kettle as quietly as she could.

She was just stirring a dollop of honey into her tea when Mrs. Hubbard appeared in the break room.

"You're raising those boys right, my dear," she said.

Jane gave her a skeptical look. "You're biased when it comes to the twins."

"It's true. But you should have seen how they took those other kids under their wings. The boys gave Fern and Peter a tour of the kitchen and made them extra-chocolatey milk. Next, they showed them how to make their books. Of course, I *had* to give all four of them a special treat. What adorable children!"

After making a mental note to tell Edwin that he could skip tonight's dessert course, Jane said, "How nice. Did Fern and Peter get enough to eat?"

Mrs. Hubbard was affronted. "As if anyone has ever left my kitchens with an empty belly."

Jane glanced down at her teacup. "That's why I'm in the break room. I don't want to be tempted by your delectable treats when I have a dress to squeeze into on Saturday."

"You won't even try a white chocolate almond scone?"

Though scones were one of Jane's all-time favorite goodies, she grabbed her teacup and fled.

That evening, when the twins asked, "what's for dinner?" Jane pointed at the coat rack.

"We're going out."

"To Mr. Alcott's?" Hem asked hopefully.

Jane pulled on her coat and arched her brows. "Maybe."

"Maybe usually means no. But this time, I think it means yes!" Fitz cried. He and his brother exchanged fist bumps.

On the drive to the village, Jane thanked her sons for spending time with Peter and Fern.

"They're cool," said Hem. "They told us lots of stories about New York City. They live in an apartment and ride the subway every day. Can we go there, Mom?"

"One day," Jane said. "Did Fern or Peter seem upset?"

Fitz, who was sitting in the front seat, pivoted to look at his brother. Their eyes met, and they shook their heads in unison.

"They seemed happy," said Fitz. "They love Storyton Hall. They said that they don't ever want to go home."

As a mother, Jane longed to shield the Gilbert children from their grief. She also wanted to punch Tris and Todd in the teeth for possibly causing Fern and Peter more pain. However, she didn't want to put a damper on a night out with her three favorite men, so she pushed all thoughts of the awful couple aside and raised another subject.

"How's Ms. Miller's pick-me-up project coming along?"

Hem spoke first. "We're done. Mrs. Hubbard helped me. I'm giving Ms. Miller some tea, and a card that says, *You're Tea-Riffic*. Get it?"

Fitz didn't wait for Jane to respond before saying, "Ms. Kota helped me. We made a cupcake with one of those sponge thingies you use in the shower. We put a bar of soap from the spa inside the cupcake thingy. My card says, *I Soap You Have a Great Valentine's Day.*"

Jane laughed and told her sons that Ms. Miller was bound to be delighted by her gifts.

"Does this mean we can have dessert tonight?" Hem asked.

"I know you helped Fern and Peter and made special cards for Ms. Miller, but you should do those things because you're a good person. Not for extra dessert."

Jane parked in front of the Daily Bread Café. She let the boys enter the restaurant first, feeling a mix of pleasure and guilt when she saw their faces light up at the sight of Edwin. He opened his arms wide and they rushed forward to hug him.

"You're lucky. I don't get nearly enough of those," Jane said to Edwin.

Fitz whispered, "We'd hug you if we could have dessert."

Jane pretended to swat him.

Edwin watched this exchange in amusement. "You might not have room for dessert. I have lots of tasty dishes for you to try. Have either of you gentlemen heard of tapas?"

The boys shook their heads.

"Instead of having one plate for dinner, you get lots of small plates. That means you can try six or seven different things in one meal. For example, I'm going to bring you a plate of olives. You don't want an entire meal of olives, but it's fun to eat a few."

"I could eat a whole plate of olives," said Fitz. "Especially the green ones. I like them."

"I like the black ones," said Hem, just to have the last word.

Edwin showed them to their table and pulled out Jane's chair.

"I'll serve each tapa as soon as it's ready," he explained. "You don't have to eat any dish that you don't like, but try *one* bite of every dish. That's how you become an adventurous eater. World travelers are always adventurous eaters."

The twins promised to try everything, no matter how bizarre.

Edwin breezed in and out of the kitchen. He served them olive medley, prosciutto-wrapped dates, roasted beets with goat cheese, shrimp and pork meatballs, sautéed spinach, grilled lamb chops, and tortillas filled with egg, chorizo, and potato.

The twins tried one bite of every dish, though it took a bit of goading to get them to sample the charred octopus. They asked for a second serving of garlic shrimp, and Edwin was happy to oblige.

The restaurant's other patrons seemed to be enjoying the new tapas menu. Magnus, the manager, acted as host, server, and sommelier. He said hello to Jane and topped off the twins' water before moving to another table to take drink orders.

A party of two occupied the four-top table behind Jane. She examined their reflection in the window but didn't recognize the elegant, elderly woman with the white bobbed hair or her male dining companion. The man was small in stature with a thin, dark mustache and a pointy beard. His sharp nose and facial hair lent him a devilish appearance.

Jane idly studied the pair until Edwin appeared with another helping of garlic shrimp. The boys fell on the six pieces of shrimp like a pack of hyenas, and Jane was about to tell them to slow down when she heard a familiar name from the table behind her.

"Gloria's late again," the man said.

The woman released a theatrical sigh. "I don't see why you bothered inviting her. She won't give you what you want."

"Never underestimate the power of food and copious

amounts of wine," the man said. He had an oily voice. A salesman's voice.

The older woman grunted. "It takes more than a mediocre Spanish red to part a treasure from a collector. Forget Gloria. You should concentrate your efforts on me."

The man raised his hand and signaled for Magnus.

"My fine fellow," he said in his oily voice. "Strike the Spanish red order. Bring me a bottle of your best champagne instead."

Gloria? Jane thought as Magnus walked away. *Are they referring to our missing paint-off judge?*

Jane looked at the pair's reflection in the window again. The man and woman sat across from each other. The third chair held their coats and the woman's purse. The fourth chair was empty.

If that seat had been meant for Gloria Ramirez, then where was she?

Missing.

The word tiptoed into Jane's mind and embedded itself there.

Where is Gloria Ramirez?

When Edwin returned with the dessert menu, Jane waved it away, telling him that they'd have to pass on dessert. She thanked him for an amazing meal and reached for her coat. It was time for her to go.

Chapter Eight

Jane waited until the boys were in bed before calling Sterling. He was in charge of the resort's surveillance system and could often track a guest's movements by reviewing the footage recorded by their security cameras.

"One of our guests might be missing," Jane said when Sterling answered. "I had the front desk call her room, but there's no answer. She wasn't at the paint-off this morning either, even though the whole thing was her idea. Tonight, the boys and I had dinner at the Daily Bread. A man and a woman were seated behind us. Our missing guest was expected to join them, but she never showed."

Sterling replied without hesitation. "We should look into this right away. We've seen people disappear for hours at a time, but not in this weather. No one would have gone on a long hike or outdoor excursion today. What's the guest's name?"

"Gloria Ramirez. I don't know what she looks like, so you'll have to ask Sinclair for a photo. And could you contact Mrs. Templeton? Have her talk to the staff member servicing Ms. Ramirez's room. Housekeeping will have to perform a late turndown service. It's the only way we can make sure Ms. Ramirez isn't in her room, waiting for someone to find her. She could be sick or injured. We need to check on her."

Sterling told Jane that he'd start investigating as soon as he got off the phone.

After setting her alarm, Jane walked over to the window and looked out. A handful of stars glowed in the inky sky, but her eye was drawn to the moon. Blurred halos of light surrounded its electric-white center.

A snow moon, she thought.

The window glass was cold to the touch, and the bare branches on the trees jerked and shuddered as the wind pushed them around. There were no signs of life outside. No animal calls or owl hoots. The world was frozen and somnolent. It was the perfect night to burrow under a comforter and read, but Jane was too unsettled to focus on her book.

Turning away from the window, she slipped a robe over her pajamas and went downstairs to make a cup of chamomile tea. While the kettle heated the water, she made a list of things she had to do in the morning. Tomorrow was going to be a busy day. The families booked for the Valentine's weekend were due to arrive, Storybook Village would open, and, in the evening, the Storyton Players would perform *Charlie and the Chocolate Factory*.

Despite of all the activities Jane had to oversee, the first thing on her to-do list wasn't a thing at all. It was a name.

Kristen Burke.

It was time to check in with Sheriff Evans. He must have learned more about the dead woman by now. And if Gloria Ramirez wasn't found by tomorrow, Jane would have to report her disappearance to the sheriff. Though people weren't officially missing until forty-eight hours had passed, Jane felt that two days was too long to wait.

So much could happen to a person in forty-eight hours. Especially if that person was lost, hurt, or, heaven-forbid, abducted.

Then again, she could be sightseeing over the mountain. Her car might have broken down. She could be in another person's room. She could be in a secret relationship. Jane couldn't trespass on a guest's privacy without just cause, but if Gloria Ramirez didn't turn up by tomorrow morning, Jane would search for her. She and her staff would look in every room, stairwell, and closet if need be. And if she couldn't be found inside Storyton Hall, they'd scour the grounds.

As if mocking Jane's plans, the wind picked up force. It raced over the roof and slithered down the chimney, creating a deep *whoosh* that echoed through the living room.

"No, you don't," Jane said and switched on the gas logs.

With her teacup on the coffee table and a soft blanket thrown over her legs, Jane wriggled into a comfortable position on the couch and reached for her laptop. She'd made some cursory notes since Lachlan had showed her Eloise's engagement ring, but she needed to hone those ideas into something extraordinary. A dazzling, shining moment that would be forever etched into her best friend's memory.

It didn't take long before Jane was completely captivated by photographs of gazebos illuminated by thousands of tiny lights, garden paths lit by luminary bags, garlands of wild roses, and *Will You Marry Me?* messages drawn in the snow.

It was too cold for wild roses, but Jane could make evergreen garlands. She had loads of white lights. They were used for all Storyton Hall weddings and made every celebration a bit more magical. Jane could also move the small white pedestal table that typically held the guest book into the gazebo. She'd drape the table with a flowing, gauzy white cloth—almost like a wedding veil—and load its surface with a variety of pillar candles.

Battery-powered candles, Jane wrote on her list as the wind whipped her house. *All white.*

With these basics in place, she now needed to figure out how to personalize this white, snowy, light-filled setting by adding books to it.

"Not books," Jane murmured. "*The* book. Eloise's favorite. *Jane Eyre.*"

The challenge was to find as many copies as she could and have the novels delivered to Storyton Hall by Saturday night. Sunday morning at the latest. Jane only patronized Run for Cover, but she knew there was a chain bookstore over the mountain. After examining their online inventory, Jane decided that she had a very good reason to shop with another bookstore.

She used her credit card to pre-pay for the books. Since delivery wasn't guaranteed until Monday, someone would need to collect the books tomorrow. The drivers would all be busy fetching families from the train station, so it would have to be a member of the waitstaff. That person would have to set out first thing in the morning and be back before lunchtime.

Before the snow comes, Jane thought.

She added this task to her list, shut down her computer, and folded the blanket.

Suddenly, she was tired. The cozy room and the hot tea had done the trick, and though her bed was calling to her, she couldn't rest until she got an update on Gloria Ramirez's whereabouts.

Sterling answered her call by saying, "I'm in her room now. There's no sign of trouble. Her clothes are unpacked and put away. Her toiletries are in the bathroom. She's reading a book called *Dear Mrs. Bird*. A Baxter Books bookmark shows that she's about halfway in."

"What about the bed? Was it slept in last night?"

There was a brief pause and then Mrs. Templeton came on the line. "Sandy worked this floor today. She cleaned the room at ten-thirty this morning. When she made the bed, she remembered thinking that the guest must have been a heavy sleeper because only one side of the bed was rumpled. The pillows on the other side are untouched. There was a book on the nightstand and another on the reading chair. Having opted to reuse her towels, Ms. Ramirez had checked off the 'go green' box on the sign hanging from the bathroom door handle. Two of the towels were still a bit damp, so Sandy left them on the hook instead of refolding them."

Sterling reclaimed the phone. "We believe our guest slept here last night and showered this morning. I've conducted a cursory search of the room. Nothing seems out of place. Would you like me to start a more thorough search?"

"No," said Jane. "I don't want to invade Ms. Ramirez's privacy any more than we already have. If she comes back later tonight, I want her to find her room exactly as she left it. There's still the possibility that she spent the day with another guest or someone who lives nearby. Her personal life is none of our business. If she doesn't appear in the morning, I'll tell the sheriff."

Sterling promised to review the surveillance footage as soon as he returned downstairs. He would inform the other Fins if the footage revealed anything unusual but would only disturb Jane's sleep in case of emergency. Jane thanked him for his diligence and asked him to encourage Mrs. Templeton to go home.

"Tomorrow's a big day. She should get some rest."

Taking her own advice, Jane climbed into bed and turned out the light. She didn't want to go to sleep without telling Edwin why she'd left the restaurant in such a hurry, so she called him.

"Is everything all right?" he asked.

After sharing her concerns about Gloria Ramirez, Jane confessed that she hadn't quite gotten over the shock of finding Kristen Burke's body.

"What makes it worse is that her death seems so sense-less. She was so young. And I can't stop thinking about the fairy-tale elements. The valuable book. What Kristen was doing in Storyton in the first place." Jane's exhale was laden with frustration and fatigue. "If Gloria is missing, then I have even more to worry about. Lots of kids are heading to Storyton Hall. I want them to be safe, Edwin. I want all of us to be safe."

"If you feel like a storm is brewing, then it probably is." His voice softened. "I know that you can handle anything that comes your way, but if you need someone to lean on, I'm here. I'm right down the road. I can be at your side in minutes. You can share your worries with me. My shoul-ders are strong. I can bear the weight."

Jane wanted to be with Edwin right now. She longed to feel his arms around her, to be warm and happy inside their protective circle. But she couldn't ask him to come over. She'd imposed restrictions of their relationship. For the sake of her sons.

Why does the right thing have to be so hard? she thought miserably.

"I love you," Edwin whispered. "When I go to sleep tonight, I'll look for you in my dreams."

This was a lovely sentiment, but Jane didn't see Edwin in her dreams. The images that haunted her sleep weren't the least bit romantic.

In Jane's dreams, Storyton was assaulted by a winter storm. A mid-winter blizzard dumped several feet of snow onto their little valley. The sky was white. The ground was white. The trees were swathed in white. The wind sent barbed snowflakes in every direction, reducing the visibility to zero. No plows operated. No one shoveled paths or driveways. The snow piled up around the shops and houses. It walled over doors and blanketed parked cars. It smothered all noise. All life.

In the dream, Jane watched the storm from her bedroom window in despair. None of the families would make it to Storyton Hall for their Valentine's weekend. They'd be stuck at airports or train stations. It would be days before regular activities would resume.

And what about Gloria? How could they search for her in the middle of a blizzard?

If she'd left a trail of footprints in the snow, they'd already be erased. If she'd fallen somewhere, she had no hope of rescue. By this point, the snow would have covered her body. She'd be a frozen, snow-covered sculpture.

As in the way of dreams, the narrative suddenly shifted. Jane saw a figure struggling to cross the Great Lawn. She was a blur of dark hair and a red coat. She had no hat. No gloves. Each step through the deep snow looked exhausting. Desperate.

"Where are you going?" Jane called to the woman.

She banged on the window, but the woman didn't turn. As Jane looked on in helpless terror, the woman in the red coat suddenly vanished. Jane stared at the place where she'd been, but there was only an eddy of snowy air. It spun around and around like a desert dervish before rising into the gray sky.

Jane woke with a start. She'd kicked off all her blankets and was shivering with cold. She sat up to reclaim the comforter and realized that her room was much darker than it had been when she'd gone to sleep. Getting up to peer out her window, she saw that it was snowing.

The next morning, Jane made sure the twins were safely on the school bus before hurrying to her office to call Sterling.

"Any news on Ms. Ramirez?"

"I couldn't find her on yesterday's footage, so I went back to the day before. I tracked her arrival. She went up to her room about thirty minutes after checking in. I saw her once after that, but only for a minute. She was heading into the Ian Fleming Lounge. She'd changed from the pantsuit and ankle boots she'd been wearing earlier to a dress and heels. The time stamp read 6:24 p.m., which meant she was probably grabbing a drink before dinner."

Jane stared at her empty coffee cup and wished it would magically replenish itself. She'd been in such a hurry to get an update on Gloria that she hadn't stopped at the lobby urns to fill her cup. Without that hit of caffeine, her mind felt sluggish and fuzzy. "You didn't see her leave the lounge?"

"She probably walked out when the camera was pointed in a different direction, but I expected to spot her later in the dining room or the café. I plan to show Ms. Ramirez's photo to the bellman working the front door last night to see if he remembers her leaving Storyton Hall."

"Have you called her room?"

Sterling said that he wanted to leave that decision to Jane. She checked her watch. 8:12. Early but not too early.

The phone in Gloria's room rang and rang. Reasoning that Gloria could be in the shower, Jane headed out to the lobby for coffee. She returned to her office, sipped from her mug several times, and then called Gloria's room again. No one answered.

Jane's next move was to speak with one of Gloria's coworkers. Examining a spreadsheet on the conference attendees, she saw that Reggie, the man with the pink mustachios, was an in-house illustrator with Baxter Books. She dialed his room number.

He answered with a cheery, "'Morning!"

Jane wasted no time explaining the reason for her call.

"Oh, my." Reggie's joviality disappeared in a flash. "I didn't see her at *all* yesterday. I even asked one of the editors if she was sick. I mean, the paint-off was her brain-child. And it was *such* fun! I couldn't imagine her missing a second of it, let alone the whole thing."

"What did the editor say?"

"He thought he'd seen Gloria at breakfast, but he wasn't sure."

Jane's anxiety was increasing by the moment. "What about your first night here? Did you bump into her at dinner? Or in the lounge?"

"Yes! In that fab Ian Fleming bar. All that wood panel-ing, leather furniture, and crystal glassware—Bond would have approved. Anyway, Gloria was there. She was wear-ing a gorgeous dress. A structured, dark green number. She was perusing the cocktail menu when I saw her."

Jane thanked Reggie for the information. "Would you talk to your coworkers before the morning session starts? If Ms. Ramirez hasn't been seen since the day everyone ar-rived, then I'll have to report her missing to the authorities. I don't want to alarm or embarrass anyone, so if you could get back to me as soon as possible, I'd appreciate it."

Thirty minutes later, Reggie called to report that no one had seen Gloria since the day before yesterday. Her closest friend at work, a woman named Sasha, said that

Gloria loved to hike. When Gloria didn't show up for the paint-off, Sasha assumed that she'd gone on a hike and lost track of time. The two women hadn't signed up for the same afternoon session, but Sasha hadn't expected to see Gloria again until today because Gloria had said that she had dinner plans with someone who didn't work at Baxter Books.

"Did Sasha know his or her name?" Jane asked Reggie.

"Gloria never mentioned it. She didn't even say if he worked for a publisher or if he was a freelance artist or an author. Not a clue. She did say *he,* though. Not *she.*"

The man with the devilish features, Jane thought.

It was time to call Sheriff Evans.

"Ms. Steward, this is a coincidence," he said by way of greeting. "I'm on my way to see you."

Jane's apprehension flared, but she kept her voice steady. "I'll have coffee waiting."

After ordering a whole pot, Jane assembled a folder on Gloria Ramirez that included a copy of her driver's license photo and the personal information she'd provided when booking her room. Jane also typed a brief timeline indicating when Gloria had last been seen, and which coworkers the sheriff might want to interview first.

When the sheriff arrived, his nose and cheeks were rosy from the cold. His brown hat was dusted with snow. He took it off and lowered it to his side. White flakes drifted to the floor.

"Sorry," he said, looking around for a place to put the offending accessory.

With his red cheeks and sheepish expression, Evans looked like a boy expecting a scolding. Jane smiled and said, "There's a hook on the back of the door. You can hang your coat and hat there. Is it really cold out?"

"It's awful. It's the kind of icy air that gets right under your collar and into your bones." He sat in the chair opposite Jane and reached for the coffee cup she'd just filled. "Thanks for this."

Jane asked, "Are you here to talk about Kristen Burke?"

"Yes. The ME has the preliminary lab results. The apple lodged in Ms. Burke's throat contained peanut oil. The oil was probably injected into the apple. Ms. Burke bit into it and swallowed a small piece. Undigested apple was found in her stomach. Her throat may have already begun to swell by the time she took her second bite. This one was fatal. Her airway closed around the food and she couldn't breathe. I expected to find scratch marks on her neck. People often do this when their air supply is cut off, but her scarf was thick, and she probably didn't have the strength to get around it."

"How terrible," Jane whispered. "She must have been so scared."

The sheriff dipped his chin in silent agreement.

Jane glanced out the window and watched the snow fall. The world was filled with a quiet beauty. It seemed impossible that violence could have tainted such a picturesque scene. But it had.

"Are you treating this as a murder case?"

"I'm afraid so," said Evans. "I'd like to speak with the staff members who helped build or decorate the Storybook Village. I have no suspects, but I'm hoping that a Storyton Hall employee saw or heard something of note."

Jane was stunned. "What about Kristen's friends? Or relatives? Don't they know why she came here?"

"She has none to speak of. And while I was able to find out basic facts about Ms. Burke, I have to rely on the police in her township to provide me with a complete picture. The trouble is, Ms. Burke's café is located a town away from the largest protest march in New Jersey's history. I don't know if you saw the news this morning, but yesterday's march got way out of hand. Authorities from three counties were called in to deal with looting, vandalism, arson, and multiple cases of aggravated assault. I can't expect assistance from these officers until things calm down."

Jane shook her head in dismay. "Why do people hurt each other? Whether it's a riot involving thousands, or one woman poisoned by an apple, I don't understand any of it." She made a sweeping gesture. "I used to believe that Storyton Hall was a sanctuary—a book-filled haven far removed from violence and perversity. But I'm older and wiser now, and I know that no place is truly crime-free. There's light and there's shadow."

Sheriff Evans leaned toward Jane. His gaze was kind and earnest. "A million years ago, when I was a young deputy, the sheriff I worked for kept a big blackboard in our conference room. He wrote a quote at the very top of the board. In permanent marker. I read those words every day, and they made an impression on me."

Now, it was Jane's turn to lean closer.

The sheriff continued, "The quote was from Desmond Tutu. 'Do your little bit of good where you are; it's those little bits of good put together that overwhelm the world.'"

The words touched Jane. Her heart felt lighter as she said, "I believe that's true."

The sheriff's tone became businesslike again. "We'll keep working to find out what happened to Ms. Burke. In the meantime, tell me about Ms. Ramirez."

It didn't take long to share what little she knew. When

Jane was done, the sheriff got to his feet and moved to the window. After a long moment, he turned back to Jane.

"If Ms. Ramirez lost her way or was injured while hiking, her situation could be dire. I need to get to the station and put out an alert. I'll send Deputy Emory over to conduct interviews with anyone who saw or spoke with Ms. Ramirez before she went missing."

Jane handed him the folder she'd prepared. He opened it, scanned its contents, and nodded.

Reaching for his hat, the sheriff said, "I'll be honest with you, Ms. Steward. I don't like the sudden disappearance of a second woman on the heels of your finding the body of another woman on your property. Tell your staff to keep their eyes and ears open."

"I will," Jane promised.

When the sheriff was gone, Jane sent a group text to the Fins.

Emergency meeting in fifteen minutes. The usual
spot.

The usual spot was the surveillance room, a cramped space containing a table and chairs, a bank of security monitors, and the copy machines. The room was also a catchall space for office supplies and an assortment of random items that needed a permanent home but never seemed to find one.

Butterworth was the first Fin to arrive. He wheeled a cart with a coffeepot, cups, and a plate of ham biscuits into the room. Finding his path blocked by a limbo stick, he frowned. He put the stick in a corner and then grunted in displeasure at the sight of the Mardi Gras masks strewn across the table.

"The theater would be a better place for such bric-a-brac," he grumbled as Sterling, Sinclair, and Lachlan entered the room.

Jane shut the door and took her place at the head of the table.

"One woman was found dead. A second woman is missing," she began, looking at her friends and protectors. She repeated everything that Sheriff Evans had just told her. "The sheriff can't expect help from the New Jersey cops, which means we need to learn everything we can about Kristen Burke and Gloria Ramirez. Lachlan, one of Ms. Ramirez's coworkers thinks she might have gone out on a hike yesterday and never returned."

Lachlan widened his eyes in surprise. "It was so cold. I can't imagine anyone going out for a walk in the woods."

"If she did, it'll be a miracle if she survived the night." Jane's tone was grave. "Can you try to track her? Despite the snow? Sterling, we need to see what she looks like."

Sterling played the video footage of Gloria entering the Ian Fleming Lounge. "This is our last sighting of Ms. Ramirez." He looked at Jane. "As for Ms. Burke, I watched three days' worth of footage and she never appeared on camera. I have no idea how she ended up on our grounds."

Jane acknowledged this with a nod and turned to her head librarian. "Sinclair, I'd like you to round up Gloria's coworkers. Everyone from Baxter Books must be interviewed. Deputy Emory is on her way, and I'd like you to sit in on the interviews. I'll join you when I can. I want to take a look at Ms. Ramirez's room first. Butterworth, I'd like you to come with me."

"Of course." Butterworth wrapped two ham biscuits in a napkin and handed the bundle to Lachlan. "You might require extra fuel if you're venturing out in this weather."

Jane asked her Fins to report back to her with any news. After telling Lachlan to bundle up, she and Butterworth headed for the staff staircase.

Using her master key, Jane unlocked the door to Gloria's room and stepped inside.

It was neat as a pin. There were no clothes on the floor. No papers on the desk. Two dresses, three blouses, and three pairs of slacks hung in the closet. The drawers held folded pajamas, socks, hose, bras, and underwear. In the bathroom, Gloria's toiletries were meticulously organized in a multi-compartment cosmetic case.

Butterworth entered the master code into the wall safe's keypad and withdrew a handbag containing Gloria's wallet, a set of keys, a small makeup bag, two pens, gum, and a day planner.

Setting the other objects aside, Butterworth flipped through the planner. "The paint-off is clearly marked in her diary, as is the afternoon session on 'Poetry in Picture Books.' It looks like she meant to attend both events."

"What are we missing?" Jane asked, glancing around the room. "She left without her purse, which implies that she didn't need money where she was going."

Butterworth pointed at the nightstand to the left of the bed. "There's a phone charger, but no phone."

"As soon as we're positive that it isn't here, we need to look up her number. Sheriff Evans might be able to use her cell phone to find her location."

Jane walked over to the nightstand. The charger sat on top of a hardback copy of *Dear Mrs. Bird*. Jane picked up the novel and flipped to where the Baxter Books bookmark was nestled between the pages. The Baxter Books logo, a puppy pulling a wagon filled with books, was charming.

Next, Jane opened the drawer to the nightstand. The

drawer was empty, save for a notepad. The Storyton Hall motto that marched across the top of the notepad—*Their Stories Are Our Stories*—reminded Jane of her conversation with Mrs. Templeton. The housekeeper in charge of this room had noticed a book on the reading chair.

Turning away from the nightstand, Jane crossed the room to where the chair was angled toward the window. Gloria must have moved it to get a better view of the blue hills and the vast sky. As Jane peered over the chair back, she saw the book resting on the floral cushion. Jane walked around the chair to read the title.

It was *Fairy Tales* by Hans Christian Andersen.

Jane's blood went cold.

She didn't need to handle the book to know that it was old. The slight discoloring of the cream boards, the gilt lettering, and the Roman numerals on the spine lent it a unique patina.

There'd been an old book near Kristen Burke's body too.

Another book of fairy tales.

"Butterworth." Jane's voice was a tremulous whisper. "I think we're too late."

Chapter Nine

Butterworth donned his gloves and picked up the book of fairy tales. He then followed Jane to Sinclair's office so she could look up the book's current market value.

"Over six thousand dollars," she said.

Jane and Butterworth stared at the book. There was nothing remarkable about its white cover. Its gilt lettering. The silhouettes of ladies in fancy dress and a man in his top hat on the endpapers. Like the Grimm Brothers book, the illustrations in the Hans Christian Andersen book were by Arthur Rackham.

"Why Rackham? Why fairy tales?" Jane muttered angrily. "Are we going to find Gloria Ramirez in an Andersen story setting? Will she be stranded on a tower of mattresses? Or frozen, her pockets filled with matchsticks?"

Butterworth put his hand over Jane's. "Steady on, Miss Jane. If Ms. Ramirez is on the grounds, Mr. Lachlan will find her."

Dead or alive? Jane thought grimly. Aloud, she said, "The two fairy tale books have some significance. I'll let the sheriff know that we found a second one in Gloria's room. In the meantime, I want to find the couple I overheard last night at the Daily Bread. Especially the man. He invited Gloria to dinner and was obviously disappointed that she didn't show up. The other woman wasn't pleased over sharing the man's attention and didn't seem to care about Gloria's absence."

"What did the man look like?"

Jane began scanning the photographs pinned to Sinclair's wall. "Like the devil."

Butterworth didn't immediately react, but when he saw that Jane wasn't kidding, he began examining photos on the other end of the room.

A few minutes later, he removed a printout from the board and showed it to Jane.

"That's the man," Jane said, and quickly read the pertinent details. "Malcolm Marcus. Age fifty-eight. Rare book dealer from Alexandria. He checked in yesterday and is leaving Storyton Hall later today after exercising the late checkout option. He didn't register for the conference, nor has he signed up for any of the special events."

Butterworth gestured at the book of fairy tales. "Perhaps this belonged to Ms. Ramirez, and she intended to sell it to Mr. Marcus."

"It's possible," said Jane. "Malcolm didn't use the terms buying or selling, but the other woman said that she wouldn't give him what he wanted without being wooed first. I don't see that woman's photo on this board, so we need to find the book dealer and question him."

"His cell phone number is listed. I'll call him right away." Butterworth reached for the phone next to Sinclair's computer. Before dialing, he turned to Jane. "Where would you like to meet him?"

"The Daphne du Maurier Morning Room. I want our guest to feel at ease," said Jane. "I also want to keep an eye on the snowfall."

"According to Mrs. Templeton, it'll be over by noon.

The ache in her hip is a more reliable barometer than any high-tech meteorological gadget."

Jane couldn't help but smile over this, but her smile slipped when she spotted two familiar faces on the board. Todd and Tris Petty. She looked at the arrogant tilt of Todd's chin and sour-lemon pucker of Tris's mouth and frowned.

Butterworth had no problem reaching Malcolm Marcus. The butler kept the conversation short and to the point. He explained that Ms. Steward, the resort manager, had recently found an unusual book and wondered if the dealer would be kind enough to take a look at it. After giving Malcolm directions to the drawing room, he ended the call.

"He was practically foaming at the mouth, and I didn't even mention a specific title." Butterworth shook his head. "But we've seen our fair share of zealous collectors, haven't we? To them, the thrill of the discovery is paramount."

"It's true. The acquisition gets their blood racing. I just hope that a woman's life is worth more than six thousand dollars."

Butterworth glanced at Gloria Ramirez's photo. She was a handsome woman in her early forties. Her pixie cut called attention to her high cheekbones and dimpled chin. Her eyes were large and dark, and her nose was a bit crooked, as if it had been broken and didn't heal completely straight. There were laugh lines around her mouth, and a beauty mark grazed her upper lip. Based on her portrait, Gloria looked like a friendly, approachable woman.

She reviewed Gloria's pertinent details. "Age forty-three. Lives in Brooklyn. Unmarried. Hobbies include urban gardening, volunteering at her local library, and working with the Boys & Girls Clubs of America. Senior editor at Baxter Books. She sounds like someone I'd like to meet." Jane swallowed hard. "I hope I get the chance."

"Mr. Marcus should be heading to the drawing room,"

Butterworth reminded her. "I'll stop by the kitchens for a tea tray and join you later. The tea gives me a reason for being in the room."

Jane smiled fondly at Butterworth. "If the book dealer doesn't behave, he'll regret it."

As she hurried through the staff corridor, Jane received two texts from Sterling. The first said that the bellhop who had worked the door last night didn't remember seeing Gloria Ramirez. The second was to inform Jane that Deputy Emory had arrived. She and Sinclair were currently holed up in the conference room with Sasha Long, Gloria's coworker.

Jane tried to find comfort in the thought that everyone was working together to find Gloria. When she entered the Daphne du Maurier Morning Room, with its oversized fireplace and walls lined with bookshelves, her eye went straight to the picture window. The great lawn was covered in snow and the flakes were still falling, forming a curtain of white outside the window.

"Ms. Steward?" came a man's voice.

Jane turned to find Malcolm Marcus standing in the doorway.

"Thank you for joining me." She gestured at one of the loveseats. "I've ordered tea, but if you'd prefer coffee or something else, let me know."

"Tea's fine, thank you." Malcolm sat down and gave the floral chintz cushion a pat. "This room looks like it was magicked here from Manderley and then given a contemporary update. It has all the romance without any of the gloom."

Jane warmed to her guest. "That was the idea. Have you been to Menabilly? The inspiration for Manderley?"

"Oh, yes. I'm very lucky. I have ample amounts of money and freedom, which means I can travel when and wherever

I'd like." He spread his hands. His fingers were bony, and his nails were long and tapered. "My parents were successful entrepreneurs. They bankrolled my business and encouraged me to pursue my passion for collecting rare children's books. They've since passed away, but their generosity toward me continues. Like I said, I'm very lucky."

Malcolm sounded sincere. He didn't use the oily voice Jane had heard at the restaurant, and she wondered if he reserved that tone for potential book buyers or sellers.

"I want to be up front with you," Jane said. "I know you by sight because I was sitting at the table behind you last night."

"Were you? I'm afraid I was too focused on the tapas to pay attention to other diners," Malcolm said. "I hadn't expected to find such excellent food in a small town in the middle of nowhere, but excellent it was."

After telling Malcolm that she'd convey his compliments to the owner, Jane said, "I couldn't help but overhear that your third dining companion didn't show. Gloria Ramirez?"

Malcolm didn't hesitate. "Yes, and I don't know why she stood me up. I emailed her weeks ago, inviting her to dinner. She accepted the next day. We're not close, so I didn't expect to hear from her again until we met at the restaurant. I'm surprised she didn't call to cancel."

"Forgive me for prying, but was this a business dinner? Did Gloria own rare books? Was she hoping to sell you something?"

Malcolm was taken aback. "I don't understand why you're asking about Gloria. I thought you wanted me to look at one of *your* books."

At this opportune moment, Butterworth breezed into the room carrying a heavy silver tray.

"Good morning, sir," Butterworth said as he set the tray down on the coffee table. "Would you care for some tea?"

Malcolm said that he would. His tone was pleasant but guarded.

Jane waited for Butterworth to pour before saying, "The book I wanted you to see was found in Ms. Ramirez's room." She handed Malcolm a pair of Sinclair's white cotton gloves. "If you don't mind."

Clearly intrigued, Malcolm pulled on the gloves. Butterworth removed the book from the interior pocket of his livery coat and offered it to Malcolm.

The man's small eyes glimmered as he studied the cream-white cover. "Very nice," he whispered. As he carefully turned the pages, he seemed to forget about Jane and Butterworth. He was completely captivated by the book. "Yes. Very nice."

"Was Ms. Ramirez planning to sell this to you?" Jane asked.

Malcolm gave her a bemused look. "I didn't think she owned anything like this. Her collection has always been very specific, focusing on illustrated children's books printed in America. She particularly liked Raggedy Ann and Andy, Christmas stories, and books featuring famous American locales like Boston Harbor or Coney Island."

"Was there a particular item in her collection that you wished to buy?"

Malcolm glanced at the book in his lap. "It wasn't this. Gloria owned a first edition of *Raggedy Ann and the Lucky Pennies* inscribed by the author. I already own a copy, but mine is in good condition and has no inscription. I was hoping to buy Gloria's, which is in very fine condition. I've been trying to get that book away from her for years. It wasn't until last month that Gloria finally agreed to consider my offer. Her father has Alzheimer's and she's paying for his care. I believe it's quite costly."

"Thank you for the explanation." Jane studied Malcolm

as Butterworth offered him a lemon poppy seed scone. "And the Andersen book? Have you seen it before today?"

Malcolm broke off a piece of scone. "I own a similar copy, but mine has red boards instead of white."

Jane reclaimed the book and casually asked another question. "The elegant woman you dined with at the Daily Bread—does she know Ms. Ramirez?"

"No. Audrey lives in Charlottesville. She has an impressive collection of young detective novels. Nancy Drew, Trixie Belden, and such. From time to time, she'll part with a few first editions. I drove to Storyton to wine and dine her and Gloria at the same time. Normally, I'd meet with them separately, but there's an antiquarian book show in Richmond on Saturday, and I want to be there when the doors open at nine."

"Do you know anyone else from Baxter Books? I was wondering if one of Gloria's coworkers was also a collector."

Malcolm fixed a shrewd gaze on Jane. "I don't think you asked me here to look at a book. You keep asking questions about Gloria. Do *you* know why she didn't show up for dinner? Is something wrong?"

Jane saw no reason to lie. "Ms. Ramirez hasn't been seen since the day she arrived. No one knows where she is. We're especially concerned because one of Ms. Ramirez's coworkers told us that she enjoys hiking. If she's lost or hurt, we need to find her without delay."

"Oh, God." Malcolm glanced at the snowy landscape outside the window. "How *awful*."

Malcolm's concern seemed a bit theatrical. Jane didn't think he truly cared about Gloria's well-being. He had shown more genuine interest in her Raggedy Ann book.

Jane got to her feet. "Thank you for meeting me. If you hear anything from Ms. Ramirez, please let me know. I have to go, but you're welcome to stay and enjoy the rest of your tea."

Malcolm jumped up and held out his hand. "Ms. Steward, I'm sure I'm not the first collector to express an interest in your books. I just want you to know that I always pay more than the other guy. Keep me in mind should you ever wish to sell."

After the shortest handshake possible, Jane hurried from the room.

She made a quick stop in her office to grab a notebook and a dollop of hand sanitizer. She rubbed the liquid into her palms on the way to the William Faulkner Conference Room.

Deputy Emory stood in the doorway, speaking to a tall blonde in a book print shirt dress. She had her arms crossed over her chest and her pretty face was creased with worry.

"We'll do everything we can to find her," the deputy promised.

"Was that Sasha?" Jane asked when the woman was out of earshot.

The young deputy, who looked like the subject of an Edward Burne-Jones painting, pushed a wisp of auburn hair out of her face. Other tendrils had escaped from a loose bun and brushed against Emory's freckled cheeks.

"It was. She gave us Ms. Ramirez's cell phone number, which I passed on to the sheriff." The deputy led Jane into the conference room. Sinclair, who'd been taking notes at the far end of the table, immediately stood up.

"Other than the cell phone number, the most crucial piece of information we received was that Ms. Ramirez purchased a new pair of hiking boots several weeks ago. She planned to use them here. Did you see hiking boots in her guest room?"

Jane remembered the shoes in Gloria's closet. There'd

been a pair of plain pumps, black strappy heels, black riding boots, and slippers. "No hiking boots. Now that yc ' mention it, I didn't see any outerwear. No gloves, hat, or heavy coat."

Deputy Emory consulted her notepad. "Ms. Ramirez arrived wearing a black, knee-length parka. According to Sasha, she's cold-natured and always bought high-quality outerwear."

Thinking of the snow-covered ground and snow-encrusted trees, Jane said, "I hope she owns the best coat and boots money can buy. Because either someone is deliberately trying to lead us astray, or Gloria Ramirez went out for a nature walk and never came back."

Emory frowned. "There's a discrepancy between Ms. Ramirez being cold-natured and going for a hike on a frigid winter day."

"That troubles me as well." Sinclair glanced from Emory to Jane. "Perhaps Ms. Ramirez went out for another reason. What if something beyond exercise or a desire to commune with nature compelled her to leave the warmth of Storyton Hall?"

Jane envisioned a handwritten note being slipped under Gloria's door. "I need to ask housekeeping about recovering the trash from her room."

"I've already spoken with Mrs. Templeton about that," Sinclair said. "She has three staff members sorting the trash. Luckily, the housekeeper on Ms. Ramirez's floor ran out of standard trash bags midway through her shift. She found an old box of white kitchen bags in the supply closet and added the contents of Ms. Ramirez's trash into a white bag."

"It's a small victory, but I'll take it," said Jane.

Sinclair was distracted by movement in the hallway. "I

believe our next interviewee has arrived. Are you staying, Miss Jane?"

"Just for this one. As soon as it's over, I'll go to the lobby to greet the incoming families. I have Storyton Hall Wonka Bars to distribute."

Jane was glad to see that the coworker waiting to enter the room was Reggie.

"Come in," Deputy Emory called.

Reggie entered and, to everyone's surprise, sank to the floor in front of Jane.

"I should have known she was missing!" he cried. "I should have said something when she didn't come to the paint-off! It was *so* weird that she wasn't there!"

Jane took his arm and coaxed him into a chair. "This isn't your fault. Everyone assumed she would turn up later in the day. There was no reason to think otherwise."

Reggie moaned. His eyes were red-rimmed, and a fresh round of tears threatened. "When she didn't show up at the paint-off, I should have looked for her. But I wanted to paint for the kids. I put my feelings and my art before Gloria, and now she's in trouble!"

"We don't know if that's true," said Jane. "In the hotel business, guests often disappear for periods of time. Usually, they're sleeping one off or . . ."

"Sleeping with someone else?" Reggie asked, recovering a bit of aplomb.

Jane nodded. "Guests have also left the resort to visit nearby towns or to spend time with one of the locals. We encourage guests and villagers to mingle, which is why many of our events are open to the public. We also value our guests' right to privacy, and we don't like to ask about Ms. Ramirez's personal life. In this case, however, we must."

At this point, Emory took over. "Another coworker

said that Ms. Ramirez was nervous about running into someone at this conference. Someone in the book business. Someone she used to love. Do you know who that person might be?"

Reggie was puzzled. "Gloria's in a serious relationship right now, but I have no idea who she dated before." He ran his finger over his mustache. "She and her man have been together for a while. They moved in together around Christmas. I've never met her guy, but Gloria loves him. You can tell."

"The former relationship, or whatever it is, might not even be relevant. We're just trying to gather as much info as we can," said Emory.

Jane touched Reggie's hand. "Please don't feel guilty about the paint-off. Ms. Ramirez's absence is not your fault. Besides, you created a piece of art that brought joy to a young lady. She and her family have been through a rough time, so the smile you put on her face is a gift."

A tear slipped down Reggie's cheek. Sinclair offered Reggie his handkerchief while Jane looked to Deputy Emory to wrap up the interview.

Emory waited until Reggie had composed himself before saying, "I'd like to confirm your contact information." After she'd checked the information against the printout in her folder, she thanked Reggie and said that he was free to go.

As soon as Reggie was gone, Sinclair pulled out his cell phone and read the message on his screen. "Mr. Sterling is pulling up out front. He has a family of five in his car."

Jane told Deputy Emory that she'd be in the lobby and left the room. She hurried into the lobby and ducked into the coat room to retrieve a basket stuffed with candy bars. Taking up position next to Butterworth, she watched as Sterling exited a forest-green Rolls-Royce Phantom.

"It stopped snowing," she said.

"It has. Storybook Village is almost ready to receive guests," Butterworth said without taking his eyes off the door. "Three sleds from Hilltop Stables are standing by. The horses are in the old barn across from the mews. The fairy-tale cottages will be warm and welcoming by one o'clock."

An unbidden image of Kristen Burke's body appeared in Jane's mind. In an attempt to push it away, she focused on the candy bars. She didn't want to picture the dead woman. She wanted to picture rosy-cheeked children visiting the cottages. She wanted to see their shining eyes and dimpled cheeks, not Kristen's swollen lips and glassy stare.

A woman tapped Jane on the arm. "Are those for the guests?"

Jane turned to find Tris Petty ogling the contents of her basket.

"They're for the children arriving today," Jane said and forced a smile. "But if you attend tonight's play, you'll receive a candy bar when you enter the theater."

"I don't suppose the tickets are free," Tris said. Her tone was petulant, and a deep frown line appeared between her brows.

Jane was used to dealing with all manner of people. In general, she liked the guests who chose to stay at her resort. But every now and then, someone like Tris came along. Someone pushy and rude. Someone who tried her patience. "They aren't free. However, the price is very reasonable considering the quality of the production. People come from quite a distance to be entertained by the Storyton Players."

Tris snorted. "I go to plays on *Broadway*. No rinky-dink local theater company could hold a candle to what we have in New York. Even off-off Broadway is bound to be better."

"You don't get free chocolate bars in New York though, do you?" Jane asked in a sugary voice.

Just then, a bellhop opened the front door and a family entered Storyton Hall. A brother and sister, very close in age, stared in open-mouthed wonder. A mother and father smiled from ear to ear. The father held a little girl by the hand. When she whispered, "Wowee," the whole family laughed.

"Welcome to Storyton Hall," said Butterworth. He offered champagne to the parents while Jane told the children to take a chocolate bar.

"Are you a princess?" the little girl asked Jane.

"No, but I know of a place where little girls are being turned into princesses."

The girl's eyes went saucer-round. "Where?"

"It's called Storybook Village. It's in the woods. You have to ride in a horse-drawn sleigh to get there," Jane said. "It's not just for princesses, either. It's for pirates, knights, artists, and people who like hot chocolate with lots of marshmallows."

The children immediately begged their parents to take them to the Storybook Village.

Jane rescued the mother and father by saying, "It doesn't open until after lunch, so you have plenty of time to unpack and explore first."

The parents finished their champagne and herded their children toward the front desk. Jane saw that Tris and Todd were watching the family with matched expressions of disapproval.

"Why write children's books if you dislike children?" Jane whispered to Butterworth.

Butterworth glanced at the sour-faced couple and grunted. "They certainly seem ill-suited for the job."

As more and more families were dropped off by

Storyton Hall drivers, Jane was able to forget about Todd and Tris Petty.

Jane loved greeting the new guests. Every person was unique. Regardless of the differences in their skin, hair, and eye color, the one thing they all shared was amazement over Storyton Hall. That, and their delight in receiving a glass of champagne or a Wonka Bar.

"Are there golden tickets inside?" a boy asked Jane after receiving his.

"You don't need a ticket to enter our chocolate factory. Tomorrow, we'll bring the factory to you."

The boy clearly didn't understand what Jane meant, but his mother told him to say thank you and move along, so that's what the boy did.

After an hour or so, there was a lull in arrivals. Most of the drivers were on their way back to the train station to collect more families, which gave Jane time to resume her worrying.

"I'm going to my office. Call me when the next family pulls up," she told Butterworth.

Once she was alone, Jane checked her phone for texts or missed calls. There weren't any. The lack of communication from both the sheriff and Lachlan felt like a bad omen.

She called Sheriff Evans. When he came on the line, he told Jane that Gloria's phone couldn't be tracked to a precise location.

"We're using triangulation to narrow down the area," he explained. "Now that the sky's cleared, we're getting a stronger signal. We'll get there. Did you learn anything from Ms. Ramirez's coworkers? Other than a text saying that she was still conducting interviews I haven't heard from Deputy Emory."

"All signs point to Gloria having gone for a hike. She

had outerwear, hiking boots, and her phone. She left her purse and the rest of her belongings in her room. It would seem that she went out and lost her way. Except for one thing."

The sheriff sighed. "Which is?"

"The book of fairy tales in her room. Like the book Kristen Burke had, this one is also valuable. It's worth around six thousand dollars."

Sheriff Evans whistled.

Jane went on. "I don't know if the book belongs to Gloria or someone else. Two expensive fairy tale books. Two women in peril—one of whom was likely murdered— has me fearing the worst."

"Could these books have anything to do with your, er, special collection?"

The sheriff was referring to the secret library. "I don't see how. Still, I could look for similar fairy tale books," Jane said. "I can't do that now, but if nothing else pans out, I'll find time to search the collection."

There was a knock on her door and the front desk clerk softly called, "Mr. Butterworth asked me to tell you that another family is arriving."

"Thanks. I'll be right out."

Jane took a compact from her desk drawer and touched up her lipstick. Her stomach gurgled, reminding her that it was lunchtime. Since she wouldn't be eating soon, she popped a mint in her mouth and left her office.

She was halfway down the lobby when her phone buzzed.

Doubling back, Jane stepped into the staff corridor and pulled out her phone. She had a text from Lachlan.

Jane read it once. Twice. She didn't realize how much her hands were shaking until she tried to call Sheriff

Evans. She had to press the phone hard against her ear to keep from dropping it.

"Lachlan found Gloria Ramirez," she said. In the empty corridor, her voice sounded thin and ghost-like. "She's in the woods off the service road. We can't save her. She's already gone."

Chapter Ten

Butterworth was busy welcoming the latest arrivals, so Jane stood in his line of sight and waited for him to notice her. When he glanced her way, she gave the smallest shake of her head. Her grave face made it clear that Gloria Ramirez had been found. Found but not saved. Butterworth responded with a nod. His eyes were soft with sympathy as he held Jane's gaze. It was the kind of gaze that felt like a steadying hand under the elbow. Strong and supportive.

Turning away, Jane walked through the kitchens to the mudroom. She put on her winter coat, hat, scarf, gloves, and knee-high rubber boots. She then exited Storyton Hall, hurrying through the snow-covered herb garden, and entered the garages. The keys to one of the pickup trucks hung in the key box, and Jane hoped the snow tires would get her where she needed to go.

Inside the truck's cab, her breath misted the inside of the windshield. She set the defrost on high and slowly drove toward the mews. A figure wearing a jean jacket, teal mittens, and a red hat with a multicolored pom-pom stood in front of one of the cages. A long braid of brown hair trailed out from under the hat. Hearing the truck's approach, the woman turned toward it. Jane saw that she was quite young. Not a woman, but a teenager.

The girl locked eyes with Jane. At first, her expression was furtive. Then, it changed to defiance. Though Jane didn't like what she saw, she couldn't stop to find out what the girl was up to. She had to drive on. And when she glanced in her rearview mirror, she saw the girl slip inside the building.

Jane assumed she'd just caught her first glimpse of Zoey, Mrs. Templeton's niece. Jane had asked Lachlan to introduce Zoey to the birds. At the time, it seemed like a good idea. But the girl shouldn't be alone at the mews. Lachlan would never leave the birds in the care of an un-trained handler, which was probably why Zoey looked guilty.

Jane couldn't worry about Zoey right now. She had one destination, and as bleak as it might be, she had to keep moving toward it.

The sun fell on the snowy ground, burnishing it with a golden hue. But when Jane passed from the clearing into the woods, the light shifted. The service road was sun-dappled in places. In others, there were blue shadows. Cold shadows.

What brought you here, Gloria?

The stark trees flanking the road held no answers. They stood as silent and unyielding as a regiment of soldiers.

The truck was doing well in low gear, but Jane felt as if she were crawling forward. She wanted to go faster but didn't dare run the risk of fishtailing in the middle of the woods.

Where are you, Lachlan? What are you about to show me?

She didn't have long to wait for answers. After rounding the next bend, she saw Lachlan standing on the right-hand side of the road. He didn't wave. His hands were folded over his chest in a universal gesture of self-preservation. Butterworth had taught Jane that people who adopted this posture were trying to place a barrier between themselves and a potentially harmful situation.

Jane could sense the gravity of what lay ahead. After parking the truck, she was torn between talking to Lachlan and rushing into the woods. She wasn't eager to confirm Gloria's death, but she needed to know what had happened to her.

"Wait," Lachlan said, stepping in front of Jane. "I have to prepare you for what you're about to see. This wasn't an accident. It was carefully planned. Whoever did this had a point to make. I don't know what that point is, but it's disturbing. Follow behind me and try to step in my boot prints. Even though I doubt there's evidence on the path I made, I don't want to compromise the scene."

"You're sure she's dead?" Jane asked. The air stung her skin and sank into her bones. Its breath was more potent than the winter sunshine.

"Yes. You'll understand in a minute."

Jane followed Lachlan into the woods. Their boots crunched as they broke through the snow crusts. They didn't speak. Theirs was a walk toward death.

The birds were unaware of the solemnity of their silent march. Chickadees, nuthatches, and wrens flitted among the bare tree branches, making celebratory noises because the snow had stopped, and the sun was shining. Jane wished they'd be quiet. Their lively, industrious chirping felt like an insult to Gloria.

"It's up ahead," Lachlan warned. "You'll see everything as soon as we pass those two pine trees ahead—the ones with the thick trunks."

Jane was frightened, but she steeled herself and kept walking.

When Lachlan passed the pines, he stepped aside, beckoning for Jane to proceed to the edge of a small clearing.

"Don't go any closer," he warned when she reached the end of his boot tracks.

Jane couldn't have taken another step had she wanted to. Shock rooted her in place.

Gloria Ramirez's body had been arranged in a sleeping princess pose. She was on her back with her hands folded demurely over her chest. She wore a thin blanket of snow. It had fallen unevenly over her, leaving lumps in places and unobstructed views of her clothing and face in others. The gaps allowed Jane to take in details, to form a picture that she would never forget.

Gloria wore a long, sea-blue parka, most of which was snow-covered. The coat's hood was pulled up so that the white faux-fur trim framed her face. Her eyes were closed. Her skin was like variegated marble streaked with blue. Her lips looked bruised. There were frozen rivulets of dried blood on her chin and jawline. She didn't seem human. She was more like an ice carving. Or a snow angel.

Jane's eye was drawn to a wink of sunshine near Gloria's left elbow. Craning her neck, she tried to see if a piece of metal was reflecting the sun's light.

"It's glass," Lachlan whispered. "I don't know where it came from, or if there's more under the snow."

Jane nodded. She couldn't speak yet.

"I'll go out to the road and call the sheriff. I can't get reception in the middle of all these trees." Lachlan hesitated. "Will you be okay?"

Without looking at him, Jane nodded again.

She didn't hear Lachlan's trek back to the road. She didn't hear his boots crushing the snow. She didn't hear the twittering of the birds. Every part of her was homed in on the glint of light off glass. It reminded her of something. Of a story. A story she hadn't thought about for a long time. But which one?

Jane's gaze roved over Gloria's body. She took in the snow on her clothes. A dusting in places. Small mounds in others. She stared at the bits of ice in the coat's faux-fur trim. The moon-white skin of her face. Those bruised-looking lips. Her utter stillness. She was the white of snow. She was the blue of ice. She was a princess, frozen in sleep.

Again, there came the wink of light.

A woman made of ice and snow, Jane thought. *A piece of glass.*

Suddenly, she knew which story she'd been trying to remember.

Gloria's killer was familiar with Hans Christian Andersen's fairy tales. He or she knew of a particular tale that had been divided into several parts, the first of which was "Which Has to Do With a Mirror and Its Fragments."

In the story, the devil made a magic mirror. Anything beautiful and good would look ugly and worthless in its reflection. When a person gazed into it, they'd see the basest side of themselves. It was a wicked piece of glass, created by wicked hands.

The devil gave the mirror to his hobgoblins and told them to share it with all the world.

The hobgoblins were delighted to use the magic mirror to deceive and frighten people. After they'd shown it to every person in the world, they decided to take it to the heavens and force the angels to look at it.

Higher and higher they flew. The mirror began to tremble, but the hobgoblins didn't stop. They kept flying. Suddenly, the mirror shattered. Millions upon millions of pieces rained down from the sky. Some were as large as coins. Others were the size of a splinter. Some were too small to be seen by the naked eye.

If one of these microscopic fragments fell into a person's

eye, that person would only see negative things from then on. Their world would become ugly and tainted. If a fragment pierced the skin and traveled through the bloodstream to a person's heart, the glass would turn their heart to ice.

The fragments did not fall at once. Some were swept around the sky by the wind or tucked into the folds of clouds. These didn't drift down to the world for a very long time.

Upon seeing the unhappiness and havoc he'd caused with his mirror, the devil laughed and laughed.

But the story wasn't really about the devil. It was about good triumphing over evil. Jane remembered it being about a brave little girl who risked her life to save her best friend. The girl embarked on a long and dangerous journey. At the end of the world, she reached a palace made entirely of ice. The palace of the Snow Queen.

"Miss Jane." Lachlan put a hand on Jane's arm, startling her. "Sheriff Evans is on his way. I'll lead him here while you wait in the truck. It's too cold for you to stay outside."

"I need to watch over her for a little longer. I need to be cold—to suffer the smallest fraction of what she must have suffered."

Lachlan was puzzled by this remark. "Why? You couldn't have prevented this. No one could."

Jane thought of the magic mirror. "Except the devil who did this to her."

By the time Sheriff Evans and Deputy Phelps arrived, Jane was shivering. The cold pierced her coat, hat, scarf, and gloves, but she watched the sheriff walk a wide circle around Gloria's body without speaking.

The sheriff told Phelps to photograph the scene from multiple angles. He then came over to stand with Jane.

"You should go back to Storyton Hall. I can talk to you when we're done."

"It feels like a betrayal," Jane said in a small voice. "To go inside and be warm. To have the option to drink hot coffee or sit in front of roaring fire."

The sheriff exchanged a worried glance with Lachlan.

"I'll walk you to your truck," said Evans. "The coroner will be here soon, and there are things I need to do before then."

Though Jane knew she was being ushered away from the crime scene, she didn't resist. After she and the sheriff passed the large pines marking the entrance to the clearing, she looked back and saw only trees and boot prints.

"Did you see the piece of glass near her elbow?" she asked the sheriff. When he said that he had, she looked at the ground and frowned. "You might find more pieces under the snow. Do you have a way to speed up the melting process?"

Evans nodded. "I have more deputies coming. They're bringing a portable generator and a heat fan. We need to see what the scene looked like at the time of Ms. Ramirez's death."

"After her death, you mean. The killer obviously posed her."

The sheriff hesitated for a moment before replying. "It would seem that way. But why?"

"Kristen Burke wore a red coat. She carried a basket. She died after biting into a poisoned apple. Red Riding Hood was probably created by Charles Perrault, the original Mother Goose, but it was a tale told all over Europe. As was the story of Snow White. The Grimm Brothers collected these stories and wrote them down. The only person to equal their fame as recorders of fairy tales is Hans Christian Andersen."

The sheriff gave her a sharp look. "The book found in Ms. Ramirez's room. It's tied to the murder scene."

By this time, they'd reached the pickup. Jane's hands were shaking, so Evans unlocked her door and started the engine. He blasted the heater and waited until Jane was settled in the driver's seat before closing the door. She rolled down the window and pointed at the woods. "I think the killer was re-creating a scene from *The Snow Queen*. It's one of Andersen's most memorable stories. Parts of it are very dark. I can only imagine how many children had nightmares about the devil, hobgoblins, thieves, or the Snow Queen after hearing that tale."

"Is Ms. Ramirez meant to be the Snow Queen?" the sheriff asked.

"That question is at the heart of the killing. Is Gloria the villain? Or is she Gerda, the heroine? In the fairy tale, pieces of glass symbolize wickedness. Did the killer cut Gloria? Did he punish her for wickedness? What about Kristen? Did he punish her too? Maybe the killer is delivering a message using these twisted tableaus. I don't know what it is, but I believe both deaths are connected to these old, old stories."

The sheriff rested a hand on the truck's roof. "I'm sorry that you're caught in the middle of this. Especially this weekend. With so many children visiting, you might consider closing the Storybook Village."

"I'll consider it," Jane promised. "But I don't think the killer would hurt a child."

"What makes you say that?"

Jane wasn't sure. She sat still for a moment, the warm air from the heaters blowing across her legs. "In Victorian times, certain stories were written to keep kids in line. They were called morality tales. The tales were filled with warnings and veiled threats. If you talk to a stranger in the woods, that stranger could be a wolf that eats your grandmother. If you're lazy like the pig that built a house of straw, a wolf might eat you. I feel like someone wanted to teach these women a lesson using stories."

"Write down any theories that might tie these deaths to fairy tales," the sheriff said. "You know more about this stuff than I do, and I have a feeling it's going to take many minds to catch this person."

Jane waited until he was gone before turning the truck around and heading toward home.

The road was empty. The woods were postcard perfect. The sun streamed down through the tree branches and stippled the snowy ground with light.

"Are you in there?" Jane asked in a low, hostile voice. "Are you hiding? Because we're going to find you."

She was angry. She was also afraid. She feared for her guests, her friends, and her family. A murderer was stalking Storyton Hall. Jane didn't understand this person's motive. And she didn't know where to begin the search for a killer.

As she drove, Jane made a mental list of what she did know.

To start, the killer was familiar with fairy tales. He— though Jane wasn't ruling out the possibility that the killer was female—had convinced his victims to meet him in the woods. Had they trusted him? Had they been anticipating a romantic tryst? Or was the killer a blackmailer? Had he held a terrible secret over their heads in order to lure them to where he waited—to where he was going to write the final words of their story?

The only way to know how the killer was connected to the victims was to examine their lives through a microscope. She and the Fins needed to scour their social media pages, acquire in-depth background reports, investigate

their employment history, real estate holdings and tax
documents, familial history, and more.

*That's how we'll find the common thread between Kristen
and Gloria. That thread will lead us to the murderer.*

"To the Fairy-Tale Killer," Jane whispered.

And despite the warmth blowing through the air vents,
she shuddered.

Sinclair was waiting in her office. He'd warmed a blanket by the fire and insisted on wrapping it around Jane's
shoulders. Next, he handed her a cup of whiskey-laced
coffee. After several sips, she nodded. She was ready to tell
Sinclair what she'd seen in the woods.

"Another murder," she began in a grim voice. "Two
women gone. I have no idea why."

Sinclair pulled his chair closer to Jane's. Their knees
were nearly touching, and Jane was comforted by his proximity. The loveable librarian made her feel grounded, and
it didn't hurt to know that Sinclair would do battle against
anyone Jane named as an enemy.

"Tell me what you saw," he said. "Every detail."

Jane did. When she finished, Sinclair folded his hands
and said, "I hope we didn't miss a clue inside the Grimm
Brothers book. Something tucked inside the spine or
hidden under an endpaper? An underlined passage?"

"I don't know about the Grimm, but I looked at every
page of the Andersen book. There were no marks. No
loose binding or separation between the endpapers and
covers. Nothing."

Sinclair gave her an affectionate smile. "I taught you
well."

Jane tried to return the smile, but she couldn't manage

it. "There's a message in the fairy tales. It could be a lesson on morality."

Sinclair grew pensive. "That's a good theory. To validate it, we need to discover what transgressions Ms. Burke and Ms. Ramirez might have committed. Today's interviews told us that Ms. Ramirez was an ambitious senior editor who was well liked by her authors and coworkers. She liked to bake and would often surprise her friends at Baxter Books with homemade treats. She worked hard and was known for being friendly and honest. She devoted much of her free time to volunteer work."

"She certainly doesn't sound like someone who'd attract enemies. She sounds lovely."

If Sinclair noticed Jane's use of the present tense, he didn't let it show. "You probably haven't had time to review my background check on Ms. Ramirez, but she worked for two other publishers before joining Baxter Books. The first was a small company specializing in children's books for the hearing and sight impaired. Prior to that, she worked at Peppermint Press."

"How many years ago?"

Sinclair, whose memory was nearly photographic, replied, "Fourteen. She spent ten of those years with Peppermint Press. Four at a small press called Sound and Light Books."

"We should speak with Nia and Gunnar," Jane said. "They might have useful insight on Gloria. A person can change a lot in fourteen years. We also need more information on Gloria's boyfriend."

"My thoughts keep returning to this mystery person Ms. Ramirez was excited about seeing here. Someone in the book business. Someone she once cared deeply for. Was this a romantic interest?" asked Sinclair. "Everyone we interviewed spoke of how well things were going between Ms. Ramirez and her significant other, a gentleman named Brandon Parks."

Jane frowned. "Have any of Gloria's coworkers met him?"

"Dr. Parks is a physician at New York Presbyterian. Both he and Ms. Ramirez had demanding careers. Because of their busy schedules, they had very little free time. When they had any, they spent it with each other. No one else. Dr. Parks is moving to a new practice in April and his schedule is supposed to loosen up after the move. That's when Ms. Ramirez was planning to introduce him to her friends."

"Sounds reasonable. If it's true." Jane wrote a few notes on a legal pad. "I'll speak with Nia and Gunnar. Keep researching Gloria. Lachlan will probably stay at the crime scene until Sheriff Evans asks him to leave. Any update on the trash from Gloria's room?"

Sinclair glanced at his phone screen. "Not yet. I asked the crew to sort through all letters, receipts, or notes. I imagine they're working as we speak."

Jane handed the blanket back to Sinclair. "This weekend is supposed to be a celebration of love. What we're dealing with is the opposite of love."

"The next few days can still be everything you dreamed it would be." Sinclair fixed Jane with a firm gaze. "There's a shadow, yes. At times, it seems like we're plagued by shadows. But don't be disheartened, my girl. If anyone can chase away the darkness, it's you."

"Then I'd better get to work. There are only so many hours until nightfall."

After Sinclair left, Jane sent a message to Butterworth, asking him to arrange a sit-down with Gunnar and Nia following the afternoon tea service. Next, she sent a text to

Sterling. Even though he'd already reviewed hours of surveillance footage, she wanted him to do it again.

This time, I want a list of every person who left Storyton Hall the day Gloria Ramirez went missing. Staff included. Gloria went outside. Which means the killer did too.

Jane was about to shove her phone in her pocket when she suddenly murmured, "What if the killer isn't staying here?"

She called Betty.

"Cheshire Cat. How can I make you smile?"

Jane said, "I know you're probably busy with the lunch crowd, but I need a favor."

"Ask away."

"Have you or Bob heard of any strangers in Storyton other than the conference-goers? Do any of the locals have friends or family visiting?"

Betty responded with a "hmmm." Jane could imagine a slideshow of faces running through her friend's mind. Eventually, she said, "Last night's customers were mostly locals, and none of them mentioned having visitors from over the mountain. There were also some folks from the conference at the table near the dartboards. One of them was still wearing his badge."

"What about the night before that?" Jane pressed.

"I'll ask Bob and get back to you. The food is up for the gents at the bar, and I don't want their stew to go cold."

"Of course."

Betty hung up.

Jane called Eloise next.

"I only have a minute," Eloise whispered into the phone. "Birdie Bloom is here signing stock. As soon as she's done, I want to talk her into doing a reading for the local children."

Jane hated to put a damper on Eloise's euphoric mood, but she had no choice. "Turn away so Birdie can't see your face. Tell me when you're ready."

Eloise was instantly concerned. "What's wrong?"

Jane told her. She knew Eloise's first questions would be about Jane's welfare, so after assuring her friend that she was fine, she said, "I need your help."

"Anything. Just ask."

This was how it always was with Eloise. She was the most selfless and generous person Jane had ever met.

"I need you to think about common themes in fairy tales. Specifically, in *Red Riding Hood*, *Snow White*, and *The Snow Queen*. The killer is making a statement using fairy tales, but I don't know what he or she is trying to say. You're the most book-savvy person in Storyton, so will you put your bookish brain to work?"

"I will," she promised. "I'll ask Violet too. She's our fairy-tale guru. She even took a college course on fairy tales. They discussed gender roles, morality, the use of magic, and more."

"Okay, we have to keep this quiet. Sheriff Evans would have my head if he learned that people were talking about the case while he and his team were still out in the woods."

After vowing not to breathe a word, Eloise said, "I need to go. Birdie's done signing stock. She's wandering around the bookstore and I have to catch her before she goes."

Lucky Birdie, Jane thought. *What I'd give to spend the afternoon in Run for Cover, chatting with Eloise and perusing the shelves.*

But that wasn't to be. Because of the Fairy Tale Killer, a dark fog of worry and fear had replaced all of Jane's rosy visions of the future.

Her final call was to Edwin.

"I'm coming over," he said after she told him about the second murder. "I can meet the twins' bus and keep an eye on them until you can get away. Today's the special children's tea, right?"

Jane glanced at her watch. "Yes. In two hours."

"I'll wrap up the lunch service and head over. And Jane, I think I should stay at your place tonight." Before Jane could utter a word of protest, he barreled on. "I'll sleep on the couch. I'll tell Fitz and Hem that I wanted to cook with them and help them work on their valentines. I'm the master of glitter and glue, after all."

"Edwin—"

"I know you want to keep our relationship separate from your family, but I can protect the twins," Edwin said. His voice was a harbor in a storm—calm and steady. "I'd give my life for them, and you can't spare a Fin to babysit."

Jane made a silent vow to show Edwin just how much she loved and appreciated him as soon the Fairy Tale Killer was caught.

"Knowing you're with the boys would be a huge weight off my shoulders," she said, infusing her words with gratitude. "They won't want to miss today's tea, so there's no need for you to rush. And thank you. Thank you for watching over them."

"I'm staying until the danger passes, Jane. If I have to sleep on the welcome mat, I'm staying. And if that makes you angry, you can throw snowballs at me. I'll see you soon."

Jane was smiling as she said good-bye.

She wouldn't smile again for many hours to come.

Chapter Eleven

It would be up to Sheriff Evans to break the news to Gloria's family, just as it would be up to him to run the murder investigation. When he was ready, he would tell Jane exactly how she and her staff could assist his department. Until then, she was expected to wait.

But she wasn't going to do that. Gloria Ramirez had been a guest of Storyton Hall. She'd died on Storyton Hall property. She was Jane's responsibility. And the quicker Jane hunted down the killer, the quicker she could focus on taking care of her living guests. Writers, publishers, parents, and children.

Jane wasn't being rebellious. Nor was she being pig-headed. She recognized Sheriff Evans's authority and respected his abilities. But he and his team had to follow a protocol that Jane and her Fins could ignore. She didn't need a warrant to enter a guest's room. She could strike up a casual conversation with a guest without raising suspicion. She could even buy guests drinks to loosen their tongues. She could monitor their movements, watch their interactions, and take note of everything they ate or drank. She could rummage through their trash.

The hospitality business had its own rules, but with a murderer on the loose, Jane was willing to break them all.

She used the two hours leading up to the children's tea service to delve deeper into Gloria's background. Jane concentrated on Gloria's social media accounts while Sinclair made calls to her landlady and to the assisted living facility caring for her father.

Gloria's social media presence raised no red flags. She posted about work, family, special meals, favorite books, movies, and causes. She supported her public library and was passionate about increasing access to books in underprivileged areas.

Brandon, her boyfriend, appeared in several posts and photos. He seemed camera shy—always smiling but never looking directly at the camera. He didn't have his own social media accounts, a fact that Gloria mentioned on Facebook. She joked that while her man was too busy making the world a better place to post cat videos, he had tons of them on his phone.

Brandon was devoted to his cats, Rachel, Monica, and Phoebe. He'd found the tiny kittens in a drainage pipe two years before meeting Gloria, and the three felines had captured his heart. Sinclair had gleaned this information from the couple's landlady. Supers were often reluctant to gossip about their tenants, but not this woman. Sinclair had barely introduced himself as an attorney lining up potential witnesses before the landlady started talking.

"Oh, boy! I feel like I'm on *Judge Judy*! What kind of case is it? Murder? Domestic abuse?"

Sinclair had explained that he wasn't at liberty to discuss the details. This hadn't bothered the landlady a bit. She'd still been happy to cooperate.

And so, she talked. And talked. Sinclair heard about the couple's favorite restaurants. He learned that Brandon's cats preferred Fancy Feast. He learned that Gloria liked salsa music while Brandon listened to classic rock. He learned that Gloria's parents had been to the apartment twice while Brandon's family had never visited.

"They're a very private couple," the landlady continued. "Not in a snobby way. They're both as nice as can be. But they don't ask people over. I guess it's because they hardly have any time together. They both work long hours. Him more than her, but she volunteers too—such a good girl. She works at the library. Does food and book drives. They're a sweet couple. I've got no complaints. If you want to hear about bad tenants, I'll tell you about the morons in 14B."

Sinclair ended the call before the landlady could describe the residents of 14B. He then spoke with the head nurse at the Alzheimer's unit, the volunteer coordinator at Gloria's library, and the founder of Books For All, the organization delivering new books to kids in low-income neighborhoods. All three women spoke highly of Gloria, using phrases like "she's generous with her time" and "she's very caring" and "we couldn't do without her."

You'll have to, Jane thought glumly as she listened in on Sinclair's conversation.

The more she learned about Gloria, the sadder Jane grew.

Sinclair noticed. When his calls were done, he put his hand on Jane's and said, "Ms. Ramirez wasn't a saint. She irritated her neighbors with her music. When she volunteered at the library, she had a tendency to vocalize ideas for improving a system that no one else viewed as broken. She was late making payments to the facility caring for her father. At work, she'd drink the last of the coffee without making more. She interrupted people in her enthusiasm to get her point across."

"If those are her worse transgressions . . ." Jane let the rest of the sentence trail off.

"All I'm saying is that she wasn't a saint. No one is. But she was clearly a good woman. People will mourn her loss. Her passing will leave a void. We're not discovering tawdry secrets or skeletons in closets. We're learning that a good woman was killed in our backyard."

"But why?" Jane jabbed a finger at her laptop screen. "Nothing on her social media sites so much as hints at an enemy. There are no nasty comments. No trolls insulting her. We found nothing negative about the authors she represents, either. People left less-than-stellar reviews for some of their books, but that's normal. So why kill her? Why kill Kristen?"

"In light of where the bodies were found, I can only assume that the killer's message is meant for someone staying at Storyton Hall."

Jane shut her laptop lid. "I didn't expect us to solve this in two hours, but I thought we'd find a lead. No matter how tenuous. But all I have is a fresh dose of rage. I want to hit someone, but I can't. I need to go to a tea party now. A goddamn tea party!"

Sinclair understood her frustration. "'Rage, rage against the dying of the light.' Hold on to that feeling, my girl. Let it drive your actions. And keep in mind that you can drink tea and smile at children without betraying the memories of the victims. Your life requires the wearing of multiple hats. It's that simple."

He was right.

The cyclone of thoughts and questions in Jane's mind quieted the moment she saw the children and parents lined up outside the Agatha Christie Tearoom. All the little girls were wearing blue dresses with white aprons, white knee socks, and patent-leather Mary Janes. The boys wore shirts or sweaters with bold prints, dark pants, and top hats. The parents weren't in costume but sported a pair of bunny ears. Some had gone the extra mile by adding pink lipstick noses or black eyeliner whiskers.

As she moved up the line toward the door, Jane complimented the families on their attire. Upon entering the tearoom, she felt as if she'd truly fallen down a rabbit hole.

Mrs. Hubbard had commissioned a group of staff members to paint a canvas floor mat for the event. Its black and white squares grew smaller in size from one end to the other, creating an optical illusion. It felt like the entire room was tilting downward, an effect emphasized by the mural on the back wall. The mural featured a row of diminutive doors.

Jane glanced from the floor to the tables, but the red hearts dancing around the base of the black tablecloths didn't help her regain her equilibrium. She focused on the centerpieces, which were either Cheshire Cats with crooked grins perched atop lopsided cushions or arched caterpillars lounging on an off-kilter clump of psychedelic mushrooms. There were so many colors and patterns in the room that it was hard to know where to look.

"Got your sea legs yet?" Mrs. Hubbard giggled from behind the buffet.

"It's a lot to take in," said Jane.

"I won't tell you to check out the cake, then." She tried to hide a smile behind her hand but failed. "The twins are having their tea in the kitchens. Apparently, Mr. Alcott met them at the bus stop and is waiting for them at your place. The boys are so excited to hang out with him that they're gobbling down their food."

"That's nothing new." Jane edged closer to the buffet. "So many beautiful treats."

The spread was as zany and colorful as the rest of the room.

Going from left to right, Jane saw glass bottles with

DRINK ME labels. The bottles contained juices of every color. After selecting a drink, the guests could pick a fruit kebob crowned with a paper EAT ME sign. A vase filled with celery, cucumber, and cherry tomato flowers sat next to a platter of chocolate-covered strawberry teacups. Radishes shaped like mushrooms encircled a bowl of creamy ranch dip. Finger sandwiches cut into rectangles waited to be plucked from a tiered stand. Each corner of the bread contained a red jam heart, turning the sandwiches into edible playing cards. There were also caterpillar grapes on skewers, pocket watch shortbread cookies, pink flamingo sugar cookies, checkerboard cheese sandwiches, white rabbit cupcakes, and the pièce de résistance, Mrs. Hubbard's cake.

Mrs. Hubbard rarely lingered to see how the guests responded to her tea spreads. She was too much of a control freak to leave the kitchens for long. Today, however, she stood behind her cake, looking resplendent in her Queen of Hearts costume. Her face had been powdered, a crown sat atop her red wig, and her lips were a bold red. Her gown had a black-and-white-striped bodice that gave way to a black skirt covered in red hearts.

"You look positively regal," Jane said.

"Every woman should be queen for a day," replied Mrs. Hubbard.

Jane pointed at the stack of mismatched teacups at the end of the buffet. "Is this teacup Jenga?"

The teacups had been precariously positioned. If one didn't gingerly remove the top cup, the whole lot of them would come crashing down.

Mrs. Hubbard giggled. "I can't take credit for this. One of my sous-chefs came up with the idea to put the cups on transparent stands. They look unstable, but they're not. They won't fall. I also roped that sous-chef into being the White Rabbit. He'll pour tea or hot cider, and a server will carry the cups to the table. Less danger of spills or burns that way."

"As usual, you've thought of everything." Jane pointed at the cake. "Are you going to shout, 'Off with their heads!' before cutting the first slice?"

Mrs. Hubbard grinned. "One of the children will do the honors. I plan to be the nicest Queen of Hearts they've ever met."

Just then, the White Rabbit came in through the staff entrance. The chef wore a three-piece suit and a pink bowtie. A watch chain dangled from his vest pocket. Like the parents waiting in the hall, he also wore bunny ears. His entire face was painted white and someone had used makeup to create very realistic bunny features. He'd also donned a pair of white gloves.

"You're a *very* dapper bunny," Jane told him. To Mrs. Hubbard, she said, "Ready?"

"As Lewis Carroll said, 'It's always teatime.'" She picked up a scepter topped with a shiny red heart. "The Queen is prepared to serve her subjects."

Jane stepped into the hall. Max and Alika Gilbert caught her eye and waved. Fern and Peter were too engrossed in conversation with the kids behind them to notice her, but Jane was happy to see their smiling faces.

Holding her hand high in the air, Jane waited for the chatter in the hallway to cease.

"Alices, Mad Hatters, and White Rabbits, welcome to your tea party," she said. "You're about to fall down our rabbit hole. At the bottom, you'll find lots of tempting treats. Later, when you're done trying the magical food, you can head to the ballroom for fun and games. We have some wonderful Wonderland activities for you. For example, you can challenge your family members to a game of indoor croquet. We also have a paper teacup stacking game, a giant-sized chessboard, a Mad Hatter ring toss, a contest to see who can make the tallest playing card tower, and more."

The children bounced up and down with glee while their parents grinned, sharing in the excitement.

Jane opened the tearoom door with a flourish. "Let the Mad Hatter Tea Party begin!"

Once inside the room, Jane stayed near the door so she could see the reactions of the first guests. Eyes went wide. There were whispers of "wow" and "amazing" and "look at that!" Children pointed at the floor. Parents pointed at the doors painted on the opposite wall. When their focus turned to the food table, they gasped in delight.

Though the parents warned their kids not to pile their plates too high, it was impossible to resist such colorful food. The children wanted one of everything. They wanted a complete EAT ME and DRINK ME experience.

When the first child reached the end of the buffet, Mrs. Hubbard bowed and smiled.

"Good afternoon, Alice," she said. "I'm the Queen of Hearts. In Mr. Carroll's story, the queen isn't very nice, but the only mean queen here is the Queen of Cakes. Still, I don't think we can have a proper Mad Hatter tea until someone yells, 'Off with their heads!' Would you like to do that? After you do, I'll cut the cake."

The little girl nodded shyly.

"Mad Hatters and Alices, I think our friend needs a little help." Mrs. Hubbard's voice boomed across the room. "On the count of three, please shout, 'Off with their heads!' as loud as you can." She waited a heartbeat before continuing. "One . . . two . . . three!"

The children made so much noise that Jane thought the teacups would tumble off the table.

Mrs. Hubbard beamed at the little girl and said, "As a

reward for helping, I'm giving you the seven of hearts cookie from the tippy top of the cake."

"I'm seven!" the girl cried.

Mrs. Hubbard gave her a wink. "You don't say."

She skillfully cut a piece from the top-hat layer and offered it to the girl.

"Thank you," the little Alice said. "You are a nice queen."

Mrs. Hubbard shot her sous-chef a meaningful look. "Remember that when I'm yelling at everyone during the dinner service."

The White Rabbit rolled his eyes and asked the little girl if she wanted tea or cider.

"Whatever the real Alice had," she replied. "With extra sugar, please."

This made Mrs. Hubbard laugh so hard that she nearly sliced the cake from top to bottom.

Jane wished she could remain in this vacuum of food, color, and bubbly chatter for the rest of the day. She served food to her guests and helped the White Rabbit with tea or cider refills. For ninety minutes, she was able to concentrate on something other than murder.

However, when she overheard one of the parents say, "If you knew Time as well as I do, you wouldn't talk about wasting it," Jane involuntarily glanced at her watch.

The Mad Hatter quote jerked her back to reality. She had to leave this festive setting and make her way to the Henry James Library.

There was nothing wrong with the library. On the contrary, it was one of the most beautiful rooms in Storyton Hall. Every wall was lined with books. It had comfy reading chairs and a mammoth fireplace. Its tall windows faced the garden, and sunlight streamed in through the glass and stippled the wood floor with luminous patterns.

The old globe on a stand creaked when it was spun. The thick rugs absorbed extraneous sounds. Despite the high ceilings, the library was cozy. Intimate. It smelled of paper and beeswax. It had a real card catalog. Complimentary bookmarks poked out of a biscuit tin on Sinclair's desk. On occasion, a plump tuxedo cat dozed in a chair.

Jane loved every inch of the library. What gave her pause was the task awaiting her. The moment she left the company of these merry families, she'd have to resume her investigation into Gloria's death by interviewing Gunnar Humphries and Nia Curry.

The interview would be a challenge because Jane couldn't let it be known that Gloria was dead. It was up to the sheriff to decide when that news would become public knowledge. Until then, Jane needed to keep up the pretense that she and her staff were still searching for their missing guest.

Butterworth had fulfilled his end of the bargain by arranging the meeting. He was standing, soldier-stiff, outside the library doors and didn't relax his posture at Jane's approach.

"Miss Jane, you have the room," he said sotto voce. "I had to pull Ms. Curry from a conference session without explanation, so you might not receive the warmest welcome. Also, Mr. Humphries is unwell. He didn't mention being under the weather, but it's quite obvious that he should be in bed. I'm going to make him a pot of tea. I'll return with it shortly."

Jane entered the library and found Nia and Gunnar in wingback chairs facing the fire. Pulling up a third chair, Jane thanked her guests for meeting with her.

"I won't beat around the bush," she began. "I asked to see the two of you in private because we have an urgent situation on our hands. Have you heard that Gloria Ramirez of Baxter Books has gone missing?"

Nia's expression had been stony when Jane first entered the room, but at the mention of Gloria's name, her features softened. "We heard. It's been hard to concentrate on our session knowing that she might be in trouble. Everyone's really worried."

"There's been no trace of her at all?" Gunnar asked. "I know this place is isolated, but someone must have seen her."

When Jane turned to the older man, she saw that Butterworth was right. Gunnar wasn't well. His skin was wan and puffy. He seemed beyond exhausted, and Jane wondered if pain had kept him up all night. She didn't know why he needed a cane, but he clearly wasn't well rested.

"Our local sheriff is on the case," Jane said. "He's a dogged and intelligent investigator, and I have great confidence in his abilities. However, we want to assist him in any way possible. That's why I called this meeting. We're speaking with those who had a connection to Gloria, no matter how brief or tenuous. We were told that she started her publishing career with Peppermint Press."

Nia glanced at Gunnar. "I didn't know that. Must have been before my time."

Instead of answering, Gunnar rooted in his pocket until he came up with a tissue.

As he blew his nose, Nia kindly drew attention away from her boss by talking to Jane. "My road to a publishing career wasn't exactly direct. I worked for a marketing firm, had a brief stint as an elementary school art teacher, and wrote articles for a children's magazine before I was lucky enough to land an assistant editor position at Peppermint

Press. From there, I worked hard until Gunnar promoted me to the publisher position."

There was a gentle knock on the library door. Butterworth entered, pushing a trolley.

"Forgive the interruption," he said. "I wanted to offer some refreshment before returning to my post. Ms. Curry? Mr. Humphries? Could I interest you in a cup of fortifying mint tea? I find the blend of peppermint, raspberry leaf, and nettle to be the perfect pick-me-up, especially toward the end of a long day."

"That sounds lovely," Nia said.

"As long as the mint isn't too strong," Gunnar said. "I might carry peppermint sticks in my basket, but they're for the kids. I'm not a big mint fan."

Butterworth began to pour. "It's quite subtle, I assure you."

After placing a shortbread stick on each saucer, Butterworth served the tea. He then silently exited the library, leaving the trolley near Sinclair's desk.

"That man moves like a cat," Nia said. "A cat that gives you cookies."

Gunnar ignored his shortbread and took a sip of his tea. He closed his eyes, exhaled slowly, and took a second sip. He seemed to sink deeper into the chair cushions, as if giving himself permission to relax.

Nia shot a worried glance at her boss and said, "I wish I could help, Ms. Steward. I've seen Gloria at other publishing functions, but we've never actually met. However, I've only heard good things about her. None of her authors has left her to take up with one of our editors, so she must be great to work with. She definitely knows her stuff when it comes to acquisitions. She has an impressive book list, and all of her authors make money for Baxter Books."

There wasn't a hint of jealousy in Nia's remarks. She was a successful woman praising another successful woman, and Jane liked her for it. She thanked Nia for her observations and looked at Gunnar. The heat of the fire and the warmth of the tea had brought a little color back to his cheeks, but he was obviously struggling against pain, weakness, or a combination of both.

"What was Gloria like when she worked for you?" Jane asked.

Gunnar put his teacup aside. "She was a hard worker—put in lots of long days. She was also a visionary. She had dozens of ideas on how Peppermint Press could dominate the children's book market. She wanted to start a new imprint focusing on a different kind of book, and I gave her my blessing. She put her heart and soul into that project for almost two years, but things didn't pan out. To be honest, Gloria and I didn't see eye to eye on that imprint, and I wasn't sorry to see it fold. She was. In the end, she decided to move to another house. There were no hard feelings between us, though. People jump houses all the time."

"That's true," agreed Nia. "It's rare for a person to stay with one company for their entire career. Authors, editors, sales reps—we all move around."

"It's been a long time since Gloria worked for me. I'm embarrassed to admit this, but we didn't keep in touch after she left," Gunnar said. His voice was thin. The hand gripping the glass knob of his cane trembled. "Like Nia, I saw her at professional functions. We'd wave or say a quick hello, but that was it."

Jane wasn't getting anything from these two. Suppressing her frustration, she asked, "Was there any conflict between Gloria and her Peppermint Press coworkers?"

Gunnar shook his head.

"Was she in a relationship?"

"She never mentioned one to me," said Gunnar. "Not that I would have asked. It isn't fitting for an employer to ask an employee about her romantic life. I've always tried to conduct myself with integrity—"

A coughing fit interrupted the rest of this thought. The coughs sounded dry and rasping. They made Gunnar's entire body quake.

Nia jumped out of her chair and pressed Gunnar's cup into his hands. "Try to drink this."

Gunnar took a sip of tea. He coughed once more and then let out a low moan. He was the picture of misery.

"I'm sorry," he finally gasped.

Nia looked at Jane. Her gaze was direct and unyielding. "He needs to rest."

Gunnar might have been the boss, but Nia was taking charge. And her meaning was clear. The interview was over.

Jane moved to Gunnar's side to help him to his feet, but he wanted to stand on his own. Leaning his cane against the chair, he wiped his sweaty palm on his pants. For the first time Jane was able to get a close-up view of the cane's knob handle. A beautiful orange flower bloomed inside the glass.

"I hope I didn't cause you any distress," she said as Gunnar struggled to stand. "Would you like me to call the local doctor? He's wonderful."

"No, no." Gunnar waved off the suggestion. "I'm just fighting a cold. Nothing a bit of rest and a bowl of soup can't cure."

"Our head cook makes the best chicken noodle soup in the state. I'll have some sent up to your room."

Gunnar paused at the doorway. "Thank you, Ms. Steward. I pray you find Gloria very soon. She's a lovely person. We might have had our differences of opinion when we worked together, but that's all it was. I was a stubborn old goat back then. Now, I'm a joy to work with. Right, Nia?"

Nia gave him a warm smile. "Right."

Gunnar coughed again, and Nia ushered her boss from the room.

Feeling defeated, Jane trudged to her office and closed the door. No messages were waiting from Sheriff Evans or her Fins. Not knowing what else to do, she called Lachlan.

"Do you have news for me?"

"Only that there were more pieces of glass under the snow. Because I helped the deputies set up the generator and heaters, I got to see the whole picture. After that, I scouted the woods for signs of entry or exit paths. I didn't find anything. Last night's snow covered everything, including any tire tracks left on the service road. Even without the snow, the winter ground makes for difficult tracking. I'm sorry I don't have anything more."

Jane decided to focus on what had been found. "Was there anything else near her body other than the glass?"

"No. Just those pieces. They were irregular in shape and were scattered around her in a crude circle."

The glass fragments gave Jane's Snow Queen theory more weight. "There was dried blood on her face. Was she cut?"

Lachlan hesitated for a moment before answering. "Not that I saw. I'm no expert, but I think it's another case of poisoning. There was a pool of dried blood on the ground, near her mouth. Like she turned her head to spit it out—to keep from drowning in it."

Jane stifled a cry of horror over this image. As she fought to regain composure, she looked out the window, toward the woods. Shadows were gathering around the trees. The night was closing in. Soon, the darkness would snuff out the light.

"I don't remember poison in *The Snow Queen*," she said when she trusted herself to speak again. "The mirror was a kind of poison, I guess. If the tiniest speck got into a person's bloodstream, their hearts would freeze."

Jane thought about Gloria's woodland tomb. Her body had frozen. She'd been covered in snow. A sculpture of flesh, clothing, and snow. All whites and blues. Except for the red blood.

Suddenly, Jane's thoughts shifted to the memory of the girl in the denim jacket skulking around the mews.

"With everything that's been going on, I didn't ask if you'd had the chance to work with Zoey."

"We've had a few feeding sessions," said Lachlan. "She likes the birds."

Jane recalled the guilt on Zoey's face and the furtive way she'd entered the building. "Did you give her a key to the mews? Because I saw her go inside on my way to meet you in the woods."

"*What?* No, I did not." He sounded angry. "I need to go down there. I need to make sure the birds are okay."

Jane couldn't let him hang up just yet. "Lachlan, wait. Could Zoey be involved in these murders? She's a stranger. She's always angry. She doesn't seem to like anyone or anything."

There was a pause before Lachlan said, "Is Zoey from the New York area? Because if not, I don't see how she could be connected to the two women."

"Mrs. Templeton's sister lives in Connecticut."

"That's close enough." Lachlan sighed. "I'll handle Zoey. You have enough to deal with."

After saying good-bye, Jane opened her notebook. She reviewed her scattered thoughts and reread the question she'd meant to ask Gunnar Humphries.

Were Tris and Todd Petty at Peppermint Press when Gloria was there?

Because the interview had been cut short, she didn't have the answer. It was information she had to obtain before day's end. The Pettys were not good people. They were bigoted, disparaging, and envious. They could be cruel to children. To Jane, that meant they were capable of other, even more sinister cruelties.

"They're the kind of people who cultivate negativity. They're human poison ivy. And I need to invite them to have drinks with me," Jane murmured miserably.

She called up to her great-aunt and great-uncle's apartments. When Aunt Octavia answered, Jane said, "I need your help. Could you pretend to fawn over a loathsome pair of picture book authors in order to extract information from them? I wouldn't ask if it weren't important."

After a pause, Aunt Octavia said, "You *do* realize that it's my cocktail time."

"Trust me, you're going to need a stiff drink to face these guests. They're horrid, but we need to impress them," Jane said. "Tell Uncle Aloysius to break out the good stuff."

Chapter Twelve

Tris and Todd were busy fawning over Aunt Octavia's collection of Meissen figures and Staffordshire teapots when Jane entered the room.

"Ah, here's my lovely niece." Aunt Octavia smiled at Jane. "I was just telling Mr. and Mrs. Petty how much I adore their books. Some people go starry-eyed over actors or musicians. Not me. Authors are the only celebrities I want to meet."

Todd gave a small bow. "Most people don't consider us celebrities. In fact, authors are pretty invisible. Our books go out into the world while we stay at home. I can't tell you how many times Tris and I have sat at a book signing without talking to anyone. It's hard on the ego, to be ignored like that."

"It's downright humiliating," Tris said over the rim of her crystal tumbler. "The last time we did a signing at a chain bookstore, the only person to speak to us was looking for the restroom."

"That's awful," Jane said, and meant it. As much as she disliked the Pettys, she'd never stopped to consider that an author's life might be filled with isolation and insecurity.

Aunt Octavia clucked her tongue in sympathy and

gestured for the Pettys to sit on the sofa across from her. She then glanced at Jane. "Pour a drink and join us, dear."

Jane examined the contents of the cocktail cart. Uncle Aloysius had certainly opened the good stuff. Picking up the bottle of twenty-year-old bourbon, Jane inhaled subtle orange and peach aromas. She studied the fox on the label, thinking that it was the perfect symbol for this meeting. Aunt Octavia needed to have a fox's cunning to deal with Todd and Tris Petty.

"May I top off your cocktails before I sit?" Jane asked her guests.

"Why not?" Todd held out his glass.

Tris gulped down the rest of her cocktail before saying, "Just a splash. I don't like to drink on an empty stomach."

Aunt Octavia told Jane to pour generously before turning a radiant smile on Tris. "There'll be no empty stomachs, sweet lady. I took the liberty of calling down to the kitchens and ordering some nibbles for us. They should be arriving any minute now."

Their drinks refreshed, the Pettys began to talk about what it was like to be a career writer. By the time the food trolley appeared, they were on their third round of cocktails. Their eyes were bright, their cheeks were flushed, and their speech had become loud and animated.

"Oh, I love these pig-in-a-blanket thingies," Tris said, loading her plate with food.

"Reminds me of that local grocery store guy who pitched to Gunnar," Todd said derisively. "As if anyone wants to read about pigs. Dirty, stupid animals. He should write a book about bacon instead."

Jane bit back a retort. She wanted to defend Tobias Hogg and pigs everywhere, but she didn't dare cross swords with the Pettys until she'd gotten what she needed from them.

Tris barked out a laugh. "Aspiring authors are such a sad bunch. They're *so* desperate. They'd trade their first-born children for the chance to be published. We were lucky. We never had to suffer through humiliating pitch sessions or write query letters. Gunnar contacted *us* after reading our stories in a national children's magazine. We never had to grovel. We just did what we do best, and now, we're on bookstore shelves all over the country."

"It must be marvelous to work for someone who recognizes your talent," said Aunt Octavia. "How long have you been with Peppermint Press?"

This question opened the floodgates, allowing Tris and Todd to share countless grievances about their employers. Listening to them complain about illustrators, publicists, cover artists, marketing reps, and other authors, one would assume that the Pettys had always hated working for Peppermint Press.

"Don't get me wrong, we were happy in the beginning," Tris said at one point. "Things were better when Gunnar steered the ship. *He* discovered us. *He* offered us a contract. Not *her.*"

"He treated us with the respect we were due," Todd was quick to add. "But when that uppity Nia took over as publisher, things went downhill. She doesn't know how valuable we are. Gives no-talent hacks like Birdie Bloom all the attention."

"And a big marketing budget," Tris said before emptying her glass for the fourth time.

Todd's use of the word "uppity" made Jane squirm. Unable to hide her disgust, she walked over to the cocktail cart and refilled her club soda. She carried the glass back to the sofa and cast a sidelong glance at Aunt Octavia. She responded with a brief nod. Now that the Pettys were sufficiently lubricated, it was time to find out what they knew of Gloria Ramirez.

"I was beginning to think this trip was a total waste," Tris said before Aunt Octavia could get a word in. "Your invitation has been the first nice thing to happen to us since we left New York."

"The honor is all mine," Aunt Octavia gushed. "I'm sure you needed a distraction. I heard that everyone is focused on the missing woman. You're both in the know when it comes to the publishing world. What can you tell me about her?"

"Gloria Ramirez?" Todd shrugged as if a missing woman was of no consequence. "She started out as an assistant editor. Did a decent enough job and got promoted. After a few years, she and Gunnar were thick as thieves. Rumor has it that she refused to stay in her lane, so Gunnar let her go. She wanted to make all kinds of changes—said the company would become more profitable by being forward-thinking—but it was *his* company. He wanted to keep things as they were. He was right too. Nothing wrong with sticking to tradition."

Aunt Octavia looked genuinely puzzled. "Forgive me, but there are certain idioms I'm not familiar with. What does 'stay in one's lane' mean?"

Tris put a hand on Todd's arm, signaling that she'd answer the question. "Gloria was making decisions above her pay grade. She wasn't the CEO of Peppermint Press. She had all these crazy ideas about which direction the company should take—"

"She wanted to control everything. Even us," Todd interrupted, his cheeks flushed with outrage. "She told us to write more inclusive stories, whatever the hell *that* means. We ignored her. We know what kids like. They like fights between good guys and bad guys. Monsters and heroes.

Buried treasure and magic. Our characters eat candy, not kale. Gloria didn't get it."

Tris nodded in agreement and continued her narrative. "Gloria kept pushing her ideas on everyone at Peppermint Press. Gunnar finally put her in charge of a new imprint— probably just to keep her busy—and she signed a bunch of new authors and had a huge launch party. But her grand scheme failed. Gunnar shut down the imprint soon after his daughter died."

"That's right," added Todd. "He took a leave of absence. When he got back, he was a different man. He wanted Peppermint Press to go back to the way it had been before Gloria came along. He wasn't interested in market trends or pumping out politically correct garbage. He kicked Gloria to the curb, and she went to work for Baxter Books."

"She ruined things for us," Tris said. "Between Gloria screwing up and his kid dying, Gunnar was mad at the whole world. There were no more dinners with our editors and agents. No more lunches celebrating a new contract. No one invited us to swing by the offices for coffee and a chat. Gunnar lowered the portcullis. He raised it later for Birdie and a new wave of authors; those of us who were at Peppermint Press during Gloria's time got pushed into a dark corner. Thanks to her, we became the ugly stepsisters. A bunch of the older authors left—moved to other publishers. But we're loyal. We stayed."

I bet you didn't get any other offers, Jane thought.

Aunt Octavia smiled sympathetically at Tris. "That must have been very difficult." She gestured at the food trolley. "Won't you have something else to eat? Our head cook will be very disappointed to find leftovers."

As the Pettys filled their plates for the second time, Aunt Octavia resumed control of the conversation.

"It sounds like you survived a time of genuine turmoil

at Peppermint Press. Changes in direction. Uncertainty about the future. Mr. Humphries taking a leave of absence. Exactly how did he lose his daughter?"

Todd was uncertain. He looked at his wife. "Car accident?"

"No, it wasn't a car accident. It was a shock, though, because she was young and healthy. I think she was pregnant too. I remember our editor mentioning something about a baby." She pointed at a platter of fried dumplings. "Anyone want these? Otherwise, I'll gobble them up."

Spoken like a witch in a fairy tale, Jane thought.

After telling Tris to help herself, Aunt Octavia fell silent. She and Jane waited for the Pettys to elaborate on the sudden death of Gunnar's daughter.

Instead, they focused on themselves, repeating many of the same complaints they'd mentioned while still on their first cocktails.

Jane observed them as they spoke. Tris or Todd hadn't liked Gloria. But would they punish her for something that happened so long ago? Did they blame Gunnar for their declining success and lack of job satisfaction? Or did they blame Gloria?

Todd tossed back the contents of his glass and set it down on the antique cherry side table. Jane hurriedly retrieved the glass before a moisture ring could stain the polished wood.

When Tris thrust out her empty tumbler, Jane took it without offering a refill. She'd had enough of the truculent couple.

In that, she wasn't alone. Aunt Octavia made a show of looking at the mantel clock. "How quickly time passes. I should freshen up before dinner. Thank you for entertaining an old woman. If any new details come to mind regarding Ms. Ramirez, please let Jane know. We're all very concerned about her."

Todd got to his feet and tugged his sweater down over his belly. "I wouldn't worry about Gloria. She's probably slumming it with one of the local yokels."

Aunt Octavia's eyes turned hard. "I may not recognize certain idioms, Mr. Petty, but I don't need an urban dictionary to deduce the meaning of that phrase. I would like to remind you that *I* am a local yokel. Should any of Storyton Hall's guests choose to *slum it* with me, I'd be most pleased. Good evening."

Too late, Todd realized his mistake.

"I, ah, what I meant is—"

Todd's stammered backpedaling was interrupted by the appearance of Muffet Cat. Though the portly tuxedo had probably been snoozing under the sofa, he seemed to have materialized from thin air. He now sat on his wide haunches, glaring at Aunt Octavia's guests with the silent hostility only a feline can muster.

"It's a cat," said Tris with a mixture of trepidation and revulsion.

Muffet Cat's glower intensified.

"Don't mind him." Aunt Octavia beamed at the pudgy feline. "He doesn't scratch. He *has* been known to bite, but not out of malice. If he smells food on a person's hand, he can get confused and . . ." She made a chomping sound with her teeth.

Tris hopped up and edged toward the door, murmuring something about dinner plans.

Aunt Octavia waved imperially. "Don't let me keep you." She then patted one of the many pockets of her leopard-print housedress. "Would you like a treat, my handsome boy?"

Muffet Cat growled in the Pettys' direction before jumping onto Aunt Octavia's lap.

Todd and Tris practically ran out of the apartment. Jane took no small measure of satisfaction in slamming the door behind them.

"Vermin." Aunt Octavia shook her head in distaste. "Their surname suits them perfectly. They keep score of everything and are envious of everyone. They're quick to insult and to judge others harshly. The fact that Muffet Cat felt compelled to abandon his evening nap to defend us speaks volumes."

"They're awful people. But are they murderers?"

"Mrs. Petty said that Ms. Ramirez ruined everything for them. If ever two people could hold a grudge, it's that couple." Aunt Octavia sighed. "To think they write books for children. It's hard to imagine. Children are like cats. They know when people dislike them."

"In this case, kids like the stories, not the authors. The Pettys write books for beginning readers. The books are straightforward and repetitive, with lots of rhyming words—good elements for a child learning to read. I can see why Gunnar is asking them to be more imaginative, though. Compared to many books at the same level, theirs are a bit flat."

Aunt Octavia stroked Muffet Cat's head. He turned on his back and wriggled until his belly and throat were exposed. Aunt Octavia scratched under his chin, and he purred loudly.

"They don't like children." Aunt Octavia put her hands over Muffet Cat's ears. "They don't like cats. They don't like their boss or their coworkers. The success of other authors sickens them. They're the type of people who can never be satisfied. Which begs the question. What makes these people happy? What motivates them?"

Jane thought carefully before answering. "Money. Status. Recognition."

"Does Ms. Ramirez's death help them achieve those things?"

"No. Not even when the media gets wind of what's happened here. The killer is anonymous."

Aunt Octavia looked worried. "For now. When I think of the fairy-tale books and the tableaus created by the killer, I get the sense that these murders might be acts of vengeance."

"I'll have to speak with Gunnar again tomorrow. I need to know what kinds of changes Gloria made and whose toes may have been stepped on in the process. She obviously made an enemy. She did something serious enough to enrage her killer."

"You should also find out what happened to his daughter. Losing a child changes a person. Forever. If Mr. Humphries took his grief out on the Pettys, they won't have forgiven him for it. He could be in danger."

Recalling Gunnar's pallor and weakness, Jane's heartbeat quickened. What if he wasn't coming down with a common cold? What if someone had deliberately made him ill?

Jane thanked Aunt Octavia and raced down the staff stairs. After locating Butterworth, she pulled him into a quiet corner and asked if he'd delivered chicken soup to Gunnar Humphries yet.

"Less than an hour ago," said Butterworth. "After meeting you in the library, Mr. Humphries rested in his room. I called to make sure he was awake before delivering the soup. He ate it all, along with a buttered roll. When I returned to collect the tray, he'd rallied a bit. There was more color to his cheeks. I asked if he required any medicine. He demurred, stating that the soup had done him a world of good. He planned to read in bed before retiring for the night. I offered to stop back in an hour or so with a pot of sleep-inducing tea, and he accepted my offer."

"I'm glad he's feeling better. However, we need to monitor everything he eats and drinks from now on." Jane shared her concern that Gunnar could be the next victim. "Kristen was poisoned. Lachlan thinks Gloria was too. So now I'm wondering if Gunnar's cold is just a cold."

Butterworth put a hand on Jane's shoulder. "I believe Mr. Humphries is under the weather and that he'll be better tomorrow. However, I'll keep a close eye on him. After the dinner service, I'll return to his room with tea. I will also deliver a breakfast tray in the morning. Speaking of meals, isn't it time for you to head home? Mr. Humphries isn't the only one who can pay a price for overdoing it."

"I'll go as soon as I catch you up on the evening's events." Jane quickly summarized the meeting with the Pettys. When she was done, Butterworth promised to share the information with the other Fins.

"Ask Sinclair to find out what happened to Gunnar's daughter," Jane said as she turned to go. "I don't know if it's relevant, but tragedy can change a person."

Looking solemn, Butterworth helped Jane into her coat. "Try to let this go until morning. Sheriff Evans may have news for us by then."

Jane pulled her hat over her ears. "It's hard to leave knowing a killer might be wandering these halls tonight."

Butterworth's expression turned steely. "If so, I'll be waiting."

Jane hurried through Milton's Gardens and across the Great Lawn, pulling her coat collar closed as the night air tried to wriggle under her scarf. Temperatures had dropped since sunset, causing the melted snow to freeze. Frost kissed the grass, and a skein of ice covered the walkways. The night sky was a cloudless, deep plum. A slim moon gave off very little light.

Opening her front door, Jane stepped into a bubble of warmth and laughter.

"Mom? Is that you?" Fitz shouted from the kitchen.

"Yes!" she called back.

Hem darted into the hallway. As Jane unbuttoned her coat, Hem wagged a finger at her. "Don't come into the kitchen. We're working on a surprise."

"I hope it has to do with food. I'm starved."

Hem's face glowed with pleasure. "You have to wait and see. Can you stay in the living room?"

"Sure. Unless you want me to set the table."

"*No!*" Fitz bellowed from the kitchen.

Jane laughed. "Edwin, are things under control in there?"

"You'd better listen to my assistant chefs or you'll be having gruel for supper."

"Don't go all Mr. Bumble on me," Jane said. "I'll do as I'm told."

She went upstairs, kicked off her shoes, and shrugged out of her suit coat. After changing into jeans and a sapphire-blue wool sweater, she unwound her hair from its bun and ran a brush through it. She then slid her feet into well-worn slippers and headed back downstairs.

Her current read, Neil Gaiman's *Neverwhere*, sat in the middle of the coffee table, along with a martini glass.

"Did the Cocktail Fairy pay me a visit?" she called out.

"Yep!" Fitz shouted back. "That's your pom granite martini."

Jane heard Edwin's chuckle, followed by a flurry of whispering, before Fitz added, "Pomegranate."

Grinning, Jane raised the glass to her lips. In addition to the pomegranate, the cocktail had lime and orange notes. It was bright and crisp with a hint of citrus, and it instantly eased some of the tension from Jane's shoulders.

She managed to enjoy several sips and an equal number of pages before Hem entered the room with a white dishtowel draped over his forearm. Without a trace of self-consciousness, he bowed and said, "May I show you to your table?"

"I didn't realize I'd be dining at a fancy restaurant," Jane said as she looped her arm through her son's. "I should have kept my work clothes on."

"You always look pretty, Mom," said Hem.

Jane smiled and thanked him. He pulled out her chair, and Fitz zipped forward to place a napkin on her lap.

Edwin appeared in the doorway between the kitchen and the dining room. With an inscrutable expression that would have done Butterworth proud, he intoned, "Dinner is served."

The boys scooted back into the kitchen to fetch the food.

"These are fried mozzarella hearts," explained Hem as he put his platter on the table. "Don't take one yet. They're hot, and I have to get the marinara dip. It's like a mini pizza, and it won't taste as good without the sauce."

"This is our vegetable," Fitz said, setting his platter down with a flourish. "Roasted rainbow carrots. Mr. Alcott said that rainbow carrots taste better than regular carrots."

Jane glanced at Edwin. "I can't wait to try them. And the mozzarella hearts too. This food is beautiful, gentlemen."

"Beautiful food for a beautiful woman," said Edwin.

The twins exchanged eye rolls, which made Jane and Edwin laugh.

Dishes were passed around. Edwin filled glasses with

water and added lemon slices to each glass. While they ate, the twins talked about their class Valentine's party.

"Ms. Miller liked our cards the most," Fitz said, reaching for another mozzarella heart. "She didn't say it, but we could tell."

"We were the only ones who made something. Everyone else got *their* stuff at a store."

Jane gestured at the food on the table. "I love that my three favorite guys had the talent to create this wonderful dinner. But even if you'd ordered pizza from over the mountain, I'd still be happy. The best part about it is that you wanted to do something special for me. Ms. Miller was happy because her students wanted to make her feel special. It doesn't matter how they did it."

Hem shrugged. He was too busy submerging his mozzarella heart in marinara to respond to his mother's short lecture.

Fitz speared a carrot on his fork but didn't eat it. "She got a *huge* box of chocolate too. The biggest one in the Pickled Pig! It looks like a giant pink flower."

"Mr. Hogg said that he orders one every year just to see if someone will buy it," Jane explained to Edwin. "If no one does, he buys it for his girlfriend."

"She's lucky," Hem murmured. "There's like, a thousand pieces of chocolate in there."

Jane remembered seeing the giant, rose-shaped box on the highest shelf in the market's candy section. Its unusual shape and hot-pink hue made it impossible to miss.

"You should have seen the card that came with it," Fitz went on.

"It was a pop-up, like we made," Hem added. "But *way* better."

Fitz turned to him. "It was just some flowers and a question mark. That's not better."

Edwin rubbed his chin. "I wonder what this mystery person wanted to ask Ms. Miller."

"He's not a mystery person. It's the man who taught us how to make the pop-up books. And he probably wants to kiss her," Hem said.

Fitz locked eyes with his brother. "I hope they don't do it at school."

The boys sniggered before attacking their food with fresh gusto.

Jane waited until they were distracted before looking at Edwin. He grinned at her before blowing her a kiss. She caught the air kiss and pressed her closed fist against her heart.

"Save some room, Mom," Fitz warned when Jane resumed eating.

Hem glanced down at his empty plate. "We have another course."

Dessert was an array of exotic fruits. They were so exotic that Jane couldn't identify any of them.

"Remember when you came to the restaurant the other night, and I asked the boys if they wanted to be adventurous eaters?" Edwin asked Jane. "I told them that being adventurous means trying new things, even if those new things look or smell strange. I thought we'd start our culinary adventure with fruit because it's usually sweet. For this evening's dessert, Fitz and Hem learned to peel and slice three new-to-them fruits. They are now ready to taste kumquat, lychee, and jackfruit."

Jane had never heard of jackfruit, let alone tried one. After sampling a slice of each fruit, the diners ranked them from favorite to least favorite. When every piece had been eaten, Edwin offered to clean up the kitchen while Jane and the twins set up a board game.

"Can we play backgammon?" Fitz asked.

Hem's eyes were shining. "Please? We've been practicing."

Edwin had taught the twins to play months ago, and they'd been using the backgammon set he'd bought them in Turkey almost nightly. Jane did chores in the kitchen to the rattle of dice hitting wood and the sound of her sons reacting to each other's moves.

"Great idea," said Edwin. "You two play first. I'll take on the winner when I'm done helping your mom."

Fitz wiped off the table while Hem retrieved the backgammon set from the cupboard where the board games and jigsaw puzzles were kept.

Hem opened the folding case and said, "I want to be black this time. If I win, you have to call me Lord Vader."

"And if I win, you have to call me Moon Knight. He's the only cool superhero with a white costume."

"What about Storm?" Edwin asked.

Fitz was affronted by the suggestion. "I don't want Hem to call me a *girl*."

Jane tried to think of another hero who wore white. Stepping in the room she said, "What about Gandalf? He was Gandalf the Grey until his battle against the Balrog. After that, he became Gandalf the White."

Fitz shot Hem a look that said, *What's wrong with these people?*

Turning to Jane, he said, "He's a wizard, which is awesome, but he's *old*."

Edwin raised a finger in objection. "Moon Knight is even older than Gandalf. He's the Egyptian moon god's avatar on earth, which means he's really, *really* old."

Fitz's mouth dropped open in astonishment. "You read comic books?"

"I used to. And I've kept most of them," Edwin said. "One of these days, I'll show you my favorites."

Later, when Jane poked her head in the boys' room to say good night, Fitz whispered, "Can Mr. Alcott come over more?"

"Yeah. He's the coolest grown-up we know," added Hem.

Jane smiled. "He's the coolest grown-up I know too. Thanks for my wonderful dinner. See you in the morning."

Downstairs, Edwin stoked the fire while Jane opened a bottle of wine. Once she and Edwin were snuggled under a blanket on the sofa, she toasted his successful dinner. They sipped their wine and spoke in hushed whispers about tomorrow's play, the popularity of the Storybook Village, and the special Valentine's events Jane had planned for the visiting families. Finally, they talked about the murders.

Jane told Edwin everything. She shared snippets of conversation, known facts, and wild theories. When she was done, she lamented the presence of the shadow of worry and fear that had fallen over Storyton Hall.

"I want to believe that the killer will be apprehended tomorrow. I want to believe that the weekend I planned for our guests won't be completely ruined by the horror of two deaths. But right now, it's hard for me to feel positive. I'd give anything to forget about the things I can't control for a little while."

Edwin stroked her cheek with the back of his hand. He then slid his arm around her waist and pulled her closer. Jane pressed her palm against Edwin's chest and felt the drumming of his heart. To her, it was the most beautiful music in the world. It was a love song.

Edwin put a finger under her chin, tilting her mouth upward. He then leaned down to kiss her. Just before his lips met hers, he whispered, "I might be able to help with that."

Chapter Thirteen

Jane felt like a teenager as she tiptoed to her room after kissing Edwin good night. He promised that he'd be gone before she and the boys woke the next morning, and he was. The only sign that he'd spent the night on the sofa was the blanket draped over its arm.

The aroma of freshly brewed coffee floated out of the kitchen, and Jane drifted over to its source. She found that not only was the carafe filled to capacity, but Edwin had also laid out a coffee cup, spoon, and napkin for her. A yellow sticky note peeked out of the coffee cup. Jane picked it up and read:

Good morning, Love.

Breakfast is in the oven. It's cooked. It just needs to be warmed up. I'm off to Hilltop Stables to borrow a horse. I'm going to ride through the woods from Broken Arm Bend to Storyton Hall. I know Landon searched the area, but I can cover more ground on horseback. I believe the Big Bad Wolf approached the fairy tale village by the access road, which means he either walked from town or parked a vehicle out of sight. When I'm done, I plan to

cozy up to the bookseller with the devilish beard.
Call me if you need anything. Be careful.

—E

When Jane opened the oven, currents of butter-scented air wafted out. A tray of ham and cheese biscuits sat under a tent of aluminum foil. The biscuits were golden-brown, but the cheese was still stiff. All Jane had to do was heat the oven long enough to melt the cheese.

"He made homemade biscuits while we slept," Jane said, glancing around the tidy kitchen in astonishment. "I am the luckiest woman alive."

The twins were thrilled by the breakfast sandwiches. They ate two each and begged to split a third.

"Can we have these again tomorrow?" Fitz asked.

Jane shook her head. "Nope. It's pancake day. You know I love making silly shapes for you guys."

"Okay, but I want rhombus pancakes," Hem teased.

Fitz grinned. "I want parallelograms."

Jane flicked the dishtowel at her sons. "You think you're *so* smart. Wait until I fold this towel into a *triangle*. Are you watching? Once I have my shape, I'll twist it around and around like so. And then, I'll use it on anyone making fun of my pancakes."

Flicking her wrist, she sent the end of the towel into the air. It made a threatening snapping sound.

"That wouldn't hurt a fly," said Hem.

"Oh, yeah? Come here, Fly Boy." Jane raised the towel.

The boys squealed and ran around the kitchen island. Jane chased them for a bit, snapping the towel inches away from their backsides.

After much laughing and shrieking, she called for a timeout.

"Mom needs coffee." Jane tossed the towel next to the

sink, picked up her coffee cup, and smiled. This was one of those mornings she'd store away in her mental file cabinet. Aunt Octavia was right. Happily ever after wasn't a huge event. It was a hundred small moments of happiness. A moment just like this.

I bet a day doesn't pass without Gunnar missing his daughter, Jane thought. The older man's loss made her more aware of her good fortune.

After breakfast, Jane reminded Fitz and Hem about their martial arts lesson with Sinclair.

"You need to do your Saturday chores before you go. I'll be inspecting your room, so if you want to build a candy house today, don't hide things in the closet or under your bed."

Ignoring their groans, Jane went upstairs to shower and dress for work.

She and the boys decided to exchange valentines after dinner, and Jane had cards and a comic book for each of her sons. She also had a special book for Edwin. It had come from Storyton Hall's secret library and was very valuable. Jane could have sold it and put the money toward the future restoration of Flaubert's Folly, but some books were meant for certain readers. This was such a book. It was meant to be touched. For gentle fingers to turn its pages. For eager eyes to drink in the words and images. It was meant to be cherished by Edwin.

During a meeting of the Cover Girls, Eloise had once told Jane that there was nothing more thrilling than watching a reader turn to the first page of a book.

Jane reflected on that evening with her friends as she wound her hair into a loose bun. If the Fairy Tale Killer wasn't apprehended within the next few hours, she would call the Cover Girls and ask for their help.

After running pink gloss over her lips, Jane stepped

into the twins' room to see how they were coming along with their chores.

Hem had the vacuum out and was waiting for Fitz to pick up his dirty clothes. Fitz was sprawled on his bed. He wore headphones, but Jane could hear the audiobook narrator from where she stood.

She gave Fitz a poke in the shoulder and made a *gimme* gesture.

Fitz reluctantly surrendered his iPod.

"I'm sure Hem would rather be on his bed, listening to a book, but he's doing what he's supposed to be doing." Jane put the iPod on Fitz's desk. "I'm going to leave this here because I trust you to do the right thing. Apologize to your brother and get to work."

It was only when Fitz started scooping clothes off the floor that Jane left the room.

Inside Storyton Hall, Jane hung up her coat and went to join Butterworth by the front entrance.

"How is Mr. Humphries today?" she asked.

"Much improved," said Butterworth. "He plans to participate in the morning's roundtable discussion. The staff knows that any food or beverages consumed by Mr. Humphries must come directly from the kitchens. Seeing as we've made this request for guests with severe food allergies in the past, no one found it unusual."

Butterworth paused to open the door for a family of four.

"Will we be the first people at Storybook Village?" a little girl asked her father.

"It depends how fast we get there. Do you think our sleigh can fly?"

The girl giggled. "No, silly. That's Santa's sleigh. He has magic reindeer."

"Maybe we have magic horses," the father said and swept the little girl into his arms.

Butterworth watched the family climb into the horse-drawn wagon. There wasn't enough snow on the ground for the sleigh, but Sam's wagon, with its hay bales and plaid blankets, was just as charming. Sam clucked at the horses and the wagon eased forward, the bells on the harnesses ringing merrily.

Butterworth wiped a smudge from the brass door handle and turned to Jane. "Sheriff Evans called. He'll be heading this way in twenty minutes or so."

Jane nodded. "Does Sinclair have news for me? I want to share everything we've discovered so far with the sheriff."

"Mr. Sinclair is waiting for you in the Henry James Library. I'll let you know when Sheriff Evans arrives."

Jane thanked Butterworth and headed for the library. Despite her anxiety over the impending meeting with the sheriff, she managed to smile and say a cheerful "good morning" to every guest. She should have been pleased by how relaxed and content they all looked. Instead, worry gnawed at her insides. Storyton Hall was occupied by families and by people devoted to the creation of children's books. Jane wanted to keep them all safe, but she doubted her ability to do so. Two murders had been committed on the grounds, and she and her Fins were no closer to identifying the killer than they had been yesterday.

"I hope you have something for me" were her first words to Sinclair.

"If you're referring to Mr. Humphries and his daughter, then I do." Sinclair led Jane into his office and shut the door. "It's an unhappy tale. The Humphries, Gunnar and

Elsa, had one child. Her name was Penelope, but everyone called her Poppy. Poppy was clearly the apple of her father's eye. There are many photographs from Peppermint Press events showing Poppy as a baby in her father's arms, a toddler on his shoulders, and a young girl holding his hand."

Jane let out a heavy sigh. "I hate knowing how this story ends."

"It's very sad." Sinclair's gaze strayed to the black-and-white photo of Gunnar Humphries attached to his background check sheet. "Toward the end of her junior year of college, Poppy met a young man named Charlie Stackhouse. The pair dated for a few months before calling it quits. Not long after the break-up, Poppy discovered that she was pregnant. Mr. Stackhouse wanted nothing to do with the baby, which was fine with Poppy and her parents. I gleaned this information from the receptionist at Peppermint Press, a Mrs. Brighton. She's been with the company for twenty years and is a bit of a gossip."

"So Poppy kept the baby?" Jane asked.

"According to Mrs. Brighton, Poppy had her parents' full support. Here's a photo taken shortly before the baby was born." Sinclair handed Jane a color printout. "The happiness on their faces is genuine."

So genuine that it made Jane's heart hurt to see it. Poppy stood between her parents. She had a freckled face and a halo of blond hair. Her smile was dazzling, and joy radiated from her blue eyes. Gunnar had a protective arm around his daughter's shoulders, and Elsa's hand was cradling her daughter's round belly. Both parents were beaming.

"The baby?" Jane repeated.

"Poppy delivered a healthy baby boy. However, she did not survive the birth." Sinclair was silent for a long moment. Eventually, he went on. "After Poppy's death,

Mrs. Humphries became very involved with the March of Dimes. She spent a great deal of time and money on legislation that would warn women about the dangers of pre-eclampsia. This was the condition that led to her daughter's death."

"Those poor parents." Jane looked at Gunnar's current photo. He didn't look like the same man. There were shadows of sorrow in his eyes and he'd aged beyond his years. Even his smile held a trace of sadness. Jane felt so sorry for the older man that she couldn't speak right away. After dabbing at her wet eyes with a tissue, she said, "Please don't tell me that Poppy's boyfriend claimed the baby."

Sinclair shook his head. "The baby, christened Aiden Humphries, was formally adopted by his grandparents. The father had no objection."

"I'm glad that Poppy's parents were allowed to raise her son," Jane said. "Though it was probably really hard at times. All the joy and wonder must have been mixed with heartache. I'm sure Aiden reminds them of Poppy. They lost a child and gained a child."

Sinclair took Jane's hand. "You'd understand the challenge more than most. You raised two children without your husband."

"Yes, and every day, I wished I could tell William some detail about the twins. I wanted to share their milestones. Complain when they were driving me crazy. Talk about how they made me laugh." She fought to keep her voice steady. "I didn't have William, but I had you. I had Sterling and Butterworth. Aunt Octavia and Uncle Aloysius. My sons had all the family they needed. They've had a magical childhood. I hope Aiden Humphries has a magical one too."

Jane's phone buzzed with an incoming text message.

"The sheriff's here," Jane said as she got to her feet.

"What happened to Gunnar's daughter is truly awful, but I don't see a connection between her death and these murders. Kristen and Gloria didn't work in the medical field." She glanced at the wall of photos and facts. "I wish I understood the killer's motive. Without that, it's impossible to predict his next move."

"Sheriff Evans might have a fresh lead," said Sinclair.

"In which case, I shouldn't keep him waiting."

When Jane entered her office, she saw a tray with a coffeepot and two cups on her desk. Sheriff Evans stood by the window, hat in hand.

He gestured at the tray. "You always have a warm welcome for me, no matter what."

"I can't take credit. This is Butterworth's doing." Jane poured a cup of coffee for the sheriff and waved at the guest chair facing her desk.

Evans dropped into the chair. He looked wrung out with fatigue. His uniform was wrinkled, and several ink stains bloomed along the base of his shirt pocket. He obviously hadn't had time to shave, and the lower half of his face was covered with salt-and-pepper bristle. Evans caught Jane assessing him and smiled wanly.

"I was at the ME's until late last night. And what I learned there kept me from sleeping."

"And from eating?" Jane guessed. She wanted to help this dedicated, dogged lawman. "I'm ordering breakfast for you. Don't bother arguing because I won't listen. You need fuel to lead this investigation. The least I can do is give you decent coffee and nourishing food."

After making a quick call to the kitchens, Jane said, "The ME must have discovered something pretty bad. You must have been exhausted by the time you got to bed."

The sheriff ran a hand over his cheek and frowned. "I never went home. I have a cot in my office, and I spent hours staring at crime scene photos. You'll understand why my mind wouldn't stop spinning when I tell you how Ms. Ramirez was killed."

Absently, Jane reached for the ninja stress ball she'd received as a Secret Santa gift. Squeezing the poor ninja until his head was in danger of exploding, she waited for Evans to continue.

He took a sip of coffee and lowered his cup. He squared his shoulders and looked Jane in the eye.

"While we were working the scene, Mr. Lachlan said that he believed Gloria Ramirez had been poisoned. The blood on her chin and the ground supported this theory. This was bad news. Identifying a specific poison takes time. Time is one thing we don't have."

The red heart on Jane's wall calendar made her think of Kristen's coat. And of poisoned apples. "I wouldn't have expected the killer to use food again. Not with the glass fragments scattered around her body. Food wasn't important in *The Snow Queen*."

"Yesterday, I read as much as I could about Andersen's creepy tale. The story doesn't mention poison outright, but the evil mirror is poisonous. Its pieces can distort the truth or cause death. Which is why I was afraid that we'd find glass in Ms. Ramirez's throat."

Jane shuddered at the thought.

"The ME didn't find glass. What she found is much stranger, and I can't connect it to any fairy tale. I'm hoping you can provide some insight."

At that inopportune moment, someone knocked on the door.

Assuming it was a member of the kitchen staff with a heavy tray, Jane hurried to open the door. Sheriff Evans moved the coffee service out of the way, creating a space for a tray laden with sausage rolls, fresh fruit, and bacon.

Jane thanked the server and waited until he left before saying, "I already ate, so don't hold back on my account."

"Let me finish telling you about the case first. I can't eat until I get this out," said Evans. "The object in Ms. Ramirez's throat? The ME identified it as a watch battery."

Jane frowned. "A battery? Did it block her airway?"

"The answer is a bit gruesome. Let's say you took the battery out of your watch. Since your watch has been running, the battery is clearly holding a charge. If you add that electrical current to water, like the moisture inside a person's throat, you get a chemical reaction."

"Like a burn?"

"Yes. The ME explained that the current breaks down water molecules. This process produces hydroxide and hydrogen gas. If you think about the size of a watch battery, it can easily get stuck in a human's throat. At that point, the chemical process begins, creating small bleeds in the surrounding tissue. Ultimately, Ms. Ramirez's aorta broke down, leading to a massive hemorrhage."

Jane covered her mouth with her hand, sickened by the thought of Gloria's suffering.

The sheriff gave her time to compose herself by putting food onto a plate. When he had a nourishing supply of bacon, rolls, and fruit, he gestured at his meal and said, "This looks insensitive after what I just told you. But you're right. I need fuel. It's going to be another long day, and your coffee and breakfast will keep me going."

Jane murmured something unintelligible, but she wasn't really listening. She was back in the woods with Gloria Ramirez. She saw Gloria's body again, recalling how she'd looked like a woman made of snow and ice. Death had stolen the color from her flesh. There'd been only a rivulet of dried blood on her chin. That small pop of red couldn't begin to convey the agony Gloria must have felt in the last minutes of her life.

Grabbing a napkin from the breakfast tray, Jane blotted her wet eyes. "It would take an intense hatred to cause another person that much pain. The killer isn't just cruel. He's barbaric."

"He's likely known by his victims. Both murders were acts of rage. And maybe, of vengeance," Sheriff Evans said.

"There must be something in Kristen's and Gloria's backgrounds to tie them to another Storyton Hall guest. Or to a villager."

Evans put down the remains of his sausage roll. "We'll have to interview everyone registered for the children's book conference. For now, we can keep the families out of the investigation. But if we don't catch the killer soon, we'll have to confine all guests and staff until we do."

"I understand. We've been doing our best to find answers too, and I'll tell you everything I know. As for the watch battery, I have no idea how that fits with a fairy tale. But I'll research watches, clocks, time—anything that might give us a lead."

While the sheriff ate, Jane shared what they'd learned from speaking with Nia, Gloria's landlord, and Tris and Todd. She concluded by telling him about Gunnar's daughter.

"Neither Kristen nor Gloria have a medical background, so I don't see how they could have influenced Ms. Humphries's fate," the sheriff said, arriving at the same conclusion Jane had reached earlier that morning.

Jane had a sudden thought. "What about Gloria's boyfriend? He works in a hospital."

"He's on a plane from New York as we speak, so I'll be interviewing him in person soon. However, he has airtight alibis for the past few days. Lots of hospital personnel can vouch for him. Seems like he works more than he sleeps. He's not our guy."

"Our guy could be a woman." Jane felt compelled to point this out, though it was hard to imagine a woman pinning Gloria to the ground and shoving a watch battery down her throat. Whatever the killer's gender, the act couldn't have been easy. Had Gloria fought back? Did her assailant have bruises? Scratches? Bite marks? Jane raised these points to the sheriff.

"The ME believes Ms. Ramirez was sedated," he answered. "He's asked for a rush on the lab results, but I doubt we'll see them this weekend. Speaking of rushes, I pressured a judge to grant me a warrant to search the guest bathrooms for a possible murder weapon. In other words, if we find sedatives, we might find the killer."

"If the guests are prevented from returning to their rooms for an hour or two, no one will realize that you're hunting down this lead. If your deputies keep a record of the medication in each room, Sterling can compile a master list for you."

Evans nodded. "Good. I'd like to get started immediately, please. And we need to gather the conference attendees so I can tell them about Ms. Ramirez."

Jane checked her watch. "They'll be taking a break from their morning sessions in ten minutes. I'll have Butterworth funnel them into Shakespeare's Theater. My staff will observe how people react to your announcement."

The sheriff wiped his hands on a napkin. He was ready to act. "I'm grateful for your cooperation and assistance, Ms. Steward."

"And I'm grateful that Storyton has a sheriff who loses sleep over his cases," said Jane.

Together, they left the office and walked through the lobby toward Butterworth.

"I need every Fin in the Shakespeare Theater in five minutes," Jane told the butler. "As soon as the morning conference sessions break, usher the guests into the theater."

Butterworth glanced at Sheriff Evans who'd moved off to make a call. "Mr. Lachlan is watching over the families visiting the Storybook Village. Should I pull him from that detail?"

"No. I feel better knowing he's there. I also need you to contact Mrs. Templeton. She and the housekeeping staff have some snooping to do."

"She'll be delighted to assist, I'm sure."

Though Jane couldn't tell if Butterworth was being sarcastic or not, she didn't have time to puzzle over his tone. After explaining that all medicines needed to be cataloged by room number, she waited for him to use his walkie to call Sinclair, Sterling, and Mrs. Templeton.

"Without delay," he added, injecting his voice with the stern authority of a headmaster.

The three senior staff members appeared in less than three minutes. Jane beckoned them into the staff hallway and hurriedly explained what was happening.

At the mention of murder, Mrs. Templeton burst into tears.

"I'm sorry!" she cried. "With the play, it's all just too much. We have so many children here. We need to protect them from such horrors!"

Sinclair pressed a handkerchief into Mrs. Templeton's hand while Sterling put an arm around her shoulders.

"Which is exactly why we must work together," Jane said. "We're all responsible for Storyton Hall and the safety of our guests. Can I count on you to assist the sheriff and his team?"

With a final sniff, Mrs. Templeton said, "Yes, of course."

Jane told her about the search for sedatives, and the head housekeeper bustled off.

"Sterling. What did you find out about rental cars?"

"Only three conference attendees have rentals. One is a woman who plans to visit her sister in Harrisonburg after the conference. Next, there's a young man whose pregnant wife might deliver any day. He wanted to have a car in case he had to rush off to the airport. Finally, there's Birdie Bloom. Apparently, she's known for skipping conference activities in favor of exploring the local area. I was told that she's always searching for inspiration for her next book."

Jane looked at Sinclair. "Is Birdie her real name?"

"No. It's Elizabeth Bloomington. She uses Birdie because it's more child-friendly."

"Has she been at Peppermint Press long enough to know Gloria?"

Sinclair gazed into the middle distance as he rifled through cards in his mental file cabinet. "Only for a matter of months."

Birdie was a slight woman. Jane couldn't picture her overpowering Gloria, but everyone connected to Gloria, no matter how briefly, had to be examined under a microscope.

"One of us should sit in on the sheriff's interview with Ms. Bloom," said Jane. Her phone buzzed and she glanced at the screen. "The sheriff is ready to address our guests. God help us, Sinclair. I never thought we'd be doing this again."

In the theater, Jane walked to the front of the room, turned on the microphone, and thanked the attendees for their cooperation. She waited until the theater doors were closed before introducing Sheriff Evans.

The sheriff cleared his throat and began to speak.

Witnessing the reactions to Gloria's death was gut-wrenching. There were loud cries of dismay, as well as mute expressions of shock. People reached for each other. All around the theater, people were holding hands.

Having hosted several book-related conferences, Jane knew that the publishing world was a small one. Writers, editors, cover designers, literary agents, publicists, sales-people—they all knew each other. There were people in this room who'd never met Gloria, but they'd heard of her. She belonged to their tribe. And now, she was gone.

Butterworth, Sterling, Sinclair, and the sheriff's deputies studied faces, looking for a tell. Jane was also scanning the crowd when her eyes locked on two men in the last row. One had dark eyes, a sharp nose, and a pointy beard. Malcolm Marcus.

The other man was Edwin. He was turned toward Malcolm and was murmuring close to his ear. As Jane watched, the bookseller's mouth curved into a sly smile and he began to nod.

Jane had expected Malcolm to be sulking. Following the discovery of Gloria's body, the sheriff had asked Malcolm to stay in town. This meant missing the book show he'd been so eager to attend. Not only that, but he also hadn't gotten the books he'd wanted from Gloria.

What had Edwin said to make him smile?

She glanced away before Malcolm could catch her staring, and her gaze fell on other familiar faces. Gunnar, Nia, Reggie, Sasha, the artist who'd led the pop-up book workshop, and Birdie Bloom.

Birdie's hands were clasped just under her chin. Her

eyes were wide and moist with unshed tears. The woman in the next seat patted her shoulder.

Jane had seen murderers behave grief-stricken or give Oscar-winning performances of sympathy. Others had shown no emotion at all. She'd seen more than her fair share of killers by now, and not one of them looked or acted like a predator. Jane knew that the most dangerous kind of criminals could blend in with a crowd. They were true wolves in sheep's clothing.

Big Bad Wolves, whispered a voice in Jane's head.

After giving the attendees a minute to absorb the news, Sheriff Evans went on to say that Gloria Ramirez's death was under investigation.

This elicited a buzz of agitated murmuring. Jane understood her guests' anxiety. It was bad enough that one of them had been killed. To find out that there were unresolved elements concerning her death was distressing. On top of that, they were all being put through the ordeal of an official interview. Just like that, their day had been derailed. Everything had become uncertain, and uncertainty was frightening.

The sheriff concluded his announcements with a warning.

"This is an open investigation, which means you must refrain from discussing the case. I'd like to remind all of you of the children staying at Storyton Hall. They do *not* need to hear about this." He paused for a moment; his stern gaze fixed on the crowd. "We will address questions during the individual interview sessions. If you have urgent information, please see Deputy Phelps right away."

At the front of the room, Phelps raised his arm.

"Ladies and gentlemen, we're pressed for time," the sheriff said. "If you want justice for Ms. Ramirez, then please do whatever you can to assist us."

Around the large room, people nodded in resolve. They wanted to help. They wanted to honor Gloria by doing their part to balance the scales. They wanted to restore peace. As a rule, they were good people. They were book people.

There are always exceptions to the rule, Jane thought.

She looked back to where Malcolm and Edwin had been sitting, but the seats were empty.

Chapter Fourteen

Though Jane would have liked to sit in on the guest interviews, she had a resort to run. Her main goal was to continue distancing the families staying at Storyton Hall from the sheriff's investigation. If all went well, their Valentine's weekend would be filled with fun and laughter. She didn't want the shadow cast by two murders to touch them.

Fortunately, most of the families were visiting Storybook Village. But Jane, her Fins, and the sheriff would have to work fast to apprehend the killer before Jane was forced to share the news with the rest of her guests.

The race against the clock was affecting Jane's mind and body. A headache throbbed behind her eyes, making it hard to think. She needed help. She needed the special kind of support that close friends knew how to give.

"I need the Cover Girls."

She remembered that Eloise, Mrs. Pratt, Mabel, and Betty had volunteered to assist with the candy house workshop. Knowing that she'd be in their company made Jane feel miles better.

She sent a text to her four friends, asking them to arrive earlier than scheduled. Jane wanted to pick their brains over lunch. Her friends always helped her to see things from a different angle. They'd ask a question no one else thought to ask. They'd turn a theory on its head. They were smart, loyal, and determined. And Jane knew they wouldn't let her down.

After the Cover Girls agreed to meet at noon, Jane walked to the kitchens to place a lunch order with Mrs. Hubbard.

She was in the middle of the lobby when Peter Gilbert barreled into her.

"Where's the fire?" Jane teased, holding Peter by his shoulders to keep him from falling.

"Sorry!" He looked abashed. "I forgot my hat. Mom says it'll be cold at Storybook Village."

Jane smiled at the little boy. "She's right. Luckily, you can get hot chocolate to warm you up."

Peter's eyes sparkled. "I want the caramel hot chocolate."

"You have excellent taste in paintings and in hot chocolate flavors," Jane said. "Where's your family? Already outside?"

Peter indicated a sofa farther down the lobby. "Over there. That tall guy by the front door said that we have to wait for the wagon."

"That's Mr. Butterworth." Jane lowered her voice. "He used to be a secret agent."

Peter shot a nervous glance at Butterworth. "Is he nice?"

"He looks super tough and serious, but he's just a big teddy bear. I've known him since I was your age. He used to put me on his shoulders and let me wind the clock." Jane pointed at the old grandfather clock.

Peter looked at Butterworth. "That's cool."

A chime rang out from behind Peter, signaling the arrival of the elevator. The little boy stiffened. It was a very slight movement, but Jane noticed.

"Speaking of nice and not nice, I saw you and your sister hold the elevator for a man and woman yesterday. That was very polite." Jane smiled approvingly. "But the people didn't get in. Instead, it seemed like they said something mean to you. Did they?"

Peter glanced at his family. If he could teleport to their location, he probably would.

Jane felt guilty about pressing him, but two women were dead. She had to know exactly what Tris and Todd were made of, so she whispered, "It's okay to tell me."

After another hesitation, Peter blurted, "They said that they didn't want to share the elevator with a pair of monkeys."

Jane tried to hide her anger. Her indignation wouldn't erase the hurtful words, but it was difficult not to react to such nastiness. "I'm so sorry," she told Peter. "Those people were wrong to say that."

Peter shrugged. "Mom says that when people are mean, I should tell them my story. She says that people get stuck in their own stories and that we need to show them what our life is like. But I didn't have time to tell that guy and lady anything. I don't really want to, either."

"You don't have to see them ever again. That's a promise," said Jane. "Thank you for telling me. And I hope you have lots of fun at Storybook Village. Don't forget to get a tattoo."

"I'm getting *three*!" Peter cried and raced over to his family.

Jane wished she could take away the damage the Pettys' insult had caused. And though she couldn't rewrite the past, she could prevent the Pettys from verbally abusing anyone else. As soon as the sheriff finished with them, Jane would be having words with the author couple.

Reciting her speech in her mind, Jane marched to the

kitchens. She placed her lunch order and headed back to the lobby. When she spotted Gunnar Humphries limping toward the William Faulkner Conference Room, she hurried to catch up to him.

After a quick hello, she asked after his health.

"I'm much better, thanks to you and Mr. Butterworth," he said, stopping to lean on his good leg. "I didn't mean to cause a fuss, especially now that Gloria . . ." His throat seemed to tighten, cutting off his words.

"Let me get you a glass of water," said Jane, coaxing Gunnar into an empty conference room.

Gunnar accepted the water and took a grateful sip. He then checked his watch and said, "I'm meeting with the sheriff in five minutes."

"You might as well wait here, where it's comfortable." Jane pulled out a chair for him. "I know you must be upset about Gloria. I don't want to add to your distress, but I'd like you to tell me a bit about Todd and Tris Petty."

"Todd and Tris? Why? Have they done something?"

Jane decided to be direct. "Since their arrival, they've made several racist comments. One of these was directed at two children."

Gunnar let out a groan.

"Have the Pettys exhibited intolerant behavior before?"

"They've had issues," Gunnar replied, averting his gaze. "The Pettys I hired all those years ago were so different from the people they are today. They used to be lively, funny, and devoted to their craft. Back then, they planned on having lots of children. But it wasn't meant to be. They spent every dime on fertility treatments. With every failed attempt, the best parts of Tris and Todd withered away. After years of disappointments, they became angry. Envious. When they finally decided to adopt, they were rejected by every agency in the tri-state area."

Jane arched her brows. "Why?"

"Todd didn't tell me until much later." Gunnar stroked the glass knob of his cane as if seeking comfort from the orange flower trapped inside. "We were at an awards dinner. Todd had had too much to drink. He was angry that his book hadn't been nominated. He was angry that he'd been given the wrong dessert. He was angry about everything. He thought I'd understand because he and I were both childless. But that wasn't true. I had a child. A daughter. Even though she died, I was still her father. You never stop being someone's dad."

"I'm so sorry." Jane covered Gunnar's hand with hers.

He nodded mournfully. "It happened a long time ago. But to me, it was yesterday. I miss her so much." He waved his free hand. "Anyway, at this awards dinner, Todd confided that he and Tris were rejected as potential parents because they wanted a white baby or no baby at all. I assume their reasons for refusing to consider a child of color revealed deep flaws in their character."

"I saw Tris and Todd when they spoke to the children. I didn't hear what was said, but I saw hatred in their eyes. In the curl of their lips. How can you hate a little kid? For crying out loud, Tris and Todd write books for kids."

Gunnar released a lugubrious sigh. "They seem to hate anything that's joyful, hopeful, or youthful. They've wasted their lives wanting what others have. On the other hand, they've also helped countless children learn to read. If they'd chosen to be more positive, their days could have been filled with children. The Pettys could have spent their time visiting schools and libraries. They could have gotten involved with the Boys & Girls Club. They could have helped children learn to read. Instead, they became embittered, unlikable curmudgeons."

"Do their books still resonate with today's readers?"

"They do. Otherwise, I would have cut them years ago." Gunnar drank more water. "I'd cut them now, but their work is all they have. It would be cruel."

Jane sat back in her chair. She wasn't made of stone. She felt sorry for the Pettys. But only a little. Tris and Todd had made a mess of their lives. Fear and prejudice had dictated their actions. They were bullies, and Jane knew how to deal with bullies.

"Can people like Tris and Todd find happiness?" Gunnar murmured.

Though the question seemed rhetorical, Jane answered it. "They can feel a temporary thrill of success in undermining others, but those are hollow victories. That's not happiness."

Gunnar's gaze had turned glassy. He was lost in a memory.

Though Jane didn't want to disturb him, she needed to ask the most important question of all.

"Do you think Tris and Todd are capable of murder?"

Gunnar met her gaze. "I've been asking myself the same thing all morning. They didn't like Gloria. They didn't like her ideas. And now, I have to admit that they probably didn't like the color of her skin. But why go after Gloria years after she left Peppermint Press?"

Opportunity, Jane thought. Storyton Hall was remote. It was the polar opposite of New York City. In New York, Gloria was surrounded by people. She worked in a busy office, shared an apartment with her boyfriend, and volunteered with several organizations.

She ruined things for us.

That's what Tris had said. To Jane, that sounded like a motive. With motive and opportunity, the Pettys now sat at the top of Jane's suspect list.

At that moment, Deputy Phelps poked his head into the

conference room. "I thought I heard voices. Mr. Humphries, the sheriff is ready for you."

Gunnar got to his feet and moved to the door. He then paused and looked back at Jane. "I should have been a better leader. I ignored comments I shouldn't have ignored. I wish I could wave a magic peppermint stick and take back whatever Tris and Todd said to those children."

Jane smiled at him. "You're producing books those kids can identify with. That'll do more good than a truckload of peppermint sticks."

"I hope so," Gunnar said. Leaning heavily on his cane, he followed Deputy Phelps out of the room.

Mrs. Pratt surveyed Jane's cramped office. "This is nice and cozy, Jane. But why are we having lunch here?"

"I need your help." Jane gestured at the platter of sandwiches and the bowl of green salad. "Go ahead and eat while I talk. I have lots of ground to cover before the candy house workshop starts."

Jane took a hearty bite from her ham and cheese sandwich and then moved to the blank whiteboard attached to the wall behind her desk. She wrote the names KRISTEN and GLORIA at the top of the board.

"These two women seem to have nothing in common. If we could find a single common denominator, it might break the case wide open."

While her friends selected their sandwiches and began eating, Jane listed the victims' current and past professions, addresses, and relationship status.

Mrs. Pratt stared at Brandon's name. Frowning, she said, "No one from Baxter Books has met Gloria's live-in boyfriend? To me, that's a red flag. Does this Brandon have an alibi?"

"Airtight," said Jane. "He's an orthopedic doc. Dozens of patients and medical personnel can vouch for him. The sheriff got a copy of the cases he worked, and there's no way he could have flown down from New York, killed his girlfriend, and flown back. He was too busy."

"Plus, he'd have no reason to kill Kristen," added Betty.

Mabel pointed at the board. "Are there any guests without alibis for Kristen's murder? I think she's the key to this whole thing because she wasn't registered for this conference. She traveled down here—wait. How *did* she get here?"

Jane's eyes widened. "That's a great question. If she drove, there's probably a car with Jersey plates parked in one of our lots or somewhere in the village. Her car might hold a clue."

"Why would she make such a long trip in the first place?" Eloise mused aloud. "Why agree to such a strange meeting place? She must have known the killer. Either she trusted this person, or she was being blackmailed."

"Did she need money?" Mabel asked.

Jane nodded. "She was barely scraping by. Her salary covered her bills. That's all. She had no savings. No vacation fund. Nothing. According to her coworkers, she constantly talked about the things she wanted but couldn't afford. She'd spend every break on her phone, scrolling through photos of clothes, jewelry, handbags, houses, cars, vacation spots—you name it."

"Poor thing." Mrs. Pratt glanced at her friends. "We're not rich, but we have so much. Comfortable homes. A beautiful place to live. An exciting social life. Marvelous friends."

"And we love our jobs," Eloise added. "Kristen's list shows that she didn't stay at any of her jobs for long. Maybe she kept hopping around in hopes of finding a better salary. Or maybe, she was trying to find her passion."

Mabel shrugged. "There's a third option. Maybe, those were the only jobs she could get."

Jane tapped the board.

"Kristen was in her early thirties. Gloria was in her mid-forties. Kristen lived alone in an apartment in New Jersey. Gloria shared a Brooklyn apartment with Brandon. She spent her free time volunteering and hanging out with her boyfriend. On her days off, Kristen liked to stay in and watch TV. These women didn't cross paths as children. Or at college or work. They appear to be strangers."

"To each other, maybe, but not to the killer," said Mrs. Pratt.

Eloise picked up the dry erase marker from Jane's desk and circled the words PRESCHOOL TEACHER under Kristen's name, and EDITOR AT PEPPERMINT PRESS under Gloria's name.

"Here's a link. Kristen used to teach little kids. Gloria edited children's books. She also volunteered with an organization that delivered books to low-income neighborhoods. What if Kristen's preschool was in one of those neighborhoods?"

"It's a good theory, but the preschool was on Manhattan's Upper West Side," said Jane. "The annual tuition cost as much as tuition at a prestigious college. The lead teachers are paid well, but Kristen was an assistant. Assistant salaries weren't great, but after two years, an assistant can apply to be a lead teacher. Kristen left the school right before her second anniversary."

Jane realized that she now had another lead to run down. Why had Kristen quit weeks before she could apply for a promotion?

"Can we circle back to my alibi question?" Mabel asked Jane.

"Sure. We discovered Kristen's body Monday afternoon after our book club meeting. The ME believes she was killed within an hour or two of our tour. My staff was still working on the Storybook Village on Sunday, so the murder couldn't have happened then. Some of the conference guests checked in on Monday. They could have met Kristen near that cottage. But the attendees who checked in on Tuesday could have stayed elsewhere before coming to Storyton, which means many of them could have arranged the meeting."

Mrs. Pratt groaned. "Too many possible suspects."

"Yes," Jane glumly agreed.

"Let's not focus on alibis right now." Eloise pressed the marker into Jane's hand. "What about motive? Kristen didn't have any money. Did she break someone's heart? Did Gloria? Could this be a revenge crime?"

Betty clapped her hands, startling everyone. "The fairy-tale elements! Eloise, on the way here, you said that the stories the killer picked featured evil queens. What if the killer identifies with the evil queens? In their mind, Kristen and Gloria deserved punishment."

"The killer could be an evil queen or a man who sees himself as the Big Bad Wolf," said Eloise.

Suddenly energized, Jane wrote two more names on the whiteboard. Tris and Todd Petty. "How about one of each? An evil queen *and* a Big Bad Wolf?"

"Why would children's book authors hurt these women?" Mrs. Pratt asked dubiously.

"Because they're deeply unhappy." Jane told her friends everything she knew about the Pettys.

By the time she was done, and the Cover Girls had uttered angry exclamations over the couple's deplorable behavior, especially toward the Gilbert children, their lunch hour was spent.

Jane eyed the mound of salad left on her plate. She could do with a serving of greens before entering a room filled with candy. When she was stressed, she tended to overindulge on sweets, and there was a staggering supply of sugary treats waiting in the Madame Bovary Dining Room. But there was no time, so she led her friends out of her office and into the dining room.

"I should have eaten my salad," Jane told Eloise as the women looked around.

White-frosted cookie houses and an array of candy-filled bowls sat on each round table. The little houses were edible blank canvases, just waiting to be decorated with pink, red, and white candy.

"How much of this candy will actually end up on the houses?" Betty asked with a smile.

Mable chuckled. "The kids will need to run around Storyton Hall five times to burn off their sugar high. Otherwise, they won't be able to sit through tonight's play."

"We have games set up in the ballroom," said Jane. "Most of them involve jumping. Lots of jumping. And hula hoops. After the games, the kids have over two hours to rest. By the time the play starts, they should be good as gold."

"You should hand out the Storyton Hall Wonka Bars at the *end* of the performance, not the beginning," Mrs. Pratt suggested.

Looking at the bowls of cinnamon red hearts, red licorice, pink bubble gum, Conversation Hearts, pink taffy, red gumdrops, white mints, strawberry wafer cookies, Valentine's M&Ms, red Swedish Fish, pink rock candy, white jellybeans, Atomic Fireballs, peppermint pinwheels, and red, white, and pink sprinkles, Jane decided to heed Mrs. Pratt's advice.

Five minutes before the guests were to be admitted, Fitz and Hem entered through the staff entrance.

"How was your lesson?" Jane asked.

"We broke boards with our elbows!" Hem happily exclaimed.

Fitz rolled up his sleeve and pointed at his elbow. "This is a deadly weapon. I wish we could have broken more boards, but Mr. Sinclair made us practice our forms while he worked on his computer."

Jane beckoned for her sons to come closer. "Remember how I told you that a Rip Van Winkle was found in Storybook Village?" She waited for the twins to nod before continuing. "Well, Mr. Lachlan found another one in the woods. All of us, Mr. Sinclair included, are trying to find out what happened to these two guests. I'd like both of you to keep an eye on the other children. Help me keep them safe. Can you do that without mentioning the Rip Van Winkles?"

"Yes, ma'am," the boys responded in unison.

"You're sitting with the Gilberts. Keep making Fern and Peter feel at home. And try to remember that the candy is for your house, not your bellies. Have fun!"

After the twins raced off to locate their place cards, Jane assigned each Cover Girl an area of the dining room to manage.

"If a table runs out of a certain candy, you can get a refill from the staff member at the bar. Don't let the kids get the refills. The candy might not make it back to the table."

Mrs. Pratt pointed at a bowl of licorice. "If I were a kid, I'd eat those by the handful while I worked on my house. I wouldn't be able to help myself."

"You can have the licorice. I'll take the chocolate," said Eloise. Turning to Jane, she whispered, "Should we be looking for suspects?"

Jane checked her watch and signaled the staff member waiting by the door. It was time to welcome the guests. "None of these people were in Storyton when Kristen was killed. That's why the sheriff is focusing on the conference attendees."

Betty looked a little disappointed. "No one in this room is under suspicion?"

At that moment, Jane saw Mrs. Templeton's niece dart in through the staff door and creep over to the bar. After scanning the selection of candy refills, her hand shot out and closed around an unopened bag of licorice. When the staff member manning the bar protested, Zoey responded by blowing him a kiss.

"I take it back," Jane said in a dangerously soft voice. "There *is* someone in this room who's been acting cagey. And I'm going to confront her right now. Hold the fort for me, ladies."

As families streamed into the dining room, Jane slipped out the rear exit. Zoey wasn't in the lobby or in the staff corridor, but Jane had a feeling she knew where the teenager was headed. After all, she was wearing a coat and her pom-pom hat.

"Where are you off to?" Mrs. Hubbard asked when Jane passed through the kitchens and began buttoning her coat. "Hasn't the candy house workshop started? Is something wrong?"

"Everything's fine. Did Zoey come through here?"

Mrs. Hubbard blinked. "Mrs. Templeton's niece? I haven't seen her since this morning when I caught her filching my madeleines. That girl likes to poach food. I didn't say anything because Mrs. Templeton has enough on her mind, but that child needs a tongue lashing."

"She's about to get one," said Jane.

In the garage, she grabbed a set of Gator keys and drove to the mews. Lachlan obviously hadn't had the chance to confront Zoey about entering the building without his permission, nor had he figured out if she had a connection to Kristen Burke or Gloria Ramirez. Like the rest of the Fins, Lachlan was running himself ragged trying to fulfill his Storyton Hall duties while protecting their guests. Jane wasn't upset. She could deal with Zoey herself.

The door to the mews was unlocked, and Jane entered the building as quietly as possible. Once inside, she stood very still.

"Don't worry, they're clueless," she heard a female voice say. "It's ridiculously easy to play them." An arrogant laugh reverberated around the space. "You should see the stuff I've gotten so far. Old books, a silver tray, some fancy candlesticks. I just need a few more things, and a way to pawn them, and we'll be all set. You and me will get out of here, and no one will even know what happened."

This short monologue was followed by lots of rapid banging.

"That's for you. The candy's for me for later. I still have a sandwich and those amazing cookies I swiped from the kitchen. I also got fish, chicken, and milk. Don't worry about getting caught. No one knows about us. They're too busy with their stupid teas and their stupid meetings about books. But we'll leave soon. I promise."

Zoey received no reply.

Jane sent a text to Lachlan, telling him to drop everything and meet her at the mews. She listened for another minute, but Zoey had stopped talking. She was now humming. It was a pleasant, soothing sound.

What's with this girl? Jane thought.

She glanced around for something to use as a weapon and had to settle for a chisel-tooth rake. Holding the rake with the teeth facing outward, Jane tiptoed toward the humming.

When she reached the empty cage at the end of the building, she almost dropped her rake.

Zoey was squatting in a bed of fresh straw, watching a large blond tabby devour a mound of tuna fish. The cat had resplendent white whiskers, a white chin and chest, and a pink nose. He gulped down the food as if he hadn't eaten in days. Zoey sat very close to him and hummed. As the cat chewed a chunk of tuna, he edged closer to the girl. The light illuminated his sea-green eyes. Zoey reached out and tentatively stroked his neck.

"What's going on?" Jane asked in a soft voice.

She hadn't meant to startle the cat, but he immediately stopped eating, flattened his ears, and retreated to the far corner of the cage. He moved like he was permanently off-balance. It was a sad sight, and Jane's heart ached for the animal.

As for the cat, he tried to make himself as small as possible while staring at Jane with eyes nearly black with fear.

"Look what you did," Zoey hissed. "It's taken me days to get close to him. Now, he's totally freaked out again."

Jane put the rake down and lowered herself into a catcher's stance. "Is he hurt?"

"Because of how he walks? I don't know." Tears slipped out of Zoey's eyes. "That's why I named him Wobbles."

"Is Wobbles the reason you stole the keys to the mews? To give him shelter?"

Zoey nodded. Letting her tears flow freely now, she said, "I found him right after Mr. Lachlan showed me how to feed the birds. I was supposed to sweep in here, but when I came in to get the broom, I heard a cry. I knew it was a cat, and he sounded hurt. This guy was standing on the edge of the woods, meowing like crazy. He had leaves sticking to his fur and he looked *so* hungry. I took the ham out of my sandwich and tossed it to him. He ate every bite."

"You must have been very patient to have coaxed him inside." Jane studied Wobbles without moving any closer. "He looks pretty healthy. I guess a diet of chicken, tuna, and milk has done him good."

"He likes whipped cream too," said Zoey, wiping her face with the back of her hand.

Jane sighed. "I don't understand you, Zoey. You treat people like dirt, but the way you've taken care of this cat shows that you have a good heart."

"Animals don't judge you. They don't try to change you. They love you exactly as you are. People don't do that. They make you feel like you're never pretty enough, skinny enough, smart enough, cool enough."

Jane heard the pain in Zoey's voice. The sorrow and loneliness. Very gently, she asked, "What would make you happy?"

"To help Wobbles. To be able to keep him. But my parents would never let me. Dad's allergic to fur or whatever. I've never had a pet, but I love animals. I always have."

After speaking with Zoey a little longer, Jane knew that the teen had nothing to do with the murders. The secret she'd been keeping involved a stray cat. That was all.

"I'll make you a deal," Jane said after telling Lachlan that he didn't need to come to the mews after all. "I'll ask the local vet to pay a house call as soon as he's free. We need to see if Wobbles belongs to someone before we make any more decisions. For now, keep taking care of him. You've done a great job so far."

Zoey sent the cat a loving glance before turning back to Jane. "What do you want from me?"

"I might need you to sabotage tonight's play."

Zoey's smile instantly transformed her from a sulky teenager to a vibrant, confident young woman. "I like where this is headed," she said and reached out to pet Wobbles.

At first, he shrank away from her touch. But Zoey continued to caress his neck, murmuring softly as she stroked his fur.

In the quiet, Jane heard a rumbling sound, like a small engine firing. Or a cat's heart speaking to a girl's heart.

Wobbles had begun to purr.

Chapter Fifteen

Jane missed most of the candy workshop. By the time she returned to the dining room, the kids were putting the finishing touches on their Valentine's houses. As Jane moved from table to table, complimenting the candy artists on their creations, Eloise sidled up to her.

"Where'd you go?"

In a low voice, Jane said, "When we talked on the phone the other day, do you remember me telling you about Mrs. Templeton's niece?"

"Zoey? The girl who seemed hell-bent on making life miserable for everyone, including herself?" Eloise looked puzzled. "Lachlan said that she was good with the birds. I was hoping he'd get through to her."

"He made some progress, but Zoey's built up a pretty high wall. I think she likes animals more than people."

"At times, I do too."

Jane smirked. "Same here. Animals don't go around murdering my guests. Anyway, Zoey found a stray cat, and she's been sneaking food from the kitchens for him. She's also been pocketing Storyton Hall books and decorations. I think she plans to run away with the cat."

"She must be really unhappy." Eloise's expression turned sympathetic. "It's hard to be a teenager these days. There's so much pressure. And on top of all that, Zoey's mom is sick. No wonder she loves animals. They give without asking for much in return."

"I'm going to do what I can to help her. In the meantime, I can cross her off my suspect list. I'm glad the workshop is winding up because I need to see which names the sheriff still has on his."

From the other side of the room, Mrs. Pratt waved at Jane. Jane didn't like the look of urgency on her friend's face.

"Thanks for being here, Eloise. I'll see you tonight."

Eloise grabbed Jane's elbow before she could walk away. "The four of us are going to hang around this afternoon. If we mingle with the conference folks, we might hear some gossip. At the very least, there'll be four more pairs of eyes on them. Hopefully, Sheriff Evans will have his man—or woman—before we dress for dinner."

Jane thanked her best friend and hurried over to Mrs. Pratt.

"What is it?" Jane asked, scanning the table for broken houses or spilled candy.

Leaning close to Jane, Mrs. Pratt whispered, "As soon as the guests leave, I need to show you something."

Something had obviously upset Mrs. Pratt because she'd dug her fingers into the meat of her palms hard enough to leave marks.

At that moment, Mrs. Hubbard entered the room. She and her sous-chef applauded the participants.

"Willy Wonka would have loved every one of these marvelous houses," Mrs. Hubbard announced to the room at large. "But they're yours and will be delivered to your rooms. That means you're free to head to the ballroom for your Candy Land games."

"Thank you for coming," added the sous-chef. "I hope you can all hula hoop out of the Molasses Swamp and jump over the Gumdrop Mountains."

The kids had clearly eaten lots of candy. They were either bouncing in their seats or already skipping toward the exit, their parents hurrying to catch up.

It took less than five minutes for the room to empty. Only the Cover Girls, several Storyton Hall servers, and Jane's sons remained.

"Mom, do you like my house?" Hem asked.

Jane put a hand on her son's shoulder as she admired his house. She then put her free hand on Fitz's back and focused on his house. She found the physical contact reassuring. Her sons were okay.

"We both found paper inside our houses," said Fitz, pointing at the small, round window over the door. "It was sticking to the icing."

Hem touched the gumdrops encircling his window and said, "Mrs. Pratt wouldn't let us throw it away."

"I'm sure someone in the kitchen left them there by accident," Jane said. "Are you two ready to play with the rest of the kids? If so, I'll move your houses to the kitchens, and you can carry them home after the games. I hope you didn't stuff yourselves on candy."

Fitz and Hem exchanged guilty glances, thanked Mrs. Pratt for helping, and loped out of the room.

"Such cherubs." Mrs. Pratt beamed. Suddenly, her face went taut and she grabbed Jane's arm. "Someone needs to watch over them. Look what they found inside their houses!"

Mrs. Pratt thrust two pieces of paper at Jane. They were the size and shape of fortune cookie missives. They had the same nondescript font too. But these bits of paper didn't offer sentiments like YOUR SMILE IS YOUR PASSPORT INTO THE HEARTS OF OTHERS or THE GREATEST RISK IS NOT TAKING ONE.

The words on the first slip were CALL OFF THE KING'S MEN.

The second one said OR TWEEDLEDEE AND -DUM ARE NEXT.

Jane's blood went cold. She slapped the papers down on the table and pressed her hand over them. Hiding the words didn't help. Jane could close her eyes and every letter would still burn in the darkness behind her lids.

"That's a threat, isn't it? Someone's threatening Fitz and Hem?" Mrs. Pratt was nearly whimpering. "It's an insult too. The boys are *nothing* like those roly-poly characters."

"'The king's men' must refer to the sheriff and his deputies," Jane said. "I need to show these to him right away." She scanned the room with wild eyes. "The houses were placed on the tables hours ago by the kitchen staff. They would have come and gone through the back door, which means the killer must have used the main door."

Jane sent a frantic text to Sterling and dropped the slips of paper into a clean napkin. She was in too much of a hurry to explain the threat to the other Cover Girls. Knowing Mrs. Pratt would do it for her, Jane rushed out to the lobby.

She saw Sheriff Evans refilling his travel mug at the coffee urns. It took all the self-control Jane could muster not to shout his name.

Moving quickly, she walked up behind him and said, "Sheriff. I need to show you something."

Her sudden proximity startled Evans, and he jerked the hand holding his mug. Hot coffee dripped from the urn onto his skin.

"Sorry," Jane said, offering him a napkin from the pile on the table. "I didn't mean to sneak up on you, but the killer left me a message. He hid it in my sons' candy houses."

The sheriff put the lid on his cup. "Show me in the conference room."

Together, they walked to the William Faulkner Conference Room. As soon as they were alone, Jane took out the napkin containing the slips of paper and handed it to the sheriff.

"The killer might be trying to tell us that his goals have been accomplished, and if there's more violence, it'll be because we forced his hand," Evans said. "He feels the walls closing in, which makes him more dangerous than ever." The sheriff gave Jane a fierce look. "I won't let anything happen to your boys. Where are they now?"

"Playing games with the other kids. My friends are with them." Her phone buzzed and she stole a glance at the screen. "Looks like Edwin is on his way to the ballroom as well. Eloise must have told him about the notes."

"You probably feel pulled in a hundred different directions right now," the sheriff said in a soft voice. "If you want to be with your sons, you should be with them. I can review our leads with Mr. Butterworth or Mr. Sinclair."

Jane was torn. Of course, she wanted to be with her sons. She wanted Edwin and the Fins to arm themselves to the teeth and make a protective circle around Fitz and Hem. But if she focused all of her energy on watching her boys, the killer might get away.

Mother, Guardian, Manager. She couldn't give these roles equal attention.

"No one will be safe until we catch this scumbag," Jane said, her voice steely with anger. "I have two leads to share with you, and I'd like to see your suspect list now that the interviews are done."

The sheriff gestured at the chair at the head of the table. Jane took it and he sat down next to her.

"I keep circling back to the fairy-tale elements of the crimes," Jane said. "The scenes pay homage to evil queens. One queen used a poison apple. The other used a wicked mirror. I can't explain the watch battery. The rabbit in *Alice in Wonderland* checks his pocket watch all the time, and that story features another evil queen, so maybe that's how the watch battery is connected. But that story isn't a fairy tale."

After writing a few notes on his legal pad, the sheriff said, "We can't confirm alibis for Malcolm Marcus, Todd and Tris Petty, or Birdie Bloom. Mr. Marcus drove his car here, and no one can verify when he left home or arrived in Storyton. Mr. and Mrs. Petty took the early flight from New York Monday morning. Since their room wasn't ready upon arrival, they claim to have passed the time wandering around the house and grounds. Ms. Bloom rented a car at the airport and drove to Storyton Hall. After checking in, she had lunch with another author. Despite her lunch date, she's not in the clear because she could have met Ms. Burke before checking in. She is low on my suspect list because she lacks an obvious motive."

"It's hard to imagine such a happy, positive person resorting to murder, but stranger things have happened."

The sheriff studied his notepad. "She also makes good money, loves what she does, has a supportive family and several close friends. Unless she's putting on an act, she's content with her lot in life."

Jane couldn't disagree. "I liked her before I met her in person. Because she writes such incredible books. Then again, I thought everyone involved in the production of children's books would be wonderful. But that's not the case. One of them is rotten to the core. Just like a poisoned apple."

"The Pettys certainly aren't content," the sheriff went on as if Jane hadn't spoken. "However, I can't find a single thread connecting them or Malcolm Marcus to Kristen Burke."

"And we have no way of knowing if Kristen owned rare children's books."

"The police searched her apartment this morning. She didn't have much." Evans consulted his notes. "Past-due bills on the counter. Secondhand furniture. Dated TV and laptop. The laptop was password protected. It'll be days before someone on the squad gets to it. Ms. Burke had two credit cards. Both maxed. Seems she bought new clothes, makeup, and jewelry the week before her road trip. None of the charges were from a gas station, though she does own a car. A 2008 silver Ford Focus with Jersey plates."

Jane took in this glut of new information. "Either Kristen wanted to look good for the person she planned to meet here, or she wasn't worried about paying off those credit cards. It doesn't sound like she owned the kind of books Malcolm Marcus likes."

"No books in the apartment at all," the sheriff said. "Not even a cookbook."

Jane was about to say that a home without books wasn't very inviting when a thought struck her. "If Kristen was struggling financially, then I don't see why she'd cross paths with the Pettys. They don't appear to be wealthy."

"They're not. They're getting by, but they have no retirement savings."

"Which means they desperately need their Peppermint Press contracts. Gunnar Humphries said that their work is all they have left. Would Todd and Tris kill to protect their careers? At one point, they saw Gloria as a threat to their future. But Kristen? She doesn't tie in."

The sheriff spread his hands. "That's my dilemma. I can't tie her to any suspect."

Jane recalled what Eloise had said over lunch. "Kristen was a preschool teacher for almost two years. She had the chance to become a lead teacher, which would have meant a higher salary. Why did she leave right before a possible promotion? And why didn't she ever work with children again?"

"Good questions. It's Saturday, so the school will be closed, but we should try to get a hold of the director or another staff member. I'll put Deputy Emory on that. Is Mr. Sterling free to search for Ms. Burke's car?"

"I'll ask another staff member to do that. Sterling's reviewing video footage. Whoever left those notes in my sons' candy houses entered the dining room through the main door. We might have the killer on camera."

A glint of excitement appeared in the sheriff's eyes. "Wouldn't that be something?"

Edwin was waiting for Jane outside the ballroom. He put his arms around her and gave her a firm squeeze.

"The boys are safe. They're busy teaching some other kids how to hula hoop." Releasing Jane, he said, "I won't leave their side. You can focus on catching the killer."

"Speaking of which, I saw you with Malcolm Marcus this morning. Did you learn anything useful?"

"After riding around the woods and finding nothing, I stopped at my place and took a photo of the book I acquired on my last mission. I knew Malcolm would sell an organ for the chance to add it to his collection, so I pretended that the owner might be coerced into selling it."

Jane heard squeals of laughter coming from inside the ballroom and smiled inwardly. Unlike the conference attendees, the families were having a ball.

Glass half full, she thought.

To Edwin, she said, "I saw Malcolm's face in the theater. Considering he wanted to be first in line at a book show in Richmond, he didn't seem very put out."

"That's because the book in question is a first edition of the 1922 classic *The Velveteen Rabbit.* The last time a first edition sold at auction, it brought sixteen thousand dollars. This copy is in excellent condition and is signed by Margery Williams. I'll be returning it to one of her descendants next week. It was originally stolen by a carpenter who worked on her home."

Jane was captivated by the story of the old book. "How did Malcolm react?"

"I've never actually seen someone foam at the mouth, but the guy came close. I told him I'd put in a good word with *The Velveteen Rabbit*'s owner if he could get me a list of people who'd recently purchased both the Grimm Brothers and Hans Christian Andersen editions found at the crime scenes."

"What reason did you give him for wanting that information?"

Edwin shrugged. "I told him that I collected fairy and folk tales from around the world and that I was looking to buy a comprehensive collection. When I said that money was no object, Malcolm took a liking to me. He sees me as a fellow zealot and is working on the list as we speak. I should have it before the play starts."

Jane gave Edwin a quick kiss. "Thank you. For tackling Malcolm. For keeping the boys safe. For lots of things. I have to review camera footage now, but call me if anything comes up."

* * *

In the security office, Sterling was leaning so close to one of the monitors that his nose almost touched the screen.

"The person who hid the papers was clever," he told Jane when she sat down beside him. "They waited until the conference folks were grabbing their box lunches from the lobby. With so many people milling about, it's almost impossible to see who goes into the dining room. But someone definitely went in. Watch."

Sterling rewound the footage a few seconds and pointed at the right-hand side of the screen. "They come from this direction. They're wearing a brown jacket with the hood up, which means they're aware of our cameras."

Jane watched the figures onscreen. People holding white boxes gathered in small groups, undoubtedly whispering about the investigation. The lunch times had originally been staggered, which would allow attendees plenty of seating in the lobby, but the sheriff's announcement had thrown off the schedule and both sessions had ended at the same time.

"There's Reggie," she said, seeing the illustrator join three other people in front of the dining room doors. "Oh, and there's Birdie. I'm so glad she didn't plant those notes. I really didn't want to learn that she was a killer."

Sterling tapped the screen. "Here comes Brown Jacket."

The figure was taller than Reggie and Birdie, but since they were both small of stature, it wasn't much help. Brown Jacket kept his back to the camera and walked well behind Reggie and Birdie's group. They didn't even notice him.

"I can't see anything. No skin, no hair, nothing," Jane said with a groan. "What about when Brown Jacket comes back out?"

"He doesn't. He must have used the staff exit. By then, the room was probably set up for the workshop and the staff was already back in the kitchens."

Jane ran her hands over her face. "I thought we'd get *something* out of this. What about the room search? Were any sedatives found?"

Sterling handed Jane a printout. "As you can see, lots of our guests use either sedatives or pain pills. Over half take some kind of medication."

Jane scanned the list for familiar names. Nia Curry was on thyroid medication, Gunnar Humphries took pain meds, Tris Petty and Reggie Novak had prescriptions for sleeping pills.

Jane fixated on one name in particular. "The Pettys were already my top suspects," she said, shaking the print-out. "But this should earn them a ride in the sheriff's car. I'm going to call him. Can you review the footage from the midmorning break until the time Brown Jacket shows up? I want to see if you can spot that jacket earlier. If not, see if any of the attendees go to their room before lunch. To change clothes, perhaps?"

"We could conduct another room search," Sterling suggested.

"No. We've lost the element of surprise. That jacket is well hidden by now. Even if we had the time to look for it, the sheriff can't get a DNA match from hair or skin samples in the next few hours. But if Sheriff Evans takes the Pettys to the station, we'll search every inch of their room. They didn't rent a car, so they have no place to stash damning evidence."

"Speaking of cars, I asked one of the bellhops to drive around the parking lots. Right before you came in, he found a silver Ford Focus with New Jersey plates."

Jane couldn't suppress a smile. "Finally, a tangible clue. Well done, Sterling."

Ten minutes later, the sheriff joined them in the security office. Sterling replayed the footage of the figure in the brown jacket.

"I can't tell if that's a man or a woman," the sheriff said. "None of the staff saw a guest in the employee-only areas?"

Jane shook her head. "As soon as Sterling finished reviewing the footage, the department heads called an emergency meeting to ask if anyone on staff had seen a guest in the employee corridors. No one had. None of the housekeepers remember seeing a jacket of that description either." She pointed at the list of medications to the sheriff. "What about this?"

The sheriff put his hand on the list. "After faxing a copy to the ME, I called to tell her that I need her to look at this right away. She'll know which meds can pack a punch after being mixed with food or a beverage. Ms. Burke wasn't given a sedative, but Ms. Ramirez was. One can only hope she slept through the pain."

Thinking of how both women had suffered fueled Jane's anger. It burned in her chest like a living thing. A beast with sharp teeth and claws. She wanted to hurt the person who'd hurt Kristen and Gloria.

Evans put a hand over Jane's clenched fist. "We're closing the net. They won't get away."

The conviction in the sheriff's eyes gave Jane a measure of comfort. She wasn't the only one feeling pressure. Evans was just as anxious to put an end to this nightmare—to ensure that no one else was written into a fatal fairy tale.

When she'd mastered her emotions, Jane told the sheriff that Kristen's car had been found. His reaction to this news mirrored hers. There was a lift in his voice when he radioed Deputy Phelps.

"I need eyes on Tris and Todd Petty. Don't let them out of your sight. The same goes for Malcolm Marcus. None of the conference guests are to leave Storyton Hall. Not for a walk. Not for a beer at the Cheshire Cat. Not for any reason. They're to be confined inside."

With Sterling reviewing more footage, Butterworth guarding the front door, and Sinclair searching for a home or cell phone number for the director of Riverside Day School in New York, Jane asked Lachlan to drive her and the sheriff to the upper parking lot. By the time she and Evans donned their coats and hats, one of the Storyton Hall pickups was idling outside the loading dock.

Though Lachlan had the heaters turned on, they hadn't kicked in yet. Jane didn't even notice. For once, the bite in the February air didn't bother her. She was too focused on getting to Kristen's car.

As Lachlan drove up the long driveway to the top parking lot, Jane silently prayed that something inside Kristen's car would break the case wide open.

Let there be a clue, she repeated. *Let this end right here, right now.*

Lachlan parked behind the Ford Focus, and they all exited the truck. Sheriff Evans passed out examination gloves. While Jane and Lachlan wriggled into theirs, the sheriff tugged on the driver's-side door handle.

"Locked," he said.

After trying every door, he turned to find Lachlan brandishing a long reach tool.

"Guests lock themselves out of their cars all the time," Jane explained. "Sterling is our resident expert, but Lachlan's a close second."

"She's all yours," said the sheriff.

Lachlan carried the long wire with its scratch-proof coating and hoop-shaped end to the passenger door. It took him under two minutes to lasso the interior door handle with the wire hoop and open the door.

"I'm glad you're on this side of the law," the sheriff said. He slid into the driver's seat and popped the trunk. Lachlan volunteered to search the trunk while Jane checked the back seat.

"Definite signs of a road trip," she said, poking at take-out cups and food wrappers.

"There are two gas station receipts in her cupholder," said the sheriff. "The New Jersey receipt has a 4:16 AM timestamp and the Virginia receipt has a 9:33 AM timestamp. She paid cash at both locations."

Jane stared at the debris on the floor. "She left before dawn to be here for an early morning meeting. That's a long drive." Sticking her head back outside, she asked Lachlan, "Did she pack anything?"

"Other than an emergency road kit, the trunk's empty."

"I have her purse," the sheriff said, prompting Jane to open the passenger door.

The sheriff began taking items out of the scuffed leather handbag and lining them up on the passenger seat. "Dead cell phone. We'll charge it, but if it's password protected, it won't do us much good."

In addition to the cell phone, the purse contained a small hairbrush, a tube of dark red lipstick, spearmint gum, dental floss, a mirrored compact, hair ties, receipts too faded to read, pens, and a pink wallet. The wallet held three credit cards, a punch card for a nail salon, a wad of grocery store and restaurant coupons, Kristen's driver's license, and a little over a hundred dollars in cash.

"Where are her keys?" Jane asked.

The sheriff glanced at the cup holders, opened the center console, and pulled down the sun visor. With a shrug, he looked at Jane. "Check the glove box."

The glove box held the car's owner manual and receipts for what must have been every maintenance service Kristen's car had received. Because most of these papers were duplicates of the original, they were pink or yellow. Only one was white, and Jane decided to examine it.

It wasn't a receipt but a printout of a map along with detailed driving directions from Kristen's home to Storyton. The map was a satellite view of Storyton Hall. The upper parking lot was circled.

There were several handwritten lines at the bottom of the page. Unfortunately, the paper was heavily coffee-stained. The blue ink had bled, making the words illegible.

Jane could read one thing. Only it wasn't a word. It was a name.

Passing the paper to Sheriff Evans, she watched him scan the driving directions and study the map image.

Finally, his gaze locked on the name.

"Petty," he said.

Jane felt a rush of triumph. Here was a concrete connection between Kristen Burke and Todd and Tris Petty. The Pettys had lured Kristen to Storyton Hall and killed her. Jane didn't know why, but that mattered less at this moment than the fact that Sheriff Evans would be removing the despicable couple from the premises.

Sheriff Evans didn't waste a second conveying his wishes to his deputies.

"Take Mr. and Mrs. Petty out to the loading dock. Use the staff corridors. Emory, I'd like you to oversee their room search. Be very thorough. We need to collect all the evidence we can. I have a feeling these two will put up quite a fight once we get them to the station."

Jane glanced around at the trash, old receipts, and the contents of Kristen's purse. Here was another kind of evidence. The evidence of a young woman's final hours. The items seemed insignificant. Immaterial. But they weren't. They were proof that Kristen had once occupied this space. She'd sat in the driver's seat. She'd sung along to the radio. She'd eaten potato chips and drank Cherry Coke. These things served as proof of life. Jane stared at them and felt a crushing sadness.

Unaware of how Jane was feeling, Sheriff Evans held out Kristen's lipstick, label side up. Jane leaned in to read the name on the label.

"Poison Apple," she whispered.

Her mind conjured an image of the pretty young woman in the red coat lying in the grass behind a Storybook cottage. Jane thought of Kristen's glassy eyes and swollen lips, and of the apple lodged in her throat.

Jane fought back tears.

"I know," Sheriff Evans said, giving her hand a gentle squeeze.

Jane responded with a nod. This was not the time to grieve. There was more work to be done. And that was a good thing, for Jane was very eager to gather nails for the sheriff to drive into Tris and Todd Petty's coffins.

Chapter Sixteen

When Jane reentered Storyton Hall through the kitchens, she was told that Todd and Tris Petty were now sitting in the back of a sheriff's department cruiser.

"You should have heard the language that came out of their mouths." Mrs. Hubbard fanned her face with a saucepan lid. "Thank goodness our guests weren't subjected to such filth. It was shocking enough for my staff. And for *me*."

Jane sat on a stool, her shoulders sagging in relief.

Mrs. Hubbard moved to her side. "You poor lamb. It's always something, isn't it? But I know how to make you feel better."

A few minutes later, she presented Jane with two chocolate chip cookies and a glass of milk.

"Try to forget that you're a grown-up for a minute. Forget about your responsibilities. Forget about that awful couple. Dunk your cookies in milk, let your feet dangle off the stool, and think of the fun events waiting for you. The hard part's over, sweet girl."

Jane took Mrs. Hubbard's advice. She ate both cookies and drank the glass of milk. The warmth and familiar din of the kitchen was as comforting as a hug. After thanking

Mrs. Hubbard for her kindness, Jane headed to the Great Gatsby Ballroom to pick up the twins.

Inside the room, the games were winding down. The kids were clearly running out of steam, and their parents looked more than ready for a little peace and quiet.

Edwin was helping Peter Gilbert step out of the pillowcase he'd used for a sack race when Jane caught his eye. He sent her a questioning glance, and she crossed her wrists to indicate that an arrest had been made. He responded with a dazzling smile. She smiled back before scanning the room for her sons.

She found them holding the ends of a long jump rope. They turned the rope while Fern jumped in the middle. All three children were singing, and though Jane was too far away to hear the words, she was close enough to see grins on Max and Alika's faces.

Jane watched this scene for several minutes, delighting in the thought that the Gilbert family had enjoyed a respite from their grief. They'd always carry their loss with them, but it was Jane's hope that the past few days had fortified them with a fresh batch of happy memories.

Eventually, Fern had a misstep. The rope caught one of her feet and she put her hands on her hips, trying to catch her breath. Jane used the break to wave at her sons. Seeing her point at her watch, they knew that it was time to go.

Instead of running straight to Jane, Fitz and Hem raced over to Edwin. They each tugged on a hand until he threw back his head and laughed.

"They're so cute with him," said Eloise.

Jane hadn't heard her friend approach. Turning to Eloise, she asked, "Why does everything have to be so complicated? He's crazy about the boys. And they're crazy about him. I didn't want them to see Edwin as a father figure because of his secret life. But I think it's too late. They've fallen for him. Just like I did."

Eloise looped her arm through Jane's. "Maybe you should invite Edwin in, warts and all. You and your sons are a package deal. You can't separate parts of your life—or your heart—because you want to play it safe. Soon, your secret life will be a thing of the past. And who knows? Maybe Edwin will hang up his robber spurs in the near future."

"All I know is that we're going to tonight's dinner and play as a family," said Jane. "And that feels right. It feels right for us to be together."

"Maybe it's not so complicated, after all," Eloise said, giving Jane a playful nudge.

Jane told her that the threat to Storyton Hall had been lifted and that the murderers had been taken into custody. "Which means you and the Cover Girls can rest before the play."

"Best news ever!" exclaimed Eloise. "Instead of looking for bad guys, we can focus on having a good time."

"We'll see plenty of bad guys, but they'll be fictional," Jane said, referring to the Storybook Supper. "Which is fine by me. You can't have a good story without a villain."

Jane walked home with the twins, with Edwin promising to join them later. He wanted to see if Malcolm had finished compiling his list of fairy tale collectors before leaving the manor house.

With Edwin searching for Malcolm and the boys upstairs reading comics on their beds, Jane had some precious time to herself. She used it to review her to-do list for Lachlan's proposal. Her office was already piled with candles, lanterns, and white string lights, and a front desk clerk had graciously volunteered to pick up the books she'd ordered from over the mountain. These, too, were now in her office. She had everything she needed to turn the gazebo into an unforgettably romantic setting.

Jane figured it would take over an hour to prep the gazebo. She planned to start on it during teatime tomorrow. Not only would she need Lachlan's help to string the lights and turn on the battery-powered candles and lanterns, but she also wanted to include him in what was bound to be one of the most poignant moments of his life. Just thinking about him getting down on one knee and taking Eloise's hand had Jane feeling giddy with anticipation.

Stretching out on her couch, she called Lachlan. As she waited for him to answer, she scanned her list. All the props were ready. Lachlan had the ring. But how would he lure Eloise to the gazebo without raising her suspicions?

When Lachlan came on the line, Jane asked him this very question.

"I haven't come up with anything yet," he confessed. "I'm not good at this stuff."

"You are," Jane argued. "You're using her favorite book as part of the proposal. You found the perfect ring. And you love her. Trust me, you've got this."

Lachlan thanked Jane for her confidence in him and then said, "The tough part is coming up with a reason for her to be outside. We don't normally take walks in the middle of February."

That was a predicament.

Suddenly, Jane had an idea. "If you tell her you've been feeding an injured bird—a hawk or an owl—at the gazebo, you'll have an excuse to go there. You could pretend to be taking food to this wild bird."

"Carrying a frozen chick in my pocket doesn't sound very romantic."

Jane chortled. "You're just *pretending* to be feeding a bird. The only thing you need in your pocket is the ring. Leave the frozen chicks behind, please."

"I also need the quote I'm going to read."

"Oh? Is it from *Jane Eyre*?"

Lachlan hesitated before answering. "It is. Does it seem like a shortcut to use someone else's words to ask Eloise to marry me?"

"No," Jane was quick to reply. "Writers know how to speak to our souls using the right words. If a line from Eloise's favorite book moves you, then it's sure to move her too."

They spent a few minutes discussing the timing of the big event before Jane remembered that she needed to do something about Wobbles. Knowing Lachlan and the local vet were friendly, she asked him to see about arranging a house call for the lost cat.

Lachlan readily agreed. "Dr. Mack is coming to the play. He won't mind showing up a little early to see Wobbles. I can update Zoey on the cat's health before the curtain goes up."

At the mention of the play, Jane realized that it was almost time to get dressed. She'd promised the Cover Girls that she'd meet them in the lobby to take photos before they took their seats, and if she didn't get a move on, she'd be late.

She was just rinsing the shampoo from her hair when the shower door opened, and Edwin entered the steamy stall.

"Can I wash your back?" he asked.

Jane handed him a bar of coconut soap from the Walt Whitman Spa. He lathered his hands with soap and began to massage her tense shoulders. He then worked his fingers into the knots under her shoulder blades and eased the ache from the muscles of her lower back.

Next, he rubbed conditioner into her hair. His fingers gently kneaded her scalp before combing the conditioner through her wet strands. He told Jane to rinse. When she was done, they traded positions so that Edwin could stand under the water's stream.

"If you worked for Violet, her appointment book would always be full," Jane said, moving in for a kiss.

After a long, deep kiss, Edwin nibbled on Jane's earlobe. When she pressed her body against his, he whispered, "How much time do we have?"

"Enough," Jane whispered back.

Later, as Jane, Edwin, and the twins walked across the great lawn to Storyton Hall, Jane reached for Edwin's hand. He shot her a surprised glance because Jane never held his hand in front of the twins. She'd always been careful to make their relationship look platonic when Fitz and Hem were around.

"Is Mr. Alcott your valentine?" Hem teased.

"Yep," she answered. Lowering her voice, she added, "Even though he's *old*."

Edwin was dressed as Geppetto from *Pinocchio*. He wore a white wig, round spectacles, and an old-fashioned suit. Jane was a resplendent Blue Fairy. She wore a sparkly dress with a tight bodice and a full, fluffy skirt. When she walked, it looked as if she were floating.

The twins had come up with the idea to be two different versions of the famous puppet. Fitz was the lying Pinocchio. He wore a long fake nose that made his voice sound funny. Hem was the donkey-eared Pinocchio. After much cajoling, Jane had given in and allowed him to carry a beer stein filled with yellow gelatin so that he could look the part of the immoral boy.

"Look at you four!" Eloise cried when they entered the lobby. Her Jill costume consisted of a pink dress with a grass-stained apron and a wooden bucket filled with blue tissue paper. Lachlan, the Jack to her Jill, was standing by the theater doors. His bucket was by his feet and his head was bandaged, presumably from his tumble down the hill. The knees of his trousers were also grass stained.

The rest of the Cover Girls had dressed as characters from *Sleeping Beauty*. Betty was a delightfully sinister Maleficent, and Violet was a charming Aurora. Mrs. Pratt, Mabel, and Phoebe were the three fairies, and Anna was almost unrecognizable as the fire-breathing dragon.

"Not a prince in sight!" declared Phoebe with pride.

"My prince will be arriving tomorrow," Mrs. Pratt said with a coy smile. "I can't wait to see what my late Valentine's surprise will be."

Jane deliberately avoided looking at Eloise. She didn't want her best friend to see the glint in her eyes and become suspicious. Instead, she chatted to Mrs. Pratt about her beau.

After the women had praised one another's costumes, they posed for photo after photo.

"Let me take one of you and Edwin with the boys," Eloise said when they were done.

As Jane stood with her sons and the man she loved, she was nearly overcome by how lovely it felt for the four of them to pose for a family photo. She realized that she needed to embrace this feeling of unity, not run from it.

Fitz and Hem were eager to get to their seats, so Jane let them go while she and Edwin stayed in the lobby to watch the families arrive.

The costumes were bookishly creative and altogether wonderful. A family of five, who'd come as the Berenstain

Bears, headed into the theater. They were followed by the Ingalls family and the Peanuts gang. A couple wearing Hansel and Gretel costumes held the hand of a young witch. The witch turned to talk with a Tigger and a Piglet. Their parents had come as Winnie the Pooh and Christopher Robin. A family of four wore the Hogwarts house colors, while another family came as Hermione, Ron, Harry, and Dumbledore. There were hobbits, as well as characters from *Peter Pan*, *Babar*, and *Madeline*. And of course, there was the Gilbert family. They looked amazing in the *Charlotte's Web* costumes Mabel had made.

Most of the conference-goers attending the play were also in costume. Jane saw a group of illustrators dressed as the Three Musketeers. A pair of editors came as Curious George and the Man with the Yellow Hat. A marketing team featured the lion, the witch, and the children from *The Chronicles of Narnia*. Birdie Bloom was channeling Pinkalicious. She wore a fuchsia dress and bubble-gum-colored sneakers and carried a plate of pink cupcakes made of paper.

Other attendees honored Roald Dahl with their costumes. A tall gentleman was clearly the BFG and a group of illustrators, including Reggie Novak, were characters from *James and the Giant Peach*. Nia Curry came as Matilda. She walked with Gunnar Humphries, who'd turned into Cat in the Hat by donning a red bowtie and a red-and-white-striped top hat.

Because the theater was quickly filling, Jane told Edwin and the Cover Girls to take their seats. She wanted to make a quick call to Sheriff Evans before sitting down.

In her office, she dialed the sheriff's direct line. She didn't expect him to answer, knowing he had the Pettys in custody, but he did.

"I'm not getting anywhere with this couple." He sounded

frustrated. "Even though we've separated them, their stories match up. They both swear that they've never met Kristen Burke. They both admit to having disliked Ms. Ramirez and aren't the slightest bit bothered by her death. The only thing they're upset about is the possibility of missing their free dinner. I don't think I've ever met such a self-absorbed couple."

"How do they explain the handwritten note on the paper in Kristen's glove box?" Jane asked.

The sheriff sighed. "That's another wrinkle. According to the Pettys, anyone at Peppermint Press could have copied their signature. Mr. Humphries keeps a signed copy of every book his company publishes on a row of shelves in the hallway outside his office. The books are accessible to dozens of people."

Jane felt the edges of panic. "What about their guest room? Any evidence there?"

"Deputy Phelps found a receipt for the Hans Christian Andersen book you discovered in Ms. Ramirez's room. While the seller's information is printed on the receipt, the buyer's isn't. The shop's closed now, but we're trying to contact the owner."

"I suppose Todd and Tris know nothing about the book."

"Not a thing. They don't collect books other than their own."

Jane stared at her whiteboard and tried to think of a way the Pettys might be provoked into a confession.

"There's more," the sheriff went on. "The ME doesn't think Mrs. Petty's sleeping pills were the sedative ingested by Ms. Ramirez. Without that link, our case is flimsy. I can hold the Pettys overnight, but if we don't find more solid evidence, I'll have to let them go tomorrow."

Jane promised to do whatever she could to help and

ended the call. The happiness she'd felt moments ago vanished, replaced by an all-too-familiar feeling of worry.

There was a soft knock on her open door. Jane turned from the whiteboard to find Sinclair standing behind her guest chair. "I have some news."

"I hope it's good," Jane said, gesturing at the chair.

"I'm afraid not." He sat down and opened a file folder. "I was finally able to connect with Ms. Burke's former employer, Catherine Howe. Mrs. Howe has been the director of Riverside Day School for the past two decades. Though she was very reluctant to talk about Ms. Burke, I was able to convince her to tell me why Ms. Burke quit. Prepare yourself, my girl. This is a difficult story to hear."

Jane reached for her stress ball and said, "Go on."

"According to Mrs. Howe, Ms. Burke was an excellent teacher's assistant. She was wonderful with the children and got along with their parents too. She'd often supplement her income by babysitting for select families on weekends. Her favorite charge was Aiden Humphries, Gunnar Humphries's grandson."

The stress ball fell from Jane's hand onto the floor. "Kristen and Gunnar. They were connected."

"Yes. Now, we come to the hard part." Sinclair put a hand on the file folder. "One evening, Ms. Burke watched Aiden while his grandparents went out to dinner with friends. While they were gone, Aiden bumped into a side table, breaking a lamp and spilling Ms. Burke's soda onto the carpet. Ms. Burke didn't want the glass from the lamp to cut the little boy, so she put him in his room and gave him a pile of books to read. With her charge suitably entertained, she vacuumed every last splinter of glass and then turned her attention to the carpet stain."

"She did exactly what I would have done," said Jane.

Sinclair gave her a sympathetic look. "While Ms. Burke was cleaning, young Aiden was looking at a book on construction vehicles. It had sound effects and flashing lights. Aiden was a curious child. Left to his own devices, he decided to find the source of the lights and sound. He peeled off the paper on the back cover, revealing the battery compartment. He removed the button battery and swallowed it, undoubtedly thinking it was a piece of candy."

Jane's hand flew to her mouth, muffling a cry.

"I've read what happens when small children swallow these batteries. It's horrific. When Ms. Burke went to check on Aiden, she probably saw blood in his mouth. He might have told her that his throat hurt. When she saw the blood and the damaged book, she called 911. The little boy died soon after reaching the hospital."

This was too much for Jane. She pulled a wad of tissues out of the box on her desk, covered her face, and sobbed.

Suddenly, Sinclair's arm was around her. He spoke to her in soothing tones, patiently letting her process the tragic death of a little boy named Aiden. Gunnar's grandson.

"That poor baby," Jane said in a choked voice. "And poor Kristen. The torment she must have felt. And she didn't do anything wrong. It was just a terrible, terrible accident." Jane grabbed Sinclair's hand. "We were looking for a reason someone might want to punish Kristen and Gloria. Is this the reason?"

Sinclair gently extricated himself from Jane's vise-like grip. "Yes. Mr. Humphries has a prescription for pain medicine. I've researched his medication. If ingested in large doses, it can cause loss of consciousness."

"Oh, God. He's in the theater right now. He's sitting near the twins!"

Sinclair raised his hands to stop her from flying out of

the room. "Mr. Butterworth and Mr. Lachlan are standing at either end of their row. Mr. Alcott is sitting with your sons. He left the theater for a few minutes to collect some documents from Malcolm Marcus, but someone had eyes on Masters Hemingway and Fitzgerald the entire time. These are the documents Mr. Alcott wanted you to see."

Jane took the proffered papers and began to scan what appeared to be a long list of book titles. Next to each title was the bookseller's name and addresses. The second column showed the buyer's name and address. Two entries had been circled in black ink. The first was the Grimm Brothers book from Kristen's basket. The other was the Hans Christian Andersen book found in Gloria's room.

The books had been purchased from independent bookstores in Texas and California and shipped to Peppermint Press. They'd been paid for by G. Humphries.

Jane couldn't contain herself a second longer. She jumped out of her chair and headed for the door. But she didn't make it out of the room.

Instead, she took a deep breath, returned to her desk, and called the sheriff.

Their conversation took less than five minutes. When it was over, Jane gave Sinclair the printouts and said, "Sheriff Evans will need those. He'll be waiting for Gunnar in the lobby."

"The play's under way. How will you get Mr. Humphries to leave without causing a commotion?"

Jane flashed him a humorless grin. "I have a man on the inside. Or, should I say, a teenage girl? She and I made a plan in case something like this happened, and I know she'll see it through. I need to speak to her right now."

Sinclair followed Jane through the staff corridors to the back of Shakespeare's Theater. The door opened next to the stage stairs. Jane waited until the spotlight shifted to the opposite side of the stage before creeping up the stairs.

To her immense relief, Zoey, aka Veruca Salt, was backstage, waiting for her next scene. Jane was able to tiptoe next to her and touch her lightly on the shoulder.

Zoey turned and smiled at Jane with unconcealed joy.

"Guess what?" she whispered. "Wobbles is okay. He just has an ear infection. That's why his balance was all messed up. The vet gave him some drops. He said that Wobbles should be totally fine in a few days. I talked to my aunt, and she's willing to adopt him if no one else comes forward to claim him. If he has a family, they'd better come looking for him because if they don't love him like I do, then they don't deserve him."

Onstage, Charlie and his grandfather were heading to the chocolate factory. Very soon, Veruca and the rest of the actors playing children would take their cue and join him.

"I'm thrilled about Wobbles," Jane whispered. "But I'm here to ask you for that favor. Do you have time to tell the other actors what to do?"

Zoey's mouth curved into a crooked grin. "Yeah. Who are we taking out?"

Looping her arm through Zoey's, Jane led the girl to the edge of the curtain. "See Mr. Butterworth?" At Zoey's nod, Jane continued. "See the man in the third seat from where Mr. Butterworth is standing? He's wearing glasses, a white shirt, and a red bowtie."

"The Cat in the Hat? I see him."

"That's the man. Do whatever it takes to get him out of this theater."

Zoey couldn't hide her delight. "I've totally got this."

She rushed away to whisper instructions to another group of actors waiting in the wings.

Jane was far too nervous to sit, so she climbed down the

stairs and pressed herself against the back wall. Though she was completely hidden in darkness, she tried not to look in Gunnar's direction. She didn't want anything to alert him as to what was about to happen.

Despite the searing glare of the spotlight and the clear voices coming from center stage, Jane couldn't focus on the play. She couldn't stop thinking about the little boy who'd been killed by a book. If not by the book, then by the battery inside of it.

Gunnar had lost Poppy, his beloved daughter. Next, he'd lost his closest tie to his daughter. He'd lost Poppy's son. A little boy named Aiden. A boy he and his wife had legally adopted. Aiden was much more than a grandson. He was Gunnar's world. And not long after Aiden's death, Gunnar's wife had also passed.

Gunnar, heartbroken and alone, had waited years to exact revenge against the woman who'd been watching his grandson the day he died. And Gloria? What had she done to deserve her cruel fate?

Jane reviewed what she'd learned about Gloria.

Gloria was ambitious. She'd wanted to take Peppermint Press in a new direction. Gunnar had let her start a new imprint. It hadn't succeeded and Gloria had left the company. Gunnar had said she'd left on friendly terms.

Had that been a lie?

Jane remembered Gunnar's outburst over children's books enhanced by sounds and lights. Is that why Gloria had gone to Baxter Books? Had she been interested in producing the kind of book that had killed Aiden Humphries? A book with a button battery?

Though some things were clicking in Jane's mind, not all the pieces were falling into place. She didn't see how Gunnar was able to convince Kristen to drive to Storyton.

Had he offered her money? Had he pretended that all was forgiven and that he wanted to atone for blaming her for Aiden's death?

And what about Gloria? Would she have shared a drink or a meal with Gunnar? Had they truly still been friendly? If so, how had he managed to drug her and drive her into the woods? How could he carry her? He couldn't walk without a cane.

These questions would soon be answered, for at that moment, the Storyton Band struck up the Oompa Loompa song. The actors playing Charlie, Violet, Mike, and Veruca congregated on stage left as the actors holding the Oompa Loompa puppets maneuvered around them.

Veruca Salt took a step forward. Signaling to the conductor to lower the volume of the music, she sang, "Someone in the audience is in for a treat. When the Oompa Loompas come for you, jump up from your seat. You don't want to miss this surprise. It's extra special neat!"

"You brilliant girl," Jane whispered as the cast continued to sing the scripted lyrics.

Veruca led the Oompa Loompas off of the stage and up the right-side aisle. They marched all the way to the back of the room, crossed over the middle, and marched down the left-side aisle. When they reached Gunnar's row, an Oompa Loompa pointed right at him. Veruca Salt began to clap. The audience, delighted to be included in the theatrical surprise, joined in.

Gunnar didn't jump up as Veruca suggested. The Oompa Loompas had to beckon him several times before he finally pasted on a smile and left his seat. Jane noticed that he barely limped as the Oompa Loompas led him out of the theater, Butterworth following on their heels.

Lachlan and Sterling were waiting for Gunnar by the

exit. Sinclair held the door open, allowing Lachlan and Sterling to enter the lobby a step ahead of Gunnar.

The Fairy Tale Killer left the theater surrounded by Fins.

Several minutes later, Veruca Salt and the Oompa Loompas returned to the stage and the play continued.

Jane knew she'd have to smooth Mrs. Templeton's ruffled feathers tomorrow, but she regretted nothing. The man who'd murdered two women had been caught. The all-too-real drama that had taken over the lives of everyone at Storyton Hall was very close to being over.

Jane was about to slip out through the back door into the staff corridor when she caught a movement out of the corner of her eye.

Someone else had left their seat and was moving, head bowed, toward the same exit she was about to use.

Retreating into the shadows cast by the stage curtain, Jane waited for the person to approach.

As the figure drew closer, Jane recognized her at once. It was Nia Curry.

She's trying to escape.

Suddenly, things became clearer to Jane. Gunnar couldn't have killed Kristen and Gloria on his own. He'd had help. The Cover Girls had pointed out that the Fairy Tale Murders had included a Big Bad Wolf and an evil queen. Gunnar Humphries was the wolf.

Nia Curry was the evil queen.

Chapter Seventeen

Nia exited the theater, and Jane slipped out after her.

When the theater door closed, Jane was keenly aware that she was now alone in an empty corridor with a murder suspect. She knew that she should be afraid, but she was too angry to be scared.

"Are you lost, Ms. Curry?" she asked the figure up ahead.

Startled, Nia swung around. Her body went taut and her dark eyes flashed. Her fight or flight response was on full display. She reminded Jane of a cornered animal, and her fear made Jane feel powerful. After days of feeling worried and helpless, she finally had control.

Nia wasn't going to raise her hands in surrender, though. Within seconds, she'd mastered her emotions.

Glancing around in feigned confusion, she asked, "Did I go out the wrong door? I have a nasty migraine and can't think straight. It came out of nowhere." She pressed her fingers to her temples for emphasis. "The noise in the theater was making it worse. I just had to get out."

Nia's acting skills wouldn't land her a spot with the Storyton Players, but Jane pretended to believe every word. "I'm sure you're desperate to escape. Why don't I show you the fastest way to the lobby?"

Though Nia's panic was almost palpable, she held fast to her charade. "That's nice of you, but what I really need is some fresh air. A place away from other people."

"I'll take you to the loading dock. At this time of night, it'll be deserted. You can take in the night air in peace. It'll just be you and the moon." Jane injected her words with such sugary sweetness that she worried she'd overdone it, but Nia responded with an eager nod.

The corridor wasn't wide enough for the women to walk shoulder to shoulder, so Nia fell into step behind Jane.

Jane didn't like this one bit. If Nia had assisted in the premeditated murder of two women, then she was callous and cunning. Jane's years of martial arts training wouldn't do her much good if Nia stuck a knife in her back.

"Can I get you anything for your pain?" Jane asked, darting a quick look over her shoulder.

"No, thanks." Nia's words came out as a groan. "I just need air. Later, I'll lie down."

Jane picked up her pace, hoping to reach her destination without incident. She didn't expect to run into any staff members because they'd already prepped the Madame Bovary Dining Room for dinner. They wouldn't return until it was time to fill water glasses or show guests to their tables.

"One of my friends gets migraines," Jane lied. "She says that medication doesn't really help. Is that true?"

"Ibuprofen helps a bit. That, and a dark room."

By this time, they'd reached the door to the kitchens. The muffled sounds of culinary activity could be heard through the thick wood.

"We'll pass through here to reach the loading dock." Jane put her hand on the door and gave Nia a reassuring smile. "No one will pay attention to us. Just walk straight through."

Nia hesitated. Jane could almost hear the other woman's

wheels spinning. She was probably so focused on what she'd do after getting outside that she didn't realize she was being herded toward the break room.

Passing by prep stations and cooktops with gurgling pots, they received polite smiles or nods from the kitchen staff, and Jane could sense Nia's panic subsiding. All she had to do was get outside. After distancing herself from the woman in the sparkly blue dress and fairy wings, Nia could make a break for it.

She must have the keys to Kristen's car, Jane thought. *Nia drove the women to the woods.*

Those keys were evidence of Nia's guilt. Jane had to ensure that they ended up in the sheriff's hands. She could not let Nia escape.

Suddenly, Mrs. Hubbard appeared in the doorway between the kitchen and the hallway leading to the break room. She carried a milk jug in one hand and a block of cheddar cheese in the other.

"Look at you!" she cried as she took in Jane's costume. Dumping the supplies from the walk-in on a counter, she clasped her hands over her heart. "You're such a lovely fairy! And what about those darling boys? Are they going to come by and show me their costumes?"

Ignoring the question, Jane gestured at Nia. "Mrs. Hubbard, this is Nia Curry. She's one of our guests. She isn't feeling well, so I'm taking her outside for some air. Is there an extra coat lying around? I thought she could use the one from that Rip Van Winkle event."

When Mrs. Hubbard's smile faltered, Jane knew that her message had been received.

"That's okay," Nia protested weakly. "I won't be out there long. My migraines are strong, but they don't last."

"You poor lamb! I know just what you need." Mrs. Hubbard took Nia's arm and steered her toward the break room.

The second Nia's back was turned, Jane grabbed a knife from the wooden block at the end of the counter. She slid it into the pocket of her skirt, silently thanking Mabel for sewing deep pockets into all of her garments.

Jane's sleight of hand hadn't gone unnoticed by the prep cook chopping carrots. He shot a glance at Mrs. Hubbard and Nia before taking his phone out of his pocket. When he looked at Jane and raised his brows in question, she responded with a firm nod.

By this point, Mrs. Hubbard and Nia had reached the end of the proverbial road. The loading dock door was perpendicular to the door to the break room, and Mrs. Hubbard had stationed herself right in front of the exit. She wasn't a small woman, and there was no chance Nia could squeeze by her without using force. As Nia weighed her options, her glance flicking from the woman blocking her path to the door, Mrs. Hubbard continued to fuss over her.

"You need to sit down in a quiet place with a cup of ginger tea. That'll be much better than catching your death outside."

"Ginger tea is an excellent idea," Jane said. Hurrying forward, she opened the break room door and waited for Nia to step inside.

Nia didn't move. "No, thank you. I just want some air."

She made to slip around Mrs. Hubbard, but Jane didn't give her the chance. She pressed a palm against Nia's shoulder and shoved her into the break room.

Nia reeled sideways but didn't fall. When she recovered her balance, she faced Jane and shouted, "What the hell?"

Jane brandished her knife. "You're not going anywhere. You're no Matilda. You might be smart. You might love books. But you're not kind, and you're certainly not good. You're an insult to Roald Dahl and the heroine he created.

He would have written you as a villain. He would have seen that you got your comeuppance in the end. Well, *this* is the end."

Nia forced a laugh. "If this is some kind of joke, it's not funny. I'm leaving."

Instead of moving, her eyes widened. She then retreated farther into the room.

Jane looked back over her shoulder. Four chefs stood behind her. Three of them held very large knives. The fourth wielded a cleaver.

"Sit down, Ms. Curry," Jane commanded. "You don't have a migraine. You have a case of I'm-about-to-get-caught. And there's no cure."

Nia's body tensed again. Preparing for a fight, she scanned the room for a weapon. Other than writing implements or utensils, there wasn't much available.

Jane handed her knife to one of the chefs. Part of her wanted Nia to give up without a struggle. The other part was looking for an excuse to strike the woman in front of her.

"Gunnar Humphries's soul was twisted by grief. He lost his daughter, his grandson, and his wife. The best parts of him probably died with the people he loved most. He was willing to throw his life away for the chance to punish those responsible for his misery. But you? Why would you take such a risk?"

"Do you know what motivates me?" Nia asked. Her mouth formed a crooked smile. "Success. I didn't want a piece of the action; I want to run the show. I want my own publishing business. I'm not working this hard to make someone *else* rich. I haven't coddled Gunnar all these years for nothing." Her eyes sparkled with anger. "Those days are over. It's time for me to be on top. To call the shots. To have the corner office. I want *my* name on the door and on every Peppermint Press business card. In *gold* letters."

"How does killing Kristen and Gloria accomplish that?"

Behind Jane, she heard murmuring. She assumed the cook's 911 call had been relayed to the sheriff and that he'd made his way to the break room, but she didn't turn around to check. She wanted Nia to keep talking. She wanted to understand why a woman who seemed to have everything going for her had been compelled to add murder to her résumé.

She studied Nia's face and saw the rage boiling in her dark eyes. Jane didn't shrink from it. She walked toward the other woman, her own anger blooming in her chest.

"Gunnar signed Peppermint Press over to me," Nia said triumphantly. "Come Monday, I'll be the new owner. And I didn't kill *anyone*. Have fun proving that I did."

"Even if you didn't poison those women, you lured them to their deaths," Jane said flatly. "That's accessory to murder. How's *that* going to look on your *gold* business cards?"

Nia's expression turned stony. "I'm done talking to you."

Jane felt a hand on her elbow. "I'll take it from here," said the sheriff.

The curious chefs made a path for the sheriff and Deputy Emory. Jane waited for Nia to be cuffed and Mirandized before moving so close to her that their noses almost touched.

"You murdered two women. You scared my guests. You threatened my sons." Jane's voice was dangerously soft. "Being in charge isn't about profit margins or a title on your letterhead. It's knowing that the heart of your company is its people. I owe everything to the people of Storyton Hall, not the other way around. And I'll be honoring their hard work and dedication by making sure that someone like you will never be in charge."

Deputy Emory put a hand on Jane's shoulder. "We're going to take her in now."

Jane nodded. She didn't trust herself to speak.

"I would never hurt your sons" were Nia's parting words.

"No, you wouldn't," said Jane. "Because you wouldn't have gotten past me."

It wasn't until Nia was escorted outside that Jane felt like she could breathe again. She stood in the break room doorway until her heartbeat slowed. Once she'd calmed down, she turned to thank Mrs. Hubbard and the chefs who'd come to her aid. To her surprise, the entire kitchen staff broke into spontaneous applause. They whooped and hollered, patted one another on the back, and shouted phrases like "Did you see that?" and "We got her!"

Adrenaline and relief made Jane want to shout too, but she was the manager of Storyton Hall, so she settled for a big smile. She approached every chef who'd picked up a weapon to defend her and gave each of them a hug.

By the time she reached out for Mrs. Hubbard, the head cook was blubbering like a child.

"Oh, my dear! That's the most exciting thing that's ever happened in this kitchen! And I don't think I liked it. No, I don't think I liked it one bit!"

Jane led the head cook over to a stool, forced her to sit down, and wiped her face with a clean napkin. Next, she whispered into a waiter's ear and he dashed off to fetch a large mug of whiskey-laced coffee.

When he returned, Jane pressed the mug into Mrs. Hubbard's hands and urged her to drink. After a few sips, Mrs. Hubbard stopped sniffling. She gazed around her domain and nodded.

"Thank you, Jane, but I can't sit here sniveling with dinner starting in twenty minutes. I'm better now. Whiskey cures most ills." Getting to her feet, she began barking orders.

Her staff, pleased to see their intrepid leader take the helm again, got back to work.

"It was the thought of someone hurting the twins that made me blubber," Mrs. Hubbard murmured to Jane in between shouts. "You and the boys are my family. I love you to pieces."

Jane took Mrs. Hubbard's hand and said, "We love you too." She then moved to the center of the room and yelled, "It's Valentine's Day. Let's celebrate love!"

This was met by a chorus of cheers. Suddenly, everyone was exchanging hugs.

Jane whispered, "My work here is done," and disappeared into the staff corridor.

Though Fitz and Hem had thoroughly enjoyed the play, they were too focused on filling their empty bellies to discuss it. Jane told them to get in the buffet line while she and Edwin relaxed with glasses of red wine.

"Part of me is afraid to believe that it's over," Jane told Edwin when the twins were out of earshot. "I thought Tris and Todd Petty were responsible for the crimes, but I was wrong."

"Your guests are safe and are having the time of their lives," Edwin said. "That's what matters right now."

Jane took his hand. "That's true. And I'm with my family. Fitz, Hem, and you." She stared into his eyes, which were always lit by a spark of mischief and a hint of laughter. Jane liked how his gaze softened whenever he looked at her.

"I don't want to compartmentalize my life anymore,"

she said. "I've learned that life is messy. Families are complicated. All families. I love you, Edwin. My sons love you. Can you ignore everything I said to you last fall about trying to separate the woman who loves you from the woman who is mother to Fitz and Hem? Will you commit to all three of us?"

Edwin leaned over and whispered, "What man wouldn't want to join a family made up of a blue fairy, a liar, and an ass?"

Jane laughed and was about to offer a rejoinder when Edwin stopped her words with a kiss. He then placed an envelope on the table and said, "I'm glad we're on the same page, Valentine."

"That doesn't look like a book," Jane said. "We exchange books on holidays."

"Rules are meant to be broken."

Opening the envelope, Jane muttered, "Rascal. Rake. Rapscallion." She was about to continue insulting Edwin when she saw that the envelope held four first-class plane tickets to London and a hotel brochure.

"You deserve a vacation. A family vacation," Edwin said. "And we're not crossing the pond to ride a giant Ferris wheel or tour the city in a red bus. We can do those things too, but this wouldn't be a gift for *you* unless books were involved."

Jane was dumbfounded. "London? Books?"

"We're going on a literary tour of England. Austen, Shakespeare, Beatrix Potter, Dickens, Tolkien, Lewis, Brontë, and more. We can't forget Harry Potter, so we'll go on the London studio tour before boarding a train to Edinburgh."

"Scotland," Jane said dreamily. She then tried to give Edwin a stern look. "We give each other books on holidays.

This is *not* a book. This is magic. I'm the Blue Fairy. *I'm* supposed to make the magic."

Edwin cupped her chin in his palm. "You do. Every day. For many people. But it's high time you took a break, sweetheart."

The twins returned to the table just as Jane was thanking Edwin with a tender kiss. Before they could roll their eyes or make a snide comment, Jane thrust the hotel brochure at them.

"Guess what? We're going to London! All four of us!"

After exchanging ecstatic glances, Fitz and Hem began firing questions at Jane.

"Can we have a spot of tea in Buckingham Palace?" Hem asked.

"Oy, guvnah. Can we ride *the tube*?"

Fitz's Cockney accent was atrocious, but Hem couldn't wait to mimic it.

"I hope our flat has a hoity-toity *lift*."

Jane sighed and squeezed Edwin's hand. "They're going to do this until we touch down in Heathrow, you know."

Edwin laughed. "Let's get some food. Maybe they'll be over their Oliver Twist impersonations by the time we get back."

When Jane returned to her seat with a plate of braised balsamic chicken, salad with mango vinaigrette, potato croquettes, and glazed carrots, the twins were ready for dessert. Jane told them to stick with two items. Hem selected a heart-shaped brownie and strawberry cheesecake while Fitz went for the red velvet cake with maraschino cherry cream and chocolate mousse. The boys ate exactly half of each dessert before swapping plates.

"That's one way to get four desserts instead of two," Edwin said.

When the twins were too full to cram in another bite, they asked Jane if they could bring a plate of chocolate-covered strawberries to Uncle Aloysius and Aunt Octavia.

"Yes. That would be very nice," said Jane, smiling at her sons. "Your valentines are at home. You can open them whenever you want."

"We put yours in the kitchen," Fitz said, giving his mom a quick hug.

Hem hugged her next and said, "You're the best mom ever."

The boys gave Edwin high fives and shouted, "See you tomorrow!"

"Tomorrow?" Jane called after them, but her question was lost in the din of talk, laughter, and the clinking of silverware.

"I asked your great-aunt and great-uncle if the twins could spend the night," Edwin said, looking very pleased with himself. "I was counting on the fact that you'd identify and catch the Fairy Tale Killer before the night was out, and you did."

"With a lot of help, including yours."

Edwin brushed the back of her hand with his lips. "You'll want to check in with the Fins and the sheriff before you leave, so I'll find Malcolm Marcus and buy him a drink. The man might be a zealot when it comes to book collecting, but I don't hold that against him. And though he won't end up with *The Velveteen Rabbit* he wants so badly, I do have a gift for him."

Jane was about to protest Edwin's plan to reward the bookseller. But when she paused to reflect on her reasoning, she realized that she'd judged Malcolm based on his looks as well as his desire to add to his personal collection. She'd been unfair. She'd seen him as greedy instead of passionate. She'd assumed he was manipulative when, in truth, he'd been perfectly transparent with her and everyone else from the start.

"It was generous of you to get him a gift," Jane said to Edwin. "What is it?"

Edwin placed a book-shaped object wrapped in brown paper on the table. "This character reminds me of Malcolm. I don't think he'll be insulted by my choice. In fact, I think he'll be thrilled. It's a first edition from 1886 and is in excellent condition."

He gestured for Jane to pull the twine bow holding the paper in place. After doing so, she peeled back just enough paper to read the book's title. It was *Little Lord Fauntleroy.*

Thinking of the spoiled little boy in the novel, Jane laughed. Edwin did too. They sat at their table, surrounded by families of every kind, and laughed.

This is love, Jane thought. *This is happiness.*

After dinner, Jane asked the Fins to join her in the Daphne du Maurier Morning Room.

"I don't want to keep you from enjoying your night off, but I want to be sure that we're doing all we can to help the sheriff wrap up his investigation. Sterling, have you been able to find any security footage that could incriminate Gunnar or Nia?"

Looking like the cat who'd caught the canary, Sterling handed Jane a printout. "Another camera picked up the figure in the brown jacket before they approached the dining room. The face is hidden under the hood, but as you can see in this freeze-frame image, the person has a tattoo of a bird with four wings on their neck."

"Nia Curry!" Jane cried.

"Ms. Curry wasn't wearing that jacket when she first arrived at Storyton Hall. She wore a bright blue coat. The brown jacket was meant to provide camouflage when she was in the woods."

Butterworth spoke next. "It appears that Ms. Curry had a suitcase devoted to coats. Inside this case, we found price tags taken from the brown jacket, the red coat Ms. Burke was wearing when she was found, and the fur-trimmed coat Ms. Ramirez was wearing when she was found."

Jane's anger threatened to flare again, but she shoved it aside. She needed to focus on seeking justice for Kristen and Gloria, and the news about the price tags was excellent. "We have concrete evidence linking Nia to the murders. I don't see how she can explain that away."

"We expect Mr. Humphries to confess," said Sinclair. "He's not interested in self-preservation. That was plain to all of us when Mr. Humphries saw the sheriff waiting for him in the lobby. His impending arrest wasn't the only reason Mr. Humphries deflated like a tire. It was coming face to face with Brandon Parks, Ms. Ramirez's beau."

Jane frowned. "I don't understand. Did Gunnar know Brandon?"

"Dr. Parks assisted in the knee replacement surgery Mr. Humphries received a year ago," Sinclair explained. "The surgery was a success. After six weeks of physical therapy, Mr. Humphries could walk without discomfort. In short, he didn't need a cane. Dr. Parks was clearly surprised to see Mr. Humphries, and even more surprised to see him using a cane."

Jane held up her hands. "Wait a minute. Did Gunnar know that his doctor was Gloria's boyfriend at the time of his surgery?"

"Dr. Parks and Ms. Ramirez had just started dating at the time. She hadn't told anyone about her new beau, let alone her boss. But the effect of running into Dr. Parks in this setting—a man who could testify as to Mr. Humphries's physical condition—proved to be too much. As I said, Gunnar Humphries deflated. The fight has left him."

Putting aside her questions about the investigation for the moment, Jane's thoughts turned to Brandon. "That poor man. I need to talk to him—to make sure he has everything he needs. The least I can do is see to his creature comforts."

"Dr. Parks accompanied the sheriff to the station," said Butterworth. "Before he left, he told me that he came to Storyton to visit the place where Ms. Ramirez was found. Tomorrow, he'd like to spend time alone there. To say good-bye. As for tonight, his main interest is knowing that her killer will be brought to justice."

"*Killers*," Jane said. "To me, Nia is just as guilty as Gunnar."

Sinclair let her remark hang in the air before continuing, "Having heard what she said in the kitchens, we believe that Ms. Curry will do anything she can to avoid prosecution."

Jane fell silent, wondering how Nia would handle her arrest. Would she deny her involvement? Would she refuse to speak at all? Would she sit in an interview room, stubbornly gazing at a point in the middle distance while Sheriff Evans tried to get answers from her? Would she immediately demand an attorney?

"We need to help Evans convince her that coming clean is her smartest move," Jane told the Fins. "Making her believe that cooperation could mean less jail time is the key. She wants Peppermint Press. She committed unforgivable sins to get it, and I think she'll continue to do whatever it takes to fulfill that dream."

"We should get the video footage and the price tags to the sheriff right away," said Lachlan. "Ms. Curry might need to see the evidence against her before she'll give in."

"I'll go to the station. I know the footage better than anyone." Sterling smiled at Lachlan. "Besides, isn't your valentine waiting for you?"

Lachlan's cheeks burned. "My love life comes second to my responsibilities as a Fin."

"We might have to reexamine those priorities in the future. Love lives should come first," Jane said. Getting to her feet, she glanced at each of her Fins in turn. "For once, the crimes committed at Storyton Hall have nothing to do with our secret library. That should be a relief, but it isn't. It'll take another year or two to empty the library of its treasures, and there's no guarantee that we'll have peace once the shelves are bare."

"Peace sounds quite dull," said Butterworth. "And rather lovely."

Jane continued to look at the four men who'd sacrificed so much to keep her and the secret library safe. If she paused too long to consider all they'd done for her, she'd become too emotional to speak, so she hurried on.

"Valentine's Day is traditionally a holiday for couples. Not here. This weekend, we've been celebrating familial love. Such a celebration applies to us as well. We're a family. And I wanted to take a moment to tell you how grateful I am to each of you. I don't have boxes of chocolate or sappy cards for you, but I do have a small token of appreciation."

Jane reached into the shopping bag next to her chair and pulled out four jewelry boxes.

"If this is a proposal, I accept," Sinclair joked.

Butterworth's brow twitched. "Mr. Alcott is likely to object."

"The four of us could overpower a single Templar," Sterling said, raising a clenched fist.

Instead of adding a comment, Lachlan opened his box. When he saw the gold arrow-shaped cuff links inside, he smiled at Jane.

"This is my first pair. Thank you."

Butterworth was aghast. "Your first pair of cuff links? *Your first?*"

The other Fins poked fun at Lachlan until Jane said, "Maybe he hasn't been invited to a function calling for a tux and cuff links. Now, he'll be ready for *any* black-tie event."

Lachlan knew she was referring to his possible nuptials and flashed her a conspiratorial smile.

Sinclair cleared his throat and stood up. "Before we separate for the evening, might I also recognize the people in this room by quoting a famous man?"

"Please," said Jane.

Sinclair's gaze was filled with affection as he spoke, "'Not even a mighty warrior can break a frail arrow when it is multiplied and supported by its fellows. As long as your brothers support one another and render assistance to one another, your enemies can never gain the victory over you.'"

Holding the jewelry box close to his heart, he got to his feet, turned to Jane, and performed a small bow. "Thank you."

"Those words are so perfect for this group. Who said them?" Jane asked.

"The quote is attributed to Genghis Khan."

Jane threw up her hands in mock exasperation. "Because nothing says Valentine's Day like a genocidal warlord."

"We're far more fortunate in our choice of leaders," said Sterling.

Sinclair gestured at the door. "But our leader needs to go home. The suspects will be waiting in the morning. As will Sheriff Evans. The rest of this night doesn't belong to the Guardian or to the manager of Storyton Hall. It belongs to a woman in love. Good night, dear girl."

After embracing each Fin, Jane made her way home.

Home.

Where Edwin was waiting.

Chapter Eighteen

The next morning, Jane woke before sunrise. Her room was dark and still. She felt the warmth of Edwin's body and heard his slow, steady breaths. He seemed to be sleeping deeply, and Jane was tempted to curl up against him and close her eyes again. Instead, she slipped out from under the blankets. She had things to do.

First, she needed to call Sheriff Evans and ask him if the charges against Gunnar and Nia would stick. Jane couldn't concentrate on her departing guests or on preparing the gazebo for Lachlan's proposal until the sheriff confirmed that the Fairy Tale Killers would remain behind bars for the immediate future.

Jane showered and dressed as quietly as she could and went downstairs to brew a pot of coffee. After filling her travel mug to the brim, she laid out a clean spoon and mug for Edwin. She drew a heart on a sticky note, pressed her lips to the paper, and tucked it inside the mug.

With her coat and keys in hand, Jane paused at the front door. She took a moment to savor the thought that Edwin was upstairs, asleep in her bed. She loved knowing he was there. It felt so right.

When she stepped outside, the air stung her cheeks and

wriggled under her coat collar. The sky was a bruised purple and a few stars clung to the horizon. Tentative streaks of pale light had started to penetrate the darkness, but the world was still cloaked in slumber.

Jane hurried through the kitchens. It was too early for the aroma of baking biscuits and the mouthwatering fragrance of fresh cinnamon buns to distract her from going straight to her office, and within minutes, she had Sheriff Evans on the phone.

"I was wondering if I'd hear from you before the sun rose," he said.

Though Jane had many pressing questions, she was also concerned about the sheriff's well-being. "Did you get any rest last night?"

"Enough," he said. "Here's how things stand right now. Gunnar Humphries has signed a written confession. Though he provided many details, none include Ms. Curry. He refuses to incriminate her, which leaves his confession full of holes. He's been charged with two counts of first-degree murder. From now on, he'll be dealing with lawyers and judges."

Hearing that Gunnar had confessed brought Jane no satisfaction. Everything about this case was tragic. Pain had irrevocably changed Gunnar. He'd then inflicted pain on others. These acts of violence wouldn't bring him peace. He'd only created more loss. More suffering.

"Why didn't Gunnar fight the manufacturers of button batteries?" she asked. "Why didn't he try to bring down the companies using them in books or toys? That would have been a noble way to honor his grandson's memory. He could have saved other children from the same fate."

"I'm afraid Mr. Humphries became obsessed with the

people connected to Aiden's death. Plotting the murders gave him purpose."

Jane slapped her desk blotter. "His *purpose* was publishing books for children! He kept playing the part—hobbling around with a cane filled with peppermint sticks—until he came up with the idea to sponsor a conference at our resort. He picked Storyton Hall as the setting for his revenge. I guess nothing mattered to him but that. Not even Peppermint Press."

"I believe Ms. Curry has been running the company for some time now. She wasn't receiving the salary or the recognition she craved, but she expects all that to change on Monday."

"Did she stonewall you all night?"

The sheriff grunted. "Pretty much. Even after seeing how much evidence is stacked against her, her confidence didn't waver. It's a confidence bordering on arrogance."

"Arrogant people are usually insecure," said Jane. "Maybe Nia's like Holden Caulfield from *The Catcher in the Rye*. He acted superior to hide his loneliness. What if Nia is doing the same thing? You could use that to get her to talk."

There was a moment of silence as the sheriff mulled this over. Finally, he said, "I understand what you're saying, but I don't know how to go about it."

"I do," said Jane. "It involves a bit of fabrication, but since she and Gunnar borrowed from storybooks to create murder scenes, I don't see why we shouldn't use fiction too."

"I'll try anything as long as it's legal," the sheriff said.

Jane ended the call, put her coat back on, and refilled her travel mug from the urns in the lobby. She then prepared a second cup for Nia Curry and told Butterworth that she was heading into town.

"Let Mr. Sterling drive you," he said. "You can organize your thoughts on the way."

Jane was soon settled in the passenger seat of Sterling's favorite car, a 1977 Rolls-Royce Silver Wraith. Though the car oozed elegance and luxury, it wasn't good in snow. Jane was glad that the flurries predicted for their area wouldn't occur until the afternoon.

Sterling pulled up in front of the sheriff's department, a charming cottage-style building. Like the rest of the village, the station looked like it belonged in the British Cotswolds. It had a low roof, a quaint front garden, and a wood door polished to a high shine.

The interior had a more industrial feel. Fluorescent light fixtures, nondescript floor tile, and the steady clamor of ringing phones and conversation created an atmosphere of constant activity.

The desk sergeant led Jane down a short hall to an interrogation room. Deputy Emory was waiting for her inside.

"I'm going to sit in the corner and observe," she said. "The sheriff thought it would be a good idea to have another woman present."

Jane sat down at the table. "I'm always happy to have female backup. Can I offer coffee to Nia? I'd like to use it as an ice-breaker."

"As long as you're not hiding handcuff keys in there, it's fine."

"Trust me, I want this woman behind bars until her hair turns gray."

A few seconds later, Nia was escorted into the room.

Despite a night in detainment, Nia looked fresh-faced and rested. She entered the room as if she owned it, unfazed by her cuffed wrists or orange jumpsuit.

I hope you like that color. I'm going to make sure you

wear it every day, Jane thought. She then wordlessly scolded herself for being as arrogant as Nia.

"I'm not here to talk about Kristen or Gloria," Jane said after Nia was seated. "You're still a guest of Storyton Hall, so I came to make sure you're being treated well."

"I'd rather be in my room, packing my things. Monday's a big day for me. I have things to do. Important things."

Nia's tone was flippant, designed to provoke a reaction, and Jane fought to keep her ire from rising.

"I bet Storyton Hall coffee is better than what they have here." Jane pushed the cup toward Nia. "I don't know how you take it, but I added a splash of cream."

Nia looked at Deputy Emory and said, "Perfect. I only add sugar to really bad coffee."

Jane waited until Nia had taken a few sips of coffee before asking if she'd had anything to eat.

"I don't want food. I want to leave. Can you do something about that?" Nia asked. "Because if you can't, you should go."

"You're my guest, and I'm here to help," Jane said. "You're not my only concern, either. Many of the conference attendees are about to become your employees, right?"

Nia's eyes glittered with excitement. "Yes. By this time tomorrow, I'll be their boss."

"Your employees might need guidance before they head back to New York," Jane said. "I could record a message from you using my phone and play it for the whole group. That way, they'll know what to expect from the new captain of their ship."

Nia puffed up with pride and smiled at Jane. "That's a good idea. Maybe you *do* want to help. But don't record until I give the signal. This'll be my first directive. It'll set the tone for how things will be from now on, so I want to nail it."

Jane took out her phone and opened her voice recording app. With hunched shoulders and a slightly bowed head, she said, "Whenever you're ready."

Nia's response to Jane's submissive body language was immediate. The more Jane tried to shrink in her chair, the taller Nia sat. Looking down her nose at Jane, she declared, "Ready."

She watched Jane hit the red record button and began speaking in a clear and confident voice. "Friends and colleagues of Peppermint Press, this is Nia Curry. It is with genuine regret that I must tell you of Gunnar Humphries's decision to retire. Our intrepid leader has given his heart and soul to Peppermint Press for many years, and now, he's ready to slow down. I know this seems abrupt, but Gunnar has been preparing for this transition for quite some time. He would have delivered this message in person, but he has pressing legal matters to see to. You'll hear about those soon enough, which is why I want to assure you that Peppermint Press is in good hands."

Nia paused to tent her hands, and Jane sensed that she was practicing her boardroom look.

You won't step foot in a boardroom, Jane silently vowed. *Just a courtroom.*

"It's my privilege and pleasure to tell you that Gunnar has entrusted me with his beloved company. I'll do everything in my power to continue his fine work and to break new barriers. I'm sure you have many questions, and I'll address those when I return to the office. There may be a delay before I take the reins—piles of legalese to wade through—but I'll monitor things from wherever I am. I look forward to making Peppermint Press even more successful. Safe travels, everyone!"

Nia made a slicing gesture across her throat to indicate that she was done. Jane pretended to hit the red button as she pulled the phone close to her body, but the app continued to record.

"That was great." Jane gave Nia a doe-eyed stare. "I liked what you said about breaking barriers."

"As the first woman of color running a successful publishing house, I'm already smashing barriers." Nia's eyes turned glassy. "I'm just getting warmed up."

Jane grinned. "Good for you. I bet you'll also be the first CEO with a neck tattoo. What kind of bird is that?"

Nia brushed the tattoo with her fingertips. "It's a four-winged blackbird. I got it when I was in college. I wanted everyone to ask me what it means. Some do. Most people ignore it."

"I'd love to know what it means," Jane said.

"Salvador Dali said, 'Intelligence without ambition is a bird without wings.'" Nia spread her hands. "I wanted people to see that I had both. In spades."

Jane liked the quote and how Nia had used it for inspiration. In other circumstances, she would have cheered Nia on, celebrating the fact that she was a force to be reckoned with. She had many admirable qualities, but her thirst for power had led her astray. She'd used her intelligence to murder two other women. Innocent women. That was unforgivable.

"You must have lots of plans for Peppermint Press," Jane said. "Will you keep publishing traditional children's books, or will you add books with bells and whistles to your list?"

Nia raised a finger. "I have two goals. First, I want to see more books featuring kids of color." She raised a second finger. "Next, I want to increase profits. If books with bells, lights, or confetti cannons make money, then I'm going to publish them."

Jane caved in her chest, making herself seem even

smaller. "Would Gunnar want that? After what happened to his grandson?"

Nia flicked her wrist dismissively. "The old man's time is up. His rules are not *my* rules. What happened to that boy is sad, but the books aren't to blame. Blame the person who was watching the kid. Kristen messed up. The kid died. Now, she's dead. End of story."

Jane nodded. "I guess you *should* do things your way now that you're in charge. It's not your responsibility to keep other little kids from swallowing button batteries."

"What happened with Gunnar's grandson was a fluke. Kids don't eat batteries," Nia scoffed. "Something was wrong with that Aiden kid. Too sheltered, maybe. No street smarts."

Jane felt a surge of triumph. She'd gotten what she'd come for.

Let's see if you still want to protect your protégée after hearing this, Gunnar.

After pressing the pause button, Jane handed the phone to Deputy Emory.

"All set?" Emory asked. Her eyes gleamed.

"All set." Jane got to her feet and smiled down at Nia.

Nia glanced from one woman to the other. As she took in their expressions, her smugness evaporated. "What's going on?"

"You're going to pay for what you did," Jane said as she left the room.

Fifteen minutes later, Sheriff Evans found Jane in the lobby. He grabbed her hand and pumped it up and down.

"Your plan worked. After listening to the recording, Mr. Humphries filled in all the blanks. He told us how he and Ms. Curry arrived before the rest of the conference-goers. Ms. Curry met Ms. Burke in the parking lot. The two women had become friendly. They'd spoken on the phone several times, and Ms. Curry had even visited the coffee shop to give Ms. Burke an envelope of cash. The money was a good-faith offering—proof that Mr. Humphries regretted having accused Ms. Burke of neglect and for shaming her into quitting her job as an assistant teacher."

"Why would Kristen trust Nia? She didn't know her at all," Jane said.

Sheriff Evans spread his hands. "More than anything, Ms. Burke wanted forgiveness. Yes, she needed money. But what she really craved was absolution. Ms. Curry was offering her what she wanted most."

"That poor woman. Could you imagine the desperation she must have felt? To drive all this way in hopes of forgiveness? If I were her, I'd wonder why Gunnar didn't just meet me in New Jersey. How did Nia convince Kristen to make the trip down?"

"They had to convince her. They needed her car. They couldn't use a rental for their criminal activity. It was too risky," the sheriff said. "Ms. Curry met Ms. Burke in the parking lot as scheduled. She gave her more money and the poisoned apple. After her death, they tossed the apple in the woods and Gunnar reclaimed the money."

Jane frowned. "I assume they used Kristen's car to transport Gloria's body too."

"Correct. As for why Ms. Burke agreed to make the drive, it was because she was promised a free vacation at a five-star resort. She told her coworkers that she was headed to the Poconos because they knew she couldn't afford a place like Storyton Hall. She didn't want to tell anyone about Ms. Curry or Mr. Humphries because she didn't want anyone to learn of her connection to Aiden Humphries."

Jane imagined Kristen packing her new clothes, loading her car, and cranking up the heater. Had she sung along to the radio, feeling hopeful and happy for the first time in years, as she drove through the dark night toward Storyton Hall? Had she dreamed of a massage and room service? Had she fantasized over what she'd do with the money Gunnar had promised? Had he offered enough to compensate for her foiled teaching career? For her guilt and self-loathing?

"She came here expecting a fresh start," Jane said softly. "With Gunnar's money, she could pay her debts and buy new things, all after vacationing in a beautiful place. And she'd finally be forgiven for her part in Aiden's death."

Seeing Jane's glum expression, the sheriff put a hand on her arm. "Mr. Humphries knew about Ms. Burke's peanut allergy from her time as Aiden's babysitter. He injected the apple with peanut oil. Because Ms. Burke had come to trust Ms. Curry, she accepted the apple. Within minutes of her first bite, Ms. Burke was dead. Ms. Curry and Mr. Humphries dressed her in the red coat and left the basket with the book at the scene."

"Nia had the murder weapon." Jane's body tightened in anger. "She's just as guilty as Gunnar."

Sheriff Evans nodded. "Mr. Humphries prepared the murder weapons. Ms. Curry delivered them. In Ms. Ramirez's case, Mr. Humphries mixed crushed pain-killers into a travel mug of hot tea. Ms. Curry invited Ms. Ramirez on a scenic drive in order to discuss ideas for closing the diversity gap in children's books. Ms. Ramirez was eager to discuss the topic. As they set out on their short drive, Ms. Ramirez accepted the cup of tea and drank from it."

"Did she pass out?" Jane asked.

"Yes. Ms. Curry then took the service road into the woods to where Mr. Humphries was waiting. They carried Ms. Ramirez's body to a small clearing where Ms. Curry dressed her in the coat with the fur-trimmed hood and placed the glass shards around her body. Mr. Humphries pushed the watch battery into her mouth."

Involuntarily, Jane pressed her hand to her lips. "Monsters," she whispered.

The sheriff stood close to Jane, offering wordless comfort.

"Where did Kristen's stuff go?" she asked. "Her clothes? Her coat? And what about Gloria's coat?"

"Packed into trash bags and dropped in the Cheshire Cat's dumpster. Fortunately, it doesn't get emptied until tomorrow. Deputy Phelps is on his way to the pub now. You'll probably hear him grumbling about dumpster diving in sub-arctic temperatures as you pass."

Jane managed a small grin. "I'm sure Bob and Betty would lend a hand, especially if it meant bringing two killers to justice."

"Of that, I have no doubt. Storyton's citizens are special people. That includes you, Ms. Steward." Sheriff Evans gave Jane a weary smile.

"Before I go, I'd like to ask you one more thing. Why did Gunnar create the fairy-tale scenes? And why did he include those valuable books?"

The sheriff ran a hand over his unshaven chin. "Mr. Humphries curated an amazing library of children's books for his daughter. He read to Poppy every day when she was young, and the Grimm and Andersen stories used to create the crime scenes were her favorites. I think the books were Mr. Humphries's way of including his daughter in his acts of vengeance."

"Grief, loss, blame. They consumed Gunnar. Ambition and pride were Nia's undoing." Jane began buttoning her coat. "They acted so warm. Positive and playful. Surrounded by their authors and illustrators, they seemed so *good.* This friendly pair who made children's books were murderers. It's hard to wrap my head around the contradiction."

"Every time I struggle to accept a contradiction like this, I think of a poem by E. E. Cummings. A million years ago, I had to say it in front of the whole class. I still remember it."

Jane liked the idea of a young Evans standing in front of the blackboard, reciting poetry in a crisp, clear voice. "Would you tell me a few lines?"

After a quick nod, he began:

> *"'If earth was heaven and now was hence,
> And past was present, and false was true,
> There might be some sense
> But I'd be in suspense
> For on such a pretense
> You wouldn't be you.'"*

Jane didn't know if it was the rhyming verse, the message of acceptance, or how the sheriff had looked like a young boy during the recitation, but the poem made her feel better.

"I'm glad you're you," she said to him.

He smiled. "Deputy Emory will follow you to Storyton Hall. If you'll gather the conference attendees, she'll announce the arrests and field questions. The news should come from our department. Two women died near Storyton Hall, Ms. Steward, but you're not responsible for their deaths. I want that made clear to everyone."

Jane thanked him and left.

The case was closed. The murderers had been apprehended. The questions had been answered. And yet Jane didn't feel a sense of relief. Like the aftershocks of an earthquake, she knew that the crimes would continue to disturb the peace. Once the media caught the scent of blood, Storyton Hall would be featured on the front pages of countless magazines and newspapers. Photographs of the grounds would circulate through cyberspace. Gunnar Humphries was a big name in New York City, and every journalist worth his salt would look for an angle on the Fairy Tale Murders.

Jane expected to see that headline everywhere. Or something like THE STORYBOOK SLAYINGS. Such headlines made her glum.

Witnessing the effects of Deputy Emory's announcement about the arrests increased Jane's despondency. The shock and horror reflected on the faces of the conference attendees were heartbreaking. Their colleagues had turned out to be murderers, and that was a hard truth to accept.

Jane consoled as many people as she could. She passed out cups of hot tea or coffee, answered questions, made assurances, and held hands. Eventually, the guests started to collect their luggage and depart. The majority planned to catch the midmorning train, and Jane hoped that the forty-five-minute drive through the pristine blue hills would soothe their pain.

The families checked out later. They filled the lobby with movement, chatter, and laughter. They'd clearly made new memories together. Wonderful memories. Jane was pleased to see the Gilberts glowing with happiness.

Some of the parents would change their minds about Storyton Hall. Once the story of the murders broke, Jane expected to receive irate phone calls from the same people who'd just thanked her for the best weekend of their lives. When they called, Jane would patiently explain that she'd done everything in her power to safeguard their families.

When the last family had gone, Jane looked around the

empty lobby and thought, *I have a day or two until the press invades. I should enjoy the peace and quiet while I can.*

She started off by having lunch with Edwin, the twins, Aunt Octavia, and Uncle Aloysius. The boys were eager to tell Jane about *Bedknobs and Broomsticks*. It was their first time seeing the film, and they wanted to discuss every detail.

"You said that you wouldn't like such an *old* movie," teased Aunt Octavia. "But you wanted a movie set in London, and I found you one."

"As usual, my beautiful bride made an excellent choice," said Uncle Aloysius.

Even though it was February, he wore his customary fishing hat. Jane thought she detected several new flies attached to the fabric above his left ear.

Apparently, Edwin noticed them too. Soon, he and Uncle Aloysius were swapping fishing stories while Aunt Octavia recommended other London-based films to the twins.

"Don't mention *Olivier Twist*," Jane whispered to her great-aunt. "Unless you want them calling you *guvnah* for the next three months."

Aunt Octavia laughed so hard that the table shook. The teacups rattled in their saucers and the flatware skittered sideways. Seeing this, the twins started laughing. So did Jane.

"What's so funny?" asked Uncle Aloysius. He'd taken off his hat to show Edwin his handmade flies. His white hair was sticking straight up like the bristles of a hedgehog.

His puzzled look incited a fresh round of laughter, and it wasn't long before he and Edwin joined in.

Listening to the musical sound, Jane knew that she'd recover from the tragic events of the past week. Her family had the power to revive her optimism and strength. The precious people gathered at this table, as well as the Cover Girls and the Fins, would help restore her balance.

After lunch, Jane set to work preparing for Lachlan's proposal. She and a handful of trustworthy staff members loaded supplies into a pickup truck and drove to the gazebo.

"Everything needs to be ready by dusk," Jane told her helpers as they hung white string lights from the gazebo's rafters. "It should be dark enough for the lights and lanterns to glow, but not so dark that Eloise won't be able to see the book pages."

"Look!" someone cried. "It's snowing!"

Fat flakes drifted down from the darkening sky. Jane reached out and caught a single flake on the back of her mitten. The snow was as soft and feathery as a dandelion puff.

An hour later, the gazebo was ready. Draped in thousands of lights, it shone like a lighthouse beacon. The white table in the center of the gazebo held dozens of copies of *Jane Eyre*. The books had all been opened to the same page. Bookmarks made of pale pink ribbon with heart cutouts rested in the gutter of each book.

There was one exception. A single copy remained closed and a piece of blush-colored ribbon was wrapped around it so that it looked like a gift. Inside, on a page marked with Eloise's favorite quote, was the ring Lachlan had bought for her.

Jane threw handfuls of dried rose petals over the books and the floor. Satisfied with the results, she backed out of the gazebo. The rest of the staff had gone, so Jane was able to take in the magical scene in silence.

All the lanterns and battery-powered candles had been turned on, creating a pathway of flickering light from the terrace steps to the gazebo. The snow continued to fall, dusting the world in spotless white. The snow muffled all sound, creating a winter paradise just for Eloise and Lachlan.

Suddenly, Jane heard voices. She'd lingered too long, and Eloise and Lachlan were now heading her way.

With nowhere else to go, she dashed toward the shrubbery behind the gazebo, hugging the shadows at the base of the structure so that Eloise wouldn't notice the trail of fresh footprints. She managed to squat down behind a robust holly bush seconds before she heard an audible gasp.

"Landon! What is all this?" Eloise was breathless with wonder.

Jane heard the sound of hushed footfalls as Lachlan led Eloise into the gazebo.

"Please open that book," he said, his voice thick with emotion.

Several seconds passed before Eloise cried out in joyous surprise.

"'Wherever you are is my home—my only home,'" Lachlan began, and, even with the limited visibility of her hiding place, Jane saw him drop to one knee. "'I ask you to pass through life at my side—to be my second self and best earthly companion.'"

Eloise was crying, and tears ran down Jane's cheeks too. Though she felt guilty for eavesdropping, she was still incredibly moved by Lachlan's proposal. It was so full of love, sincerity, and fear that she prayed Eloise would hurry up and answer him.

Finally, she did. And her acceptance was another *Jane Eyre* quote.

"'All my heart is yours, sir: it belongs to you.'" She sniffed, and Jane knew that her best friend was smiling through her tears. "Yes, Landon. For the rest of our lives, *yes!*"

Jane turned away, allowing the lovers' kiss to belong to them alone. She waited in the bushes, listening as her best friend and the man she loved exchanged more kisses, quiet laughter, and excited murmurs.

She didn't feel the least bit cold.

The days leading up to this magical moment had been marked by coldness. And death. There had been fear too. And anger. Now, there was only petal-soft snow, candle-light, and love.

When Eloise and Lachlan left the gazebo, heading for a roaring fire and glasses of champagne, Jane stood in the lantern light and looked down at the books. Taking off her mittens, she spread her hands over the pages.

She caressed the paper, traced the lines of ink, and ran her fingers along the neat edges.

"You came through," she whispered to the books. Her voice was filled with warmth and affection. "Like you always do."

As the light danced over the words, Jane didn't feel at all alone. She felt like she was among friends. Which, of course, she was.

Epilogue

The Cover Girls were gathered in Jane's kitchen. Anna, Phoebe, and Violet sat at the little table by the window. Mabel and Betty were arranging the food on the center island, and Mrs. Pratt was fanning a stack of paper napkins.

Jane was at the sink, preparing to pop the cork of a prosecco bottle. She didn't like the popping sound, so she muffled it with a dish towel. After opening a second bottle, she lined up champagne flutes and poured a splash of white peach puree into the bottom of every glass. Next, she added the brut prosecco, watching as the bubbles climbed to the rim. She then topped the cocktails with a sprig of mint.

She was wiping a dribble of wine off the counter when Eloise called out a merry "hello" from the living room.

"The food's almost ready," cried Betty.

"And I have *big* news to tell everyone before we eat!" bellowed Mrs. Pratt.

Eloise entered the kitchen, looking positively radiant. Her blond hair shone like sunlit hay, her cheeks were petal-pink, and light danced in her eyes. She wore a fuzzy, gray sweater and a pair of jeans. After placing a pile of books on the counter, she stuffed her hands in her pockets and leaned over the island to inspect the food.

"I'm starving," she said. "But I won't steal one of these

risotto cakes, even though they look amazing, until you share your news, Eugenia. We've been dying to hear about Roger's Valentine's Day surprise."

Mabel laid a pair of tongs next to a platter of empanadas before swinging around to face Mrs. Pratt. "You're fixing to burst, so let it out."

Mrs. Pratt loved being the center of attention, and her friends knew that she'd draw out this moment as long as she could. After taking a deep breath, she clasped her hands together and glanced around, making eye contact with every Cover Girl.

"Do you remember our last meeting?" she asked. "We were talking about what kind of business we hoped would move into the space Spokes had vacated?" She waited a beat before continuing. "Well, I know what the business is. Anyone care to guess?"

Though they'd rather fill their plates, the Cover Girls exchanged quick nods. They'd humor Mrs. Pratt. The sooner she told her story, the sooner they could eat.

Mabel went first. "A bakery?"

Mrs. Pratt shook her head.

"A chocolate shop?" Anna guessed.

Another shake of the head.

"I hope it's not a bar," said Betty. "We've been Storyton's only pub for decades."

"No, no, and no." Mrs. Pratt grinned at her friends. "It's going to be an antique shop. The owner will sell furniture, textiles, clocks, books, and *objets d'art*. There'll be vintage items as well as antiques. Just wait until you hear the shop's name."

Jane wagged a finger at Mrs. Pratt. "We're not going to guess that one. Our cocktails might go flat before we get it right."

Slightly put out over being rushed, Mrs. Pratt fiddled

with a pull on her sweater. When she was satisfied that her friends were waiting with bated breath, she said, "It'll be called the Old Curiosity Shop. Isn't that darling?"

The other women agreed that it was.

"How does Roger fit into this equation?" asked Eloise, even though the answer was obvious.

"*Roger* is the proprietor!" Mrs. Pratt exclaimed. "He bought a house in Storyton and is moving at the end of the semester. He plans to work in the shop while teaching two online courses. He's transitioning into retirement."

Betty put a hand over her heart. "Goodness, what a bold move. After all, Storyton is the polar opposite of New York City."

"That's true," said Violet. "And where do *you* fit in with these plans, Eugenia?"

Mrs. Pratt blushed prettily. "Roger wants to commit to our relationship. He understands how much I value my independence and has no interest in changing me. He's asked to continue courting me, but from across the street instead of several states away."

"He wasn't kidding when he said that he had a surprise for you," said Mabel. "Are you happy about how things turned out?"

Mrs. Pratt's smile said it all. "I'm thrilled to bits. I love being with Roger. I never get tired of talking to him. He makes me laugh. And he makes me think too. He challenges me with trivia questions, crossword puzzles, and Sudoku. He makes me feel young and alive but also peaceful and calm. I can be myself with him. It's the kind of comfortable feeling that I hope you'll all experience one day."

"We definitely need to raise our glasses to this news," Jane said to Mrs. Pratt. "What a wonderful surprise. Roger Bachman is a lucky man."

After Violet and Anna distributed glasses, Jane held out hers in a toast, "To Eugenia and Roger."

"To Eugenia and Roger," the rest of the Cover Girls echoed.

Jane took a tiny sip of her cocktail and said, "Before we eat, Eloise wants to share her ideas for our next read. I know we usually do this at the end of our meetings, but she needs to do it now. She'll be quick. Eloise, the floor is yours."

Eloise grabbed her stack of books and walked over to the table where half of the Cover Girls sat. Mabel, Betty, and Jane moved behind their friends' chairs so that they could see the book titles too.

Eloise balanced the books on her left hand while using her right hand to pull off the topmost book and place it on the table. By positioning her hands this way, she was able to hide her ring.

Mrs. Pratt reached for the first book. "*The Bride Test* by Helen Hoang. Sounds like a romance, which means it'll be right up my alley."

Phoebe picked up the next book. "*The Wedding Date*. We haven't read anything by Jasmine Guillory, have we?"

"No, but we've read Elizabeth Gilbert before," said Anna. She held up the third book, which was Gilbert's novel, *Committed*. "This could be a reference to a person's relationship status or their time in a psych ward."

The women laughed.

Mabel pointed at the next book. "I love Jojo Moyes. Just thinking about *Me Before You* makes me teary-eyed. *Ship of Brides*, eh?" She studied Eloise. "I'm sensing a theme here."

Eloise held up the second-to-last book, *Happily Ever After* by Nora Roberts. She then raised the final book, which was Carson McCullers's *Member of the Wedding*.

"I can't have a happily ever after without the Cover Girls, so I hope that you'll all play a part in my special day."

Eloise laid the books on the table, leaving her left hand resting on top of *Happily Ever After*.

The second Mrs. Pratt's gaze landed on Eloise's ring, she let out such a high-pitched shriek that Jane half expected her champagne flute to crack.

"You're engaged!" Mrs. Pratt screamed.

The other Cover Girls joined in with their own squeals, cries, and gasps. Though the noise eventually died down, the excitement didn't. The women took turns hugging Eloise and wiping tears of joy from their faces. After offering their congratulations, they began firing questions at Eloise.

Jane cut them off with a time-out gesture. "Eloise can tell us more over dinner. Load up your plates, ladies. And if you need a cocktail refill, let me know. We're having peach-flavored cocktails tonight because Eloise is getting married in August, so we're having a taste of summer to celebrate our future summer bride."

Over dinner, the women begged Eloise to share every detail of the proposal.

Jane listened as raptly as her friends, for even though she'd been lucky enough to witness the magical moment, Eloise described it with such heartfelt emotion that Jane felt like she was experiencing it for the first time.

When Eloise was done, Mrs. Pratt, Mabel, and Betty had to wipe away a fresh round of tears. As they did so, they looked at one another and laughed.

"It's crazy to think back on all that happened last week," said Violet. "Famous children's book authors, two murders, *Charlie and the Chocolate Factory*, Valentine's Day, and a marriage proposal." She reached across the table and squeezed Eloise's hand. "I'm glad it ended on such a high note."

"Me too," Jane said. She looked at Eloise. "I was honored when Lachlan asked for my help. But to tell you the truth, setting the scene for your proposal was a gift to *me*. I'd spent the past few days embroiled in a murder investigation, and even though the killers were caught, I felt bruised inside. The murders happened on our grounds, in or near a fairy-tale village built to delight children. The whole experience wore me down. I was sad and scared. And angry. Being asked to create your shining moment was a balm to my spirit. I'm grateful to Lachlan for including me."

Eloise put an arm around Jane's shoulders. "You're lucky I'm keeping my last name. Otherwise, you'd have to call me Lachlan too."

The women discussed the pros and cons of taking a man's name until the conversation shifted to other topics. Jane overheard Phoebe ask Anna how things were going with school and her job at the pharmacy. Anna said that both work and school were great and that her boss crush was still going strong.

Suddenly, Anna turned her attention to Jane. "We've all been so wrapped up in Eugenia's and Eloise's news that we haven't heard about your Valentine's Day. How did it go?"

"Like the rest of the week, it had its highs and lows," Jane said. "Nia Curry hid threatening notes inside the twins' candy houses. As you can imagine, I was livid. If I'd known she'd written them, I would have grabbed a bow from the archery hut and shown her that my arrows are much deadlier than Cupid's."

Mabel made a *tsk tsk* sound. "I can understand Nia's desire to get ahead in this world. I know the challenges she faces as a woman of color—the barriers she had to overcome every day. But she was doing it! She was already a success story. If she'd just kept on that path, she would have reached the top of the mountain. Instead, she threw it all away."

"Did she confess?" Violet asked.

"Not exactly," Jane answered. "When I spoke with Sheriff Evans earlier, he said that Nia's attorney was trying to cut her a deal in exchange for her cooperation. She'll serve time. It's just a matter of how much. Gunnar Humphries provided a full confession and is now awaiting sentencing."

Eloise folded her arms over her chest. "What happened to that dreadful author couple? The Pettys."

"I wouldn't let them return to Storyton Hall," Jane said. "A housekeeper packed their belongings and one of our drivers drove Tris and Todd straight to the station. Knowing they'd get there hours before their train was due, I sent them with some reading material. *The Watsons Go to Birmingham, Maniac Magee*, and *Roll of Thunder, Hear My Cry*."

"Do you think they'll read those books?" Anna asked.

Jane shrugged. "I don't know, but I decided that the books stood a better chance of teaching them a lesson than I did. We've all learned from books. It's not too late for Tris and Todd. A story can still teach them to be better human beings."

Murmurs of agreement followed Jane's comment.

"Landon told me that Gloria's boyfriend flew down from New York," said Eloise. "How is he?"

"At first, he was numb with shock. But grief has set in by now. He's miserable, and there's not much anyone can do to bring him comfort. Sterling took Brandon—that's his name—to the place in the woods where Gloria was found. Brandon asked if he could place a memorial there. After exchanging ideas, we decided on a memorial bench. It'll have a plaque with Gloria's name. The seat will be plain marble, but the base will feature carvings of children's reading books. I've already contacted an area sculptor. She's going to start on the project right away."

Betty dabbed at the corner of her eyes. "We'll have to picnic there when it warms up."

"Yes," Eloise agreed. "We can bring our favorite children's books and have a grown-up story time."

"I love that idea," Jane said. "I can see us relaxing on a big, plaid blanket. The sun will stream through the trees as we sip lemonade and eat peanut butter and jelly sandwiches."

"Don't forget the chocolate chip cookies," Mrs. Pratt was quick to add.

This elicited a ripple of laughter.

"I wish I'd known what was going on up here last week," Anna said with a hint of accusation. "I might be busy, but I still want to help. Especially if your guests are in danger."

Jane felt a rush of affection for her friend. "Do you know what you do best? You, and everyone else at this table?"

"Provide scintillating commentary during our book club meetings?" Mrs. Pratt guessed.

Phoebe picked up her champagne flute. "Make killer cocktails?"

Mabel pointed at the chocolate cake in the center of the table. "Decide that it's perfectly acceptable to have double dessert?"

Jane grinned. "Those things, yes. But more importantly, you keep me grounded when I feel like I'm going to float away. When things get totally crazy like they did last week, all I have to do is call, and I know you'll come running. You'd drop anything to help me." She looked at Anna.

"You never need to prove that you're a good and loyal friend. I already know you are."

"So tell your good and loyal friends about Edwin," Anna said with a smile. "Did you do anything romantic on Valentine's Day, or were you too busy chasing bad guys the whole time?"

Jane feigned nonchalance. "Edwin and I usually exchange books on holidays, and I was planning to give him an old cartography book for Valentine's Day. He loves maps, and the maps in this book are all hand-colored."

"I bet he loved that book," said Eloise.

Violet, who was distributing servings of chocolate cake, gave Jane the biggest piece. "What book did he give you?"

"And did it have an engagement ring inside?" Mrs. Pratt asked, her eyes shimmering with mischief.

Jane wriggled the unadorned fingers of her left hand. "Trust me, the only engaged woman here is Eloise. But my gift was still amazing. Edwin is taking my boys and me on a literary tour of London."

"A family vacation!" Betty exclaimed.

"Exactly," Jane said, unable to stop smiling.

The Cover Girls asked about Jane's London itinerary before sharing their favorite vacation spots. From there, the topic switched to the mishaps they'd experienced on family trips. From missed flights to snake bites, everyone had a story about a disastrous vacation. The discussion looped back around to Eloise when Mabel asked where she and Landon planned to go on their honeymoon.

Eloise spread her hands in a gesture of helplessness. "We haven't thought that far ahead. We need to decide where to live first."

Jane couldn't believe she hadn't considered this before.

Lachlan would want to stay on the grounds, but his current cottage wasn't big enough for two.

"What about the carriage house?" she suggested. "It's been shut up since the roof leaked last year, but the roof will be replaced in March. I wanted to update the kitchen and paint the interior, but if you'd like to live there, we could work together to make it your dream home."

"Really?" Eloise glowed with delight. "It's always been my favorite building on the property."

"Then consider it yours," said Jane. "I love the idea of popping over to borrow sugar or have a glass of wine in the evening. We're going to be neighbors."

Eloise knocked the rim of her glass against Jane's. "To neighbors."

After the women polished off their chocolate cake, they cleaned up the kitchen. While her friends organized the leftovers, wiped off the counters, or loaded the dishwasher, Jane brewed a pot of decaf and took out a box filled with herbal teas. The Cover Girls carried cups of coffee or tea to the living room and settled in chairs or on the sofa.

They were supposed to discuss Kristin Hannah's *The Great Alone* that evening, and Jane was about to launch their meeting as she always did by asking her friends to share their favorite quote from the novel. She was opening her mouth to speak when Betty asked, "What will you do with Lachlan's cottage? Offer it to another staff member?"

"Normally, yes, but his cottage also needs a facelift. The carriage house, Lachlan's cottage, and the restoration of Flaubert's Folly are on my to-do list as soon as the weather breaks."

Violet picked up her purple and white polka-dot teacup, which Jane had purchased especially for her, and blew away a curl of steam. "Have you ever thought about renting the empty cottages? To large families or to people who want more privacy?"

Jane gazed at her in surprise. "Funny you should mention that. Remember the cookbook competition I mentioned? The one coming up this summer?"

Mabel gasped. "Are you kidding? The best Southern chefs will be invading Mrs. Hubbard's kitchen, and you need locals to serve as taste testers. How could we forget that?"

Phoebe raised her hand. "I volunteer to taste every cake. Twice. That's the kind of sacrifice I'm willing to make in the name of friendship."

Jane waited for the quiet laughter to die down before continuing. "One of the chefs is from a town called Oyster Bay. It's on the North Carolina coast. The chef, Michel, runs a renowned restaurant called the Boot Top Bistro. The woman who owns the restaurant is a writer. Her first book came out last year. Anyway, she called this morning to ask if she could rent a cottage on the grounds. She plans to close the restaurant while Michel's here and would like to spend that time working on her next book. She said that she needs a change of scenery and believes that Storyton Hall will provide the inspiration she's looking for."

Mrs. Pratt waved her reading glasses at Jane. "Imagine that! She could be a few houses away from you, sitting at a desk, writing a Great American masterpiece."

"I wonder if I've heard of her work. What's her name?" Eloise asked.

"Olivia Limoges."

Eloise nodded in recognition. "I read her book the week it came out. It's called *The Fruit Seller & Other Stories*. It was really good. The story about the lighthouse keeper was my favorite." She raised her brows in question. "Are you thinking of letting her stay in Landon's cottage?"

Jane's expression turned pensive. "I've been mulling it over. I've never rented a property on our grounds before, but I can understand why a writer might want their own space. Do you think I should say yes?"

In answer, Eloise opened her copy of *The Great Alone* to a page marked by a sticky note and read, "'Some people have family photos or home movies to record their past. I've got books. Characters. For as long as I can remember, books have been my safe place.'"

Running her hand over the page, Eloise said, "If books are our safe places as readers, then they're probably the safe places for writers too. What could be the harm in having Olivia Limoges spend a week in a Storyton Hall cottage?"

Jane felt the comforting weight of the hardcover on her lap. "You're right. What could be the harm? I'll tell her that she's welcome to the cottage."

With that bit of business taken care of, the Cover Girls opened to the places in their books marked by bits of fabric, receipts, paperclips, or pretty bookmarks. After sharing their favorite quotes, they began to talk about how the story had moved them. Or marked them. How it had changed them in some way, no matter how small.

They spoke of the scenes that had gotten under their skin and named the characters that had climbed into their hearts and stayed there, eliciting feelings of empathy, understanding, sadness, and joy. As the women discussed the plot, the setting, and recited compelling bits of dialogue, their words mingled with the author's words. Her story became their story.

The Cover Girls read over a hundred books a year. They were well aware of the fact that not all stories had fairy-tale endings. They didn't mind. To them, happy endings weren't that important. It was the journey they were interested in—the voyage from the first page to the last. The women relished every moment they were given to lose themselves in someone else's words. And they cherished the ending of every book, because an ending meant that they could gather together, as they had tonight, and relive the story.

With every book, and every meeting, their lives became more and more enriched. Their kind of happily ever after was made of food, friendship, and books.

It was a story they hoped would never end.

Read an excerpt from the third Secret,
Book & Scone Society Novel from the USA Today
and New York Times bestselling author
Ellery Adams . . .

THE BOOK OF CANDLELIGHT

And in this moment, like a swift intake of breath, the rain came.

—Truman Capote

Nora Pennington had no idea how much the rain would change her life.

According to the saying, spring was supposed to come in like a lion. And so it did.

It plodded into the little western North Carolina town like a wet cat looking for a comfortable place to nap. Having settled in, it was in no rush to leave.

The rain began on a Monday in early April. It was tentative at first. Gentle. The kind of rain that coaxed people into slowing their pace and speaking in softer voices. It was chilly. Thick cardigans, already packed away in anticipation of balmier weather, were unpacked. Extra cups of coffee were brewed. People craved soup and homemade bread for supper.

It rained all day. The roads glistened. The soil turned dark. The vegetation was weighed down by fat water droplets. When the storm tapered off late in the evening, the townsfolk assumed that Tuesday would bring a change. A little sunshine. A rise in temperatures.

The next morning revealed another gray sky. By lunchtime, it was raining again.

The rain fell every day that week. As the consecutive days of wet weather drove the locals and the tourists indoors, Nora's bookstore became a sanctuary for book lovers and for those searching for a cozy place to wait out the rain.

Miracle Books had never seen such a steady stream of paying customers. They bought books and hot drinks—one after the other—until Nora feared she'd run out of coffee beans or tea bags. She'd never had to stock so much milk before. By Friday, she was down to her last twenty sugar packets.

Her coffee bar supplies weren't the only things being depleted. Her stock of shelf enhancers was also thin. Shelf enhancers were what Nora called the antique and vintage items decorating her bookshelves. As beautiful as books were on their own, Nora felt they shined even brighter when surrounded by interesting *objets d'art* like an etched cranberry glass vase, a Steiff fox terrier, a hand-painted wooden rooster, chintzware candleholders, cut-glass powder boxes with silver lids, a singing bird toy in a brass cage, and, because Easter was around the corner, a selection of vintage plush bunnies, windup chicks, alabaster eggs, and handwoven baskets in every color of the rainbow.

Nora couldn't complain about the rapid disappearance of her inventory. She was selling stacks of books and a dozen shelf enhancers a day. In addition to these sales, she was taking in a tidy profit from the coffee bar, which included the sale of the book pastries made by Hester Winthrop of the Gingerbread House bakery. In short, Miracle Books was having a banner week.

By Friday, the bookshop was a mess. Not an eclectic jumble. Not charming dishevelment. A flat-out mess.

Due to gaps on the shelves, books leaned against one another like tired children. The holistic medicine section needed a good dusting, as did the shelves in Romance. Nora noticed that the display of vintage teacups she'd lined up in front of Victoria Holt's novels were no longer quaint but pathetic looking. A few days ago, the ten floral teacups had been filled with sprigs of dried lavender and rosebuds. Since then, eight of the cups had been sold and someone had removed the posies from the remaining two cups.

I can't blame them, Nora thought, listening to the steady drumbeat of the rain outside her window. *Everyone is desperate for a little color. A bit of cheer.*

After hanging the CLOSED sign that evening, Nora did some tidying up and then rode to the grocery store on her bicycle. By the time she returned to her tiny house located behind the bookstore, she was drenched. Leaving her bike on the deck, she entered what had once been a working train car. The locals called Nora's house Caboose Cottage, and as she peeled off her wet clothes, she wished she could push it onto the tracks and ride to a place awash in sunshine.

Too tired to return the phone calls or texts she'd received from Jedediah Craig, the handsome, charismatic paramedic she was dating, or any of her Secret, Book & Scone Society friends, Nora dropped on her bed and fell into a deep sleep. Neither the rumbles of thunder nor cracks of lightning could wake her.

The next morning, there was finally a break in the rain.

Buoyed by the sight of a pale sun fighting its way through the haze, Nora rode to the old tobacco barn where the flea market was held every weekend.

Hoping to find a treasure trove of new shelf enhancers

inside, she shopped the booths of her favorite sellers first. These were the people who treated her like a human instead of a burn victim. They were the people who'd look into her hazel eyes before letting their gazes stray to the octopi-shaped burn scars on her neck or the jellyfish bubbles swimming up her right arm. Eventually, they'd find the space above her pinkie knuckle. A space created by hungry flames.

Nora had been an attractive woman before the fire had marked her. She didn't regret her scars. She regretted the event that had caused them. Her recklessness had almost cost a mother and her young son their lives, which was why Nora refused to allow the plastic surgeon who'd operated on her face a few months back to repair the skin on her neck, arm, or hand.

"You already worked a miracle on my face," she'd told him during one of her follow-up visits. "If I wear the right makeup, you can hardly tell that I was burned."

She chose not to use the makeup, preferring to let her skin breathe, to let the thin scars show along her hairline where Dr. Patel had worked his magic. Nora didn't want to erase the evidence of her car accident, the fire, or the months in a burn unit. The married, suburbanite librarian she used to be had died that night, and the woman who'd left the hospital to start a new life in Miracle Springs was a better person. She was uglier, poorer, stronger, and more compassionate than the woman who'd sped along that dark highway, fueled by rage and alcohol.

"You want me to take off three bucks because of that tiny wrinkle?" a vendor named Beatrice asked Nora. "You want my six kids to starve?"

Beatrice loved to haggle. Her eyes were already glimmering at the prospect of a good back-and-forth session with Nora.

"Six? Last week, it was five," Nora said, holding back a smile. "And you know how fussy my customers are. They won't focus on the blue butterfly inside this paperweight. They'll focus on the crack."

"That's no crack. It's a dimple," Beatrice objected.

Nora put the paperweight aside and held up a vintage Bakelite alarm clock. Its yellow hue reminded her of a ripe lemon.

"What about this? If I buy both of these, will you knock five bucks off the total?"

"*Five?*" Beatrice acted affronted. "There's not a damn thing wrong with that clock."

The haggling continued for several minutes. When it was over, Nora left the booth with the paperweight and clock as well as a hammered copper inkwell and blotter.

She moved around the flea market, asking for discounts from every vendor. Though it had been a record-breaking week for Miracle Books, there was no telling what would happen next week. Life in retail was filled with uncertainty.

An hour later, Nora's backpack was stuffed with treasures wrapped in newspaper. Deciding to return for more on Sunday, she headed for the exit and ran into her friend June.

June Dixon managed the thermal pools for the Miracle Springs Lodge, the biggest hotel in town. June was in her fifties but looked a decade younger. Her café au lait skin glowed with health and her close-cropped, black curls accentuated her high cheekbones and drew attention to her best feature: her golden-brown eyes.

"Are you coming or going?" June asked Nora.

"Going. You?"

June frowned. "I stopped by to find out about booth rental. I want to sell my socks here, but it's too pricey. I'd have to knit around the clock to pay for the privilege of sitting on my ass all weekend. No, thanks."

"I told you I'd sell your socks in my shop."

"And you wouldn't burn me like the folks who run the gift shop at the lodge, but that experience made me realize that I don't want to owe anybody anything. I want to sell my stuff my way."

The two friends ambled over to the last booth in the row. Situated close to the door, the booth belonged to an artisan known to the locals as Cherokee Danny. Every weekend, he and his wife arranged their wares on tables covered with handwoven blankets. Danny was a potter and his wife was a basket maker. The couple had been at the same spot since Nora had moved to Miracle Springs, but she'd never purchased anything from them.

Living in a tiny house meant that Nora only had space for items she used on a daily basis. Other than her favorite books and a few antiques, she bought collectibles for resale only. No matter how wonderful the item, it was priced and put on a bookstore shelf.

Nora looked at the wares in Danny's booth and remembered telling Jed that he could jazz up his spartan kitchen by buying a few pieces of pottery. She now knew that most of his salary went toward his mother's medical expenses, so he couldn't afford pottery. He didn't even own a couch. He lived like a monk so that his mom could receive the very best care. Jed was a good man.

As Nora admired a bowl glazed a rich, walnut brown and stamped with swirls, she realized that she and Jed weren't the kind of couple that exchanged gifts. She wasn't sure what kind of couple they were, but she felt like buying him a gift anyway.

"Are you looking for yourself or for someone special?" asked Danny's wife. Nora didn't know her name.

Nora wasn't sure what to call Jed. She was in her forties, and it seemed silly to say that she had a boyfriend. The term sounded juvenile. *Significant other* was no good and Nora wasn't the type to use idioms like *partner in crime* or *my better half*.

"A friend," she said. "He could use a bowl like this for pasta. Or salad. If he ate salad."

The other woman laughed. "The only way I can get Danny to eat veggies is by drowning them in butter."

"Hello, I'm sitting right here," said Danny.

"I know," his wife retorted playfully. "I wasn't trying to be quiet."

There was a smile in Danny's voice as he said, "Like you've ever been quiet a day in your life." To Nora, he said, "If you've got any questions about my work, let me know."

"Can your pieces withstand everyday use? Like microwaving or dishwashing?" she asked.

"Not all," he said. "That bowl you and my girl were talking about can handle high heat, though."

Nora picked up the pot and saw the price sticker affixed to the bottom. "I'll take it."

While Danny's wife wrapped the bowl in newspaper and chatted with June about her baskets, Nora and Danny griped about the rain.

"We live thirty minutes away," said Danny. "Our house is right on the mountain, and I don't know how much longer it'll stand if the rain doesn't let up. If we get another week of this, our place will slide down the mountain like a sled."

He made a downward motion with his hand.

Wanting to offer him a little hope, Nora said that the

upcoming forecast called for two days of partly cloudy weather.

Danny shook his head. "That's wrong. More rain is coming. I've seen the signs. It's coming today, and it won't budge until it's made us even more miserable."

After thanking Nora for her purchase, Danny moved off to help another customer. His wife handed Nora the bowl, now cocooned in white paper. "May this humble pot bring many blessings to the home it enters."

Nora didn't know how to respond to the woman's words or to her warm fingers lingering on the back of Nora's scarred hand. The touch itself felt like a blessing. She managed a quick "thanks," before she and June made for the exit.

Just outside the doors, the two friends parted. June headed for her car and Nora walked to the bike racks. As she put the paper-wrapped bowl in her bike basket, it began to rain.

Cursing under her breath, Nora pulled the hood of her raincoat over her head and donned her helmet. A few hours of weak sunlight weren't enough to dry the muddy parking lot, which meant Nora had to maneuver around dozens of deep puddles. The shoulder of the main road was just as bad. In a matter of minutes, Nora's sneakers, socks, and pant legs were completely saturated with muddy water.

She rode across the bridge and entered the downtown shopping district, surprised by the number of cars on the road. Seeing a line of red taillights ahead, Nora decided to cut through the park.

This seemed like a brilliant idea until she came upon a tree branch in the middle of the sidewalk. She tried to swerve around it, but her tires slipped out from under her and she went down hard.

She'd fallen before, but not directly onto her hip and

elbow. Pain tore through her entire left side as water splashed over her pinched face. It took her a few seconds to sit upright.

Her jeans were torn at the knee. Blood soaked the frayed denim around the hole, turning the blue fabric purple.

Nora heard the sound of boots in the water. Someone put a hand on her shoulder.

"Are you okay?"

It was Hester, looking adorable in a red-and-white polka-dot raincoat.

"Yeah." Nora got to her feet. "But I don't think I can say the same for my flea market finds."

Shoving a tendril of frizzy blond hair out of her face, Hester said, "Come into the bakery. I'll make you some tea."

Hester carried Nora's backpack and the bag with the pottery bowl into her warm kitchen.

"Have you ever thought about buying a car?" she asked once they'd shucked off their raincoats. The aromas of melted butter, baking bread, and cinnamon wafted through the space, settling around Nora's shoulders like a cashmere shawl. Spilled flour, halos of powdered sugar, and bits of dried dough covered every surface.

"I don't need a car. I don't go anywhere," said Nora. She gestured around the kitchen. "What happened? It looks like a spice rack exploded."

After pulling a tray of dinner rolls out of the oven, Hester slid one onto a plate. She cut the roll in half, buttered it, and pressed the halves together. Putting the plate in front of Nora, she said, "I can't keep up with the work. I thought the rain would slow things down. Nope. People want my food more than ever. My cash box is stuffed, but I'm running on empty."

Nora took a bite of the roll and moaned. "No wonder

they line up for your stuff. This tastes like the feeling of putting on PJs at the end of a long day."

Hester smiled. "Thanks, but the bakery's popularity might also have something to do with my over-the-top April Flowers theme."

Seeing Nora's quizzical look, Hester beckoned her to the front of the store.

Nora gazed at the display cases in astonishment. They held baked apple roses, tulip cake pops, daisy lemon tarts, sunflower cupcakes, pansy sandwich cookies, and more. Every muffin, roll, and loaf of bread was shaped like a flower or embellished with a floral design.

"This is right out of *The Secret Garden*. Except the flowers are edible. Amazing," Nora said. Then she sighed. "I need to change my window display, but who has the time? I'm running back and forth between the checkout counter and the ticket agent's office like a madwoman. Last night, I was too tired to eat dinner. On Thursday night, I fell asleep in my clothes."

Hester plucked at her shirt. "This is my last clean T-shirt. And it wasn't like I was on top of things before the rain came. I can't remember when I last changed my sheets or washed my towels. My house smells like a high school locker room."

Nora understood. At home, she'd been using the same plate, fork, and glass for days. She'd wash them and leave them on the counter to dry. She didn't bother putting things in cabinets or drawers. That required too much energy.

"Are you thinking about running another ad?" she asked, returning to her roll.

Hester frowned. "Ever since the Meadows was bought, a bunch of the people who lost their jobs after the community bank scandal have gone back to work. Now, no one is interested in my part-time gig. Especially since I'm not offering any benefits. Unless you count free food."

The Meadows was a planned housing development on the outskirts of town. No houses had been built because the investment firm heading the project was run by scumbags. These scumbags colluded with more scumbags from the Madison County Community Bank to commit major mortgage fraud. The crooks had been caught, partially due to the efforts of the Secret, Book & Scone Society, and the bank had gone belly-up. The recent purchase of the development by a legitimate firm meant homes and jobs for many of the fraud victims.

Nora put on her raincoat. "My applicants were a high school kid who wouldn't work weekends, an empty nester who wanted a higher wage than I make, and a chain-smoker who couldn't name the last book she'd read."

"Ouch."

"Whoever works with me has to be a book lover. That's non-negotiable." Nora reached for the door handle and paused. "Speaking of books, should I grab my book pockets while I'm here?"

Hester slapped the counter with her oven mitt. "I totally forgot! I'll bake them right now and ask Jasper to drive them over. Otherwise, they'll be water-logged."

Nora grinned at the image of Hester's boyfriend, Deputy Andrews, transporting pastries in his sheriff's department cruiser.

"Good idea. Besides, I want to ask him if he finished *Ready Player One* yet."

Hester filled a measuring cup with flour and said, "Not everyone devours books like we do. Some people savor every page."

"I need books like I need oxygen." Nora glanced out at the rain. "A little sunlight would be nice too."

* * *

Inside the dry and cozy haven that was Miracle Books, Nora set the coffeemaker to brew and inspected the contents of her backpack.

The results were depressing.

The inkwell of the hammered copper desk set was dented, the butterfly paperweight was chipped, and the Bakelite clock was cracked. A vintage leather canteen had also been flattened. The only survivors of her fall were a Russian nesting doll and a silver plate bowl.

"Damn it," she muttered, stuffing a screwdriver into the canteen to push out a few dents.

The coffeemaker beeped, and Nora checked her watch. It was almost ten and both she and the shop were completely disheveled.

Nora looked at the hole in her pants. She didn't have time to change. Instead, she turned on lights, straightened throw pillows, and ran a rag over the dustiest shelves. With one minute to go, she switched on some music and ran a brush through her hair. As she fought with a knot at the nape of her neck, she thought, *I need to clean this cut on my leg. I need to change the window display. I need to open boxes. I need to restock the shelves.*

Her mental list scrolled on as she put the old brass skeleton key in the front door and unlocked it.

The door immediately swung open, and the sleigh bells dangling from its hinges clamored.

"Don't you get tired of that noise?" asked a doppelganger for Colonel Sanders. He removed a gray fedora and shook it out, his gaze moving from Nora's face to her torn pants. "Honey, you're a hot mess. What can Sheldon do to help you?"

Normally, Nora would have delivered a terse reply and gone about her business, but genuine kindness radiated from the man's dark eyes. She liked his fedora and his pink bowtie. She liked how his sweater vest seemed to hold his belly in check.

Before she could say a word, the man looped his arm through hers. "I smell coffee. Let's go to where the coffee-pot lives, and you can tell me everything. I'm an *excellent* listener."

Minutes later, to Nora's surprise, the short, round, bearded stranger was in the ticket agent's office, making coffee for them both.

"So many mugs! I love them," Sheldon declared. "Especially the snarky ones."

Nora watched him. She was so tired that it was a relief to sit back and let him take over.

Sheldon handed her a mug emblazoned with the text TALK DARCY TO ME, and said, "There's no problem that a Cuban coffee and a heart-to-heart can't fix. Go on. Take a load off."

Nora sat. "Cuban?"

"No talkie before coffee." Sheldon motioned for her to take a sip.

Nora was immediately smitten with the strong, sweet brew. "Magical."

"Not magical. Cuban. I'm only half-magic because I'm half-Cuban," he said. "Sheldon Silverstein Vega, at your service."

"As in, Shel Silverstein the poet?"

Sheldon spread his hands. "Mom was a school librarian who wanted her son to love words. And I do. My Cuban papa wanted me to love food." He rubbed his belly. "And I do."

Studying her guest, Nora realized that Sheldon was too handsome to be compared with Colonel Sanders. Sheldon's skin held a hint of bronze and his white hair was mixed with a generous dose of silver.

The sleigh bells clanged. Nora called out a hello before

turning to Sheldon. "Thanks for the coffee. I'd better get to work." She held out her hand. "Nora Pennington, by the way."

He took her hand as if she were a queen and he, her courtier. "Lady Nora, I've been in town for three days, and I'm terrifically bored. The inn where I'm staying is being renovated, and I didn't emerge from the thermal pools to find my chronic pain miraculously gone. I don't do yoga, I have a therapist back home, and I can't stand kale. So when I saw your shop—this glorious den of books and trinkets—I thought, here's the place for me. I can arrange the bric-a-brac, I can shelve books, I can make Cuban coffee. Whatever you need. Give my day some purpose. *Please.*"

A middle-aged couple appeared from around the corner of the fiction shelves and Nora asked if she could help them with anything. The man wanted a coffee and the woman wanted a vegan cookbook. Nora promised to make the man's coffee after showing his wife the cookbook section, but she never got the chance. By the time she returned to the ticket agent's office, the man was settled in the purple velvet chair, contentedly sipping coffee out of a Dilbert mug.

"Do you want a job?" Nora asked Sheldon. She was only half teasing.

"I might," he said. "But I'm a complicated man. I come with baggage."

Nora smiled at him. "Don't we all?"

With Sheldon handling beverages, Nora was able to load a shelving cart with inventory from the stockroom. She even managed to put out some of the new books in between making recommendations and ringing up sales.

When Deputy Andrews arrived carrying two boxes of book-shaped pastries, Nora asked if he had time to look for a new book.

"I've gotta go." He jerked his thumb out the window. "Multiple fender benders."

The mention of car accidents reminded Nora that she'd forgotten to examine the pottery bowl she'd bought for Jed.

Later, after bagging *Goodnight Moon*, *Harold and the Purple Crayon*, and *Maisy's Bedtime* for a woman who'd be babysitting her rambunctious grandson at the end of the month, Nora decided to check on both the bowl and Sheldon.

Sheldon had tidied the ticket agent's office from top to bottom. The coffee machine sparkled. The counters gleamed. He'd also lit one of the scented candles from the display in the home and garden section.

"You'll sell more candles if people can sample their smell," Sheldon said. "I mean, I had no clue what to expect from a candle called Beach Reads. It could smell like cocoa butter and sweat for all I know."

Nora grinned. "Thanks for cleaning up back here. I've been meaning to do it, but the rain has kept me super busy."

Sheldon pointed at a cardboard box. "I put your broken stuff in there. I'm guessing that the hole in your jeans and your busted antiques happened at the same time."

"I fell off my bike," Nora said as she reached for the plastic bag in the sink. She peeled off the layers of news-papers and released a heavy sigh. The rim of the bowl was chipped. Red clay peeked out from a dime-sized area where a chunk of brown glaze was missing.

Seeing her stricken look, Sheldon came up behind her and asked, "Have you ever heard the story of the cracked pot?"

Nora shook her head. She was in no mood for a story.

"It's about a water bearer who has to walk a long way to fetch water for his master. He carries a pot in each hand. One pot is flawless. The other is cracked. Every day, when the water bearer returns to his master's house, the perfect pot is full of water. The cracked one is half-full."

As Sheldon spoke, Nora searched through the newspaper for the glaze chip. She hoped to ask Danny to repair the bowl. She'd see him at the flea market tomorrow.

Sheldon continued his story. "The cracked water pot was ashamed that he couldn't carry as much water as the flawless pot. One day, he apologized to the water bearer."

"The pot speaks?" Nora asked wryly.

"Yes. Now, listen. This is the important part. The water bearer told the pot to pay careful attention to the flowers they passed on the way home. The pot did, and he saw that they were beautiful. There were flowers of every shape and color. They filled the air with a lovely perfume and brought joy to all the people on the road. The flowers existed because one day, the water bearer dropped seeds on the dirt along the side of the road. He then watered the seeds with the water leaking out of the cracked pot. The water bearer told the pot that he had no reason to feel shame. After all, it was his flaw that had created so much beauty."

Nora looked at Sheldon. He was a curious man. A quirky and capable man. She didn't know him, but she liked him.

Sheldon tapped his temple. "I know what you're thinking. Who is this marvelous Mr. Miyagi? This glam Gandalf? This winsome Obi-Wan? This dreamy Dumbledore?"

The moment had come for Nora to learn more about Sheldon Vega. Gesturing at the circle of chairs on the other side of the ticket agent's office, she said, "I'm thinking that I lucked out when you showed up today. You're like a fairy godmother." She gestured at the circle of chairs. "I always thought fairy godmothers were too good to be true. They never had any visible flaws, which made me distrust them. Why don't you tell me about some of yours?"

"Some of my flaws?" Sheldon rolled his eyes and released a theatrical sigh. "Honey, we do *not* have that kind of time."